ONCE A FAN...

The Fannish Writings of

MIKE RESNICK

I0526103

ALSO BY MIKE RESNICK FROM WILDSIDE PRESS

NOVELS:

The Branch

The Chronicles of Lucifer Jones:
Adventures
Encounters
Exploits

SHORT STORIES:

Pink Elephants and Hairy Toads
A Safari of the Mind

NON-FICTION:

Putting It Together: Turning Sow's Ear
Drafts into Silk Purse Stories

AS EDITOR:

Alternate Skiffy
I Have This Nifty Idea . . . Now What Do I Do With It?

ONCE A FAN...

The Fannish Writings of

MIKE RESNICK

Introduction by

Guy H. Lillian III

WILDSIDE PRESS

To Carol, as always

And to science fiction fandom:

> *You buy my books,*
> *You pay my bills,*
> *You stroke my ego,*
> *You provide me with lifelong friends,*
> *You are always stimulating,*
> *You make me care about tomorrow.*

> *Thank you for a wonderful 40 years.*

CONTENTS

Introduction, by Guy H. Lillian III 9
A Word to the Fore, by Mike Resnick 14

Part I: WORLDCONS

Roots . . . and a Few Vines. 16
Worldcon Memories—Part 1 24
Worldcon Memories—Part 2 36
Worldcon Memories—Part 3 53
Worldcon Memories—Part 4 69
Worldcon Programming—Then and Now. 85
Chicon 2000 Report 88
Your First Worldcon 95
Millennium Philcon Diary 112
What It Takes to be a Worldcon Guest of Honor . . . 127

Part II: BIOGRAPHIES

On the Road with Sims and Sims 134
A Giant Among Midgets—Barry Malzberg 138
10 Reasons Why I Hate David Gerrold 142
About Mark Aronson, Whom I Almost Like. 144
Michael Banks 146
Introducing Lan, Who Needs None 148
Scott and Jane Dennis: Semi-Secret Masters
        of Fandom 151
Seven Views of Kristine Kathryn Rusch 154
About Barbara Delaplace, Who Lives With This
        Skinny Hairy Guy. 157
10 Little-Known Facts About Judy Tarr 159
10 Reasons Why I Hate Martha Beck 160
Bill Cavin: Just the Facts, Ma'am 162
Laura Resnick 164
Carol Resnick. 166
About Dick Smith and This Female Person
        He Lives With. 168

Jack Williamson 171
Toastmaster: Jack L. Chalker 173
Kris Rusch and Dean Smith: Beauty and the Geek. . 176
Legendary Lou Tabakow. 179
I Remember Isaac 185
Dick Spelman: From SMIF to SMOF 187

Part III: ARTICLES
Memorable Meals. 191
Predictions for the 21st Century. 208
The Literature of Fandom 211
Uh . . . Guys—My Name Isn't Koriba 226
Orlando Safari Diary. . . . .
What Works For Me 244
Hunting Lake. 247
A Limerick History of Science Fiction 257
Introduction to *Fantastic Chicago* 258
The Best African Movies 260
The Great ERB Revival 270
How Fandom Has Changed 273
My Favorite Museums 276
Time Capsule 284
How I Single-Handedly Destroyed the Sex Book
    Field 288
My Favorite Musicals 292

Part IV: SPEECHES
Skylark Presentation Speech 319
Nolacon II Toastmaster Speech 322
1989 Worldcon Banquet Speech 333
2000 Rivercon Toastmaster Speech 336

Part V: INTRODUCTIONS TO FANNISH BOOKS
Introduction to *Alternate Worldcons*. 341
Introduction to *Again, Alternate Worldcons*. 343
Introduction to *Alternate Skiffy* 345
Introduction to *Girls for the Slime God* 349

Part VI: THE RESNICK LISTS

The 15 Best Science Fiction and Fantasy Novels . . . 352
The 10 Best Science Fiction Films 353
The 10 Best Fantasy Films 353
The 12 Best Films of All Time 354
My 25 Favorite Fanzines (And Their Editors) 358
The 5 Most Influential Sf Editors 356
The 5 Best Resnick Novels 356
My 5 Favorite Resnick Novels 356
My 15 Best Short Fiction Stories 357
The 5 Worst Worldcons I've Attended 357
The 12 Best Film Scores 358
The 25 Best Western Films 359
The 25 Best Comedy Films. 360
The 12 Best American Meals 361
The 12 Best Foreign Meals. 361
The 12 Best African Films 362
The 25 Best Musicals. 363
The 12 Best Performances by an Actor in a Musical . . 364
The 12 Best Performances by an Actress in a Musical . 364
My 10 Favorite TV Shows 365
The 25 Greatest Race Horses Of The 20th Century . 366
My 12 Favorite Museums 367
My 10 Favorite Zoos 367
My 15 Favorite African Game Parks 368
My 3 Favorite Historical Characters 368
The 5 Best Basketball Players 369
The 5 Best Big Bands 369
The 5 Best Mystery Writers 369
The 5 Greatest Novels I've Read 370
The 5 Best Film Directors 370

INTRODUCTION

by Guy H. Lillian III

Mike Resnick is a science fiction *fan.*

Well, of course, you scoff. Mike Resnick is a very well-known science fiction *writer* and *editor.* On shelves of beautiful blond wood in his beautiful Cincinnati home rest 42 science fiction novels, 12 collections, and 23 SF anthologies, all bearing the Resnick name. (That's in addition to the non-fction, how-to books, mysteries, and books about Africa.) In a display case downstairs four Hugo Awards for short fiction stand like sentinels over a wild menagerie of other trophies—a Nebula from the Science Fiction Writers of America, a *Seiun* Award from Japan's SF community, an *Ignotus* from Spain's, a *Prix Tour Eiffel*, two Polish honors called *Sfinks*, and many, many more. On his nametag at the last world science fiction convention he sported so many of the miniature rocket pins given Hugo contenders (he has 22 nominations) that his name was obscured. He's been Guest of Honor at 31 North American SF conventions, ranging from coast to coast, not to mention the five events which have so hailed him in France and the one (so far) in Slovakia. He's served as toastmaster at 12 conventions, including the 1988 World Science Fiction Convention. That's quite a resume. Of *course* Mike Resnick is a science fiction *pro.*

To which I reply, maybe. Honors, awards, and notoreity mark success in one's profession—that's obvious. But fandom—being an SF *fan*—requires something more. It requires *love.*

Love means, in this instance, commitment and involvement, for SF is not merely an accumulation of books or baubles on a shelf. SF is a long-lived, on-going community of like-minded souls, bound together by a love for the art and literature of the fantastic and the future. No other literary genre supports such an active, enthused, and creative readership. Hundreds of conventions gather within any year to celebrate SF's tenets and creators, ranging in size from a few to many thousands. To be a science fiction *fan*, a *real* one, you don't just sell to these multitudes . . . you're one of them. One of *us.*

Mike is, indeed, one of us. He began his career as a reader of grand SF and fantasy, and his collection of SF works is both enormous and impressive: a complete set of Edgar Rice Burroughs, about half of which are first editions; a first edition of Sam Moscowitz's epic *The Immortal Storm,* and an autographed copy of C. L. Moore's *Scarlet Dream* (the only book, he says, which he ever went out of his way to have signed). In 1960, during his student stint at the University of Chicago, he met his future wife Carol, and in 1963 they attended their first convention, the World SF Con in Washington. Carol is a supremely talented costume designer, and she and Mike made quite a career at worldcon masquerade competitions. Five times they took the stage in costumes Carol designed, and on four of those occasions they were acclaimed the winners. (For the encyclopediacally-minded, those years were '73, '74, '77 and '79. They won an Honorable Mention in '76.) No one creates convention costumes for money. They're done for the sheer joy of doing them. Surely that stands as a definition for *fan.*

More to the point, though, is what happens off the stage. At conventions, SF fans commingle, talk, exchange views, share experiences—and have a good time. At these activities, Mike Resnick excels. You should see him at parties, ever ready to entertain or enlighten with a pointed anecdote or a persuasive argument. You should attend one of *his* parties, surely the liveliest thrown. At the last worldcon, in Philadelphia, Mike's female fan club, the fabulous Babes for Bwana, was joined by the brilliant singer-songwriter Janis Ian, Mike's 28th collaborator on a work of fiction. Beauteous bellydancers plied their avocation. It was fun. It was epic. It was pure Resnick.

Mike hosts not only lively live parties, but has a listserv on the Internet that is as vibrant as any physical get-together. Celebrants join in conversations and arguments on topics divers and outre—basketball, horse racing (a Resnick obsession), dog-breeding (Mike and Carol used to own an award-winning kennel), and science fiction, of course. All voices are welcome—SF fans are like that.

There is one other aspect to fanac—as SFers abbreviate "fan activity"—that bears mention, since it's the reason the book you're holding exists. Since the early '30s SF fans have shared their love for the genre through the writing, editing, illustrating and publishing of our own amateur magazines: fanzines. Mike has contributed articles and anecdotes of tireless wit to dozens of these publications. You will find a sampling of these pieces here, squibs done for no other motive than love of the genre and the urge to help a fellow fan gain favor for his fanzine. I'm proud that Mike has asked me to write this introduction to this collection of his fan writing, but even more so that he includes a sampling of his work for *my* fanzine, *Challenger*. Makes a simple faned ("fan editor") feel important, it do.

But that's the point of science fiction fandom. Everyone *is* important. Mike Resnick, writer, editor, screenwriter, and most of all, stalwart of the SF *fan* community, would be the first to tell you that.

A WORD TO THE FORE

I've been writing for fanzines since 1962, but since I cherish my audience, I've spared you anything from the first 21 years. (You don't *really* want to read a serious article about how to play Martian chess [1963], or a list of where to get the best materials for your Worldcon masquerade costume if you live in Illinois [1976], or anything like that, do you?)

Anyway, I write these things as a labor of love. I accept no money for writing for fanzines, and I've had to tell a couple of Worldcon committees that I will not allow my name on the ballot for Best Fan Writer. There's an old saying in science fiction that you can't pay back, so you have to pay forward. As a pro, I've taken it to mean that I must help newcomers by teaching Clarion, writing the *Ask Bwana* column, and buying stories from new writers for a score of anthologies. But I don't think that adage holds true for fandom, I most certainly *can* pay it back for all the pleasure it's given me, and one of the ways I do that is to contribute articles as often as I can to the fanzines that I most enjoy.

My role model—not as a writer, but as a professional—is Robert Bloch, who was the best friend fandom ever had. I don't believe he ever said No to a hopeful fanzine editor; I at least try not to say it too often.

Anyway, I hope you like the articles, biographies, and speeches that I've cobbled together for *Once A Fan* . . . If we're both still around in another decade or so, I'll see you in the pages of . . . *Always A Fan.*

PART I: WORLDCONS

Ever since 1963, the Worldcon has been the highlight of my year. Some people prefer birthdays, or Christmas, or anniversaries. Not me. Science fiction has been my life for four decades, and Worldcon encompasses, in one incredibly crowded week, just about everything I love about it: old friends, new friends, pro friends, fannish friends, endless tables filled with books and magazines, art shows, parties without number, even egoboo.

So it's only natural that I've written a lot about specific worldcons, and worldcons in general. I hope you find the enthusiasm contagious; I'd like to meet you at the next Worldcon.

ROOTS AND A FEW VINES

So I'm sitting there in Winnipeg, resplendent in my tuxedo, and morbidly wondering how many fans have called me "Mr. Resnick" instead of "Mike" since the worldcon began three days ago.

I don't *feel* like a Mister. I feel like a fan who is cheating by sitting here with all the pros, waiting for Bob Silverberg to announce the winner of the Best Editor Hugo. He goes through the names: Datlow, Dozois, Resnick, Rusch, Schmidt.

He opens the envelope and reads off Kris Rusch's name, and suddenly I am walking up to the stage. Bob is sure I thought he called out *my* name, and looks like he is considering clutching the Hugo to his breast and running off with it (although that is actually a response common to all pros when they are in proximity to a Hugo), but finally he sighs and hands it over to me, and I start thanking Ed Ferman and all the voters.

What am I doing here, I wonder, picking up a Hugo for a lady who is half my age and has twice my talent and is drop-dead gorgeous to boot? How in blazes did I ever get to be an Elder Statesman?

Well, it began in 1962, which, oddly enough, was *not* just last year, no matter how it feels. Carol and I had met at the University of Chicago in 1960. We'd gone to the theater on our first date, and wound up in the Morrison Hotel's coffee shop, where we talked science fiction until they threw us out at 5 in the morning. It was the first time either of us realized that someone else out there read that crazy Buck Rogers stuff (though we might have guessed, since they continued to print it month after month, and two sales per title would hardly seem enough to keep the publishers in business.)

Well, 1962 rolls around, and so does a future Campbell winner named Laura . . . but the second biggest event of the year comes when Ace Books, under the editorship of Don Wollheim, starts pirating a bunch of Edgar Rice Burroughs novels, and a whole generation gets to learn about Tarzan and Frank Frazetta and John Carter and Roy Krenkel and David Innes all at once.

But the important thing, the thing that unquestionably shaped my adult life, was that one of the books had a little blurb on the inside front cover extolling ERB's virtues, and it was signed "Camille Cazedessus, Editor of *ERB-dom*." Well, you didn't have to be a genius to figure out that *ERB-dom*, at least in that context, was an obvious reference to Edgar Rice Burroughs.

A whole magazine devoted to one of my favorite writers? I could barely wait until the next morning, when I took the subway downtown and entered the Post Office News, Chicago's largest magazine store. I looked for *ERB-dom* next to *Time*, *Life*, *Look*, *Newsweek*, and *Playboy*. Wasn't there. I looked for it next to *Analog*, *Galaxy*, and *F&SF*. No dice. Wasn't anywhere near *Forbes* or *Fortune* or *Business Week* either.

So I go up to the manager and tell him I'm looking for *ERB-dom*, and he checks his catalogs and tells me there ain't no such animal.

I grab him by the arm, drag him over to the paperbacks, pull out the operative Burroughs title, turn to the inside front cover, and smite him with a mighty *"Aha!"*

So he promises to get cracking and find out who publishes this magazine and start stocking it, and I return to our subterranean penthouse (i.e., basement apartment) to await the Good News.

Which doesn't come.

I nag Post Office News incessantly. I nag my local bookstore. I nag the public library. I even nag my mother. (This seems counter-productive, but she has been nagging *me* for 20 years and fair is fair.)

Finally, I look at my watch and it is half-past 1962 and there is still no sign of *ERB-dom*, so I write to the editor, Miss Cazedessus (so okay, until then I'd never heard of a *guy* named Camille), in care of Ace Books, and a month later the first five issues of *ERB-dom* arrive in the mail, the very first fanzines I have ever seen, along with a long, friendly letter that constantly uses the arcane word "worldcon."

Within two months I have written three long articles for *ERB-dom #6* and have become its associate editor. There is a worldcon in Chicago that summer, not a 20-minute subway ride from where we live, but the future Campbell winner chooses

August 17 to get herself born, and we do not go to the worldcon. When she is 8 days old I decide to forgive her and lovingly show her off to her grandparents, and she vomits down the back of my Hawaiian shirt (which, in retrospect, could well have been an editorial comment), and it is 27 years before I willingly touch her again, but that is another story.

There is one other thing that happens in 1962. We are living at the corner of North Shore and Greenview in the Rogers Park area of Chicago, and right across street of us is this old apartment building, and on the third Saturday of every month strange-looking men and women congregate there. They have long hair, and most of them are either 90 pounds overweight or 50 pounds underweight, and often they are carrying books under their arms. We decide they are members of SNCC or CORE, which are pretty popular organizations at the time, and that they are meeting there to figure out how to dodge the draft, and that the books they carry are either pacifist tracts or ledgers with the names and addresses of all the left- wing groups that have contributed money to them.

We have to go all the way to Washington D.C. a year later and attend Discon I to find out that they are not draft dodgers (well, not *primarily*, anyway) but rather Chicago fandom, and that they have been meeting 80 feet from our front door for 2 years.

So I wend my way back through the audience, and I find my seat, and I hand Kris Rusch's Hugo to Carol, because I am also up for Best Short Story, and I think I've got a better chance at this, and when I run up to accept the award it will look tacky to already be carrying a Hugo. Besides, Charles Sheffield is sitting right next to us, and he is up for Best Novelette, and he is getting very nervous, and wants to stroke the Hugo for luck, or maybe is considering just walking out with it and changing the name plates at a future date. (In fact, I am convinced that if he does not win his own, neither Kris nor I will ever see *her* Hugo again. Charles will probably deny this, but never forget that Charles gets paid an inordinate amount of money to tell lies to the public at large.)

So Guy Gavriel Kay begins reading off the nominees, and suddenly I realize that I am not nervous at all, that this is becoming very old hat to me. I have been nominated for nine Hugos in the past six years. I have actually won a pair. Worldcons are very orderly things: you show up, you sign a million autographs, you eat each meal with a different editor and line up your next year's worth of work, and then you climb into your tux and see if you won another Hugo.

It's gotten to be such a regular annual routine, you sometimes find yourself idly wondering: was it *always* like this?

Then you think back to your first worldcon, and you realize that no, it was not always like this . . .

Right off the bat, we were the victims of false doctrine. Everyone we knew in fandom—all six or seven of them—told us the worldcon was held over Labor Day weekend. So we took them at their word.

The problem, of course, was the definition of "weekend." We took a train that pulled out of Chicago on Friday morning, and dumped us in the basement of our Washington D.C. hotel at 9:00 Saturday morning. At which time we found out that the convention was already half over.

(Things were different then. There were no times in the convention listings. In fact, there were no convention listings. Not in *Analog*, not anywhere. If you knew that worldcons even existed, you were already halfway to being a trufan.)

Caz (right: he wasn't a Miss at all) met us and showed us around. Like myself, he was dressed in a suit and tie; it was a few more worldcons before men wore shirts without jackets or ties, even during the afternoons, and every woman—they formed, at most, 10% of the attendees, and over half were writers' wives—wore a skirt. If you saw someone with a beard—a relatively rare occurrence—you knew he was either a pro writer or Bruce Pelz.

When we got to the huckster room—20-plus dealers (and selling only books, magazines, and fanzines; none of the junk that dominates the tables today), I thought I had died and gone to heaven. The art show had work by Finlay and Freas and Emsh and even Margaret Brundage; only J. Allen St. John was missing from among the handful of artists whose work I knew and admired.

They had an auction. It even had a little booklet telling you what items would be auctioned when, so you knew which session to attend to get what you wanted. Stan Vinson, a famous Burroughs collector who had been corresponding with me for a year, bought a Frazetta cover painting for $70. Friends told him he was crazy; paintings were supposed to appreciate, and no one would ever pay that much for a Frazetta again. I bought a Finlay sketch for $2.00, and an autographed Sturgeon manuscript for $3.50.

In the afternoon we decide to go to the panels. I do not know from panels; like any neo, I take along a pencil and a notebook. The panels are not what we have these days, or at least they did not seem so to my untrained and wondrous eyes and ears.

For example, there is a panel with Willy Ley and Isaac Asimov and Fritz Leiber and L. Sprague de Camp and Ed Emsh and Leigh Bracket, and the topic is "What Should a BEM Look Like?." (I have a copy of the *Discon Proceedings*, a transcript of the entire convention published by Advent, and to this day when I need a new alien race I re-read that panel and invariably I come up with one.)

There was a panel with Fred Pohl and a tyro named Budrys and a gorgeous editor (though not as gorgeous as the one I accepted a Hugo for) named Cele Goldsmith and even >>>>>>**JOHN CAMPBELL HIMSELF**<<<<<<, on how to write stories around cover paintings, which was a common practice back then, and which remains fascinating reading today.

There was a sweet old guy in a white suit who saw that we were new to all this, and moseyed over and spent half an hour with us, making us feel at home and telling us about how we were all one big family and inviting us to come to all the parties at night. Then he wandered off to accept the first-ever Hall of Fame Award from First Fandom. When they asked if he was working on anything at present, he replied that he had just delivered the manuscript to *Skylark DuQuesne*, and received the second-biggest ovation I have ever heard at a worldcon. (The biggest came 30 years later, when Andy Porter broke a 12-year losing streak and won the semi-prozine Hugo in 1993.)

Since we didn't know anyone, and were really rather shy (over the years, I have learned to over-compensate for this tendency, as almost anyone will tell you, bitterly and at length,) we ate dinner alone, then watched the masquerade, which in those days was truly a masquerade ball and not a competition. There was a band, and everyone danced, and a few people showed up in costume, and every now and then one of them would march across the stage, and at the end of the ball they announced the winners.

Then there was the Bheer Blast. In those bygone days, they didn't show movies. (I think movies turned up in 1969, *not* to display the Hugo nominees or give pleasure to the cinema buffs, but to give the kids a place to sleep so they'd stop cluttering up the lobby.) They didn't give out the Hugos at night, either. (An evening banquet might run $5.00 a head, and the concom got enough grief for charging $3.00 a head for rubber chicken served at 1:00 PM rather than six hours later.) They didn't have more than one track of programming. (Multiple tracks came along 8 years later, and evening programs even later than that.)

Well, with all the things they *didn't* have, they needed a way to amuse the congoers in the evening, so what happened was this: every bid committee (and they only bid a year in advance back then) treated the entire convention to a beer party on a different night. We could all fit in one room—I know the official tally for Discon I was 600, but I was there and I'll swear that there were no more than 400 or so in attendance; the other 200 must have been no-shows, or waiters, or bellboys—and the bidding committee would treat us to a small lakeful of beer, with or without pretzels, and then the next night a rival bid would do the same thing. (You voted—if you could drag yourself out of bed—on Sunday morning at the business meeting. A fan would speak for each bid, telling you how wonderful his committee was. Then a pro would speak for each bid, telling you about the quality of restaurants you would encounter. The better restaurants invariably carried the day.)

After the beer blast was over, everyone vanished. The Burroughs people, all of them straighter than Tarzan's arrows, went to bed. We remembered that Doc Smith had mentioned parties, so we began wandering down the empty, foreboding corridors of the hotel, wondering if the parties really did exist, and how to find them.

We walked all the way down one floor, took the stairs up a flight, repeated the procedure, then did it again. We were about to quit when a door opened, and a little bearded man and a thin balding man, both with thick glasses, spotted our name badges and asked if we'd like to come in for a drink. We didn't know who the hell they were, but they had badges too, so we knew they were with the con and probably not about to mug a couple of innocents from Chicago, and we decided to join them.

Turns out they were standing in the doorway to a huge suite, and that their names were del Rey and Blish. Inside, wearing a bowtie and looking not unlike a penguin in his black suit, was Isaac Asimov. Randy Garrett was dressed in something all-satin and not of this century. Bob Silverberg looked young and incredibly dapper. Sam Moskowitz was speaking to Ed Hamilton and Leigh Brackett in a corner; this was many years before his throat surgery, and it was entirely possible, though unlikely, that no one in the basement could hear him.

And every last one of them went out of their way to talk to us and make us feel at home.

Later another young fan wandered in. Much younger than me. I was 21; Jack Chalker was only 19. We sat around, and discussed various things, and then something strange happened, something totally alien to my experience.

Someone asked Jack and I what we wanted to do with our lives. (No, that's not the strange part; people were always asking that.)

We each answered that we wanted to write science fiction.

And you know what? For the first time in my life, *nobody laughed.*

That's when I knew I was going to come back to worldcons for the rest of my life.

So Guy Gavriel Kay reads off the list of nominees, and then he opens the envelope, and the winner is Connie Willis, and I am second to her again for the 83rd time (yeah, I know, I've only lost 76 Hugos and Nebulas to her, but it *feels* like 83), and everyone tells me I've won a moral victory because I have beat all the short stories and Connie's winner is a novelette that David Bratman, in his infinite wisdom, decided to move to the short story category, and I keep thinking that moral victories and 60 cents will get you a cup of coffee anywhere west of New York and east of California, and that I wish I didn't like Connie so much so that I could hate her just a little on Labor Day weekends, and my brain is making up slogans, modified slightly from my youth, slogans like *Break Up Connie Willis*, which is certainly easier than breaking up the Yankees, and I am wondering if Tanya Harding will loan me her bodyguard for a few days, and then I am at the Hugo Losers Party, and suddenly it doesn't matter that I've lost a Hugo, because it is now 31 years since that first worldcon I went to, and it is my annual family reunion, and I am visiting with friends that I see once or twice or, on good years, five times per year, and we have a sense of continuity and community that goes back for almost two-thirds of my life. Hugos are very nice, and I am proud of the ones I've won, and I am even proud of the ones I've lost, but when all is said and done, they are metal objects and my friends are people, and people are what life is all about.

And I find, to my surprise, that almost everyone I am talking to, almost all the old friends I am hugging and already planning to see again at the next worldcon, are fans. Some, like me, write for a living; a few paint; most do other things. But we share a common fannish history, and a common fannish language, and common fannish interests, and I realize that I even enjoyed the business meeting this year, and you have to be pretty far gone into fandom to enjoy Ben Yalow making a point of order.

A lot of pros don't go to worldcon anymore. They prefer World Fantasy Con. It's smaller, more intimate, and it's limited to 750 members—and while this is not official, there is nonetheless a "Fans Not Wanted" sign on the door.

That's probably why I don't go. It's true that worldcons have changed, that people who read and write science fiction are probably a minority special interest group these days, that bad movies will outdraw the Hugo ceremony . . . but the trufans are there. It just means you have to work a little harder to hunt them up.

One of the things I have tried to do with the new writers I have helped to bring into this field, the coming superstars like Nick DiChario and Barb Delaplace and Michelle Sagara and

Jack Nimersheim and all the many others, is to not only show them how to make a good story better, or to get an editor to pick up the check for meals, but also to understand the complex and symbiotic relationship between fandom and prodom.

Some of them, like Nick, luck out and find it right away. Some, like Barb, wander into a bunch of Trekkies or Wookies or Beasties who won't read anything except novelizations, who are watchers rather than readers, whose only literary goal is to tell second-hand stories in a third-hand universe, and she wonders what the hell I'm talking about. Then I drag her to a CFG suite or a NESFA party and she meets the fandom *I* know, and suddenly she understands why we keep coming back.

So I'm sitting in the airport, waiting to board the plane from Winnipeg to Minnesota. I think there are three mundanes on the flight; everyone else is coming from worldcon. Larry Niven's there, and Connie Willis, and maybe a dozen other pros, and one of the topics of conversation as we await the plane is whose names will make the cover of *Locus* if the plane crashes, and whose names will be in small print on page 37, and how many obituary issues Charlie Brown can get out of it. Then the topic turns to who you would rescue if the plane crashed: Connie and Larry and me, because you wanted more of our stories, or Scott Edelman and me, because you wanted us to be so grateful to you that we'd buy your next twenty stories. (That goes to show you the advantages of being able to do more than one thing well.)

Now, in any other group, that would be a hell of a morbid discussion, but because they were fans, and almost by definition bright and witty, it was the most delightful conversation I'd heard all weekend, and once again I found myself wondering what my life would have been like if Ace had not forwarded that letter to Caz 32 years ago.

And then I thought back to another convention, the 1967 worldcon. I was still very young, and too cynical by half, and when Lester del Rey got up to give his Guest of Honor speech, he looked out at the tables—every worldcon until 1976 presented the GOH speech and the Hugo Awards at a banquet— and said, "Every person in the world that I care for is here tonight."

And I thought: what a feeble thing to say. What a narrow, narrow life this man has lived. What a tiny circle of friends he has.

Well, I've sold 72 books of science fiction—novels, collections, anthologies—and I've won some awards, and I've paid some dues, and I don't think it's totally unrealistic to assume that sometime before I die I will be the Guest of Honor at a worldcon.

I've done a lot with my life (all with Carol's help, to be sure). I've taken several trips to Africa. I've bred 27 champion collies. I've owned and run the second-biggest boarding kennel in the country. I've sired a daughter than any father would be proud to call his own. I've been a lot of places, done a lot of things. I don't think I've led a narrow life at all.

But when I get up to make my Guest of Honor speech, I'll look around the room just the way Lester did, and, because I'm a reasonably honest man, I won't say what he said.

But I *will* say, "With three or four exceptions, every person in the world that I care for is here tonight."

for Mimosa #14

WORLDCON MEMORIES— PART I

1971: NOREASCON I (Boston)

Hank and Martha Beck had a room on the 23rd floor of the Sheraton. And on Saturday night, I wandered up there, toting a ton of books I'd bought in the huckster room, and hoping to find a nice, comfortable chair where I could sit and browse through what I'd bought.

Well, Martha had her share of comfortable chairs—but being Martha, she had more than her share of friends sitting in them. And Martha, Pat and Roger Sims, and Banks Mebane were using all the uncomfortable chairs while playing bridge. And five or six people were sitting on the bed, talking about who the hell knows what.

So I walk around the room once, hoping someone will get up or die, whichever comes first, and no one does. And then I remember: there's an outdoor swimming pool on the fifth floor. I walk to a window, make sure it's visible, and then turn to the room and exclaim that there are naked people in the pool. Lots of 'em!

I never saw a room empty out so fast. Martha led the charge down the stairs—no one was willing to wait for the elevator—followed by maybe 20 other people, and I sat down to look at my books.

Must have been good books, too, because I hardly noticed the passage of time, or that the room *stayed* empty.

About two hours later, Roger Sims, red of face and short of breath, comes back to the 23rd floor and enters the room. "I thought you were kidding," he says.

"You mean I wasn't?" I say.

So he takes me down to the pool, and sure enough, there are about 200 naked bodies in and around the water. I have about three minutes to appreciate the prettier ones of the female persuasion, and then—so help me—the cops raid the joint.

John Guidry grabs Carol and me by our arms and tells us that he's got a room on the fifth floor, and we can wait there until the fuzz leave, which is precisely what we do.

Now, you can't keep a little thing like 200 naked bodies a

secret for long at a Worldcon, and on Sunday night, some two thousand potential voyeurs show up to gape again—but it is 50 degrees and drizzling, and all the skinny-dippers know enough to stay inside, where it is warm and dry.

Other memories of Noreascon I:

Meeting Marvin Minsky, and realizing that I'd found what was said to be impossible—a man who was both smarter and wittier than Isaac Asimov (and a dear friend of Isaac's, as well).

Finally getting to meet Cliff Simak, the GOH, and quite possibly the sweetest, most decent man I've ever known.

Listening to Cliff's GOH speech. This was during the most bitter part of the feud between the Old and New Waves, and rather than speak about his career, Cliff spent most of the speech trying to make peace. It was too reasonable to have much effect.

1978: IGUANACON (Phoenix)

What I mostly remember is that Satan would have found Phoenix on Labor Day weekend *much* too hot for his taste.

We stayed in the headquarters hotel, the Hyatt. It was maybe 40 stories tall, and had a 9-story atrium. The atrium was cool and comfortable . . . but it took every bit of the building's air-conditioning power to cool the it. Everything above the 9th floor felt like the anteroom to hell. CFG (the Cincinnati Fantasy Group) had a suite on the 21st floor; we got rid of it after a day. You couldn't open the windows—they didn't want anyone jumping or falling out—and you couldn't get cool air, or indeed *any* air circulation.

The Adams Hotel across the street wasn't much better, but at least it had *some* air-conditioning. I remember that we waited until Stu and Amy Brownstein, who were staying at the Adams, went out to party each night, and then we'd borrow their room for a nap before we had to go back to the hell of the Hyatt.

Stu and I were going to wear our tuxes for some function or other. I remembered the tux, but forgot the bowtie. Carol had seen a formal-wear store two blocks from the Hyatt, so Friday morning we decided to walk to it and buy a black tie. Got almost halfway before we decided we'd never make it before we melted. On the way back, we passed five or six wrinkled old ladies trudging toward us, each wearing a sweater. I think that was when I decided that I didn't want to be immortal after all.

Then there was the Sun's Anvil—the square block of concrete (and no shade) that you had to walk across to get to the huckster room, the art show, or the programming. I *live* in the huckster room at a Worldcon . . . but I made the trip only twice in five days. Not a lot of people made it more often.

David Gerrold and I were two of the five masquarade judges on Saturday night. And it turned out that the one truly cool room in the whole damned city was the room where the judges went to deliberate. For those of you who have been wondering for two decades why there was a record number of runthroughs, I might as well lay it on you: David couldn't bear to go back to the Hyatt, and that 68-degree deliberating room kept beckoning to him. Not that the rest of us tried to argue him out of it.

One night we went out for dinner with Lou Tabakow, stately old God Emperor of Cincinnati fandom. He'd heard of this very nice rooftop restaurant. We assumed he meant "penthouse"; nope, he meant "rooftop."

We get there, take an elevator to the roof, and step out into the rays of the late afternoon sun. Lou and I immediately take off our jackets and ties. By the time the salads arrived, Lou has unbuttoned his shirt; it is gone before we hit the main course. Then, as the sun continued to beat down on us while we wait for dessert, stately, dignified, white-haired Legendary Lou looks around, sees that all the other diners except Carol are males, announces that Carol is a member of the family, and removes his pants, finishing the meal in his shorts. He was unquestionably the most comfortable diner there.

I remember being dragged off to an "authentic" Japanese restaurant by Carol, Joni Stopa, Jo Ann Wood, and other sophisticated gourmets. And while they ordered a bunch of stuff that looked like uncooked rubber, Ben Jason and I studied the menu—which was entirely in Japanese—and tried to figure out which of those words looked like meat, or at least plain broth. Guessed wrong, too.

I also remember that the entire registration on Thursday was being worked by one teenaged girl until Lynne Aronson rolled up her sleeves, recruited some workers, and saved the day.

1983: CONSTELLATION (Baltimore)

By now I was an established pro, and I found, to my unhappiness, that Worldcons were becoming more business and less pleasure.

I had just fired my former agent, and this was the convention where I'd made up my mind to find a new one. Found her, too. I hit it off with Eleanor Wood and hired her before the weekend was over. She quintupled my income the next year, and we've been together for fifteen happy and lucrative years now.

We stayed in the Hyatt, since it was attached to the convention center. Officially, no parties were allowed; I imagine we attended somewhere between 15 and 20 within the hotel.

The Hilton was six or seven uphill blocks away. I went there one night with John Guidry, got stranded on the 27th floor, walked down to ground level, and never went back.

I never did make it to the Holiday Inn, where the CFG had its annual hospitality suite. Carol did, a couple of times—and both times was almost dragged forceably into a burlesque theater by an exceptionally motivated ticket seller.

It had been a few years since we'd had a Hugo banquet, and I was really pleased that the grand old custom was back. That lasted about 10 seconds. Observation: crab feast or no crab feast, NEVER GIVE A THOUSAND FANS WOODEN MALLETS.

As we were sitting there waiting for Jack Chalker to announce the Hugo winners, a notebook somehow materialized at our table. Barry Malzberg, who was up for a Hugo, was sitting next to me. He pulled a pen out and wrote a title on the first page of the notebook: "Fear and Loathing in Baltimore." I took it away and wrote an appropriate opening sentence, then passed it on to Jack Dann, who wrote a second sentence and gave it back to Barry. The three of us wrote a 4-page round-robin, one sentence at a time. Then Sheila Gilbert pulled out a blue pencil and edited it, and her husband Mike illustrated it. I'm sure they've all forgotten it many years ago—but in 1985 I donated it to some fannish charity or other, and was told that it sold for $125.00.

1987: CONSPIRACY 87 (Brighton, England)

Not a lot of memories of this one. We were just passing through on the way to Africa. We got there on Thursday afternoon and were gone by Saturday night.

I delivered "Kirinyaga" to Scott Card. Didn't mean a thing at the time; I had no way of foreseeing the effect it would have on my career. I did just one panel, and no autograph session. Met most of my European editors and some of my foreign agents.

What I mostly remember was trying to find the Corn Exchange. It was a large building that housed the Bantam party, the biggest shindig of the con. And it was all but impossible to locate. It was half a dozen twisty, angular blocks from the con, and "clearly marked" meant that the words "Corn Exchange" were there in big, bold, 2-inch-high letters about 20 feet above ground level. I'll swear that there are pros and fans who are *still* wandering the streets of Brighton, trying to find their way to or from it.

We stayed in the "pros'" hotel (i.e., the expensive one, where they put all the pros, regardless of what we'd requested). The Metropole was the headquarters hotel, and CFG had its suite there, hosted (in Bill Cavin's absence) by Scott and Jane Dennis. Pat and Roger Sims were a few blocks away. We had dinner with them in their hotel. Then, with a sly smile, Roger invited us to see their room. I discovered the reason for the smile a moment later: the elevator was so small that the four of us couldn't fit in it—and it was the only elevator in the building.

1993: CONFRANCISCO (San Francisco)

This is the con that picked up the nickname "ConFiasco" very early on, and will never lose it. (The fact that some committee members have spent years on the computer networks arguing with unhappy attendees that they did so have a good time no matter what they think hasn't done much to eradicate the label or the taste.)

It began with the voting. The committee knew it had lost the Marriott, a huge, modern hotel across the street from the Moscone Center, but it kept that fact a secret. Then, after it won, there came the announcement that the Marriott was unavailable, and that the headquarters hotel was quite a few uphill blocks away.

CFG decided that we had voted for the hotel and we were damned well going to have the hotel, so using just our initials, we blocked 60 rooms and a hospitality suite, then passed the word to a bunch of old-time fans and pros, and sold them out instantly. The con committee was pissed because we cost them 300 room nights; but we were just as pissed that they were trying to stick us almost a mile away from the facility we'd voted for.

The CFG suite was like Rick's in Casablanca. You remember: "Everyone comes to Rick's." Well, if you wanted to meet every fan and pro with more than a couple of Worldcons under his or her belt, all you had to do was sit in the suite, and sooner or later they'd make an appearance. We opened it every night at about 9:00 and closed it every morning about 4:00; it was probably the best hospitality suite I've experienced in a more than a third of a century of Worldcons.

(In fact, it was in this suite that *Alternate Worldcons* was conceived, sold, and assigned to its writers. The story of how and why is in the book's introduction.)

I think the beggars—they preferred to call themselves "the homeless"—had one hell of an efficient grapevine. We arrived on Tuesday and walked to the Moscone Center . . . and passed one solitary beggar. By the weekend, there were thousands of them . . . and by the next Tuesday, there was only one again.

I remember the endless lines for registration. There was one to register. They you had to stand in a second one if you were on the program, a third if you wanted a program book (for which you'd paid), and a fourth if you were Hugo nominee. Bob Silverberg stopped by on his way out and offered to get me in. Since I was standing next to Mike Glyer, and I didn't want to be the star of a con report in *File 770* about former fans suddenly becoming snobbish pros, I regretfully refused and spent another couple of hours waiting to register.

I remember going out to dinner just prior to the masquerade, and seeing an enormous line of fans waiting to get in. And I remember walking by on the way back, and finding that hundreds of them had been turned away.

I was up for a Hugo, and as usual there was a very nice

spread of food laid out for the nominees. But no one had remembered to set out any chairs, and a number of nominees with physical ailments—I remember Beth Meacham's arthritis was extremely painful that night—were very uncomfortable until we were finally allowed to take our seats in the audience.

I lost the Hugo . . . but that was okay, because I got to accept the Campbell for my daughter (who was being charged by an enraged elephant in South Africa at that very moment.) On my way back to my seat, someone—it might have been Mike Glyer—asked me for a quote. I still remember it: "My stud fee just tripled!"

1997: LONESTARCON 2 (San Antonio)

So it's late on Sunday afternoon, and I've just finished doing my sixth or seventh panel or reading or something, and I'm beat. And I'm standing on the corner, waiting for the light to change so I can cross from the convention center to the Marriott and take a shower. And there's a young man standing next to me, saying how tired he is.

"Me, too," I agree. Then I see Kris Rusch standing at the opposite corner, waiting to cross to the con center. "In fact," I say, "I think what I need is a hug from a pretty woman. Like *that* one," I continue, nodding toward Kris.

The light changes, and the kid goes into a panic. "That . . . that's Kristine Kathryn Rusch!" he says in awed tones. "She's a writer and an editor and a Hugo winner and . . ."

"I don't care," I say. "She's a pretty lady and I need a hug."

"But she's married! You can't just walk up to her and . . ." The kid is actually sputtering now. I realize that I've taken off my badge, and he has no idea who I am.

We meet halfway across the street. I throw my arms around Kris. She smiles, hugs me back, and gives me a kiss.

I get to the opposite sidewalk, and I see the kid is staring at me, jaw agape.

"Sexual magnetism," I explain, and vanish into the Marriott.

I hope he remembered to shut his mouth before he went to sleep.

Other memories:

A female pedestrian was killed by a bus just a few feet from

Jack Chalker.

Linda Dunn was the first person to do a Worldcon costume from one of my books—she was Suma, from Kevin Johnson's cover painting to *Eros Ascending*—and she won a pair of prizes.

I had the first kaffeeklatsch of the con, on Thursday afternoon. I was annoyed at the timing—later in the con figured to draw better—but I managed to fill the room. More to the point, the hotel didn't quite understand that the kaffeeklatsch wasn't the Hugo pre-ceremony, and they laid out a spread that must have contained, at a conservative estimate, 20 million calories and cost a few thousand dollars. (They figured out their mistake within the hour, and all future kaffeeklatsches had to settle for wet coffee and dry donuts.)

Carol and I found a "tea room" a couple of blocks from the con center. At one point, she asked where the ladies' room was. "We ain't got none," was the answer. "You're kidding, right?" she says. The waiter fixes her with a steely eye: "This is Texas, ma'am."

Neal Barrett was an hilarious toastmaster. I know some people have criticized him for being too vulgar or too long-winded, but I was there, and the audience laughed non-stop.

An audio publisher brought out my very first audio recording, a couple of Kirinyaga stories read by a New York actor.

And speaking of *Kirinyaga*, I had sold the book to del Rey, which proceeded to treat me like a king. This is the company that used to send writers into shock if they popped for a corned beef sandwich. Well, they took Carol and me out to four different meals, and Fed Ex'd a copy of the cover painting to my hotel when I asked for it.

Had lunch with Gardner Dozois, who was as sick of business meals as I was. I promised not to try to sell him anything if he promised not to ask me to send him anything. Most enjoyable business lunch of the con.

Bantam announced a month before the Worldcon that they'd be taking a select list of invitees (five huge buses' worth; so much for "select") to a nightclub on Sunday night. It was so hot that we didn't dress formally—but a lot of writers and editors did. And then found out, after driving well out of town, that the San Antonio definition of a nightclub is almost identical to everyone else's definition of a Texas honkey tonk. I spent most of the night playing horseshoes with Andy Porter; Dean Smith lorded it over a shuffleboard game. If you didn't like barbeque sauce, you were in deep trouble.

My daughter Laura, who has a major fantasy novel coming from Tor in 1998, roomed as usual with Peggy Ranson. We met in the Marriott's bar Sunday night to exchange gossip—and I was flabbergasted to find out that she knew about five times as much as I did. The kid really gets around.

I was up for a Hugo for the 16th time in nine years, and managed to lose it. I was also scheduled to pick up Hugos for Maureen McHugh and John Clute if they had won; they lost, too. I did pick up chocolate rocket ships for all of us at the Hugo Losers Party (including one for Michael Burstein, who won the Campbell). Maureen was on a diet, so was I, and I hated to think of the condition John's would arrive in (he lives in England), so I gave Michael's to Tony Lewis to deliver, and hid the other three behind the television in the CFG suite, where I assume they are still rotting.

After about 15 business meals in a row, it was a pleasure to just relax and eat with friends on Monday. Had breakfast with Rick Katze, lunch with Tony and Suford Lewis, dinner with Dean Smith and Kris Rusch, and a late snack with some CFG members. Helped me to remember what Worldcons were like before I started writing this stuff for a living.

One other thing. At LACon III the previous year, Dimensions—the science fiction branch of Miramax—had an offer on the table for *The Widowmaker*, which included Carol and me writing the script. One of the Dimensions execs flew out from New York just to have dinner with us at the Annaheim Hilton. We'd agreed on a pick-up fee for the books, a price for the screenplay, keyline art, everything but the price of the 3-book option, and he felt we were probably one phone call away from agreeing on that, too. And when we got home from LACon III, the offer was off the table. Seems that in intervening three days, Dimensions' first science fiction (as opposed to horror) film had come out and was bombing, and Miramax wasn't sure they wanted to keep Dimensions in business. But in the year following LACon III *Mimic* came out and made a bundle, and *Scream 2* began looking like it would even outearn *Scream 1*, and suddenly, at LoneStarCon, the offer for *The Widowmaker* was back on the table. This time we didn't give them a chance to reconsider.

For Mimosa #22

WORLDCON MEMORIES— PART 2

1966: TRICON (Cleveland)

Though we had met a number of fans during the past couple of years who would become lifelong friends—Pat and Roger Sims, Bob Tucker, Ed and Jo Ann Wood, Dave and Ruth Kyle, Hank and Martha Beck—we nonetheless spent most of Tricon with the Edgar Rice Burroughs fans. After all, it had been through the Burroughs door that we entered fandom, and Burroughs would never be as popular with the Hugo voters again as he was in 1966. The Barsoom books were on the ballot for Best All-Time Series, Frank Frazetta was up for Best Artist primarily because of his ERB covers for Ace, and *ERB-dom*, on which I was the assistant editor, was up for Best Fanzine.

Camille Cazedessus, Jr.—Caz to everyone—showed up late, and found they had sold his room out from under him. In fact, they had sold *every* room out from under him, and he was forced to accept a huge suite for the price of a room. The *ERB-dom* crowd—Caz (the editor) and his wife Mary, us, John F. Roy, John Guidry, Neal MacDonald, and a new artist, Jeff Jones—spent every evening camped out there.

This was the worldcon that hosted the first Asimov/Ellison Insult Contest. It was generally considered that Isaac was winning when Harlan segued off into a lengthy description of a fistic encounter with a couple of Frank Sinatra's bodyguards, and then the hour was over.

One of the most memorable, if not the most pleasant, recollections I have of Tricon is the bagpipers. You see, back then the worldcon wasn't large enough to fill a hotel, let alone the two or three we now take over, and we shared the premises with other groups. In 1966, it was a group of happy bagpipers, who went up and down the corridors in the wee small hours of the morning, wearing their kilts, drinking their Scotch, and blowing their bagpipes. Loudly. (I don't think you *can* blow a bagpipe softly.) It was the first, and probably only, time in worldcon history when the fans complained to the hotel that the mundanes were making too much noise.

I sold my first sf novel at Tricon. In retrospect, I wish I hadn't. It's a pretty good Burroughs pastiche but a pretty awful Resnick novel, and copies of it come back to haunt me at every autograph session. (I resist the urge to tear it up, and just remind the reader that I was a teenager when I wrote it and I've gotten a lot better.)

(No, I wasn't a teenager in 1966. But it took me half a dozen years to sell that sucker. I should have listened to the first 30 editors.)

Now let me tell you about the Hugos. Back then you didn't have to be a member of the worldcon to vote. The worldcon drew maybe 600 attendees or thereabouts. *ERB-dom* had a mailing list of close to 1,000. All Caz did was copy the ballot and mail it out with the last issue before the voting deadline, and *ERB-dom* became the first Burroughs fanzine ever to win a Hugo. (And the last. I think the rules were changed the following year. They were certainly changed soon thereafter.)

Harlan won his first Hugo, and when it came time to announce the award for Best All-Time Series (a ridiculous award, since it presupposed that no series written after 1966 could possibly be better), he took the microphone away from a shocked Isaac, who was the Toastmaster, and announced that The Foundation Trilogy had won. Nowadays everyone just yawns, but on that night it was a shocker: the sf fans all thought Heinlein's Future History had a lock on it, the fantasy fans couldn't see how Tolkein's Lord of the Rings could lose, and the old-timers voted en masse for Doc Smith's Lensman series. And of course, there were enough Burroughs fans there to give Hugos to Frazetta and *ERB-dom*, so they felt certain the Barsoom series would win.

Having been to one worldcon already, I knew what the dealers room was like (and back then, it sold almost nothing but books and magazines), so we took along an empty suitcase and I filled it up, courtesy of a few dozen friendly hucksters.

I had overslept every morning, and we had an early train back to Chicago on Labor Day, and I was worried about sleeping through it. I mentioned this to John Roy the night before, and at 5:00 AM he phoned me and started reciting the longest, stupidest series of filthy limericks I'd ever heard. They were so dreadful that I was totally awake and ready to leave at 5:15.

1973: TORCON II (Toronto)

In 1972, as I was standing shoulder to shoulder with half a hundred sweating photographers trying to get pictures of some of the masquerade costumes, I noticed that the costumers all looked cool and composed and (especially) uncrowded, and I decided that I'd been on the wrong end of the camera long enough. All I had to do was convince Carol to make a costume for us to wear, and we'd finally be able to *enjoy* a worldcon masquerade.

Well, oddly enough, she thought it was a fine idea, and we spent the next couple of months trying to decide what costume to make. We finally hit upon Lith the Golden Witch and the wonderfully-named Chun the Unavoidable from Jack Vance's *The Dying Earth*.

Chun's robe was covered with eyeballs, so while Carol made an elegant flowing black velvet robe, I got a few hundred ping-pong balls, pasted irises and pupils on them, and strung them on a series of glittering wires which she then attached to the robe. Then, to make the costume complete, I carried the eyeless head of Liane the Wayfarer.

Carol's costume was a little more problematical. She would wear patterns of gold feathers on her arms and legs, and gold body paint, and gold leaves in her hair, and a gold loincloth, and she would carry a gold cage containing a frog, but what she mostly was was naked. We brought along a brass bra in case she changed her mind (i.e., lost her nerve), but she had three or four vodka stingers an hour before we were due on stage and that was enough to curb any inhibitions she might have had.

We had a wonderful time, posed for a trillion photographs, were interviewed on Canadian television (American news programs weren't wildly anxious to run interviews with a topless witch back in 1973), and won the award for Most Authentic Costume. There was no Best in Show at Torcon II, but Joni Stopa, one of the judges, later told us that she polled the other judges and if there had been a Best in Show, we'd have won it. We enjoyed the experience so much that we would do four more costumes in the 1970s (and three would be even bigger winners).

The con was held in the Royal York Hotel. I remember an endless bridge game in the N3F room, and some nice room parties, but what I mostly remember was that they nickel-anddimed you to death. You wanted matches with your cigarettes, it was an extra penny; ice with your water, an extra penny; and so on. After the masquerade, Hank Beck and I got hungry and decided to grab a sandwich. The only place open was the night-club in the basement. We didn't want to be drowned out, so we called ahead to find out when the singer was taking her break, showed up two minutes after she left the stage, ordered and ate our food, and left before she came back on—and nonetheless had to pay a substantial entertainment charge.

This was the year that the Hugo rocket ships didn't arrive on time, and the committee was able to hand out only the bases. Later that night John Guidry and I went up onto the roof to catch a breath of fresh air, and we found Ray Lafferty, who'd had a few too many, on his hands and knees, obviously looking for something he'd misplaced. We asked what he'd lost and of-fered to help him find it. He held up the Hugo base. He was pretty sure he'd won a Hugo earlier that night, but he couldn't remember what happened to the damned rocket, and he thought maybe he'd lost it up here on the roof. We gently es-corted him back into the hotel, and he picked up the rocket the next year at Discon II.

I'd pretty much lost touch with all of the Burroughs fans ex-cept for John Guidry and John Roy, but when we heard that Buster Crabbe was to be the Guest Speaker at the Burroughs Bibliophiles' Dum-Dum (which was held at the worldcon until the end of the decade), we jumped at the chance to hear him. He was a brilliant, funny speaker. In all my experience at all the hundred-plus conventions I've been to, only Isaac Asimov and Bob Bloch ever performed better.

We'd taken our Dodge maxivan to the con, so we could transport our costumes, and on the way home we offered a ride to Martha Beck and John Guidry. When we hit Michigan we stopped at Win Schuler's, one of my favorite steak houses. They began by giving you free meatballs and bar cheese while you pe-rused the menu. Martha, John and I put away a quick four or five pounds of meatballs while waiting for our meals to arrive, and finally Carol decided to take a table at the far end of the restaurant and pretend she didn't know us. It was quite some time before we even realized she was gone.

1977: SUNCON (Miami Beach)

No one knew if there was going to be a worldcon in 1977. Don Lundry's group, known as "7 for 77," won the bid without naming a city. They later hit upon Orlando, lost their hotel a few months before the con (I think they were waiting for it to be built and it was behind schedule, but I could be misremembering), and then moved to Miami Beach and the Fontainbleu. A couple of weeks before the worldcon, the Fontainbleu went into receivership, and no one knew if it would stay open. As a result, Suncon was the smallest domestic con of the decade . . . but that just meant that those of us who showed up had this enormous, semi-empty hotel in which to play and party.

Carol and I arrived a day early, and came away with a pair of collector's items because of that. We were among the first to register and get our badges and program books and giveaways. A few minutes later they closed down registration. Seems they forgot to include Harlan Ellison's copyright notice on the program book bio he did of Toastmaster Bob Silverberg, and they had to make up a hand stamp and stamp the copyright notice into every program book. We have two of the ten or twelve copies that got away before the omission was discovered.

This was the con at which Second Fandom was created. It was First Fandomite Dave Kyle's suggestion, but a number of us modified it a bit. We wanted to be able to throw a party in which the oldpharts didn't drink all our booze and the kids didn't eat all our food, so we created a group with restrictions at both ends: to become a member, you had to have started reading science fiction after the cutoff date for First Fandom (sometime in 1938, as I recall) and before the day that *Astounding* became *Analog*. We were formed solely to have parties at worldcon, and while I suppose we still officially exist, we haven't thrown one in a few years now. The person to complain to is Roger Sims, who's been our president since the beginning. (We actually did create the Groff Conklin Award, to be given to the author who did the most to interest us in science fiction, and we gave it out once—to Sprague de Camp, a worthy recipient—but we decided that awards were against the spirit of party-throwing and we never gave out another.)

The Fontainbleu was a bit shabby and run-down for a luxury hotel, but the lobby was magnificent: two thousand people could sit comfortably and visit. There was an Olympic-sized saltwater pool out back, and literally hundreds of fans spent goodly portions of their day in it. (It was *so* buoyant from the salt that it was impossible to sink; dozens of fans wiled away their afternoons floating on their backs and reading whatever they'd purchased in the huckster room.)

We attended the Dum-Dum to listen to Leigh Brackett give a speech. So did Keith Laumer, whose entire personality changed after he suffered a stroke. He became abusive and offensive, and only Leigh could quiet him down. Mainstream fans knew all about his problems, but this was Burroughs fandom's first exposure to him, and they didn't know how to react or what to do. A very awkward couple of hours.

Carol was willing to make me a costume, but she didn't want to go in costume herself. I hit upon Clark Ashton Smith's "Master of the Crabs," and tried to coordinate it by long distance with Angelique Trouvere (a/k/a Destiny), who had to cancel at the last minute. I had a number of large, realistic-looking plastic crabs on my jeweled robe, and a long white beard, and a trident, and a bunch of other stuff, but Carol decided it needed something authentic, so the morning of the masquerade she went out to the Fontainbleu's unkempt beach and brought back a bunch of seaweed, which she then hung on the robe. By masquerade time it smelled pretty awful; no one wanted to be within 30 feet of me—including me. I won Most Outstanding Costume, and two minutes later I was in the shower stall, scrubbing as hard as I could (and two minutes after that I was dousing myself with the strongest, cheapest men's cologne I could find. Neither helped much.)

The Fontainbleu had an all-night coffee shop. Lou Tabakow, who had become perhaps our closest fannish friend after we moved to Cincinnati, lived there. I think he had about 15 snacks—pie and coffee—each day with various friends, and never did order anything resembling a meal. (He also caught the costuming bug, and won a prize for a very funny fannish costume.)

Our room had a sign on the wall, asking us to please not litter the floor with food crumbs. We didn't know why until late one night, when we were using a basement passage from one tower to another, we ran into a small army of palmetto roaches, each about four inches long and ugly as sin. I went right back up to the room and made sure the floor was spotless.

Phil Foglio won his first Fan Artist Hugo. We felt partially responsible, since when we lived in the Chicago area, I was convinced Phil would go all week without eating and then visit us on the weekend and down 17 or 18 pounds of meat, and if we hadn't let him in, he would have died of malnutrition without ever having made it to a worldcon.

1982: CHICON IV (Chicago)

Chicon IV began awkwardly. We had been to Windycon at the Chicago Hyatt the year before, and had been stranded on the 22nd floor for a couple of hours. (The elevators went straight to the rooftop, then began coming down—but when they reached a certain weight level, which they always did before the 22nd floor, they expressed right to the lobby level, and then repeated the procedure.)

Now, a few years earlier, Windycon had been held in the Radisson, just across the Chicago River from the Hyatt. The rooms had been very nice, there was a great pool on the 13th floor, the elevators all worked, and the restaurant served a memorable brunch . . . so I wrote a letter to a number of our friends, detailing our experiences at both hotels, stating we would be staying at the Radisson, and recommending they do the same.

We showed up a few days before worldcon began . . . and found that the Radisson had lost our reservation. After considerable acrimony they found a room for us that was somewhat smaller and considerably dirtier than a broom closet. The corridors needed carpets and a paint job, the help was surly, there was a stale odor permeating the place. Third World facilities can nosedive like that in a couple of years, but we hadn't expected a member of a major chain on Chicago's "Miracle Mile" to degenerate so quickly.

So I left Carol there, walked half a mile to the Hyatt, found they had a room on the 5th floor, took it, went back, got Carol and the luggage, and moved to the Hyatt—and am *still* catching hell from Jo Ann Wood and a few others, partially for suggesting the Radisson and partially for deserting it.

Of course, once Larry Propp (the co-chair) found out we

were on the 5th floor—which was reserved for committee big-wigs and the Guests of Honor and did not require elevators—he spent an hour every morning trying to get the hotel to move us out. Didn't work. Finally Kelly Freas, who was the artist Guest of Honor, showed up, and Larry dragged him to our room and explained that it had been reserved for Kelly, and since Kelly was an old friend, we agreed to move to the 24th floor—only to have Kelly decide that he'd rather be with fans on the 24th than committee members on the 5th. At which point Larry left us alone for the last couple of days.

The CFG was on the 7th floor and the SFWA Suite was on the 6th, and the escalator went to the 4th, so we never once had to take an elevator. I remember Frank Robinson and Jack Williamson were stranded somewhere around the 30th floor when they were due to participate in a midnight panel, and never did make it down.

Larry Tucker was busy filming FAANS, the now-classic video starring just about everyone in Midwestern fandom, and it frequently made the 7th floor corridor inaccessible. It was worth it, though; FAANS is every bit as important to fandom as *Ah! Sweet Idiocy!* or *Fancyclopedia II.*

My first few legitimate sf novels (as opposed to the Burroughs and Howard pastiches of more than a decade ago) had come out during the year, and for the first time I went to an autograph session and didn't just sit there getting sympathetic looks from passers-by. It was also the first time an editor bought us a meal at a worldcon; Sheila Gilbert of Signet took us to Doro's, my favorite Italian restaurant, and a place we used to go to celebrate each new book contract.

We had driven up from Cincinnati, and on the way back we stopped for a housewarming at Lynne and Mark Aronson's new home in Chicago's Rogers Park. John Guidry came back to Cincinnati with us. I gave him a map of the local second-hand bookstores, bade him good hunting, and hardly saw him again for the next three days.

1988: NOLACON II (New Orleans)

This one's going to take a while to explain. To this day, everyone else complains about Nolacon II. Me, I had a great time.

But there was no reason why I shouldn't have had a great time: I was the Toastmaster, and I was given the Presidential Suite at the Sheraton.

Let me tell you about that suite. It had four bedrooms. It had six bathrooms. Every bathroom had its own television set. It had a four-poster bed on a raised platform in the master bedroom. It had a living room with a 60-foot window wall overlooking the French Quarter and the Mississippi River. It had a dining room that could seat two dozen people at the mahogany table. It had an express elevator to our front door on the 49th floor. We had a liaison (read: gofer/driver) all week long. We had complimentary breakfasts all week long. And since we were in New Orleans, and nobody eats in a hotel when the French Quarter is only a block away, we were given a substantial per diem.

Hard not to like a situation like that.

Which is not to say that the con ran smoothly. (My suite ran smoothly, but that's a whole different matter. In fact, we made up hundreds of invitations to huge parties in the suite on three different nights. We spent the first four days passing them out, and the last three days partying until dawn in the suite.)

Nolacon had asked me to edit a reprint anthology of sf parodies to be known as *Shaggy B.E.M. Stories.* (Damned good book, if I say so myself—even though the editor was never shown the galleys, and hence the final version has well over 200 typos.)

Anyway, one night John Guidry called to say that I had listed an Arthur C. Clarke story in the table of contents, but it wasn't on the disk I sent him. I said sure it was. He insisted it wasn't. I told him to put the disk in the machine and I'd tell him how to find the story. He had never worked a computer before, and was sure he'd wipe all the data from the hard disk with a wrong key stroke, and refused. I kept urging him to turn on the goddamned machine, and he began getting hysterical, so finally I told him to go out into the hall of his office building, find the first room with a light on, knock on the door, and bring whoever answered it to the phone.

Which is how I met Peggy Ranson. She turned on the computer and promptly found the story. She also mentioned that she had slipped a number of letters under the door to the worldcon office, asking for information, but had never been answered. By the end of our conversation, I realized that I was speaking to a very bright, very friendly, and (most importantly) very competent person, and I told John that I insisted on Peggy as my liaison, and that I would accept no other.

Good decision. Three years later she won a Hugo for Best Fan Artist, and she's been on the ballot ever since.

So we show up for the con, and the hotel has no idea that we're coming, or that the committee had reserved the Presidential Suite for us eight months earlier. (The Pro and Fan GOHs, Don Wollheim and Roger Sims, had first choice. Both chose huge suites in the Marriott, which was half a block closer to the Quarter.)

We get that settled, and the first order of business is the Opening Ceremonies, which goes rather smoothly. I introduce Don and Roger, a jazz band serenades (if that's the right word, and I suspect it's not), and everyone goes off to pig out in the Quarter.

The next order of business does not go quite so smoothly. It's the Meet the Pros party. Now, I haven't been to a Meet the Pros party since my first worldcon back in 1963, and somehow I do not feel culturally deprived. I would much rather meet the fans, and in smaller groups, but what the hell, I am the Toastmaster and the Toastmaster presides at this. (Or so I thought, until I was drafted to do it again in Orlando when the Toastmaster refused.)

I know from hearing the pros talk about it that every year they wear funny hats or Mickey Mouse ears or some other distinguishing thing so that the Toastmaster can identify them and the fans can spot them, and every week for a year I ask some committee member or other if they've figured out what the pros will be given to wear and I have been assured that it's under control and there's nothing to worry about. I also request that I be given a couple of spotters, one at the door and one on stage, because I don't know every pro by sight, especially the newer ones, and I don't want to slight anyone. No problem, I am told; we would never dream of embarrassing you or slighting a new writer.

So I show up and ask who my spotters are. Spotters, they say; what's a spotter?

Okay, I say, we'll get by without them. What are the pros wearing?

You're the Toastmaster. We thought you knew it was your responsibility. What did you bring for all 400 of them to wear?

So I turned around and went back to my suite, one minute into the Meet the Pros party. I have no idea how, or even *if*, it went.

My novel, *Ivory*, came out that week, I did a joint signing with Michael Whelan, who painted the cover. Autographed upward of 300 copies, at which point I thought my hand would fall off.

Since we had all these extra bedrooms, I invited my father and Laura to each take one, which they did, and I seem to think Laura invited an old high school or college friend to use the fourth bedroom a couple of nights. Laura had just started selling romance novels; it would be another 5 years before she won her Campbell . . . but since she had been raised in science fiction, she already knew most of the fans and pros, and managed to hit just about every party, escorting my father—an old party boy—to most of them.

By 1988 I was writing for a lot of publishing houses, and we were wined and dined by editors at some of the finest restaurants in town: Arnaud's, Toujaques, Antoine's, Broussard's, and Brennan's. We went to Commander's Palace, probably the best single restaurant in New Orleans, with Pat and Roger Sims, and found that our old headwaiter from some previous trips to Brennan's—the only headwaiter who ever recognized my name or read my books—had moved there. We got the best table, the best service, and, as with Brennan's, no bill. (We promptly invited him to one of our room parties, and he actually showed up—with a bunch of his friends.)

(I have to add, in all immodesty, that those were some of the best parties ever given at a worldcon. We got to see almost every one of our old friends—something that gets more and more difficult each year, as I have more and more business meetings—and that suite was so big that no one had to stand unless they wanted to. We took all the money we'd normally spend on room, board, and planefare, and blew it on food and drinks for the parties. Then we got everyone from old-time fans to Hugo-winning pros to my daughter to my literary agent to help host the various shindigs.)

Roger Sims had asked to be roasted, rather than make a GOH speech, and the committee accommodated him. I was the Roastmaster, and Dave Kyle, Jack Chalker, Jay Kay Klein, Lynne Aronson, Jo Ann Wood, and Pat Sims took their best shots at him. It was a lot of fun, especially if you weren't Roger.

Carol had to judge the masquerade on Saturday night. It was on the other side of the Quarter, and the pre-judging started early, which meant we couldn't eat together. I'd had so many 8,000-calorie meals I didn't feel like going out to a restaurant, so Fred Prophet and I went down to the second floor of the Sheraton, where all the bid parties were, hit each one, picking up some cheese here and some ham there and some cake over there, and after we'd made the circuit we felt like we'd had a huge dinner and were ready to go watch the costumers do their thing.

The Hugos were Sunday night. The committee had given me a contract, stipulating the amount of the per diem I was to receive. When we showed up, they gave me some of the money they owed me and asked us to wait a few days for the rest of it, since they were very tight for cash and would be taking in tons of money at the door, and I agreed. I asked co-chair Justin Winston for the rest of my money on Friday and Saturday, and was put off. Sunday the word was passed to me: we think we've paid you enough, we don't really need you anymore, so we're not going to pay you the rest of your per diem.

Fine, I said. I got into my tux, went down to the auditorium, and waited backstage. The room filled up. The time for the Hugo ceremony to start came and went. I stayed backstage. The fans started stomping their feet. I began reading a book. Finally a panicky message reached me: what the hell is going on? Answer: certainly not the Toastmaster, at least not until he gets the rest of his per diem. Justin gave the money to Craig Miller (an innocent bystander), and Craig got it into my hot little hand less than 30 seconds later. After which I went on stage, told some funny stories, and gave out the Hugos.

But I was so pissed that I became the first Toastmaster in history to boycott closing ceremonies.

Still, that suite made up for just about everything. As Jack Chalker told me after he toastmastered ConStellation in 1983, once you've had a presidential suite at a major hotel, you're never going to be happy with a mere room again.

Boy, was he right.

1992: MAGICON (Orlando)

We showed up a few days early, since we would be leaving for a month-long Kenya safari with Pat and Roger Sims immediately after Magicon. This gave us a chance to sample some of Central Florida's attractions. Carol, an ardent birder, had me drive her and Rick Katze to Merritt Island at (ugh) 6 in the morning, and a couple of days later I took her and Barb Delaplace back at 5 in the afternoon, just to see those birds who like to sleep as late as I do. We also hit Busch Gardens with Laura, Rick Katze, Michelle Sagara and Thomas West.

I started a tradition of taking "my" Campbell nominees out to dinner. We went to an Indian restaurant with Laura, Barb, and Michelle (who came in 2-3-4 to Ted Chiang, and came in 1-3-4 the next year, at San Francisco. Nick DiChario, who I met for the first time at Orlando, and who was also one of "my" Campbellians, came in 2nd at San Francisco.)

(Pat Cadigan, who was up for a Hugo or a Nebula, I can't remember which, berated me all weekend for only taking my Campbell nominees out, so beginning in 1993, I also took all "my" Hugo and Nebula nominees out to dinner at worldcon. Given the amounts of food these men and women could put away, giving up editing anthologies a few years later may have been the most financially prudent decision of my career.)

As always in the 1990s, I spent too damned much time deal-making and nowhere near enough partying. Still, there was one deal I was absolutely thrilled to make: St. Martin's gave me the editorship of the Library of African Adventure. (I was a little less thrilled after we brought out the first three books, and the library is now at Alexander Books, which is owned by my old friend—and sometime sf writer—Ralph Roberts.) Also, John Betancourt brought out a beautiful, leopardskin edition of *Adventures*, my favorite of my own books. More importantly, Harry Warner's *A Wealth of Fable* finally got the illustrated hardcover edition it deserved.

We stayed at the Peabody, where the B-Line restaurant, built to resemble an old-fashioned diner, was frequently empty at 3:00 PM but always filled to overflowing at 3:00 AM.

We'd used a coupon supplied by the worldcon committee to rent a Cadillac for $90.00 for an entire week, and made good use of it. We'd been to Orlando a number of times, so we knew where to go to get off the tourist trail and find the best restaurants.

On Sunday, we had some time between a reading and preparing for the Hugos, so we drove through a couple of areas called Bay Hill and Windermere, visited some open houses, and decided that that was where we wanted to retire to. (We're getting closer all the time. These days we split our year between Cincinnati and Orlando, but haven't quite gotten around to selling our house yet. Dick Spelman is already down there, as is my father, and Pat and Roger Sims plan to move there in a couple of years. Bill and Cokie Cavin keep saying they plan to move there too, and so do Greg and Linda Dunn. So we should be able to put on a Midwestcon South before too much longer.)

I remember that the Hugo was absolutely gorgeous. (The rocket ship is always the same, but the base is different each year, and this year it was made from the platform that held the Apollo moon rockets.) I really faunched for it . . . so of course I lost.

A week later I was sitting 20 yards from a herd of elephants at a water hole in Samburu, and somehow losing it seemed a little less important, at least for the moment.

1998: BUCCONEER (Baltimore)

A lot of our friends didn't show up for this one. John Guidry's father died the day before the con began, and George Laskowski had contracted liver cancer. My own father, who managed to attend a few cons this decade, was unable to leave his assisted-care home for this one. I hate all these reminders that I'm not 23 anymore.

We showed up on Tuesday—not a bad idea, since by Wednesday almost every hotel had managed to screw up their reservations list—and promptly got our room in the Marriott. After seeing all the other hotels (the Hilton, the Omni, the Holiday Inn, Days Inn, and the Hyatt), we came to the conclusion that the Marriott was the pick of the litter—but that it was a pretty ugly litter.

The hotels were spread out, which meant we missed a lot of parties, and missed seeing a lot of friends who were walking around the area looking for us while we were looking for them.

Carol, who found out the week we left that she's got a couple of herniated disks in her neck and needed an awful lot of physical therapy, cheered herself up by falling in love with the Inner Harbor and walking there every day. She and I took every water taxi on every route that existed, and while I was doing panels and hanging around the huckster room (my favorite daytime location at a worldcon, just as the CFG suite is my favorite evening location), she spent hours touring the area.

My first panel was held at 10:00 PM Wednesday (that's what I get for telling them not to schedule me in the mornings), and Lawrence Watt-Evans, Roger MacBride Allen and I dutifully trudged to the Omni for some kind of quiz. But the quizmaster and the questions never arrived, so we sat and stared at the audience for a while, and they sat and stared back, and we finally wound up the hour plugging our books and telling fannish anecdotes.

The huckster room had more books and magazines than usual, and the art show was outstanding. I had three new books out, two hardcover novels and a trade paperback collection, and they seemed to be moving pretty well. Laura's first hardcover fantasy novel had been published a month earlier, and I surreptitiously made sure it was prominently displayed on every table that stocked it (something I have never done with my own books for reasons that currently elude me.)

The SFWA Suite—Laura, who spent more time there, called it the SFWA Sauna—was as far from my hotel as you could get, and barely had room to turn around in. I went once, stayed ten minutes, and didn't return, which was pretty much par for the course. CFG had its usual hospitality suite (in the Marriott, where almost all of us stayed), and we spent the latter part of each evening there.

Thursday we went to the crab feast. (Some people never learn.) We waited half an hour, in the semi-blazing sun, for the water taxi to arrive. Once there, we discovered a) that we would be eating outside in the heat; b) that the only remaining table was about 15 feet away from a country/western band equipped with state of the art loudspeakers; c) there were no hot dogs or hamburgers [and I *hate* crabs], which means that I paid $30.00 for a drumstick and a corncob. We arrived at about 7:00. The crab feast was to continue until at least 10:00. I was ready to leave after half an hour, and much to my surprise, everyone in our party—Carol, Dick Spelman, Sue and Steve Francis, Pat and Roger Sims, Mark Linneman—felt the same, so we returned in time to hit some parties.

I did very little business at this worldcon. I had only one book to sell, and only a few publishing houses to touch base with. Friday we had breakfast with del Rey and lunch with Bantam and a drink with Tor, which took care of most of my obligations, and allowed me to revert to being a fan for the first time in maybe a dozen worldcons.

Except for Friday night, which was the Hugo ceremony. I wore a white suit—Josepha Sherman calls it my Good Humor Man suit, while Barbara Delaplace, who doesn't pull her punches, refers to it as my Italian Pimp Suit. I thought I had a decent chance with "The 43 Antarean Dynasties," since I had won the *Asimov's* Readers Poll and the *Scifi Weekly* Hugo Straw Poll . . . but I hadn't even been nominated for the Nebula, and writers can be pretty insecure people, so as usual I had no speech or notes prepared. And suddenly I was walking up to the stage to accept my fourth Hugo. I can't recall exactly what I said, but it must have been okay, because the next day about 300 people congratulated me on my moving and memorable acceptance speech, whereas only a dozen or so mentioned that I'd written a moving and memorable story, which managed to be both ego-inflating and ego-deflating at the same time.

We'd flown in with Stephen Boucher, who, being an Aussie, was helping to host the Hugo Losers Party. He pointed out that I had cheated in the past, losing Hugos on the same nights I won them, but this time I was only nominated for one, and if I won he promised to personally throw me out of the party. It was five or six blocks away, and I wanted to get out of my suit and take a shower, but I couldn't deny Stephen and Perry Middlemiss the pleasure of forcibly ejecting me, so I stopped by the Hugo Losers Party at the Hilton just long enough to be given the bum's rush, and then we spent the rest of the night celebrating at the CFG suite.

Saturday morning was the SFWA meeting. I usually make it to one a decade, and this was the one I chose for the 1990s. It was noisier and nastier than usual—our president of 36 days' standing barely survived a censure vote—and reminded me why I don't go more often.

I was scheduled to do an autographing in the huckster room in the afternoon, and to my surprise, my line was immense—a regular Ellison or Asimov-type queue. Made me feel I'd finally arrived. I still hadn't finished when my hour was up, and had to move to another table to take care of the last few people who'd been patiently waiting. I was sitting next to Gardner Dozois, who thoughtfully signed my name to a few books just to keep busy.

We ate three good meals at the worldcon, all across the Inner Harbor in Little Italy, the last of them Saturday night. We partied with our fannish friends in the CFG suite, went to bed, packed in the morning, and went home. The flight from Baltimore to Cincinnati took 75 minutes. Laura, who bought cut-rate tickets on Northwest (which she has since dubbed Northworst), reached the Baltimore airport a couple of hours after we did on Sunday afternoon, but didn't get home until daybreak on Tuesday, due to a series of snafus that found her making the final leg of the journey, from the Detroit airport to the Dayton airport, via a bus that left at 12:30 AM Tuesday morning.

All in all, a memorable con, if not always for the right reasons.

For Mimosa #23

WORLDCON MEMORIES— PART 3

1967: NYCON III (New York)

We arrived a few days early so I could visit my editors (who were not, in those days, science fiction editors) and see some plays. Walter Zacharias of Lancer (now of Zebra) told me that he had reprinted some Conan stories and for reasons he absolutely could not fathom they were catching on, and actually assigned me a science fiction novel rather than the usual Gothic or doctor/nurse book.

I had been to a charming Italian restaurant called Barbetta's the summer before I met Carol, and I decided to celebrate the science fiction book contract by taking her to it. You'd be amazed what a change seven years can make. Oh, it was still charming, and the food was still good—but the prices had gone up from about $6.00 a plate to about $50.00. Which is a lot now, and which was absolutely eye-popping (and budget-busting) back then.

The first night there we saw *Cabaret*, a far better play than Bob Fosse's movie would lead you to believe. Then we saw *I Do! I Do!*, the two-person Tom Jones/Harvey Schmidt musical, starring Mary Martin and Robert Preston. Saw it very clearly. From the center of the first row. Robert Preston sweated nonstop for two hours. On me. When the play was over, it was hard to say which of us was more drenched in Prestonsweat, but my money's on me.

The con was held in the Statler Hilton, which was not exactly in the most elegant of midtown Manhattan venues. The food was abominable. No one felt like walking 20 blocks north to the better midtown restaurants, and Jon Stopa finally discovered a working-class bar around the corner that served sandwiches in the back room. Thereafter, most of the Chicago-area contingent ate most of their meals there.

This was the last year that the Worldcon shared its hotel with another convention. And since it was the last time, it was probably only fitting that the convention we shared it with was hosted by the Scientologists. I remember that an escalator ran up from the main floor to the mezzanine; if you turned to your right, you found yourself at the sf registration desk; left, and you were lined up to register for the Scientologists.

It was instant hatred—and more to the point, it was instant competition. I don't know who converted more of which to what, but it kept up for the entire weekend.

Which was just as well. There's a reason why it's been a third of a century since there's been a Worldcon in New York. A reason above and beyond Manhattan's notion of affordability, that is. And the reason is that each of the NyCons was, each in its own way, a bit of a disaster.

By Thursday night only one elevator in the Hilton was running. By early Saturday morning, there was a lengthy period when *none* of them were running. The rooms were tiny, and the beds, even the doubles (mockingly called "king-size") were shoved against the wall to provide a little extra floor space. I remember the first morning we were there: I rolled out of bed, prepared to get to my feet—and put a serious dent in the plaster wall. Damned near broke my nose in the process.

The programming was minimal, and, we felt, overwhelmingly fannish. Very few panels with or about pros, and for those of us who'd come halfway across the country to here our idols speak and were confronted with one fannish panel after another, it was a major disappointment.

I got a real kick out of one of the costumes in the masquerade. (This was back in the days when a little creativity could go a long way, and no one spent four and five digits on a costume). Lynne Aronson, a hopeful writer at the time (she later founded Windycon), came as a rejection slip, covered with all the rejection slips she had received—including one of mine. Later Isaac Asimov put a pipe in his mouth and walked across the stage, claiming to be Harlan Ellison, who responded by pinching some girls on stage and claiming he was Isaac.

One interesting sidelight. Paul Allen, a Burroughs fan who was publishing *The Barsoomian* at the time (and later published *Fantasy Newsletter*) picked up a copy of Dick Lupoff's *Edgar Rice Burroughs: Master of Adventure*. He brought it over to Reed Crandall, who had done the frontespiece, to sign it. Reed not only signed it, but drew a little Tarzan sketch on the title page. Then Paul took it to Frank Frazetta for an autograph; Frank saw Reed's drawing, and gave Paul a full-page sketch on one of the blank pages. So did Al Williamson. Roy Krenkal wasn't there, but Paul visited him one afternoon, and Roy also gave him a full-page sketch. By the end of the con, I think he had original pen-and-inks by 12 different pro artists in the book, and was turning down thousand-dollars offers (in 1967, yet!) for it. Niftiest made-on-the-spot collector's item I ever saw.

Carol had seen some earrings she liked in the hotel's jewelry store, but they were quite expensive, and after our experience at Barbetta's, she didn't want to shell out the money for them. We were due to stay until Tuesday, but we weren't enjoying the con very much, so as soon at Lester del Rey finished his Guest of Honor speech at the Monday afternoon banquet, I bought her the earrings; we paid for them by checking out and flying home a day early.

1974: DISCON II (Washington, D.C.)

Jon and Joni Stopa, who had attended a Disclave at the Sheraton Park Hotel, told us to ask for the new wing when we sent in our reservation. The old wing was a bit of a Chinese maze, but the new wing rambled down a hill behind the hotel, with large, airy, new rooms. We did as they suggested, and wound up on the sixth of eight floors, which was actually two floors *below* the ground level of the main hotel.

So why am I telling you this?

Because the huckster room was in the basement of the main hotel—two floors below ground level. It had guards posted all around the front doors—but no one guarded the single unlocked back door, and we began using it as a shortcut. Could have stolen thousands of books and magazines if we'd felt like it.

Matter of fact, I felt like a bit of a thief anyway, because while I (and probably you, too) have heard of people selling fanzines by the pound, I'd never actually encountered it—until Discon II, where I bought 5 pounds of two-time Hugo winner *Amra* (a complete run of 70-some issues) for $2.00 a pound.

Martha Beck was just recovering from abdominal surgery, and we agreed to fly out with her and room next to her, just in case she found herself in need of a friend in a hurry. It was our own fault for forgetting that Martha can make 20 friends just by walking from one end of a room to the other. Martha and her friends gathered in her room every night at about 3:00 AM to filksing until sunrise. One night I staggered in at about 4:30, and couldn't sleep because of the singing, so at maybe 5:00 I walked over and began pounding the wall. Someone on the other side pounded back in rhythm, and soon 15 or 20 of Martha's friends were turning the walls into bongo drums. I knew when I was licked, and I never tried that again.

Jo Ann Wood and Carol love to go afield for lunch. Jo Ann had some kind of 4-wheel drive vehicle, and a guide book, and she found some fish joint in Annapolis that was supposed to be fair to middling. So she gathered up Carol, me, Martha, and John Guidry, and off we went. We didn't know any short cuts, so we spent the first 20 minutes driving through the worst of Washington's slums. Almost two hours later we pulled into this unprepossessing building at the Annapolis waterfront. I don't remember the name of the restaurant, but I *do* remember the waiter bringing over a dish none of us had ordered. We explained that he'd made a mistake, and he in turn explained that yes, it was an error, some other waiter had written down the wrong order for a party across the room—but since our table seemed willing to eat anything smaller than ourselves with enormous gusto, the restaurant had decided to make us a gift of it.

The program item I remember best is the second (and final) Isaac/Harlan Insult Contest (the first had been at Tricon in 1966). Some local reporter wandered in, took it seriously, and reported in his newspaper that two of our most famous writers started yelling at each other and almost had to be restrained. Harlan and Isaac decided it was not the kind of publicity the field needed, and reluctantly agreed not to have a third contest.

Carol had been working most of the summer on our masquerade costumes—The White Sybil and The Ice Demon, from Clark Ashton Smith's Hyperborean story-cycle—and it took us a couple of hours to get into them, since we were covered with body paint and Carol in particular had lots of make-up and had to be glued into her enormous headpiece. I think we started preparing at 5:00 in the afternoon, and the masquerade started (theoretically) at 8:00, though as always it ran an hour or so late.

This was the biggest, longest masquerade in history. This was before the 60-second limitation (and may well have been the catalyst for it). It seemed like every filksinger in the world went in costume and that each sang his or her entire repertoire. There was a Wizard of Oz group that was not content to sing one song from the film; they had to sing the entire score. There were endless skits, which I guarantee the participants enjoyed a hell of a lot more than the audience. There were green belly dancers, and blue belly dancers, and red belly dancers, and each felt compelled to dance her entire elaborate routine. I remember wishing about midnight that we'd lose so we could go back to our room, shower, and have some dinner.

But we didn't lose. We were voted Most Beautiful, Judges' Choice, and Best in Show—and the next morning our photo became the first to knock Richard Nixon and/or Gerald Ford off the front page of the *Washington Post* in this final month of the Watergate scandal.

1980: NOREASCON II (Boston)

Having experienced the Sheraton's elevators in 1971, we decided to spend the extra money and take a room in the Tower, solely to have access to the express elevator. We never once felt it wasn't money well spent, especially after hitting some parties in the main body of the hotel.

This was the first Worldcon where I participated in an autograph session. There were two of us at the table, myself and Tanith Lee. Tanith was (and is) a lovely and very busty woman, and she was wearing a low-cut dress or blouse, and her line was *enormous*. Hundreds of young men were racing around the huckster room, buying Tanith Lee books so they could stand at the table and look down at her while she looked down at the books and signed them. After awhile a buzzing commenced, to the effect that you shouldn't bring her all three books (the limit) at once, but should stand in line three times and get three eyefuls. I signed two books during the entire hour; Tanith was still signing when I left. I must confess to having had more ego-gratifying experiences.

We had won Best in Show at the NasFic masquerade in Louisville the previous year with our "Avengers of Space" costume/skit (which included Carol, Joan Bledig, Michaele Jordan, and me), and Carol had announced her retirement from costuming. But Jo Ann Wood, who was running the masquerade, twisted her arm all summer, and finally she agreed to wear to bring the Avengers out of mothballs, but only if we could do so out of competition, since the costume had already won at a major convention. So Jo Ann agreed, and we got to do our space opera burlesque skit all over again. It was still fun.

This was legendary Lou Tabakow's last Worldcon. Lou had become our closest fannish friend since we had moved to Cincinnati four years earlier, and we knew he was dying of ALS (Lou Gehrig's Disease). He didn't want any sympathy, he just wanted to have a good time at what he guessed would be his last major con. Ray Beam bought him a cane, and he agreed to use it, but that was his only concession to his disease.

But one of its manifestations was that he slurred his speech, and another was that he had a pronounced limp (hence the cane). In fact, at first we assumed he'd had a mild stroke, until he underwent a barrage of tests and got the bad news.

Anyway, he was given First Fandom's Hall of Fame Award at the Hugo ceremonies. He lost his balance climbing up to the stage and almost fell, then slurred his thanks into the microphone. And poor Bob Silverberg, the Toastmaster, who had known Lou for close to thirty years but hadn't been told of his illness, jumped to the understandable conclusion that Lou was a little tipsy, and made a joke about it. And received a lot of undeserved hell for it that night and for months (and for all I know years) to come.

CFG had two suites, facing each other, across a corridor: one was for smokers, one for non-smokers. As was usually the case when Lou was presiding, sooner or later just about every pro and BNF wandered through and visited for awhile. Lou was there every night until three or four in the morning, and I remember thinking that if he were to die right then and there, it wouldn't be such a terrible thing, for he was never happier than when he was holding forth in the CFG suite.

It's been close to 20 years, and I still miss him. On the other hand, given how many times each week we'd meet for coffee at 1:00 AM, I'm probably ten to twelve books ahead of where I'd be if he was still around.

Personally, I'd rather have had Lou's company than the books.

1984: LACON II (Los Angeles)

LACon II didn't get off to a promising start. When we ordered our plane tickets, we were told that the Cincinnati-to-Los Angeles flight was sold out, and that we'd have to take a flight from Dayton. Between the day I ordered them and the day I picked them up, things changed, and we were booked on the Cincinnati flight after all. But our travel agent didn't tell me, and like an idiot I never looked at the tickets (a mistake I've never made again).

So we drive to Dayton and hand over our tickets, and get the news: our flight is leaving from Cincinnati in 90 minutes. Could they get us to Cincinnati in an hour? Yes, but they couldn't guarantee our luggage would make it through. So we paid a couple of hundred dollars for tickets to Cincinnati (the Cincinnati airport is only half an hour from our house), we raced through the gate to catch the plane just before they locked the doors, we got off in Cincinnati, raced to make our connecting flight, and didn't know until half an hour after we landed in Los Angeles that our luggage did in fact make it on the same flight.

But things began getting better right away. The Anaheim Hilton, which was less than a month old at the time, was—and remains—the best party hotel ever to host a Worldcon. (I might argue that Chicago's Hyatt is the best overall convention hotel, since everything is contained in one building, but for parties, nothing equals the 5th floor of the Anaheim Hilton, with hundreds of rooms leading out to the various lanais, the huge astroturfed roof areas of the enormous 4-story garage.)

My father, who had never been to a Worldcon before, drove up from San Diego. He stayed with his sister, who lived in the area, but spent ten or twelve hours at the con every day, and when it was over, he'd become a fan who would attend another 25 cons in the next decade.

It had been a long time since I'd found more than four or five books I needed at any Worldcon, but LACon II was a throwback to the Good Old Days. I must have bought 30 books, including one of the rarest: a copy of *The Ship That Sailed To Mars*. I beat my dear friend Frank Robinson to it by maybe ten seconds, and he didn't speak to me for the next two days.

The con had some special deal with Disneyland, and one day a bunch of us took advantage of it: Tony and Suford Lewis, Pat and Roger Sims, Carol and me, Fred Prophet, my Dad, and (I seem to remember) Banks Mebane. We had a great time, came back after dark, and played poker until dawn. Just like a real old-time Worldcon, so Roger assured us.

I remember that one of the restaurants Carol and I went to, a few miles away, was called the Hobbit. Despite the fact that I'm not a Tolkein fan, I became a Hobbit fan that night. We were also wined and dined by Tor, which had just become my new publisher, and New American Library, to whom I still owed some books; it was the first time I'd ever had so much attention from publishers at a con, and it quite turned my head while filling my stomach.

Carol would get up to swim and exercise every morning. She later told me that the only pro or fan she ever saw by the pool before noon was Ed Bryant.

I wrote up the masquerade for *Science Fiction Chronicle*, and to thank my aunt for having us out for dinner one night, I brought her along. This was one of the last masquerades to feature nudity. My aunt turned red as a beet at the sight of the first couple of topless girls, and never viewed either science fiction or conventions in quite the same innocent way again. (The kicker: her daughter—my cousin—is a con-going fan.)

We had an Indian dinner with a bunch of NESFAns the next night, then walked back to catch the Hugo ceremony. When we got there the line was literally around the block. I couldn't understand why the Hugos had suddenly grown so popular, but I was pleased nonetheless. Then Tony Lewis pointed out that it was the line for the Star Wars Triple Feature, and that there was absolutely no line at the Hugo door. We walked in, and sure enough, the auditorium was perhaps 20% filled. Bob Bloch did his usual splendid job in what was to be the last time he would ever hand out Hugos at a Worldcon. I know there are those who think Isaac Asimov was our greatest toastmaster/public speaker, and some think it was Harlan Ellison, and a few lean toward Tony Boucher, but my vote goes to Bob

Bloch. He was not only the best friend fandom ever had—and my personal role model in that respect—but he was also the wittiest entertainer we will probably ever encounter at a convention.

That night I went out onto the lanai with John Guidry. After awhile we found a couple of empty chairs and sat down to visit with Neil Rest, who was busy fantasizing about making a Worldcon bid for a cruise ship. Before long he had attracted a hell of a crowd, and by daylight hundreds of people were urging him to make it a *real* bid. John walked away thinking if there was so little serious support for any Central Zone cities that people actually would support a cruise ship, maybe it was time to put together a New Orleans bid. So that evening saw the birth of two bids: Nolacon II, which won the 1988 Worldcon; and the Boat, which came in second in a field of four.

1989: NOREASCON III (Boston)

This Worldcon was too big even for Boston's Sheraton, which had hosted two prior ones. We spilled over into the Back Bay Hilton, the Marriott, and a couple of other hotels, which meant that every night we'd walk the circuit from one hotel to the next, trying to hit all the parties and make all the connections (and probably missing more than we made.)

We were in the Back Bay Hilton, a delightfully quiet hotel, right across the street from the Sheraton. Every night a bunch of the Back Bay Hilton residents—Dean Wesley Smith, Kristine Kathryn Rusch, Barbara Delaplace, Carol, me, maybe ten or twelve others—would gather a bunch of chairs in a circle and spend a few hours visiting/partying right there in the hotel's lobby.

I had lunch one day with Marty Greenberg (who is fast closing in on his one thousandth anthology). He asked what I was working on. I described *Bully!*, an alternate history novella featuring Teddy Roosevelt. Sometime during dessert he asked me if I had any ideas for selling our anthology. What anthology, I asked. Why, *Alternate Presidents*, he replied; you know, Teddy Roosevelt and all that. I didn't know we *had* an anthology, I said. If I sell it, he said, will you edit it? Secure in the knowledge that no one would be breaking down Marty's door to buy it, I agreed.

Marty ran into me less than three hours later, as I was coming off a panel. It's due in three months, he said. What is, I asked. *Alternate Presidents*, he replied. And sure enough, he not only sold *Alternate Presidents*, but four other brands of Alternates, and about fifteen other anthologies, and lo and behold, I was in the anthology business for the next few years, like it or not.

This was the first year I was nominated for a Hugo, and—as the cliche goes—I truly was honored just to be nominated, because I knew that being nominated was as close as I was going to come to the Hugo. I was up against a tough field that included David Brin, and David Brin was as hard to beat on Labor Day in the 1980s as Harlan Ellison had been in the late 1960s and 1970s. So I was totally relaxed when we seated ourselves and waited for Fred Pohl to start reading off the winners.

I was speaking to George Alec Effinger, who was seated just in front of me, when Carol let out a scream and poked me and told me to go up on stage and pick up my Hugo. I calmly explained to her that she must have heard wrong, that everyone knew David Brin was going to win the Hugo. Tell him, George, said Carol—but George, who is deaf in one ear and had his good ear turned to me, hadn't heard a thing. Carol kept jabbing me in the ribs and telling me I really and truly had won, and finally a bunch of pros who were seated nearby began telling me to go pick up my Hugo so Fred could get on to the next award.

So I walked up on stage, and took my Hugo, and stared at the microphone—and for the first time in my life, I was speechless. I was still trying to adjust to the fact that I'd actually won. I hope you all saw that, because it'll be a cold day in hell before I'm ever speechless again. (The fact that I've always found something to say while winning more Hugos does not mean I've grown smug or complacent; it merely means I now know that it's possible for me to win, which was something I absolutely did not know at Noreascon III.)

(Postscript: George heard well enough to run up on stage and pick up his Hugo for Best Novelette . . . and later that night, Jack Chalker and I cornered him and wouldn't let him get away until he'd agreed to become the third author in our round-robin novel, *The Red Tape War*, which came out a couple of years later.)

I had promised Barry Malzberg to call him with the Hugo results, so went to my room the moment the ceremony was over and phoned him—and left the Hugo on my dresser. The rocket ship is the same every year, but the base is different, and this base had a number of metal spheres on it. I think that simply because I didn't carry it around to the parties, mine was the only Hugo to make it home intact. The spheres fell off all the others. (I still remember Gardner Dozois going from party to party complaining that he'd lost his balls.)

The CFG suite was in the Marriott, where you had to fight your way through a huge Armenian reunion every night to reach the elevators. Nice suite, but a pain to get to.

The next day, at noon, the Worldcon had a 50th Anniversary Banquet. Isaac Asimov was the emcee, and about twenty of us had been selected ahead of time to describe our first Worldcon. I'd written a short speech, but when it was my turn the lights were so blinding that I literally could not see my hand in front of my face, so I spoke off the cuff and gave the written speech to Mike Glyer, who later published it in *File 770*.

The gist of it, a sentiment I've voiced many times, is that whoever said you can choose your friends but you can't choose your family was dead wrong. I've chosen my family, and I go to its reunion just about every Labor Day.

1994: CONADIAN (Winnipeg, Canada)

This was not a convention I was looking forward to. The opposing bid, Louisville, had asked me to be their Toastmaster, and I had my suite atop the Galt House all picked out. Then Winnipeg won the closest election in recent years.

We chose to stay at the Holiday Inn, which was attached to the convention center. It might not have been the brightest idea we ever had, because while it made the days convenient, the nights were incredibly inconvenient. There was only one suite in the whole hotel—the SFWA suite—which meant we had to walk blocks away to hit any of the parties and visit any of our fannish friends. And it rained a lot. I usually spend 20 minutes in the SFWA suite during the course of an entire Worldcon; I found myself spending a few hours there almost every evening during Conadian.

Two good friends had had open-heart surgery during the same week that summer, and both were at Worldcon. Dick Spelman, who'd felt some chest pains when hurrying through an airport, went to his cardiologist, took a stress test, and found himself getting a quintuple bypass a week later. Jay Kay Klein had had a heart attack, and got *his* bypass after the fact.

The difference between the two was like night and day. Jay Kay is fine these days, but that summer he couldn't climb a short flight of stairs without terrible pain, and he appeared uncomfortable all weekend, while Dick was his old self, zipping around here and there with an abundance of energy. Moral: get the bypass *before* you damage the heart muscle, not *after*.

Bantam/Doubleday/Dell invited all its writers to a banquet on a boat Friday night. We found ourselves sitting with Gene and Rosemary Wolfe, who offered us a ride back to their hotel in their rented car. We walked into the lobby with them, prepared to hit some parties. Gene and Rosemary just wanted to go to their room and rest. Now, Rosemary has serious problems with her legs—but the elevator Nazis had declared that everyone in the lobby would be expressed to the 21st (and top) floor, and could walk down to the party of their choice while the elevators zipped right back down for the next load. Gene explained Rosemary's problem. No one seemed to care, and the poor woman had to walk all the way down from the 21st floor to her room on the 6th. Suddenly the Holiday Inn didn't look so bad after all.

Strange thing happened with the Hugos. Only three short stories got enough nominations to make the ballot. One of them was mine. Then David Bratman, the Hugo administrator, declared that for the evening of September 4 only, Connie Willis' novelette was a short story. It won. My story came in second, beating all the other short stories. I still don't understand exactly what happened, or why her short story was a novelette again on September 5. (I don't blame Connie, who deserves all her awards and more.)

I was also up for Best Editor. So was Kris Rusch, who was unable to attend and asked me to accept for her if she won. Bob Silverberg read off the five nominees, and then announced that Kris had won. I ran up to the stage to accept, and I could tell from the shocked look on Bob's face that one of the losers had gone berserk and we were about to have a "situation." I wrestled the trophy away from him and began thanking people. My first thanks went to Kris' employer, Ed Ferman, and Bob relaxed noticeably. My pal Jack Nimersheim was up for the Campbell and lost, so except for Kris it wasn't an exceptionally successful night.

(I spent the next two days telling anyone who asked that I had no intention of sending Kris her Hugo, but that she could visit it whenever she wanted, providing she called first and left her clothes at the door. Then I ruined everything by sending it back to Oregon with Alan Newcomer.)

This was also the Worldcon where *Alternate Worldcons* first appeared. Dean Wesley Smith had shipped a couple of hundred copies to Winnipeg. They were sold out by Saturday, and by Sunday people were offering two and three times the cover price for it, despite the fact that they knew there'd be more available by the next weekend. It made a boy editor quietly proud.

1996: LACON III (Los Angeles)

We flew in with Pat and Roger Sims on Monday, rented a car that was fine for four people and totally inadequate for four people and their luggage, and drove to the Anaheim Hilton. Along the way I broke my glass frames, and had to get some new ones that afternoon. Then I ripped my canvas shoe, and had to go shoe-shopping in the evening. Just graceful, I guess.

On a previous trip, Carol and I had discovered the Gene Autry Museum of Western Americana. We had expected it to be a little storefront with some movie posters, which didn't deter Carol (who can name the horse of every cowboy and cowgirl ever to appear in a B movie). You can imagine our surprise when we found it was housed in a beautiful, brand-new $50 million building, and that it was truly a museum, perhaps the most fascinating one in the Los Angeles area—at least to a couple of overgrown kids who grew up on John Wayne movies and still think *Maverick* was probably the best TV show of all time. We were dying to see it again, and Pat and Roger caught a little of our enthusiasm and joined us when we drove there on Tuesday. Debbie Oakes and Bill and Cokie Cavin followed us in another rental car, and Bill, who collects old guns, went back again the next day to finish looking at all the Colts and Winchesters and the like. Fabulous place.

Dick Spelman had found a Norwegian buffet two blocks away from the hotel, and we ate there with fannish friends the first couple of nights, since we knew we wouldn't be able to eat with them again until the con was over. My father, who was sharing a room with Fred Prophet, showed up Wednesday morning, and Laura, who had recently signed for her first fantasy novel with Tor, arrived Wednesday afternoon. We didn't see either of them until the evening, for Carol wanted to visit this incredibly upscale shopping mall—I can't remember where it was; maybe half an hour from the hotel—and we spent the afternoon there, she shopping, me gasping at the price-tags. (Want a pair of $400 slippers, or a $1,750 sports shirt? That's the place to go.)

James White, the Guest of Honor, had been one of my favorite writers since his first book more than three decades ago, and I was thrilled and honored when NESFA, which was publishing his Guest of Honor book, *The White Papers*, asked me to write the introduction to it. I'd met him very briefly—for less than a minute, I'd guess—at Magicon; I ran into him in the lobby late Wednesday afternoon, spent an hour or so talking with him . . . and kept running into him all weekend long. By Labor Day we'd become fast friends, and we've been corresponding ever since. A fine writer, and an even finer person.

We had dinner in the Hilton's upscale restaurant with Dean Smith and Kris Rusch—we always have at least one meal with them at Worldcons—and then we helped open up the CFG suite. Bill Cavin, who is the God-Emperor of CFG, hadn't been to the 1984 Worldcon, so he didn't realize that the fifth floor was the party floor. We had a beautiful suite on the sixth floor, and all the regulars came by, but a lot of people who never left the fifth floor and the lanais never knew we were there.

Meals were wonderful, calorie-laden, and filled with business. Amy Stout, who was bidding for *Kirinyaga* for del Rey (and eventually she got it) took us to breakfast. Anne Groell, who was editing the *Widowmaker* books, took us to lunch. Beth Meacham, my long-time editor at Tor, took us to lunch. Gardner Dozois took us to lunch. Marty Greenberg took us to breakfast. (I seem to think we sneaked in one breakfast with

Laura and my father, but I could be mistaken.)

Anyway, that left the evenings for the Rich Folks. Andrew Rona, a vice president of Miramax, which had just made an offer for *The Widowmaker*, took us to dinner at the same upscale Italian restaurant that Kris and Dean had taken us to. The next night, Jean-Louis Rubin, president of Capella, which was producing *Santiago*, took us to the same restaurant. The next night Eleanor Wood, my agent, took us to the same restaurant. When Kia Jam and Tim Douglas, a producer and a special effects master who had done some preliminary work on *Santiago* and had optioned the *Oracle* trilogy, showed up Sunday and wanted to know the best restaurant in the hotel, we begged them to just get us a hamburger in the coffee shop; we simply couldn't face another $50-a-plate 8,000-calorie meal.

I did my usual share of panels, readings, kaffeeklatsches, and so on, and finally got around to the autograph session. I sat next to Joe Haldeman, and at the next table were Melanie Rawn and Jennifer Roberson. The most unbelievable event of the year then transpired: I was still signing when the three of them were done. I'm sure it was a fluke—I'd trade my royalty statements for any of theirs in a New York minute—but it made my Worldcon.

Just as well, because I was up for two Hugos—a novelette by myself, and a novella in collaboration with Susan Shwartz—and lost both of them, despite having won lesser awards already with each. Our closest Hollywood associate, Ed Elbert—he's got his fingers in five different Resnick projects and is the guy who secured our initial screenwriting assignments for Carol and me—showed up for the Hugo ceremonies. When they were over, he took us all—Carol, me, my Dad, Laura, and fellow loser Susan—to the bar for brandy and condolences. Carol and I have known Ed for years, so we were still feeling a little disappointed over losing two more Hugos (yes, I've won a lot; but on the other hand, I've lost a lot more), but Susan had never sat in a bar drinking Remy Martin with a real Hollywood producer, and she got over losing in less time that it takes me to tell about it. (As I write these words, Ed just got back from Malaysia, where he was producing Fox's 1999 Christmas movie—*Anna and the King*, starring Jodie Foster. He tells me that ever since

he signed Foster, everyone in town is answering his calls—
which is how you tell whether you're up or down in Tinseltown.)

Bantam has this habit of taking its writers off the premises
for a banquet once each Worldcon. This year we were given a
private tour of the museum at the La Brea Tar Pits, and then
caterers came in, set up tables, and served us an excellent meal
right on the premises. David Gerrold later wrote a story for one
of my anthologies explaining why he pushed me into a tar pit
during the festivities.

Laura and I spent some time at a private Japanese party—
or at least, one that had written invitations—and I renewed
some old friendships there. Dick and Leah Smith presided at a
nightly Australian party, and Boston and Philadelphia also
gave very pleasant bid parties. Somewhere along the way Rich
Lynch cornered me and got me to promise to write an article,
which appeared as "The Literature of Fandom" in *Mimosa #21*.

On closing night, we went to a party at Scott and Jane Dennis' suite across the street at the Marriott, which was very
fannish, and after all those editors and all those Hollywood mo-
guls, it was the most enjoyable time we had at the entire con.

I guess you just can't take the fan out of the boy . . .

For Mimosa #24

WORLDCON MEMORIES— PART 4

1963: DISCON I (Washington, D.C.)

This was our very first worldcon. I was a mature 21 years old; Carol, my child-bride, was only 20. You could fill a book with what we didn't know about science fiction conventions. Several books. In fact, I'm sure someone already has.

We had no money to speak of. We left Laura, who had just turned a year old, with some grandparents, and prepared to spend five days in Washington, D.C. on my $93.17 income tax refund. (The wild part is that we did it, and came home with a few dollars left over.)

We had discovered Burroughs fandom the year before, and it was through our ERB friends that we learned about the worldcon. We couldn't afford to fly to it, and our car couldn't be trusted to go 50 miles without suffering from cardiac arrest, so we took the train—a back-breaking 24-hour journey from Chicago.

What we didn't know—one of the many things—was that when we were told worldcon was on Labor Day weekend, the weekend for all practical purposes started on a Thursday. We got there Saturday morning, just in time to find out that the con was about half over.

We were met in the basement—the train actually let us off inside the hotel—by Camille Cazedessus, Jr., the editor and publisher of *ERB-dom*, for which I was the assistant editor. He waited until we got our room—an outrageous $7.00 a night despite the convention rate—and then took us down to the huckster room. I thought I had died and gone to heaven: there were 30 or 40 tables of books and magazines. No jewelry. No games. No toys. No light sabres. No clothing. No media junk. Just literature. (If it happened today, I'd *know* I had died.)

There was a sweet old guy in a white suit who saw that we were new to all this, and moseyed over and spent half an hour with us, making us feel at home and telling us about how we were all one big family and inviting us to come to all the parties at night. Then he wandered off to accept the first-ever Hall of Fame Award from First Fandom. When they asked if he was working on anything at present, he replied that he had just delivered the manuscript to *Skylark DuQuesne*, and only then did we realize that he was the fabled E. E. "Doc" Smith.

There were panels with all the writers we'd worshipped for years. And then there was the auction. Stan Vinson, a Burroughs collector, paid the highest price of the weekend for a Frazetta cover—$70, for a painting that would probably bring $40,000 or more today—but even broke kids like me were able to participate. I bought a black-and-white Virgil Finlay drawing for $2.00 and an autographed Ted Sturgeon manuscript for $3.50.

They held the masquerade Saturday night. Back then it was a masquerade ball, with a live band, and the costumes were secondary to the dancing and partying.

About that partying: Doc had told us there were parties, but he hadn't told us *where*, so we wandered up and down the various corridors of the hotel, and were finally invited into a suite by two odd-looking men who turned out to be Lester del Rey and James Blish. I don't know what they saw in a pair of kids from Chicago, but they, and every pro and fan in the suite, treated us like part of the family—and they've been our family ever since.

The next afternoon we went to the banquet, where I got my first-ever look at a Hugo. At the time it seemed like the Holy Grail: if I lived a good and pure life and kept learning my craft and wrote to the best of my ability every day, maybe someday, 50 or 60 years up the road, I might even be allowed to touch one.

1969: ST. LOUISCON (St. Louis)

By now we'd been to a few worldcons, and knew enough to get there a day early. We ran into Martha Beck in the lobby, and went to the bar with her to have some coffee and visit a bit.

Now, neither Martha nor I are drinkers, and I can't remember exactly how it came about, but somehow or other we got involved in a drinking contest. I knew enough to order brandy Alexanders, which are like chocolate malts with just enough alcohol to kill the germs; Martha kept ordering one planter's punch after another. Well-named drink; after six or seven rounds it punched her but good. We had to help her to her room, where her husband, Hank, was not amused. With either of us. (I probably had more alcohol that afternoon than I've had in the 30 years since.)

The elevators didn't work very well, and the elevator operators were surly as hell. The air-conditioning didn't work very well either, so I put on a swimsuit and thought I'd cool off in the pool. Bad idea. It was over 100 degrees out, the sun had been shining on the pool all summer, and about three seconds into my swim I realized that the pool was hotter than the water I shave with.

(We went to an Archon at the same hotel—the Chase Park Plaza—eleven years later, in 1980. The same elevators didn't work, the same surly help ignored the guests, the same air conditioners spit warm water into the rooms, and the same swimming pool was close to boiling.)

We were the only people who were satisfied with our room. In fact, "satisfied" is an understatement. I registered as a publishing company that I owned, rather than as an individual. For $14 a night, they gave us a room with a fireplace, a bathroom that could have held a relaxacon all by itself, a few couches, and enough room so that the late Bob Greenberg was able to set up a screen, a projector, and about 20 chairs and show some movies he'd been working on to some of our friends.

(I registered as publishing companies the next 15 years, some real, some imaginary. Never got another room like that. For *any* price.)

Sometime during the weekend David Gerrold and Anne McCaffery found out that I had sold three science fiction novels, cornered me before I could get away, and wouldn't leave me alone until I joined SFWA. I've been a member for 30 years now, and I still haven't decided whether to forgive them for it.)

The masquerade had what most old-timers think is the greatest costume ever done, Karen and Astrid Anderson's "The Bat and the Bitten." It also had Rick Norwood, which would later work for Freman Dyson but was just a student back then, dressed as Charlie Brown (the comic book character, not the *Locus* publisher). Rick came out with a kite, did a Charlie Brown pratfall, and inadvertently tore the huge movie screen that hung down at the back of the presidium stage.

Harlan Ellison immediately climbed onto the stage, explained that it was our duty as members of the convention to help the committee pay for the damage, and collected a quick $800, mostly in dollar bills.

Well, the next day, at the banquet, it was announced that the damage had looked worse than it was, and that the total cost of repairing the screen was only thirty dollars. Harlan, who was the Toastmaster, announced that he was donating the rest of the money to Clarion.

Instantly Elliot Shorter, who would make an NFL linebacker look small and puny, was on his feet, shouting that Harlan wasn't giving *his* money to Harlan's pet charity. Lester del Rey, on the other side of the room, stood up on his chair and echoed those sentiments. And in a matter of no more than a minute or two, hundreds of fans were screaming in protest. The results? First, the money was earmarked for a beer blast; and second, Harlan gafiated from fandom.

1972: LACON I (Los Angeles)

We showed up a few days early to hit a bunch of secondhand book stores with John Guidry, and also to see the first performance ever given at the new, state-of-the-art theater at Century City (Stephen Sondheim's brilliant and bittersweet *Follies*, with the Broadway cast; it folded after leaving Los Angeles.)

A girl from Chicago—her first name was Helen, and I regret to say I've forgotten her last name—had just gotten her driver's license, and rented a car once she arrived. One night she offered to drive a bunch of Chicago-area fans to a restaurant that had been recommended, so Joni Stopa, Carol and me, Martha Beck, and a couple of others piled into the car (cars were much bigger then), and off we went. As we were driving by a playground, we saw the street we were looking for about 50 yards ahead, and one of us said "Turn left here" — so Helen turned left *here*, right into the playground's chain link fence.

There was skinny-dipping every night. The only thing I really remember about it was seeing Frank Robinson remove all his clothes but keep on his trademark leather hat as he plunged into the pool.

The con was at the International Hotel, right by the airport. We had arrived early enough to get a room on the second floor—non-functioning elevators have always gone hand-in-glove with worldcons, and we always try to get a low room—but Martha had done even better, securing a ground-level poolside cabana for herself.

Martha likes her friends to like each other. I had sold a bunch of books ("the kind men like") to Earl Kemp, who had chaired the 1962 Chicon before moving west to edit Greenleaf Classics for Bill Hamling. I was a dear friend of Martha's, but I hardly knew Earl at all; I just sold him books. Earl was a dear friend of Martha's, but he hardly knew me at all. Martha decided all we had to do to like each other as much as she liked both of us was get to know each other, so she invited us to her cabana on some pretext or other and then left and locked us in for a few hours. We each wanted to go out and party, and do some business, and we resented being locked in there with each other. Under other circumstances we might well have become close friends; but neither of us had much use for each other after those hours of enforced togetherness.

Bob Bloch was the toastmaster—and I persist in thinking he was our best/funniest public speaker ever, even including Isaac Asimov. Fred Pohl was the Guest of Honor, and it was the first time in my memory that both the Toastmaster *and* the Guest of Honor gave witty speeches at the Hugo banquet. I also got to meet one of my heroes—well, heroines—for the only time: Catherine L. Moore. To this day, whenever my sensawonder needs a shot of adrenaline, I pick up one of her Northwest Smith stories and I'm fine thirty minutes later.

The masquerade was memorable for a number of reasons. There were some gorgeous costumes. There were more naked ladies than ever appeared before or since, and their costumes—from grandmother Marji Ellers' "The Black Queen from Barbarella" to teenage Astrid Anderson's "Dejah Thoris"—were truly memorable.

But the most memorable of all was a fellow who came as an underground comic strip hero called The Turd. His costume consisted of about five gallons of peanut butter smeared all over his pudgy body. But he forgot that he'd be under hot lights all evening. The peanut butter turned rancid, ruined every costume that he brushed against, and did some serious damage to the carpet and to some draperies he happened to lean against.

From that day forward, there has been an arcane rule that outlaws the use of peanut butter in worldcon masquerades. Now you know why.

1976: MIDAMERICON (Kansas City)

MidAmeriCon, informally known as Big Mac, was billed as the Ultimate Worldcon. Ken Keller and the late Tom Reamy promised that they would provide brilliant innovation after brilliant innovation, such as fandom had never seen before.

Their biggest fear was that people might try to sneak into the con without paying, and they decided upon one final innovation to make sure it couldn't happen. They announced that they had a foolproof method of making sure only members were admitted. Most people thought it would be some kind of unduplicatable badge, perhaps with a hologram on it, but when we arrived it turned out that in addition to the regular ID badge, each member was given a hospital bracelet that could not be removed, or, once removed, could not be put back on.

So of course, a group of fans went to a local hospital, found a little old lady who liked science fiction and was being released that day, convinced her to keep her bracelet on, and got her into every function, including the Hugos and the masquerade.

Still, there *were* innovations galore. There was the first—and, to this day, the only—hardcover program book. There was closed-circuit television of the better panels, all the speeches, and the masquerade, piped into every room of the hotel.

There was an absolutely dreadful and almost endless live play based on some of the works of Cordwainer Smith.

To counter that, there was a humor group, just getting started, called Duck's Breath Theatre, that entertained us with their hilarious rendition of "Gonad the Barbarian"—and they were still going strong, on Public Radio and elsewhere, two decades later.

There was the first fan cabaret.

There was, for the first time, a banquet with no Hugo ceremony or Guest of Honor speech, and a Hugo ceremony/Guest of Honor speech with no banquet.

At one point, I came across Ed Wood, who was doing some reviewing for *Analog*, sitting by himself in the lobby, looking like he was going to break down crying any second. He had a copy of Dave Kyle's coffee-table book on the history of science fiction with him, and at first I thought maybe Dave had died. Nope. Then I figured that he felt awful because Dave had been his dear friend for a quarter of a century and he was going to rip the book to shreds in his review. Wrong again. It turns out that Ed was heartbroken because he had looked forward to ripping it to shreds and had found only two mistakes—both typos—in the whole book. He later gave it a rave review. (If you didn't know Ed . . . well, now you do.)

Of the five masquerades in which we participated, this was only one we ever lost. So naturally I think they were our prettiest costumes—Haunte and Sullenbode, mirror-image feathered things from *A Voyage to Arcturus*. Carol lost a contact lens while we were waiting backstage to go on. She wasn't wearing much except feathers, the lens had to be somewhere in the feathers, and I must have thought that Alfie Bester, who was serving drinks to the costumers backstage, spent a little too long helping her try to find it. He later confided to me that he stopped when he got the distinct feeling that I was about to turn *him* into a demolished man.

Patia von Sternberg, a fan who was also a professional stripper, entertained the audience while the judges were deliberating. She came out, did her routine, and got down to her g-string in about five minutes — only to be told that she had to fill another 20 minutes before the judges returned. (Same thing happened to me at Chicon V, except that I wasn't taking my clothes off.)

Robert A. Heinlein was the Guest of Honor. This was right before he had surgery to cure a blockage to his brain. He was, by his own later admission, mentally impaired at the time, and his speech was embarrassing. Even more embarrasing were some ill-mannered fans who heckled him from the balcony.

Joe Haldeman won his first Hugo for the now-classic novel, *The Forever War*. We were all celebrating and partying on the roof later that night, when a bunch of skinny-dippers climbed out of the pool, grabbed Joe, and—though he did his damnedest to fight them off—threw him into the pool.

The only time I've ever seen Joe furious was when he pulled himself out of the pool. Over the years there have been a number of apocryphal stories explaining his anger—the most common was that he was carrying a large check from a publisher in his wallet and he was sure the water had ruined it—but Gay Haldeman told me just a few months ago that the real reason was simply that it was his first $100 suit.

1986: CONFEDERATION (Atlanta)

We flew in from Cincinnati, met Pat and Roger Sims at the airport (they'd flown in from Detroit), and shared a cab to the hotel. We were in the Marriott, a large hotel which boasted a nifty 44-story atrium.

The tenth floor was the most interesting of all, because it was the party floor. Nothing but party suites all the way around. (CFG had its own suite on the eleventh.)

We had our usual problems with the elevators, and one unusual problem as well. Thanks to overloading, somewhere near the top floor one of the elevators went off its track. It didn't fall all the way down to the ground, thankfully—it just kind of got stuck there—but that, if I'm not mistaken, was the origin of what has become known as the Elevator Nazis, worldcon committee members who make sure the elevators aren't overloaded during prime party times.

Worlds of If, a 3-time Hugo winner in the late 1960s, which had long been out of business, made a comeback for one single issue, which was given away free to all members of the convention. It contained Orson Scott Card's long, glowing review of *Santiago*, the best review I'd ever gotten up to that moment, so from my point of view it couldn't have made its reappearance at a better time, or with a better reviewer.

We'd been told for years that the best restaurant in Atlanta was Nikolai's, on the rooftop of the Hilton, which was next door and hosted most of the panels and the huckster room. We had three dinners there. I think our table was next to Bob Silverberg's all three times; he knows a good restaurant when he sees one.

Had a dinner in the Marriott with Beth Meacham and her

husband, Tappan King. For my money, Beth is the best book editor the science fiction field has ever had, and is long overdue for a few Hugos—and not because she is my editor. I've had a *lot* of editors; she's the only one I've ever said this about.

Anyway, I'd brought along the first hundred pages, plus an outline, of *Ivory*, the novel I was working on. I gave Beth the envelope containing the pages as we were waiting to be seated. Then, while Tappan proceeded to talk with us for the next hour, Beth looked up from the manuscript just long enough to find a few pieces of food and bring them to her mouth. This is a lady who *never* stops working. Still, when your editor would rather read your latest effort than eat an elegant meal, you can't help but be flattered.

There was an autographing at a local science fiction store, and meals with a few other editors, and panels, and a reading, and I realized halfway through the convention that this was the first worldcon at which I spent more time being a pro than a fan. I didn't like that aspect of it then; I don't like it now. But I don't enjoy World Fantasy Con—there's an invisible sign on the door that says "Fans not wanted," and *I'm* a fan—and I rarely go to the Nebula banquet, so I find, of necessity, that I line up my next year's work at each worldcon, and that means I find them a lot more lucrative and a lot less fun than I used to. It's an ongoing trend that seems to have started with this one.

Bob Shaw was the Toastmaster. It was the only less-than-stellar performance I ever saw him give. He told me later that he was fine until he walked out on stage. He hadn't been expecting the five-minute light show, and it rattled him.

The late George "Lan" Laskowski won the first of his two Hugos for *Lan's Lantern*, thereby beginning a tradition he would tease me about for the next decade, that of winning Hugos only in years in which I didn't write for his fanzine.

1991: CHICON V (Chicago)

We showed up a few days early, since Chicago is the town we grew up in and we wanted to hit a bunch of our favorite places. We spent a day at Brookfield Zoo, another with Rick Katze at Lincoln Park Zoo, a third with Barbara Delaplace at the Field Museum of Natural History, and a fourth hitting a couple of dozen second-hand bookstores with Joan Bledig.

Ross Pavlac had negotiated unbelievably low room rates at the Hyatt—so low, in fact, that for the first and only time in our lives, we paid for a suite at a worldcon (and it was still less than we had expected to spend on a room).

Louisville and Winnipeg were battling for the 1994 worldcon. I was rooting for Louisville. They had asked me to be their Toastmaster if they won, and I already had my suite picked out atop the venerable Galt House. They had parties every night, but so did Winnipeg—and Winnipeg imported a chef and gave out some really fine food, than which nothing will endear you more to fans. Came the night of the ballot counting, and Winnipeg edged Louisville in the closest election of the modern era . . . and my beautiful free suite and perks went down the drain.

The committee forgot to schedule me for an autograph session. I was pretty popular by this time, and it seemed that every time I sat down, or stood still, or even walked slowly, half a dozen people were shoving books under my nose and asking me to sign them. Flattering and annoying, all at once; at least I remembered to be annoyed with the committee and not the fans.

We've never had so many fine meals at so many excellent restaurants. Beth Meacham and Tor took us to the Everest Room; Brian Thomsen and Warner's took us to Mareva's; Ginjer Buchanan and Ace took us to the Ritz Carlton Dining Room; Eleanor Wood, my agent, took us to Truffles. And the day before the con started, Carol and I went to Le Francais, rated by Michelin as the best restaurant in America. After all those 10,000-calorie meals, it was a pleasure to have a corned beef sandwich with Gardner Dozois and *Asimov's*, and a ham-and-egg breakfast with Dean Smith and Kris Rusch of Pulphouse.

I'd agreed to emcee the masquerade on Saturday night, so I spent about an hour and a half backstage with the costumers, making sure I could pronounce all the names and read all the descriptions.

I was told that I had a "plant" in the first row of the audience. He had a set of earphones, and was in contact with the backstage gophers. They would tell him when each costume was ready to go on, and he would relay the information to me via hand signals.

Great idea. Didn't work. I've been on a lot of stages, but this one had the single brightest spotlight I've ever seen. It was so blinding that every time I looked up from the costumer's notes, which I'd laid out on the podium, I couldn't see a damned thing—including my guy in the first row. (It was a problem all the Hugo winners would have the next night when they went up on stage to pick up their awards.)

So I figured, what the hell, I'll just read what I've been given to read and not worry about it. That worked until the third or fourth costume. Then, as I was preparing to read the name and title of the next entrant, a hand shot out from under the curtains and grabbed my ankle in a deathgrip. I explained to the audience what had happened, and that I assumed this meant I was to slow down. A moment later the hand gently began stroking my leg, and I explained that this either meant I was to go faster or else that I was engaged, or maybe both.

Anyway, it took about two hours to run through maybe a hundred costumes, and then the judges went off to deliberate, and thr audience was entertained for the next half hour by a very funny professional comedian. Then someone hunted me up, explained that the judges weren't back yet, and asked if I could go out onstage and tell a joke or two until they arrived.

What do you need, I asked, as I walked out from the wings—about five minutes?

About 45, came the answer, as the light hit me in the eyes.

So I went out and did everything except a striptease for the next three-quarters of an hour. We got through it—barely—and I have never consented to emcee another masquerade.

I was back in the same place again the next night, for the Hugo Awards. I lost two Seiun Sho's (Japanese Hugos) before I even took my seat—the winners were announced informally at the pre-ceremony party, as well as formally on stage. I was up for a pair of Hugos, and when Ed Bryant, who was presenting the Best Novelette Hugo, opened the envelope, paused for a moment, and told the audience he wanted to make sure he pronounced it properly, I knew "The Manamouki" had won, as indeed it did. I thought I might have a chance for Best Novella with "Bully!," since it had beaten Joe Haldeman's "The Hemingway Hoax" in the *Science Fiction Chronicle* poll, but I ran second to him for the Hugo. (Just as well. We realized after pos-ing for Hugo Winners' photos again in 1995 and 1998 that each time one of us had won a Hugo during the 1990s, so had the other—so now I vote for Joe any time he's not in my category, just for luck, and I assume he does the same for me.)

Then it was the nightly round of parties. The Hyatt is un-usually convenient for party-hopping. All the large suites are by the fire exit door, so all you do is take the elevator up to the 32nd floor, walk to the end of the corridor, hit whatever party is going on there, then walk down a flight, repeat the process, and keep doing it all the way down to the 7th or 6th floor. Then, if it's before three in the morning, you take the elevator back up and do the whole thing all over again.

1995: INTERSECTION (Scotland)

This one was a pain to get to. Ever since Delta chose to make Cincinnati a hub, and subsequently took control of 90% of the gates at the airport, we have been the single most expensive American city to fly out of. There's no competition, and Delta has never offered a cut rate from Cincinnati to anywhere. As a result, most Cincinnatians fly from Dayton, Columbus, or Lexington; most of the people you see at the Cincinnati airport began traveling somewhere else and are just changing planes here.

Anyway, Delta wanted something like $900 to fly each of us, round trip, to London. We picked up a Sunday *New York Times*, found a bucket shop that had New-York-to-London tick-ets on United for $350 apiece, and decided to buy them. Delta wanted $300 apiece for Cincinnati to New York round trip tick-ets, so we flew round trip from Dayton—the airport's 10 min-utes farther from our house than the Cincinnati airport—for $103 apiece.

So far so good. But like an idiot, I didn't check my bucket tickets when they arrived. I went to my local travel agent, bought round trip tickets from London to Edinborough, and then found out that the flight times from New York to London had changed and we didn't have time to make the connection. I went back to my agent, but the tickets were nonrefundable, so I had to buy a second set. By the time we were done, I think the aggravation had just about offset any savings.

We had chosen to stay at the Moat House because when we looked at the map it was next door to the convention center, and the other hotels were all a mile or more away. (They weren't even close to each other. The Progress Report said the Hilton and the Sheraton were 80 yards apart—and indeed they were. What it didn't say was that they were separated by an 8-lane highway, and you actually had to walk better than half a mile to get from one to the other.)

We arrived at the Moat House, checked into our room, and stopped by the restaurant for lunch. It wasn't especially good or especially memorable, but it was 50 pounds (about $80 at that time), and we realized that this could be a *very* expensive vacation if we didn't watch our step.

Fortunately Jack Nimersheim came to our rescue. He found a pizza restaurant about a quarter of a mile away, and except for dining with editors, we ate just about all of our lunches and dinners there.

During our first night at the Moat House, the fire alarm went off. Now, we've been to enough conventions to know it was just fans being less amusing than they thought they were, but the hotel absolutely insisted that everyone evacuate it at maybe 3:30 in the morning. When it happened again an hour later, I think about 80% of us stayed in bed.

A few months prior to the convention I had been asked by the program committee if I could put together an hour videotape about our travels in Africa, and maybe narrate it as well. No problem, I said; do you need it in Beta, VHS, or PAL (the standard British format)?

Oh, VHS is fine, they said.

Are you *sure*, I asked, because every Brit I trade tapes with wants them in PAL format.

Trust us, they said; we know our convention center's video system.

I was to give the presentation in the huge auditorium—the one that hosted the Hugos and the masquerade—from 8:30 to 9:30 Thursday night, so I stopped by at about eleven Thursday morning to deliver the tape to the tech crew. They put it in their machine and hit the Play switch. No picture.

This isn't PAL, they said accusingly.

I don't know which of us got more annoyed at the other, but the gist of the matter was that they took the tape downtown to have it transferred to PAL format. The committee told me it would be back around 3:00 in the afternoon.

So I show up at 3:00. No tape. I check in at 4:30. No tape. I stop by on my way out to dinner and my way back. No tape.

Okay, I say; cancel the program and we'll do it some other year.

Too late, they say; you're giving a video presentation at 8:30.

But I don't have any video, I explain.

Nobody had an answer to that.

I show up at the auditorium at 8:00. There are four or five video technicians in the back, ready to project my African tape onto an enormous screen. Only one problem: still no tape.

At 8:25 I get onto the stage and check the microphone. I figure I'll spend 30 minutes excoriating the committee, and 30 talking about Africa.

At 8:27 a young man comes racing into the auditorium, waving a tape in his hand. It works, and nobody in the audience knows how close the committee and I came to killing each other.

Until the next day. Then I wake up to find out that the bastards are actually billing me twenty pounds for converting the tape from VHS to PAL. I explain my position and offer my opinion of this decision on the first three or four panels I'm on, as well as my kaffeeklatsch, and sometime on Sunday I am told that the worldcon has graciously decided to absorb the cost itself.

While this little battle of wills was going on all weekend, there was also a con to be attended. I got to meet many of my European agents and editors, and to sign foreign editions I'd never seen before. (Foreign publishers aren't too bad on paying what they owe. They're just terrible at sending out author's copies of the books.)

There were no parties in the Moat House. We hit the other hotels one night, but it was more effort to get to them than it was worth, so we spent most of the nights just visiting in the Moat House lobby.

On Friday John Brunner, Hugo winner and former worldcon Guest of Honor, became the first pro—for all I know, the first person—ever to die at a worldcon. It cast a pall of gloom over the rest of the weekend.

The masquerade was pretty small—23 costumes total. Most costumers are American, and it's just too much hassle (and too expensive) for them to ship their costumes to overseas worldcons.

I was only person ever to be nominated for four Hugos. Carol and I went in with Eleanor Wood, my agent, waited patiently for Diane Duane and Peter Morwood to finish their Toastmaster routines, and got ready for the Hugos. The Campbell went to Jeff Noon, a Brit who'd written a very nice first novel. Then Dave Langford won his umpteenth Hugo as Best Fan Writer. Nothing extraordinary.

But then Dave's *Ansible* beat *Mimosa* for Best Fanzine. That was surprising. And then David Pringle's *Interzone* beat *Locus* and *Science Fiction Chronicle* for Best Semi-Prozine. That was shocking. Then Jim Burns knocked off Michael Whelan and Bob Eggleton for Best Artist, and we began wondering if an American would ever win again. (I covered the Hugos for Andy Porter, and titled my article "The Empire Strikes Back.")

I lost my first Hugo of the evening—Best Editor—to Gardner Dozois. Hardly a surprise.

About five minutes later, my "Barnaby in Exile" lost Best Short Story to Joe Haldeman's "None So Blind." Okay, good story, no problem with that.

Two minutes after that, I lost my third Hugo of the night when David Gerrold's "The Martian Child" knocked off my "A Little Knowledge" for Best Novelette. Not unexpected; David had won the Nebula, too.

But now we were coming up to Best Novella, and I thought I had that one in the bag with "Seven Views of Olduvai Gorge." After all, it had beaten novellas by Harlan Ellison and Ursula Le Guin for the Nebula, and Harlan wasn't even on the Hugo ballot. Piece of cake.

Then, as Chip Delany was reading off the nominees, he came to Brian Stableford's name.

"Isn't Brian a Brit?" asked Carol.

I had forgotten. I groaned so loud that I almost didn't hear Chip read off my name as the winner.

In my thank-you speech, I seem to remember explaining that I'd be proud and happy and elated later in the evening, but at that moment I was just relieved not to have become first guy in history to *lose* four Hugos in one night.

Later, I stopped by the men's room. The huge facility was almost deserted. I think the only two other guys in it were Bob Silverberg and Joe Haldeman. Then one of them—I believe it was Bob—said, "Quick, lock the door!"

I asked why.

"We wouldn't want the fans to learn that *we* do it the same way *they* do."

I locked the door.

for Mimosa #25

WORLDCON PROGRAMMING—
THEN AND NOW

Sooner or later everyone at a Worldcon goes to a program item. It may be one of the special ones, like the Hugo Ceremonies or the Masquerade, or one of the more mundane ones . . . but it's a truism that every Worldcon attendee has attended the program at one time or another.

Did they always?

Actually, yes—and usually in far greater percentages.

And was the programming worth attending?

I think we'll leave that to the reader to decide.

I have in front of me the very first Worldcon Program Book. The convention began on July 2, 1939 with an "Informal Gathering at Convention Hall" followed by "Lunch Recess"—and that was the entire programming for the first half day.

Came 2:00 PM, and you had the following:

1. Registration in foyer

2. Official Opening of the Convention

3. Minutes of the First National Science Fiction Convention

4. Address of Welcome by Sam Moskowitz

5. "Science Fiction and New Fandom" by Will Sykora

6. "Science Fiction, the Spirit of Youth" by Frank R. Paul

7. Motion picture: "Metropolis"

8. Recess for Refreshments (30 minutes)

9. "The Changing Science Fiction" by John Campbell.

10. "Men of Science Fiction" by Mort Weisinger

11. "Science Fiction Personalities"—general introductions and discussions

12. Supper recess

In the evening they held an auction, and then broke up for the night.

The next day began with a reading of the minutes and a speech about "The Fan World of the Future."

By July 4, the third and final day of the convention, programming had slowed down to include only a softball game and a fireworks display (not put on by the Worldcon).

You kinda wonder why anyone ever came back a second time—but they did. And a third time. And a fourth.

And by the time of my first Worldcon in 1963, programming had become a little more complex and a little more sophisticated. (In fact, there was enough of it in 1962 and 1963 for Advent Books to put out Proceedings—transcripts, actually—of the entire programming for each.)

By 1963 there were panels as well as speeches. From that day to this, the finest panel I ever attended was a 1963 panel entitled "What Should a B.E.M. Look Like?" A B.E.M., for the uninitiated, is a Bug-Eyed Monster, and the panel's participants were Isaac Asimov, Willy Ley, Ed Emshwiller, L. Sprague de Camp, Fritz Leiber and Leigh Brackett—and whenever I'm stuck for a new alien race, I pull out the Proceedings, read that panel, and invariably I come up with one.

There were other fascinating panels, too. (In general, any panel with Isaac Asimov or John Campbell was, by definition, fascinating.) There was a panel on how to write a story around a generic cover painting. There was a panel in which the current crop of magazine editors held forth on what they wanted from potential writers. There were panels on writing, and illustrating, and science. There were special panels by the Burroughs Bibliophiles and the Hyborean Legion. By 1963 the Hugos were well-established, and were given out at the banquet, which featured the Guest of Honor's speech, and was usually toastmastered by Isaac Asimov, Robert Bloch or Anthony Boucher, our three wittiest speakers of that era.

And then, within a handful of years, Worldcons—and programming—got really complex. Soon there were round-the-clock movies, showing the Hugo nominees and dozens of other films. Then came multi-track programming, when it was no longer feasible for the entire convention—which had numbered in the hundreds until 1967, and numbered in the multi-thousands by the early 1970s—to attend each item.

With multi-track programming came special interest programming. Suddenly we had hard science tracks, soft science tracks, fantasy tracks, academic tracks, art tracks, fannish tracks, even children's programming. At one point, one Worldcon boasted (confessed to?) 18 simultaneous tracks of programming.

And of course there were workshops. They were held for writers, for costumers, for weapon makers, for just about every interest group you can imagine.

And it still wasn't done. Suddenly, because there were so many authors, autograph sessions were scheduled well in advance. So were readings. Then came the notion of kaffee-klatsches, where perhaps a dozen fans would sign up to drink weak coffee and eat dry donuts at a table with their favorite author and question (grill?) him for an hour or two. And somehow these all became program items, since they had to be scheduled without conflicting with any of the more traditional program items on which the participants had agreed to appear.

The Hugo banquet simply got too large to control. It was cancelled after 1977, reinstalled for a single year in 1983, and never held again. Suddenly the Hugos, like the Oscars before them, were no longer given out at a dinner among friends, but at a major ceremony, usually captured on videotape, always written up in the daily press, and attended by nominees in tuxes and evening gowns.

When all this still couldn't satisfy the growing throngs of attendees (and justify the huge jumps in the cost of memberships), night panels and nighttime readings were added.

Somehow we've gone from a bunch of kids pompously reading the minutes of the previous day's business to their friends, to a 5, 6, even 7-day celebration of science-fiction, a 24-hour a day revelry in which at least 16 of those hours are heavily programmed from Thursday through Monday, and hundreds of formal and informal parties fill in all the unprogrammed gaps.

Some people say Worldcon has gotten too big, too busy, too unmanagable. Me, I love it, and look forward to it like a kid looks forward to Christmas.

Though if we only have 15-track programming this year, I suppose I won't feel *too* cheated.

For the Chicon 2000 Programming Souvenir Book

CHICON 2000 REPORT

Food highlights:

Dinner at the Greek Islands, our favorite Greek restaurant, with Nick DiChario, Mary Stanton, and Jay Kay Klein. Great pastitso, dolmades in a thick lemon sauce, flaming saganaki.

Dinner at the Parthenon, Chicago's second-best Greek restaurant, with Rick Katze. Same meal as above, good but not *as* good.

Dinner at the Ritz-Carlton with Eleanor Wood. Great vennison steak in a cream sauce, very nice chocolate souffle for dessert. Only other con member we saw there was Bob Silverberg.

Dinner at Lawry's The Prime Rib, with Greg Benford, Dick Spelman, Tony, Suford and Alice Lewis, and Kristine Kathryn Rusch. Best prime rib in the city, plus wonderful Yorkshire pudding.

Dinner in the hotel at Stetson's, with Beth Meacham. Much better than I'd anticipated. I had a 18-ounce filet mignon.

Best meal of all: Dinner at Eli's, with Anne Groell, my Bantam editor. Chopped liver appetizers (free, and all you could eat) and shrimp de jongue, one of my favorite dishes and all-but-impossible to find these days.

Brunch with Gardner Dozois and Susan Casper. The company was better than the food.

Also had gastronomically-unmemorable business lunches and breakfasts with Shayne Bell, Josepha Sherman, Marty Greenberg, Kris Rusch, and Beth Meacham.

Business highlights:

Beth Meacham and I have agreed on the next book I'll do for Tor. Only question now is whether I want a one or a two-book contract; I'm leaning toward one.

Anne Groell wants another book from me at Bantam; we're still trying to work out which it'll be.

Gardner Dozois bought "Old MacDonald Had a Farm" from me at our brunch. He'd received it the day before he left for worldcon and actually brought it along to read, something *I* would never do at a worldcon.

Greg Benford assigned me a story for what appears to be a very high-paying non-science-fiction anthology.

Met the guys from Frequency Audio Magazine, picked up my CD (their first "issue" has pro actors reading the 5 short story Hugo nominees). They want more stories from me, so I'm going to spend a day trying to figure out what will read well aloud and then send it to them.

Decided it's time to get some more newcomers and semi-newcomers into print, so I had lunch with Marty Greenberg and gave him 8 or 9 anthology ideas. I told him I would only edit one a year, but I was willing to commit to 3 in the next 3 years if he could sell them now.

Had a long meeting with Josepha Sherman. Years ago I wrote the first 40 pages of a Young Adult sf novel called *The Hero*, and had no luck at all placing it. Since Jo writes YA books, I showed it to her a year ago and asked for some input. She offered to collaborate, I agreed, and evidently she's got some editor so hot for it that the woman has begged us to give her a 3-book outline/synopsis, which is what we came up with over an extended lunch.

Got an assignment from an anthology and made arrangements to collaborate with M. Shayne Bell on it. We had breakfast and came up with the plot.

Believe it or not, someone who isn't Marty Greenberg has asked me to edit an anthology. I can't give any details until I decide whether or not to do it. (I'm leaning against, but I'm getting a lot of pressure for; you'll understand once I can discuss it.)

Got a green light to keep writing GalaxyOnline columns.

I was approached by DUFF—the Down Under Fan Fund, that sends a fan to Australia every year—with an interesting request: would I be willing to Tuckerize (i.e., write someone's name into a story) the high bidder for the right to be Tuckerized By Resnick? I said sure, and a new groom paid $650 for his wife of 6 weeks to be written into a story. (Harry Turtledove got $665 for the same thing; highest of all was Lois MacMaster Bujold, who offered the same service for the SFWA Treasury, and got $1,000.) The story's already done; I had a major female character in the story I just sold to Gardner, and he had no problem with my changing it to the auction winner's name.

Did a TV interview with Joseph Formichella and another with Donna Drapeau. Did 3 radio interviews, I have no idea with who or for what stations. Oh, and a long print interview with Frederique Roussel, a lovely Parisian; the French seem to have staked a claim on me this year.

Parties:

The most fun I had was at the CFG Suite Sunday night. We played two hours of the most hilarious Broadway musical trivia anyone's ever seen, and then a couple of more hours in which we had to identify opening and closing lines of sf stories and books. I don't know why that 4-hour stretch was so enjoyable, but it was.

Also had a great time at the Listserv party, which drew a hell of a lot more of us than I thought would be there. At one point Brad Sinor tried to cram us all into one photo; I'm dying to see how it came out.

Tried the SFWA suite a few times, as usual; it was so crowded that I never stayed more than 4 or 5 minutes tops, as usual. Tried the Tor party; it was so jammed I didn't even make it 3 minutes before I gave up on it and went out into the hall for some fresh air—where I bumped into Mr. Tor himself, Tom Doherty, who couldn't stand the crowd and was out there, hiding from his own party, in splendid isolation. We talked for a few minutes, and one by one were joined by Ben Bova, Bob Silverberg, and a couple of others who couldn't take the noise and the jostling. It was a nice "rump party," though I didn't stay too long even in the hall.

The Frequency Audio boys put on a nice one, and Boston, as always, threw a pair of very enjoyable bid parties. I stopped in at the Torcnto and Japanese bidding parties, skipped Charlotte and Con Jose, hit Minneapolis-in-73 and the Bucconeer thank-you party.

And, as I've done just about every night for better than 20 years of worldcons, I wound up each evening in the CFG suite, usually arriving about 12 or 1, and staying until they closed up at 4 or 5 in the morning. This is still the place where most of my friends, most of the old-time fans and pros, come to gather—and we owe Linda Dunn a huge thank you—she was in charge of the SFWA Suite and didn't want to cart home all the unfinished booze, so she made a present of it to CFG. (That's

Cincinnati Fantasy Group—my home club—for the uninitiated. We're not bidding for anything, we're not running for anything . . . but we've had a hospitality suite about 90% of the worldcons during the past half-century. It's where trufen and fannish pros like Robert Bloch and Bob Tucker in the past, and me and George RR Martin and Josepha Sherman and Jack Chalker and Joe and Jack Haldeman in the present, gather late each night at worldcon to visit and unwind a bit. Stop by at 3 or 4 in the morning, and you can usually find Bruce Pelz, Craig Miller, Tony Lewis, Rick Katze, Joe Siclari, Tom Veal, and others of that ilk deciding the fate—and location—of future worldcons.)

Oh—one other party I forgot to mention. My daughter will recognize it, because she's experienced it before. Once per worldcon the Japanese put on a private, invitation-only party, and never invite more than a handful of guests, almost always writers or editors. You show up and realize that you are outnumbered about 4-to-1 by your hosts, who do *everything* for you. You look around for a chair, they rush over and carry it to you. You look thoughtfully at a food tray and it is instantly brought to you. You sit down, and are quickly engaged in conversation by some member of the hosting party who has read every one of your books and stories and can discuss them intelligently. If another guest sits down and starts talking to you, the host who *was* talking to you discreetly vanishes (but stands at the ready to talk to you again the instant your new companion departs.) It is quite an experience, let me tell you. This was the fifth or sixth year in a row I've been invited; over the years I've run into Connie there, and Silverbob, and Greg Benford, and David Brin, and Nancy Kress . . . but the only person I see there year in and year out is Rob Sawyer, who just happens to also be a Seiun winner.

Programming:

I did a really dull (I thought) panel on collaborations, a surprisingly interesting panel on all the writers and artists who had lived in or passed through Chicago over the course of the last century, a well-attended and active panel with Kris Rusch called "Ask Bwana" which included repeats of all the questions I've been answering for years in the Ask Bwana column, and an okay panel on writers who were too good to be famous or too famous to be good or some such thing.

It was when someone complained that I didn't spend as many hours talking to newcomers as I had at some worldcon 10 or 12 years ago that I pulled out my schedule to find out why—and that's when I realized just how hard they work the pros, at least the more prominent ones, at a worldcon.

I had 4 panels. Doesn't seem like much. But I also did an "official" one-hour autographing, and two unofficial ones—one at Larry Smith's table, one at Asimov's. I led a tour through the History of Worldcon exhibit, which was another 75 minutes. And I did 2 TV interviews and 3 radio interviews and a print interview; there's another 6 hours. I won't even count the two photo sessions, one for Locus, one for a French magazine. I did a half-hour online chat. I showed up for the Hugo "rehearsal" because as a presenter I needed to know where to pick up the envelope and the Hugo. I went to the pre-Hugo ceremony, and I attended the Hugos; there's 3 more hours. I did a 75-minute kaffeeklatsch. I did a 75-minute reading.

When the dust had cleared, I figured that I was onstage or oblgated or call it what you will for over 21 hours, not counting all the time it took to simply get from one venue to another—and that doesn't include 4 business dinners, 2 business lunches, and 2 business breakfast/brunches, which had to take another 16 or 17 hours. I'm not objecting, mind you—I loved every minute of it (well, except for the two minutes when I lost two more Hugos), but it does explain why I had so few blocks of time available before the late-night parties.

And I'm not unique; I can think of a couple of dozen pros who worked as hard, and poor Harry Turtledove probably worked considerably harder, given his Toastmaster duties.

The Eisenstein Art Exhibit:

All during the 1960s and 1970s Alex Eisenstein (husband of author Phyllis Eisenstein) spent the bulk of a major inheritance on science fiction art. The public finally got a chance to see it at Worldcon: he had a large room in the display area, and had most of his stuff hanging there. (Not the Frazettas, which were too valuable.) He had almost 100 paintings by Emsh, another 30 or so by Kelly Freas (including the wonderful *Martians, Go Home* cover), a bunch by Schoenherr, some Virgil

Finlays, a lot of other stuff. A truly wonderful exhibit.

The Art Show:

Not all that impressive this year. Nothing by Whelan, Mattingly, Rowena, David Cherry, Frazetta, Gurney. The only major artists represented were Bob Eggleton and Don Maitz.

The Huckster Room:

More books than usual, but I only bought two the whole weekend. Usually I go there hoping to find some new specialty editions or fanzines and semi-prozines that I hadn't previously seen, but this time they just weren't there. NESFA had a phenomenal weekend, selling close to $30,000 worth of books from their single table; and Larry Smith told me he had a record weekend. Some of the other dealers weren't as happy.

The Fan Lounge:

A wonderful idea. Huge room, divided into fan history and fan lounge. The lounge had tables and chairs, sold old magazines and fanzines (and I bought more fanzines there than books in the dealers' room). Dozens of Hugos and program books and photos and ribbons and badges from different years were on display. A very nice place to relax, located on a level between the restaurants and the dealers room, It was run by Janice Gelb and Pat and Roger Sims, and a lot of CFG members volunteered their time in various capacities.

OK, that's a preliminary overview of the worldcon. I averaged about 5 hours of sleep a night, ate like a king, and, as I do at almost every worldcon, had the most fun I'll have all year.

The same, alas, can't be said for Carol. We went to the Field Museum Wednesday, and did some shopping in the Loop on Thursday. Then, Friday morning, as she was showering just prior to going to the Art Institute, she slipped, and as she was falling, she came down hard on the little metal extension atop the water nozzle that activates the shower, and tore a goodly piece of flesh out of herself. We patched her up, cleaned the wound a few times each day, and while it didn't prevent her from going to the Art Institute Friday or the Aquarium Monday or any of her duty dances such as the Hugos, or meals with editors, she was understandably uncomfortable for the last 4 days of the con. First thing we did when we got home was take her to the doctor, who cut off some flesh but pronouced the wound Uninfected and Healing.

The Babes for Bwana t-shirt craze seems to be catching on. Kris Rusch wore one (with "President: Oregon Chapter" printed on it) to our "Ask Bwana" panel (and BJ Galler-Smith and Ann Marston were in the audience wearing theirs), and Carol wore hers ("International President and Founding Member") to the Listserv party.

I realize I was (purposely) vague about some of the books and stories I sold at Worldcon. As I sign the contracts and make them official over the next few months, I'll let you know what each of them were. And that, I think, should hold you while I try to write something that can make next year's Hugo ballot.

For Challenger #14

YOUR FIRST WORLDCON

PARTIES

You've heard endless tales about the parties. Well, there are all kinds of parties—the single events, the pro events, the bid parties, the hospitality suites. You'll get most of your info from various bulletin boards, and also from the twice-daily (and often thrice-daily) convention newsletter, which will be made available in most public places.

Every group that's bidding for a future worldcon will have at least one party, most two, a few every night. These are "open" parties and will be posted/advertised all over the hotels and in the newsletters.

For this worldcon, the bidders who will have open parties include:

- Boston in 2004.
- Charlotte in 2004.
- Glasgow in 2005.
- Los Angeles in 2006.
- Japan in 2007 (but they've never held an open party yet, and might not this year).
- Australia in 2009.
- A number of regional conventions will also have open parties to interest you in attending their upcoming cons. Almost any new con will also have an open suite to announce its existence.

The winners for the next two years usually have open suites:

- San Jose in 2002 (traditionally, next year's winner also hosts the Hugo Losers Party).
- Toronto in 2003.

And often the previous year's host has an open "thank-you" party:

- Chicago in 2000.

Then there will be open and semi-open Hospitality Suites. There will probably include:

- The Con Suite (hosted by Philadelphia).
- The CFG Suite (Cincinnati Fantasy Group)—semi-open; mention that you're on the Resnick Listserv and you'll get in.
- The N3F Suite (The National Fantasy Fan Federation Suite), for new fans. They have a suite every couple of years.
- The Science Fiction and Fantasy Writers of America (SFWA) Suite. You'll need a SFWA member to get you in the first time. If you want to return, you can probably pick up a sticker for your badge that will get you in.

There will be pro parties. They're not exactly open, and not exactly closed. Basically, you'll need a pro or a well-known fan to get you in, but once inside they won't have to stay with you or vouch for you:

- Tor always has a big party, sometimes two.
- Baen always has a party.
- Avon usually has a party.
- Bantam got tired of having its party crashed, so now it takes its authors and friends off the premises for an invite-only dinner.
- DAW usually holds a small party. Get a DAW author or freelance editor to accompany you.
- Del Rey and ROC almost never have parties.
- Asimov's and Analog will have a party, but it usually consists of renting out the SFWA suite and supplying food and booze one evening.
- Many of the semi-pro and specialty publishers will have parties. The most likely at Philadelphia will be Obscura Press, *Farthest Star*, *Tangent*, and *Speculations*.

Almost every special interest group except the Burroughs Bibliophiles, who were numerous enough to split off from Worldcon 20 years ago and hold their own conventions, will have a suite at worldcon. For example, the Resnick Listserv party was held in Gordie Meyer's Obscura Press suite one night at Chicago. If he gets another suite, we'll do it again; if not, I'll try to arrange to take over the CFG suite for our party one night. Gordie also hosted the sff.net party one night. There will be parties that specialize in Bad Book Fandom; in hearts tournements (part of Southern Fandom); there are always a couple of big-money poker games; CFG usually sets aside tables for Wizards and poker, and this year will have a table for mah jong.

Some fans and pros take out suites to split expenses and have a place to host parties. For example, Susan Shwartz, Josepha Sherman, Steve Stirling and his wife, and Listmember Ann Marston usually take out a two-bedroom suite, which gives them a living room/parlor for entertaining friends. So do a number of others; ask around (and remember that suites don't *always* mean there's a party; sometimes they're a place to hide from parties and crowds.)

Most of the computer networks will have parties. First Fandom, a last-man organization consisting of anyone who can prove he was active in science fiction prior to 1938, will have a suite and a party (it gets smaller each year).

Any foreign group with enough attendees from home will throw a party, usually not an open one. The Japanese always have one. So do the Australians. The Slovakians held one last year. If Pierre-Paul Durastanti shows up, I'm sure the French will have one, complete with oversexed French maids.

There'll be 15 or 20 rooms where fans have brought their favorite movies or tv shows, legitimate or (more likely) bootleg, and will show them to anyone who wants to watch. This won't be advertised, but just walk up and down the hotel corridors, and when you find an open door, take a peek in—it's usually a small party or a group watching videotapes.

And of course, I'm barely scratching the surface. Despite the 15-track programming and the Hugos and the masquerade and the dealers room and the art show and everything else, 70% of a worldcon takes place from 10:00 at night until 4:00 or 5:00 in the morning, at least once you know your way around.

And how do you learn where these things will be? All the open ones will be posted everywhere. As for the others, you ask. You find someone who has been around—from this List I'd suggest me, or Adrienne Gormley, or Ron Collins, or Brad Sinor. or Steve Silver, or Linda Dunn, or Roger Sims (who hosted the fabled Room 770 at the 1951 worldcon in New Orleans and must be approaching his 50th worldcon by now) or anyone else you know has been to a few worldcons, and ask. If it's a party you need a little help to get into, that's what the pros on this List are here for. If there's a writer, an editor, or a BNF (Big Name Fan) you want to meet, someone on the list can introduce you. Never be shy; pros are as approachable as fans. Most of us are just fans at heart, so never be shy about approaching a pro at any convention.

STANDING EXHIBITS

There will be a number of standing exhibits, open from 10:00 AM until 6:00 PM or thereabouts. Two are huge, most aren't; the two big ones are easy to find, while most of the others take some looking for.

- The Dealers' Room, a/k/a the Hucksters' Room. It used to sell only books and magazines, but these days it sells games, CDs, toys, clothes, jewelry, videos, anything associated with sf. Probably 40% of the dealers still sell books and magazines, which is a lot, since there will be about 300 tables and a number of booths. For new mass market books, try Larry Smith, the biggest new-book huckster of them all. For new specialty books—Obscura, Wildside, etc—they'll either have their own tables or they'll have shipped their titles to a new-book huckster. The mass market book publishers won't have tables, but many of the magazines will, including *Asimov's* and *Analog*, and so will most of the semi-prozines, including *Locus*, *Science Fiction Chronicle*, *Speculations*, and *Interzone*.

- Autograph sessions—they'll be announced well in advance—are usually held in or near the hucksters' room. But those are just the "official" worldcon autograph sessions. Most of the popular writers will also be signing at dealers' or publishers' tables as well. Last year, for example, I signed at *Asimov's*, at Larry Smith's, at the NESFA Press table, and at one other which I can't remember at the moment — 5 hours in all, counting the official session, so anyone who wanted an autograph probably got one. (And if you see a writer in the hallways, just walk up and ask for an autograph; that's part of what they're there for. You're paying a ton of money to attend, so don't be shy about asking for anything at all.)

- The Art Show. Just about every major artist from Whelan to Eggleton to Maitz will display some of his paintings here, as will hundreds of minor artists. The hangings will all be in the middle of the room; sculptures and other 3-dimensional pieces will be on tables lining the walls. Almost everything will have a minimum-bid pricetag on it. The auction rules change from year to year, so ask how you bid at the entrance to the art show—but know that 90% of what you see will be sold on Sunday and Monday, and some of it sooner.

- Kaffeeklatsches. These are one-hour (and occasionally two-hour) periods where you sign up to meet with your favorite writer or artist. They serve coffee and sweets, and usually there are 12 to a table—the writer and 11 fans. Occasionally I've filled 2 tables, but you can't count on their availability, with me or any other writer, so as soon as the con opens, sign up for the kaffeeklatsches you want. It's always first-signed first-seated.

- Fanzine room. There is always a room devoted to fanzines. Usually it's a small, unpublicized room, difficult to find, but it's worth the hunt, because it gives away dozens of fanzines. Not the perennial Hugo nominees like *Mimosa* and *Challenger* and *File 770*, but enough to get you started.

- Fanhistorica room. This doesn't occur every year, but it's present more often than not, and will be a room devoted to the history of fandom—books, photos, artifacts, famous (and incredibly valuable) old fanzines, everything you'll want to know about sf fandom from its origins in the 1930s to the present day.

  Occasionally, as happened last year, some old-time pros and fans (like myself and Listmember Roger Sims) will lead tours of the exhibit, spewing forth 60 or 90 minutes worth of anecdotes about the items on display.

- Fan lounge. The last few domestic worldcons have had a fan lounge, a practice that began in Boston in 1989. It'll be somewhere near the dealers and lecture rooms, and you'll find tables where you can plop down, relax, get soft drinks or coffee, read fanzines (which will be supplied), and meet other fans.

• Hugo exhibits. The location varies, but worldcon always displays 30 or 40 old Hugos from different years. The rocket ship is always the same, but the base differs each year. It's generally considered that the 1976 base (designed by Hugo winner Tim Kirk) and the 1991 base (taken from an Apollo launch platform) are the loveliest, and the "Rat Hugo" (1984, Annaheim, with Disney-type mice) is the ugliest.

(Other memorable Hugo bases: the Castrated Hugo [1989, with steel balls resembling planets in the base; the planets kept falling off, leading one Hugo winner, Gardner Dozois, to loudly bemoan the fact that he'd lost his balls]; the Thermometer [1991, a plastic rather than a metal rocket ship, which led me to remark after winning one that it looked exactly like a rectal thermometer for elephants, a description that seems to have caught on]; the Hollywood Hugo [1996, a huge base, a lot of film illos, and a pair of 20th Century Fox-type spotlights]; and the Diarrhea Hugo [1988, the only Hugo to be shown in flight, trailing 15 or 20 inches of solid black smoke which resembled . . . well . . . ah].)

• Forthcoming movies will have huge displays near the huckster room. I take no interest in them, but most fans seem to love them. Listmember John Guidry, movie critic and former Worldcon chairman, can probably tell you everything you need to know about then.

• Costume exhibit. This doesn't occur at every Worldcon, but when it shows up, it's stunning. It'll be a display of the greatest masquerade costumes of the past 20 years, draped on mannequins. Check to see if they have it at Philly when you get there.

• Photo exhibit. Over the years SFWA's attorney, M. Christine Valada, who is also a photographer, has taken black-and-white portraits of just about every pro who attends worldcon, and there is a standing display of all of them every year.

• Fan photo exhibit. Encouraged by Valada's traveling

photo show, fandom now has its own portrait exhibit.

There will doubtless be more exhibits, but these are the ones that tend to show up every year, or at least most years. Some years there are "one-shot" exhibits as well, as happened last year, when local Chicago art collector Alex Eisenstein (husband of writer Phyllis Eisenstein) put his 200-piece collection of paintings by Freas, Emsh, Finlay, Paul, et al on display. (His Frazettas were *not* displayed; they were so valuable the insurance costs were prohibitive.)

Anyway, hunt them all up. You do youself a disservice if you travel all the way to worldcon, pay all that money to become a member, pay even more to stay at the hotels, and then don't take advantage of all the exhibits that your money is paying for.

SPECIAL EVENTS

Along with the regular programming, which we'll get into later, every worldcon has its share of special events.

- Hugo Ceremonies.

  This is where the Toastmaster gets to shine (if he shines at all; some don't). 14 Hugos will be presented in the pro and fan categories, but that's not all. Dave Kyle, who has replaced 4e Ackerman as the administrator, will present the Big Heart Award. The Japanese will present the Seiun (Japanese Hugo) for the Best Translated Novel and Short Fiction of the Year. Depending on what perks the worldcon committee gives them, First Fandom may present the First Fandom Hall of Fame Award—but more likely they'll do it at a regional con. There will be photo ops for everybody, and you can probably watch the Hugos and the Masquerade in your room on closed-circuit television.

- The Masquerade:

  This is the biggest draw of the worldcon, but it's a mere shadow of its former self. All during the 1970s and early 1980s the worldcon masquerade used to draw well over 100 costumes and take at least four or five hours, often longer. Now, thanks to Costume Con and the proloferation of minor costume conventions, the masquerade barely draws 35 to 40 costumes...but it's still a fun event to go to. And if you're an author, nothing gives you a bigger kick than watching a fan who spent months of effort creating a costume based on one or more of your characters.

- Meet the Pros Party.

Usually held Thursday night. Last year it was a huge autograph party. Usually it's just ice cream and the like. All the pros will wear something—a funny hat or something similar—that will identify them, and you can meet them. (Warning: at least half the pros stay clear of this event. But with perhaps 400 pros attending worldcon, that's still a goodly number to meet.)

- Opening Ceremonies.

The Toastmaster introduces the Pro and Fan Guests of Honor, who will make brief speeches. You'll be told where to find everything, and then sent off to do just that.

- Bitch Session.

Always held on closing day (Labor Day), it's exactly what it claims to be. The Convention Committee listens to everyone's complaints, answers those that they can, apologizes for those that they can't—and hopefully future worldcons will learn from their mistakes.

- Closing Ceremonies.

I've never been to one. (I even boycotted the one where I was Toastmaster). So I can't say what goes on. Nothing too important, I should imagine.

- Pro Guest of Honor Speech(es).

There used to be just one Pro GOH, and 90% of the time it was a writer. These days there's usually a Writer GOH, an Editor GOH, and an Artist GOH, and each will have an hour in which to make a speech. Check the schedule; usually they're at awkward times, as they're rarely big draws.

- Fan GOH Speech.

It probably draws a bit better than the pro speeches,

which is only right and fitting. Unlike the Nebulas, Worldcon is put on by and for fans, a fact that many pros forget or are simply unaware of. Pros are an attraction and their function is to draw more fans to the con, but never make any mistake about who the con is for.

- Hugo-nominated movies.

    These will play at least twice, free of charge, before the Hugos.

- Fan cabaret

    A number of the worldcons organize fan cabarets. Do you sing? Play the tuba? Belly-dance with snakes? Contact whoever's in charge and volunteer your services—or just go and watch. The most famous group to come out of the fan cabaret was the Duck's Breath Theater, which has been performing on Public Radio for about 25 years now. Their classic, originally performed at MidAmeriCon in 1976, is "Gonad the Barbarian."

There may be other special events. If Joe Straczynski (creator of *Babylon-5*) shows up, they'll give him an hour or two in the biggest auditorium they can get their hands on, and the crowd will be Standing Room Only. (Isaac Asimov and Harlan Ellison once drew that kind of crowd, but Isaac is dead and Harlan is not quite the draw he once was.) Anyway, check your program book to see what other special events there are. They can be as diverse as a mineature golf tournament (1991), a pro vs. fan basketball game (1986), a trivia contest (just about every year), the world premiere of a science fiction movie ("A Boy and His Dog" in 1974; "Watership Down" in 1978) or the first peek at a new TV show (Star Trek in 1966).

PROGRAMMING

OK, I've mentioned 18-track programming and the like, but until you run into it, I don't think any of you can truly realize the magnitude of worldcon programming. I've got the 2000 pocket program (which used to take 2 or 3 pages of a digest-sized Worldcon program book back when I started going, and now is a separate publication, as thick as a paperback book.) Our own Listserv member Steve Silver was in charge of programming at Chicon VI, so he can answer any questions that remain when I'm done.

Let's take a typical hour. Not even a weekend. Let's say Friday. Maybe 4:00 PM, late afternoon, when some people are taking naps to prepare for the parties, others are sneaking out for early dinners, and things are going about as slowly as they ever go at a worldcon. Let's see what programming was going on then.

Now remember: all the standing exhibits—the dealers room, the art show, the fanzine room, the fan lounge, the fanhistorica room, the Hugo displays, any other special exhibits—are all up and running. In addition to that:

Grand Ballroom A:

IT CAME FROM OUTER SPACE. *The NASA Space Product Development Program.*

Grand Ballroom B:

CRITICS' VIEW OF THE RECENT CROP OF SCIENCE FICTION MOVIES. *Panel with Bob Blackwood, Paul Barnett, Randy Dannenfelser, Matthew Springer, John Flynn.*

Grand Ballroom C-D:

VOLCANOS AND ICE. *The Last Days of the Gallileo Spacecraft, A Bill Higgens slide show.*

Regency A:

MILITARY ISSUES. *Elizabeth Moon, John Laprise, John T. Major, Charles Walther, Jim Groat.*

Regency B:

THE JAMES TIPTREE AWARD AUCTION.

Regency C:

CREATION OF A PUBLISHING HOUSE. *Jim Baen, Tom Doherty, Toni Weisskopf, Lois McMaster Bujold, Mark Shepherd.*

Gold Coast Room:

21ST CENTURY FANHISTORIANS. *Joe Siclari, Filthy Pierre, Moshe Feder, Keith Stokes, Dick Smith.*

Buckingham Room:

SHOULD THE VOTE BE EARNED, A LA STARSHIP TROOPERS? *Audience panel.*

Picasso Room:

50'S-70'S VINTAGE. Using clothes from the 1950's through the 1970's for costuming.

Columbian Room:

ANCIENT AND MEDIEVAL ECONOMIC SYSTEMS (AND HOW TO USE THEM IN YOUR WORK.) Greg Costikyan, John Fast, Mike Moscoe, S. M. Stirling.

Haymarket Room:

HOW TO MAKE A MILLION DOLLARS PUBLISHING A FANZINE. Charles Brown, Ed Bryant, Gary K. Wolfe, Mark R. Kelly.

Addams Room:

IS THE SCIENCE FICTION BOOK CLUB STILL NECESSARY IN A WORLD OF ONLINE BOOK-SELLERS? Steve Miller, Andrew Wheeler, Alice Bentley, Therese Littleton.

Fishbowl Room:

BOOK TO COSTUME TO PAINT. Bob Eggtleton, Joy Day.

State Room:

LITTLE ANSWERS TO BIG PROBLEMS. Wil McCarthy, Larry Ahearn, John G. Cramer, Howard Davidson

Regent Room:

ASFA AND THE CHESLEYS. Panelists discuss the art awards. Teresa Patterson, Mel White, etc.

Crystal Room:

PRESENTATION OF THE PROMETHEUS AWARDS.

Ambassador Room:

THE FUTURE OF THE HUMAN FORM. Lee Martindale, Edwin Strickland, etc.

Embassy Room:
COMICS UNDERGROUND. Len Wein, etc.

Childrens':
CHILDRENS' BELLY DANCING

Childrens':
CHILDRENS' LIVE ACTION ROLE PLAYING

Childrens':
LAND BEFORE TIME WORKSHOP. *Hal Clement.*

Kaffeeklatsch:
Kevin Anderson.

Kaffeeklatsch:
Linda Dunn.

Kaffeeklatsch:
April Lee.

Reading:
M. Shayne Bell.

Reading:
Carol Berg.

Reading:
Mary Marshall.

Reading:
Sue Blom.

Tour of Fan History Exhibit:
Mike Resnick.

Autographing:
Nancy Kress.

Autographing:
Jerry Oltion.

Autographing:
Karen Haber.

Autographing:

Edward Rosick.

Autographing:

Orson Scott Card (who had to cancel).

And of course the round-the-clock movies were proceeding on schedule.

All this at 4:00 PM.

I could pick any other hour of daytime programming and it would be just as crowded, but I'm tired of copying from the pocket program so you'll have to take my word for it.

So understand on the front end: when you arrive at worldcon, there will be programs on writing sf, on selling sf, on criticizing sf; on hard science, on soft science, on fantasy, and on horror; on science itself; on research; on academia; on movies; on costuming; on fandom and its history; on fanzines; on art; on futurology; on editing; on publishing; and there will also be a couple of tracks for children.

Constantly. Every hour on the hour. All at the same time. Starting at 9:00 or 10:00 every morning, continuing through 6:00 PM every night. And while the number of panels diminish at that point, they do continue through midnight. Checking that same Friday at Chicon VI, there were 4 panels each at 10:00 PM and 11:00 PM, and 2 more at midnight.

Now, if Philadelphia is like Chicago, Baltimore, San Antonio and Los Angeles before it, it will publish the programming schedule a few weeks before the con on its web page. Download it and study it at home, mark those things that you feel you *have* to see, work out all your schedule conflicts . . . and you'll save 4 hours of doing the same thing at the con, where you've got better things to do, friends to make and contacts to discover.

But I hope this one example will give you a notion of exactly what goes on, hour by hour, during the day at a worldcon.

WHAT TO BRING

OK, so it's your first worldcon. What do you pack? What do you bring? What do you leave behind?

Clothing: There is no panel or party where you won't be accepted wearing a t-shirt, shorts, and sandals . . . so what else you bring depends to a great extent on what makes you comfortable and where you plan to go when you leave the hotel.

If you're dining out with editors, or simply plan to visit some upscale restaurants, bring along the appropriate clothes. If you plan to use the hotel's pool, bring along a swimsuit. (The skinny-dipping days of the 1970s and 1980s worldcons are long gone.) If you're a Hugo nominee, at least bring a suit, and a tux is not out of place (and if you're a woman, dope out the comparable items to wear.) If you're entering the masquerade, make sure you pack your costume in a way that won't break or otherwise harm it. If you plan to participate in the Regency dance (yes, every worldcon has a Regency dance, don't ask me why), you might bring the appropriate Regency costume.

If you're on any medication, bring enough to see you through the convention; it's murder trying to fill a prescription in a strange city on a holiday weekend.

I wouldn't bother bringing a laptop. First, there's too much to do (and you're paying quite a bit to do it) to waste time with your computer—and second, most of the people you want to chat with and send e-mail to are already at the con. (And most hotels will charge incredibly high connect rates, measured by the minute if not the second.)

Bring any books you want autographed. This is your one chance all year to find 80% of the major authors in the field in one place, and they're all there for your convenience. Ditto any magazines.

Bring any guide books you may have purchased. Why try committing them to memory?

If you're into photo memories, bring your camera, or videocam, with enough film, tape, and batteries that you won't have to go out to purchase any.

Bring cash and/or credit cards. No one in a strange city wants to cash your checks.

Above all, bring the one item I never do without, the most important single item you *can* bring: a small blank notebook that fits easily into a pocket.

Why?

Well, to begin with, you'll write down the titles of all the books you're looking for in the huckster's room, as well as the dates of all the magazines, before leaving home, to make your searching a little easier.

You'll want to write down the room numbers of all your friends—and that could come to a cool 100 numbers right there. Impossible to remember them all.

As you find out when and where the parties are, you'll want to write down the times and room numbers of each. That's dozens more numbers and times.

You'll want to write down those events that you absolutely don't want to miss. Still more times and places.

You might also write down the addresses and phone numbers of all the restaurants you want to visit (and, this being a holiday weekend, all the better ones, inside and outside the hotel, will require reservations.)

If you're a hopeful writer, you'll want to write down whatever it is you have sold, or promised to send, to which editor. Even if you're not, it helps to write down anything you promise to send/sell/trade with other fans.

If you're trading addresses, either street or e-mail, with new friends, you'll want to write them down.

So be sure you bring that blank book. You'll fill it up soon enough—and while you're thinking of it, bring a couple of ballpoint pens as well.

SAVING AND SPENDING MONEY

Worldcon isn't cheap. There are a few ways—not many, but a few—of saving money. To wit:

- Car pool to get there. With gas prices going through the roof, and airfares ditto, the cheapest way to get to *any* Worldcon (at least, any Worldcon on this continent) is to car pool.

- You'll hear stories of fans sleeping ten and twelve to a room. They are not an exaggeration, but it seems a bit excessive to me. Still, Philadelphia has the highest room rates in Worldcon history, and it certainly makes sense, if you're traveling on a budget, to share a room with perhaps 2 or 3 others.

- As I've explained, the initial price for an attending membership is about $50. Right now it's $145, and going up a few more times before the con. But there's a way around this. Surf the net and find someone who has an attending membership and can't use it; it can be sold and transferred to you prior to mid-July . . . after that, it has to be done at the door.

   (Example: someone who bought in at $60 wants to sell; the price is currently $160; you offer to split the difference, the seller agrees, you get an attending membership for $110, you save $50, the seller makes $50, and everyone's happy.)

- If you're a writer and you're dining with an editor, remember: the editor or publisher *always* pays for meals; the writer *never* does.

- If you see a second-hand book or magazine you want in the hucksters' room and it's too expensive for your budget, make an offer. Half the time you'll find the huckster is willing to deal.

- Don't do this every night . . . but one night, at least, you can probably fill up on all the goodies they lay out at the various parties and save yourself the cost of a dinner. If you're on a panel, you can do the same thing in the Green Room. So that's two meals. Not much, but in a city like Chicago or Philadelphia, it could save you $30 or so, even at downscale restaurants.

And now a couple of proper ways to spend money:

- The maid who makes up your room doesn't work a 7-day week, so for the best service, and just to be fair, leave a buck or two on your pillow every morning when you go out for the day, rather than leaving $10 or $15 in a lump at the end of the week.

- Most parties don't want your money. But a few hospitality suites will have a bowl out with a note asking for donations. Put a couple of bucks in, or you may never be asked back.

- If there's a bid you approve of, by all means buy a pre-supporting membership. If they win, you'll probably get a rebate on your attending membership—and if you don't buy one, and they lose, well, it's people like you who stop them from having enough money to make a winning bid (which runs about $65,000 these days, and sometimes more). Remember: all bid committees consist of nothing but unpaid volunteers; they offer their time and effort, so someone else has to chip in the money.

(I wrote this in a series of missives to members of the Resnick Listserv who were attending their first Worldcon at Millennium Philcon in 2001.)

MILLENNIUM PHILCON DIARY

Tuesday, August 28:

We landed at the less-than-impressive Philadelphia airport at 1:15 PM and actually made it to the Marriott by 2:00, an hour before we thought we'd get there. We got a corner room on the 9th floor, and while Carol was unpacking I went down one flight to the room directly below us to meet Janis Ian, the world-famous singer who had collaborated with me on a short story.

We hit it off immediately (but we knew we would; we'd been corresponding for months), and she was floating on air because our story, "Water-Skiing Down the Styx," had just knocked off Ursula Le Guin to become Fictionwise.com's current best-selling story. She had shipped about a five-foot shelf of hardcovers to the hotel so she could get them signed. It was a really strange experience, reassuring a woman who has millions upon millions of fans that these writers, most of whom haven't sold 100,000 copies of anything in their lives, would not be offended if she asked for their autographs, and that some would be out-and-out thrilled.

Janis has been a heavy sf reader all her life. In fact, she's probably better-read in the field than I am. A huge grin spread over her face when I introduced her to her first pro, and it was still hovering there between her nose and her chin when we parted six days later.

I work like hell at worldcons. I do panels, readings, kaffeeklatches, autograph sessions, fan history tours, anything I'm asked to do. I meet with my agent, with every book and magazine editor who's ever bought me or even expressed any interest in me, with every foreign agent and publisher, with every small press, with every audio publisher—and the fact that I thoroughly enjoy every minute of it doesn't make it any the less necessary or any the less exhausting. I try to line up the next year's work at worldcon so I don't have to make any trips to New York. (Even Carol's not free of these professional obligations; she has about a dozen duty dances each worldcon.)

The conventions officially begin on Thursday, and from Thursday to Monday I'm wearing my professional hat, so I always reserve Tuesday and Wednesday for my fannish friends (as well as any time I can spend with them after the con ends.) So on Tuesday night, we introduced Janis to fandom (well, SMOFdom, to be honest), and were joined for dinner by Tony and Suford Lewis, Dick Spelman, and Rick Katze. We went to a Moroccan place called The Fez; fine food, though when we were told that we would be eating with our hands, I took a quick look at my fastidious friend Dick's face and realized that this would not be his most memorable gustatory experience.

When we got back to the hotel we sat at the circular bar—a huge raised area built around a bar in the lobby—and as the various pros began checking in and passing by, I introduced Janis to each of them—Bob Silverberg, Fred Pohl, Lois McMaster Bujold. That was when she got her first major shock: before she could ask them for autographed books, most of them asked her for autographed CDs.

While I was speaking to Silverberg, a couple of girls came up and shyly asked for Mr. Resnick's autograph. I explained that my name was Mike and not Mister, and expressed the hope that they would enjoy the books. As they left, Bob turned to me and said, "You do the humble bit very well." Pause. Then, "Personally, I flunked it." If you know Silverberg, you'll be laughing too hard to read this line.

Gardner Dozois and George R. R. Martin showed up around 11:00, so Janis and I joined them for drinks. Mine was water, as usual. (Carol, who stays up until 2:00 or 3:00 AM at home, comes to cons to relax, and is rarely up after midnight.) Janis went to bed around 1:30, and I spent another couple of hours talking to old fannish friends.

Wednesday, August 29:

Carol and our dear friend Josepha Sherman, yet another of my multitude of collaborators (and the only pro who knows as much about horse racing as I do), spent the day shopping at Lord & Taylor. I got up, met Janis for coffee about 10:30, and then we went to the hucksters' room. It was closed to non-dealers, but after 38 years of attending worldcons I am not without my resources and I got us in. We shopped and visited with dealers and fans, and I introduced her to some more pros.

We registered and got our badges and program books in late afternoon, and then I noticed that my left foot felt kind of strange and that I was limping, so I went back to the room and found I had a broken blister the size of an old-fashioned silver dollar. Carol had just come back from shopping and immediately treated it with all kinds of stuff. I kept explaining that it was just a blister and nothing to get excited about, and she kept saying that I was a diabetic and if they cut my foot off all that money we spent on dancing lessons would be wasted (which at least shows where her priorities were). She won, as usual.

We had another fannish dinner, this time with a pair of CFG (Cincinnati Fantasy Group) members, Debbie Oakes and octogenarian surgeon Mary Martin (who won the 1966 worldcon masquerade as A. Merritt's "The Snake Mother" and whom I plan to marry just as soon as I work Carol to death), and Robyn Herrington from Calgary, another collaborator. B.J. Galler-Smith, still another Canadian collaborator, was supposed to join us, but she called about five minutes before we left to say she'd just arrived at the airport and couldn't possibly make it. We went to Kabul, an Afghan restaurant, and had the best of the meals that we paid for ourselves. (I stop paying for meals when worldcon starts.)

Then it was back to the hotel for the first of the Boston and Charlotte parties, and a very private single-malt Scotch tasting party up on the 19th floor. (I don't drink, but I accompanied Janis, just in case she got so heavily into it that she forgot her room number. Didn't happen . . . and it turned out to be a very enjoyable party.)

Thursday, August 30:

I injected a little coffee into a vein, then mosied over to the hucksters' room, where Walter Jon Williams and I signed autographs at the *Asimov's* table from 11:00 to noon. My line never let up, so I found an empty area and signed for a few more minutes when noon rolled around. By then I'd already lost most of my voice, which happens to me every worldcon, but usually not til Sunday or Monday.

I was distressed to find out that the *Asimov's* people had brought copies of the forthcoming October issue rather than the current September issue, which carries my story "Old MacDonald Had A Farm." No, it wasn't egomania. You see, last year a new husband won a fannish auction for DUFF (the Down Under Fan Fun, which flies an Australian here or an American there, depending on the year) and paid $650 for me to write his bride into a story. I had sold this story to Gardner for *Asimov's* that very morning, and there was no problem changing the main female's name to Julie Balch, the name of the bride. I wanted to surprise her by getting an issue signed by Gardner, managing editor Sheila Williams, and myself.

(The ever-competent Sheila arranged for me to get a copy on Friday, and I went a little overboard. I got signatures, all personalized "To Julie," not just from the *Asimov's* folk, but Bob Silverberg, Connie Willis, Lois McMaster Bujold, Nancy Kress, David Brin, Greg Benford, Greg Bear, Larry Niven, George R.R. Martin, Charles Sheffield, Pat Cadigan, James Patrick Kelly, and perhaps 75 others. I figure that particular copy of the magazine is probably worth three times what her husband paid to get her in it.)

I wasn't hungry—noon is a little early in the day for me—so I hung around the hucksters' room for a couple of hours, then went off to do a rather dull panel on "Rediscovered Authors." Jack Chalker and I were on it, and have done this panel many times. We wanted to speak about Fred Brown and Henry Kuttner and C. L. Moore and Stanley Weinbaum . . . but because we had done the intro and afterward for NESFA's Eric Frank Russell tome, and the moderator was the editor of the book, every time we discussed any other author we kept getting dragged back to Russell.

Barry Malzberg showed up as the panel ended. This was his first worldcon in 18 years, and I wanted to show him around, but I only had a few minutes to help him get registered, and then I was doing an autographing at John Betancourt's table. My latest "how-to" book, *I Have This Nifty Idea . . . Now What Do I Do With It?* was out, and selling very rapidly (as well it should have, since it contains 33 outlines and synopses that sold, including some by Silverberg, Joe Haldeman, Kevin Anderson, and others of that ilk. He told me that by the end of the con he'd sold over 120 copies, and it is not an inexpensive book.) John had also published this year's Hugo nominee for Best Related Book, *Putting It Together*, the first print-on-demand book ever to make the Hugo ballot, and I signed a batch of both, plus a collection of mine he'd published the prior year. A grinning

Janis, now making dozens of contacts on her own, stopped by to tell me that she'd checked on her computer and we were still #1 at Fictionwise.

At 5:00 I did a repeat of last year's Fan History Tour. We had a big crowd, and since everything was so spread out, I stuck to the Hugo display and told 60 minutes of funny stories about each of them and the cons they represented. I think of all the gigs I do at worldcon, this is the one I enjoy most, and I certainly plan to volunteer to do it again next year.

Since worldcon had started, tonight was a pro dinner, and a large one. We went to Rangoon, a Burmese restaurant, with Janis, Barry and Joyce Malzberg, Greg Benford and his lady, Nick DiChario, Susan Shwartz, Josepha Sherman, and Robyn Herrington. (And I want to apologize again to Robyn. I've known her for close to ten years, and I kept forgetting this was only her second worldcon, so I kept assuming she knew all the people I was introducing Janis to. I got better—I think; I *hope*—as the con went on.)

We went back to the hotel and helped open the CFG suite—Cincinnati never bids, but has a 5-night hospitality suite for old and new friends every worldcon. We don't advertise or list ourselves with all the other parties, but anyone who wants us can find us just by asking around a bit.

Then Carol and I went up to Gordie Meyer's (Mr. Obscura Press) suite, for the Resnick Listserv Party, now officially known as the Babes For Bwana Party II. The Babes were out in force, with maybe a dozen of them wearing their Babes For Bwana t-shirts. (Along with the photo of me and a rhino, and the big "Babes For Bwana" logo, each has a little personal inscription. Carol's says "President and Founding Member." Kris Rusch's is "Director, Orgeon Chapter," and so on. The newest member, Janis Ian, is "Chorale Director.")

John Teehan was there, and Donna Drapeau and Adrienne Gormley and just about all the List members who were at the con. Christy Harden Smith, surely the sexiest lawyer in or out of fandom, made chocolate fondue and all kinds of goodies. Fictionwise also supplied us with a bunch of stuff to give away—t-shirts, boxer shorts, hats, coffee mugs, mouse pads, each displaying a cover of one of the books or stories I'd sold to Fictionwise. (I brought home a *Bully* mousepad and an *Adven-*

tures coffee cup. I don't know who wound up with the boxer shorts, but one of them had the cover to *Encounters*, which under certain circumstances might well be viewed as a promissary note.)

Barry managed to lose the room number and never showed up, but Susan Shwartz, Jo Sherman, Greg Benford, Walter Jon Williams, Nick DiChario, and half a dozen other pros were there. So were two of my Clarion kids that I'd collaborated with—Tom Gerencer and Toby Buckell—and a few CFG members, and some NESFA friends, and some sff.net members, and Guy Lillian and Rosy, his new bride. (I hadn't realized that I've known her father, fellow sf writer and longtime NASA bigwig Joe Greene, for years. With that pedigree, their kid will probably chair a worldcon and win the Best Novel Hugo at it.)

Then, just when we were all having a wonderful time and it seemed like the party couldn't possibly get any better, Kent Brewster (publisher of *Speculations*, which runs my "Ask Bwana" column every issue) brought three gorgeous belly dancers to the suite. Evidently they had offered to perform in the SFWA suite and been turned down (my daughter suggests that the music would have kept the writers from talking for whole minutes at a time, a fate worse than death). We were happy to have them. They brought their own music and spent the next half hour entertaining us. At one point they draped their veils around my head, and Adrienne Gormley took some "Bwana of Arabia" photos that we'll be running for the List or on the web page pretty soon.

As they were jiggling a few inches away from me, a thought occurred, so I asked them what they were doing Saturday afternoon. They were free, so I told them to show up at Larry Smith's table at 2:00, when I was scheduled to autograph, and see if they could generate a little extra traffic.

(And I was teased mercilessly the rest of the con by various of the Babes, who claim that only *I* could talk about book promotion with three gorgeous bosoms shaking in my face.)

The party broke up about 3:00 in the morning, though Scott Pendergrast (co-owner of Fictionwise.com) stayed a little later to talk some business, and then Gordie and I talked a little more business until about 4:30.

The party really and truly was the talk of the con for the

rest of the weekend. I must have been asked about it by at least two hundred non-attendees, each more bitter than the last about missing it.

Friday, August 31:

Carol and Debbie Oakes went off to see the major art museum, and came back in late afternoon singing its praises.

I began the day by having coffee with Marty Greenberg, and we did some business. I sold him a couple of collections, and together we sold a pair of anthologies. Sheila Gilbert, editor and co-publisher of DAW Books, joined us because she had heard Janis was at the con with me and wanted me to introduce her. (It seems to me that I spent most of the weekend explaining that I hadn't brought Janis to the con, that she wasn't with me but was a free agent, and that I'd never even seen her before Tuesday.) Marty, who has the most commercial mind of anyone I know, came up with half a dozen Janis Ian projects in the next five minutes, and I agreed to put Janis (who knew nothing of this at the time) together with Marty and DAW on Saturday to see what we could accomplish.

(Sheila had been my editor at Signet in the early 1980s, and bought 13 books from me, including such totally offbeat stuff as *Adventures* and *The Branch*. We stayed at her house on one of our trips to New York, and she and her late husband Mike—a pair of devoted orchid growers—are the reason Carol fell so in love with orchids that we eventually built our current house, with a huge greenhouse, to accommodate them.)

I was supposed to have lunch with Bob Silverberg and Barry Malzberg at noon, but Barry never showed up at the right spot. We searched for him and waited as long as we could, but we both had obligations at 2:00, so at 12:20 we left without him. (We could have stayed. Bob had been touted onto the Famous Deli, quite a cab ride away. Within 30 seconds of arriving he found out they didn't serve beer, I found out they didn't serve chopped liver, and we both found out that the place hadn't been painted or redecorated since World War II. It got worse. For whatever reason, I'd have to say that Barry came out ahead on the deal.)

Barry and I did our official autograph sessions from 2:00 to 3:00 (I say official, because all the ones I do at the request of dealers and publishers are unofficial, and not listed in the pocket programs). I was thrilled to see that Barry, who was sure he'd been forgotten by fandom and would sign perhaps three books at the entire con, had a line of worshipful readers that lasted the entire hour. It's comforting to know that nobody that good gets forgotten.

At 3:00 I raced over to the program area for a panel on "Under-Plundered Mythologies," with Jo Sherman and some others. Nice panel, nothing special.

From 4:00 to 5:00 I cruised the hucksters' room, finally finding a pair of books to buy. It gets harder each year, since I have such a large collection and get so many freebies from publishers.

At 5:00 I was on another panel, "The First MacDonald's on Epsilon V," with Cory Doctorow, Severna Park (a/k/a Suze Feldman), Jim Morrow, and Ellen Kushner. Sounded dull as hell to me when the committee told me I'd be on it, but it turned out to be more interesting than I'd anticipated.

At 6:00 Carol and I went to the Eos reception (I gather they're not Avon Eos anymore) with my agent, Eleanor Wood, at the Museum of Natural History. Very nice party, tasty tidbits to eat, champagne to drink (except for me; I had water), a wonderful dinosaur exhibit including one area where if you stood in the right spot you could be menaced by T. Rex on a huge television screen. I could be mistaken, but I don't think I saw a single fan there, just writers, editors and agents. I had an appointment with Eos editor Jennifer Brehl the next day, and since I'd never seen her and I'd be meeting her alone, I needed Eleanor to point her out and introduce us.

Then we were out of there, because Eleanor, who was Robert A. Heinlein's agent and still represents the estate, had to be at the Retro Hugos to pick up the awards in case he won. So we grabbed a less-than-memorable Italian meal somewhere, and hurried back to the hotel. It was an odd meal, because usually Eleanor tries to eat with me at the end of the worldcon, so I can report on all my meetings; this time I still hadn't met any of the book editors, so we spent most of our time talking about the Broadway theatre season.

The Retros were held at 8:30, and if your name was Heinlein you did pretty well—Hugos for Best Novel, Best Novella, and Best Movie.

I think the results were the best argument against having any more Retro Hugos. Not the Heinlein wins; I would never argue that he didn't deserve everything he got and more. But there were two brilliant short stories, Fritz Leiber's "Coming Attractions" and Richard Matheson's "Born of Man and Woman," that lost to Damon Knight's one-punch humor story, "To Serve Man," probably because it was on Twilight Zone and gets reprinted all the time. Similarly, no one will argue that Bob Silverberg is one of our finest writers, but the 15-year-old Silverberg who won the Fan Writer Retro over Bob Tucker and Walt Willis won it only because he was the only name most fans recognized; clearly none of them had read any of the fannish writings from 1950, or the legendary Willis, the Dave Langford of his day, would never have come in 4th out of 5. By the same token, this was the only chance most fans ever had to vote for Virgil Finlay, Hannes Bok, or Edd Cartier, three of the all-time greats, for Best Pro Artist, but they're all long dead or retired, and they all lost, quite possibly for that reason.

Then it was off to the parties, but they were too crowded—though I did run into Michelle Sagara, who I hadn't seen in years—and by midnight I was ensconced in the CFG suite, which never seemed to have more than 25 people. Debbie Oakes, Mary Martin, and Pat and Roger Sims had the adjoining bedrooms and ran the suite, and Debbie in particular did yeoman work. Each night seemed to begin and end with people playing Wizards, a card game—the suite wasn't big enough for Mah Jong too, so they played that in another room—and by 2:00 every night all non-SMOFish conversation seemed to have vanished. And as we've said for 38 years now (*ghod*, that long???) there is no better, more pleasant way to end the night at worldcon than in the CFG suite, surrounded by old friends, old fans, and the few remaining pros who came from fandom.

Saturday, September 1:

Another day in which I didn't see Carol from when I left the room until dinner. (She had thoughtfully found a drug store on Friday and got some ointments and painkillers for my foot—the

one with the huge broken blister. I was so sleepy—I'd been getting about 4 hours each of the last 3 nights—that she managed
to cut all the dead skin off my foot without waking me up.)

Asimov's and *Analog* were having an award breakfast at
10:00. I'd gotten an invite for Janis, so I picked her up in the
lobby and we took a cab over to the Imperial Inn, where I had to
face Chinese food at 10 in the morning. (Talk about an appetite
surpressant!) They handed out certificates and bonus checks to
the winners of the *Asimov's* poll and the Anlab (this was my
third win in the last four years), and when I went up to accept
the award for "The Elephants on Neptune," I explained that of
all the many stories, well over 20 by now, that I had sold to
Gardner, this was the first he'd ever returned for revisions. He
didn't mind that there were elephants on Neptune, or that they
breathed oxygen, or that they could speak English, or that they
could forage and find food—but it bothered the hell out of him
that I'd given Neptune a solid surface when everyone knows it's
a gas giant, so I had to insert a sentence explaining that. I then
thanked Gardner for turning me into a hard science writer.

I left Janis surrounded by adoring writers and cabbed back
to the Marriott in time to make a lunch appointment with Tom
and Toby, my two Clarion kids. Barry was supposed to join us,
but he got lost again.

At 1:00 I had my kaffeeklatsch—my third scheduled meal
without a break—but fortunately the con committee was so
tight-fisted that we had neither weak coffee nor stale donuts
nor indeed anything else to eat or drink. I gave away cover flats
and color Xeroxes of some no-longer-valid Santiago-the-movie
matte paintings, and we did the usual question-and-answer for
a pleasant hour.

Then it was 2:00, and I went to Larry Smith's table to sign
for an hour, as I always do at worldcons—and my belly dancers
were there waiting for me. They started dancing, and drawing a
crowd, and instead of using feathered fans as they had at the
party they used Resnick books, posing for hundreds of photographs. Whenever one of their songs was over, they stopped
dancing and explained that they would start again when someone bought a Resnick book.

Did it work? Well, one party bought the 7 African Adventure and 3 Worldwide Adventure titles that Larry had on dis-

play—a tidy expenditure of about $175. Two different guys bought both the 4-in-1 hardcover *Velvet Comet* and the 4-in-1 hardcover *Galactic Midway* books, a quick $75 expenditure apiece. Others made more modest purchases. I think Larry did about $500 in Resnick books that hour, and I've already "contracted" the belly dancers for next year's Babes For Bwana Party and next year's autograph sessions. (They even joined the Babes, and have formed their own branch of Babes For Bwana, officially known as Bwana's Harem.)

At 3:00 I reluctantly left the dancers and wandered over to the bar for a meeting with Jennifer Brehl. It was congenial, we discussed the proposal I'd had Eleanor send her, I told her I'd expand it a bit to cover some points she had questioned, and we'll see if we can do some business. The strong indication I got is that we can and will.

At 4:00, I introduced Janis to Eleanor Wood, another of her fans. Not to make her a client; that's up to them. But I knew I was taking Janis to DAW to hear a ton of proposals and deals, some of them quite complex, and I wanted Eleanor to give her a primer on what she would hear, what it meant, what she should watch out for, and so on.

Then, while Eleanor was educating Janis, I met with Scott and Steve Pendergrast, the brothers who own the phenomenally-successful Fictionwise.com. They came up with an interesting offer for me that I have accepted—this has nothing to do with buying more of my books and stories, which they will also do—and when we sort out the details, I'll let you know more about it.

Betsy Wollheim and Sheila Gilbert showed up at 5:00—Marty had been in the bar all day, schmoozing one editor after another—and when we decided it was too crowded and there were too many prying ears, we all went up to the DAW suite, four old friends and one confused newcomer. There's one deal Marty and I had worked out that Eleanor had approved, the DAW ladies agreed to it, and they'll be arguing money with Marty on it this month, but it's as good as done. There's another much more complex one where they will have to make an offer, and Janis will have to bring it to me or, better still, to Eleanor to see where the crouching tigers and hidden dragons are.

We just had a few minutes to clean up for dinner, and then

Carol and I—and Janis, for whom I had finagled an invite (well, it didn't take much; Anne Groell, my Bantam editor, has all her CDs)—went off to the Bantam dinner. Bantam decided years ago that they didn't want fans or rivals crashing their expensive parties, so they hit upon the notion of taking their writers—even agents aren't invited—off the premises to a fancy dinner.

This one was at Spasso's, which Charles Sheffield still doesn't believe exists since it's not listed in his guide book. Nonetheless, we sat with Charles and Nancy Kress and Roger McBride Allen, and at one point Janis asked a totally innocent question about Harlan Ellison, and that was it—we were off to the races, the five of us taking turns telling hilarious Harlan stories for the rest of the meal and then equally hilarious stories about other writers and editors all through dessert and coffee.

We went to the CFG suite when we returned, and got to see the end of the masquerade—and the winners—on closed-circuit TV. The costumes were a hell of a lot better this year than last, and much deeper in quality. We also learned that Boston—our choice any time they run—just won the right to put on Noreascon IV in 2004.

I tried getting into the Tor party a couple of times, but the room was so crowded it spit me out. So, as happens most years, I wandered down the corridor until I found Tom Doherty (Mr. Tor) hiding from his own party and breathing in cool fresh air, and we had our annual chat.

I made it into the SFWA Suite for about 10 minutes—about my usual limit—and left. The Japan and Minneapolis parties weren't much better—*everything* seemed crowded—and I never did make it to Chicago or Los Angeles. I managed to introduce the Clarion kids to some agents and editors, and I remember introducing Robyn to a number of writers and editors as well, but I couldn't take the crowds, and I was back relaxing in the CFG suite by 2:00—but not before I'd picked up assignments to write four stories for anthologies and sold some foreign rights to other stories. I spent another hour there, and went to bed at 3:30, much the earliest night of the con for me.

Sunday, September 2:

Carol woke me at 10:15, after my longest sleep in a week—almost 7 hours. I got dressed, re-bandaged my foot, and went over to "The Resnick/Malzberg Dialogue—Live!" panel at 11:00. I love being on panels with Barry—we've done some at Lunacon, and did a pair in 1983 at his last worldcon—where his wit always shows through, and we kept the audience informed and laughing for an hour while agreeing on nothing except the fact that God outdid Himself when He made Sophia Loren. A number of audience members came up to me later to tell me that was their favorite panel of the con. It certainly was mine.

At noon I went off to lunch with Beth Meacham (my Tor editor), Gardner Dozois (my Asimov's editor), and Pat Cadigan (who was to have been my first collaborator before she moved to England and forgot to give me her e-mail address for years). It was just four old friends visiting for an hour. Then Pat and Gardner had to go to perform on panels, and Beth and I got down to business and agreed on the next novel I'll write for her, after I hand in *The Return of Santiago* this fall.

After lunch I finally made it to the art show, just before they started dismantling it. There were far more top artists than at Chicon last year, including Bob Eggleton, Don Maitz, Kelly Freas, Michael Whelan, Donato Giancola (who is fast becoming my favorite among the current batch), Stephen Youll, Ron Wolatsky, and others.

I had a reading at 3:00. This year for reasons unknown to me (or anyone else) they held the readings to 30 minutes, thereby making it impossible to read a novelette or even a longish short story. So I brought a bunch of 4-and-5-pagers and read as many as I could before the time was up. As always, I signed each one and handed it to an audience member when I was done.

Then Janis and I did a TV interview with Donna Drapeau (who sent me a tape of the show that contained her Chicon interview with me, and I can attest to the fact that she and her partners do a wonderful job). We finished by 4:30, and made arrangements to meet in the lobby at 6:30 (she was our guest at the Hugo reception). Then I went to my room, kissed Carol hello, kissed Carol good-night, and took a 90-minute nap.

She woke me in time for me to get dressed in a jacket and

tie (and my first pair of socks since last year's Hugo ceremony), informed me she had spent the last day and a half line-editing the first 400 pages of *The Return of Santiago* (which should answer all the people who asked where she was Saturday and Sunday), planned to reward herself with a little wine at the Hugo reception, and then off we went to it. This was the one place the con hadn't stinted on the money, and the spread was remarkable, clearly better than any since LACon back in 1996. We spent about 90 minutes there, and then went off to our seats to find out who won the Hugos.

You've all seen the results by now. I managed to lose all three for which I was nominated, none of them by close margins. (Which I prefer, if I must lose. The three times I've lost by two or three votes, I've spent the rest of the con wondering which of my friends was too lazy to vote and thinking of various ways to dismember them.) The real surprise was Harry Potter beating legitimate sf novels; and the real triumph was my pal Jack Williamson, the unquestioned Dean of Science Fiction, winning his first fiction Hugo at the age of 93.

I stopped by the Hugo Losers party for a couple of minutes, mainly to prove I'm a good loser, but it was like Tor and SFWA, just too damned crowded. I also tried the Baen party, which was emptier, and I spent a few minutes there, but eventually I wound up back at CFG, where I belong, and spent most of the night there visiting with old friends. I did make one excursion to the Kansas City party—they've decided to bid against Los Angeles in 2006—and another to Boston to congratulate them.

About 3:15 I decided to see if they'd posted the Hugo vote totals yet, and Christy Harden Smith, dressed in her sexiest Marilyn Monroe white satin dress (which she had promised to wear for me, and which was worth the price of admission), accompanied me while we looked all the hell over. Never found it, and I finally toddled off to bed around 4:30.

Monday, September 3:

One last piece of business. I met Anne Groell, my Bantam editor, for breakfast while Carol was packing, and we've agreed on my next Bantam novel, if the contract details are acceptable. Nancy Kress and Connie Willis were at the next table, and since there aren't two sharper wits in science fiction, it kind of forces you to wake up fast, since they love throwing barbs at me, a sweet gentle unassuming self-effacing Bwana who would never harm or insult a fly.

Then I went back to the room, gathered up Carol and the luggage, and flew home, where I found one contract, 3 checks, and 394 e-mail messages waiting for me.

For Challenger #15

WHAT IT TAKES TO BE A WORLDCON GUEST OF HONOR

I've been asked to write a little something about the general topic of Worldcon Guests of Honor, probably because, never having been one, I can be completely impartial.

Bad assumption. How can anyone be impartial to the recognition of a lifetime's accomplishments in a field we've devoted our lives to? Like every other pro and fan, I think that the Guest of Honorship at a Worldcon is the highest accolade to which any member of our community can aspire—and, furthermore, I think it almost invariably goes to totally deserving men and women.

Let's take the Pro Guest of Honorship. Since it's a lifetime award, what are some likely criteria?

Well, first of all, it should go to a writer of seminal works. And it has:

- Isaac Asimov—the Foundation and Robot stories
- Joe Haldeman—*The Forever War*
- Ursula K. Le Guin—*The Left Hand of Darkness* and *The Dispossessed*
- Philip Jose Farmer—*The Lovers* and the Riverworld novels
- James Blish—*A Case of Conscience* and the Okie stories
- Clifford D. Simak—*City* and *Way Station*
- Alfred Bester—*The Demolished Man* and *The Stars My Destination*
- Larry Niven—*Ringworld*
- Gordon Dickson—the Dorsai stories
- Arthur C. Clarke—too many to mention
- Frederik Pohl—ditto
- Robert A. Heinlein—more than Clarke and Pohl combined

He (or she) should have spent considerable time on the bestseller list:

- Anne McCaffrey
- Ray Bradbury

He should have pushed the envelope and explored new facets and corners of our field in new ways:

- Robert Silverberg
- Gene Wolfe
- Samuel R. Delany
- Roger Zelazny
- Theodore Sturgeon

He should not be a flash in the pan, but should show that he can adapt to whatever directions the field chooses to go:

- Jack Williamson
- Murray Leinster
- Damon Knight

He should understand that fandom is intricately linked with prodom, and must never ignore his fannish roots:

- Robert Bloch
- James White
- E. E. "Doc" Smith

He should produce a body of work that shows excellence in science fiction, fantasy, and even horror:

- Fritz Leiber
- Harlan Ellison

If he's an editor, he must be acknowledged as one of the

most influential in the field (and preferably in the history of the field):

- John W. Campbell
- Michael Moorcock
- Ben Bova
- Gardner Dozois

If he's an artist, he must be acknowledged as one of the best and most influential of his generation:

- Frank R. Paul
- Jach Gaughan
- Michael Whelan
- Bob Eggleton
- Kelly Freas
- Vincent Di Fate

And if he's a publisher, he must fill a specific niche and publish major works:

- Lloyd Arthur Esbach
- Donald A. Wollheim

Okay, I haven't named them all—I've got a word limit—but you get the idea. Many of them fall into two, three, or even four categories. Ain't no losers on that list, and this year's Pro Guests of Honor aren't going to be the first. Terry Pratchett created the Discworld, and has been living on the bestseller list for well over a decade. Phil Klass broke into print more than half a century ago, and I suspect that his failed stories can be counted on the fingers of one badly-mangled hand.

Now let's take a look at the Fan Guest of Honor criteria—and let's not forget that while the Pro has some degree of fame beyond the walls of the Worldcon and the Fan frequently doesn't, Worldcons are put on by fans, *for* fans: the Guests of Honor are chosen by fannish committees; the Hugos are voted on by fans; and in those and all other ways, the one place a Fan is truly of equal stature to a Pro is at the Worldcon.

Fandom used to be all-encompassing. These days it's splintered and gone off in dozens of directions. Excellence in any of them is a legitimate qualification for a Fan Guest of Honorship—for instance, publishing a top fanzine:

- Buck and Juanita Coulson—*Yandro*
- Bill Bowers—*Outworlds* and *Double:Bill*
- Andy Porter—*Science Fiction Chronicle* and *Algol*
- Walt Willis—*Hyphen and Slant*
- George Scithers—*Amra*
- Dick Eney—*Fancyclopedia* and *A Sense of FAPA*

Or being a tireless letterhack:

- Harry Warner, Jr.

Or being a convention worker, publisher, and actifan:

- Wilson "Bob" Tucker
- Bruce Pelz
- Mike Glickshon

Or constantly crossing the barrier between Pro and Fan:

- Terry Carr

Or hosting Worldcon's most famous party in Room 770 and founding Second Fandom:

- Roger Sims

Or being a dealer's room huckster and con worker:

- Rusty Hevelin
- Bob Madle

Or being science fiction's photographic biographer:

- Jay Kay Klein

Or for a high level of fanac over a long period of time:

- Jon and Joni Stopa
- Bob and Anne Passavoy

Or for being a pioneer of international fandom:

- Takumi and Sachiko Shibano
- Bruce Gillespie

Or being a two-time Worldcon chairman:

- Milton A. Rothman

Or being a fanzine Hugo winner *and* a Worldcon chairman:

- Mike Glyer

Or for all-round longevity:

- Forrest J Ackerman
- David A. Kyle

Once again, I didn't name them all—but there are no undeserving names on that list. This year's winners are hardly undeserving, either. Peter Weston chaired the 1979 Worldcon, and he's still around and still active. As for Jack Speer, he attended the very first Worldcon back in 1939, wrote a history of fandom, and has been fanning ever since.

The last and current Noreascons, unlike almost all other Worldcons, chose not to have a Toastmaster—but of course they will have someone as yet unnamed to preside over the Hugo ceremony, which is where most of us grade our Toastmasters anyway. Basically, the Toastmaster's only requirement is that he or she be entertaining, be able to kick the ceremony off with a 10-to-15-minute humorous routine, and be able to interject witty remarks throughout the proceedings. Probably the two greatest were Isaac Asimov and Robert Bloch, who were given the honor time and again.

One of the problems is that many of our wittiest speakers (Connie Willis and Gardner Dozois come to mind) are up for Hugos so often that they're rarely asked, since it's considered a *faux pas* to have the Toastmaster give himself a Hugo or announce that he just lost one. Still, it's quite an honor, because it means a Worldcon committee thought you were one of the wittiest speakers around.

(In fact, the few flops we've had have been Toastmasters, not Guests of Honor, since Toastmasters are chosen on hope and instinct and Guests of Honor on lifetime accomplishments.)

Anyway, that's my take of the "above the title" names that you'll encounter at any Worldcon. View them with enormous respect and affection; every one of them has earned it.

For Noreascon IV Progress Report #1

PART II: BIOGRAPHIES

Over the years I've been asked to write biographies and appreciations of many of my pro and fannish friends, usually for convention program books, occasionally for fanzines or even books.

It's an honor to be selected to share my feelings about a friend, and I don't believe I've ever turned such an assignment down. Believe me, you don't want to read all the biographies I've done (5 for Jack Chalker, 3 for the late George Laskowski, etc.), so I've chosen a representative selection here.

ON THE ROAD WITH SIMS AND SIMS

Larry Tucker wants me to tell you about Pat and Roger Sims, and I'm going to.

He probably wants me to tell you that Roger chaired the 1959 worldcon, founded Second Fandom, was Fan Guest of Honor at the 1988 worldcon, and writes Harlan Ellison stories for fanzines—but I'm not going to tell you about that, any more that I'm going to tell you that Pat is the vital financial and secretarial cog that keeps the Cincinnati Fantasy Group viable, or that she's saved half a dozen ineptly-conceived conventions by virtue of her hard work and managerial talents.

That stuff's all a matter of record, and it won't tell you a damned thing about the people behind the statistics.

You don't really know much about people until you've traveled with them. You may think you know Pat and Roger Sims, and the ConFusion committee may think *they* know Pat and Roger Sims, but take it from me, until you've stared across the breakfast table at them with growing repugnance for 31 days in a row, as I just did in Kenya, you never truly know someone. However, the following excerpts, each and every one of them true in every respect, will at least give you some slight insights into your Guests of Honor.

LAKE BARINGO, KENYA (Sept. 26, 1992):

Roger: Bird!

Mike: Where?

Roger (without pointing): Over there!

Mike: Over where?

Roger: Nine o'clock.

Mike (looking to his right): There's nothing to my right.

Roger: Three o'clock.

Mike (looking to his left): Nothing there either. Point to it.

Roger (points dead ahead): There—but it's flown away.

Mike: Roger, that's twelve o'clock.

Roger (defensively): I've got a digital watch.

LONDON (April 10, 1985):

Pat (reading map in back seat): Turn right here.

Mike (dubiously): You're sure?

Pat: Absolutely. Turn east.

Mike: It looks wrong.

Pat: Trust me. How hard is it to read a map?

Mike turns, finds himself facing three lanes of traffic coming at him on a one-way street. Screams. Pulls onto sidewalk, barely avoiding a nanny pushing a baby carriage.

Mike: I thought you said turn east!

Pat (turns map 180 degrees): Oh, we were going south, not north, weren't we? (Shrugs innocently) It's the map's fault; they printed it upside down.

SERENGETI NATIONAL PARK, TANZANIA (February 20, 1989):

Pat: Aren't warthogs adorable? They're my favorite animal.

The warthog we are watching roots in the dirt, breaks wind, moves his bowels, spreads the stool over a 30-foot-square area with his back legs, stops to scratch at a number of engorged ticks, and rapes two of his daughters.

Pat: Aren't impala adorable? They're my favorite animal.

CAIRO, EGYPT (February 10, 1989):

Pat: That's a lovely papyrus.

Ali the Merchant: Madam has exquisite taste.

Pat: How much is it?

Ali the Merchant: 300 pounds. But for Madam, 250.

Pat: I don't know . . .

Ali the Merchant: Because it is a Tuesday, 200.

Pat: Well, maybe . . .

Ali the Merchant: And because it is after noon, 175.

Pat: 175?

Ali the Merchant: To celebrate my daughter's birthday, 150.

Roger approaches from far end of shop.

Roger (to Pat): These shopkeepers love haggling. Whatever price he named, we can get it cheaper.

Pat: But . . .

Roger (decisively): Go out to the car and wait for me. I'll talk him down.

> *Pat walks out to car. We can see Roger gesticulating wildly for about five minutes. Finally he shakes Ali the Merchant's hand, money is exchanged, and he emerges with the papyrus.*

Roger: I told you they can be talked down.

Pat: What did you pay for it?

Roger (proudly): Only 350 pounds.

NAIROBI, KENYA (February 17, 1989):

Roger (setting down empty glass): Boy, I needed that!

Mike: What did you have?

Roger: Just water.

Mike: Did you remember what I told you about the water?

Roger: Absolutely. I told the bartender I wanted distilled water from an unopened bottle.

Mike: Right.

Roger (superior smirk): Water's a lot healthier than that beer you're drinking.

Mike: Probably. But they keep the beer in a refrigerator, and I hate drinking warm water on hot days.

Roger: Me, too. That's why I told the bartender to put ice cubes in it.

Mike: Did you ask him where he got the water to make those ice cubes?

> *Roger looks from Mike to the brown water trickling from the bar's faucet to his water glass, then grabs his stomach and races for the nearest bathroom.*

SOMEWHERE OVER THE ATLANTIC (August 25, 1987)

Roger: What film are they showing?

Mike: *The Black Stallion.*

> *103 minutes elapse. The horses come onto the track for the climactic race.*

Roger: That gray horse is a sharp-looking animal.

Mike: I suppose so.

Roger: I'll bet you five dollars that he beats the black one.

Mike: You're kidding, right?

Roger (pulling out five-dollar bill): Is it a bet or not?

Mike (shrugging): It's a bet.

> *10 more minutes elapse. The Black Stallion wins the race.*

Roger (sighing and handing over money): Damn!

Mike: You saw the film last month. You know that the Black Stallion won the race.

Roger: True.

Mike: So why did you bet on the gray?

Roger: I thought he looked ready this time.

So there you have it, a handful of real-life scenes from our travels and travails with Sims and Sims.

Invite them back and maybe I'll tell you what happened in Heidelberg, Copenhagen, Luxor and Brighton.

For 1993 ConFusion Program Book

A GIANT AMONG MIDGETS

"He tried to make the world the kind of place it might have been. It drove him mad."
— Justin Playfair
They Might Be Giants

Barry Malzberg tried to make science fiction the kind of field *it* might have been. It didn't drive him mad, but it has occasionally made him more morose than he might otherwise be.

It will be to science fiction's everlasting shame that he failed to elevate it, for there has been no finer exemplar of what we could have become than Barry himself.

Writing is an egomaniac's sport. You *must* believe you are the best, or there is simply no reason to continue pushing nouns up against verbs in the wee small hours when the rest of the world is sleeping the sleep of the innocent. You may be properly modest in public, but during those long nights of the soul, when it is just you and the keyboard and the story that is trying to get out, you have to convince yourself that you're writing the best story or the best book ever put to paper, or there is simply no reason to endure the psychic strain and frustration required to keep working on it. Therefore, I hope you will realize what an enormous admission it is when I tell you that I will happily settle for being the second best writer alive, behind Barry Malzberg.

I first made contact with him after doing a radio interview, back in 1980. The host pulled a question from out of left field, asking me what I thought were the two best novels of the past decade. I considered my answer during the ensuing commercial, and realized that it wasn't even close: the two best novels of the 1970s, by far, were *Galaxies* and *Herovit's World*, both by Barry Malzberg.

So I wrote Barry a postcard and told him what I had said. His answer was brief and to the point: "Where were you when I needed you?"

I wrote back, he wrote back, we met for brunch a month later in Manhattan, and we have occasionally gotten together, frequently corresponded, and have spoken on the phone literally a thousand times during the past ten years. During this time he has become my closest friend in the field of science fiction, as well as remaining one of my very few literary heroes.

One of the things you will find when you finally meet Barry is that he is a gentleman, in the true sense of the word. He is gentle, decent, well-mannered, thoughtful, considerate, self-effacing, and witty—all those traits one demands in a Boy Scout but, once exposed to the field, never really expects to find in a science fiction writer.

He is also a man of prodigious intellect and erudition. The average man—and this includes the average science fiction writer—speaks in sentence fragments, a la Richard Nixon and his hired guns. Barry, on the other hand, speaks in exquisitely-constructed paragraphs, and when you listen to him expound on any of the things that are near and dear to him—and they cover an enormous range from writing and science fiction to classical music and horse racing—you will find that his knowledge of his subjects is, in a word, profound.

He remains the most misunderstood and misinterpreted writer of his time, which has always been a mystery to me, since his method of attacking a story, while never less than eloquent, has always been straightforward and comprehensible, unlike some of the pretenders who climbed aboard his bandwagon or clung to his coattails in the late 1960s and early 1970s.

One of the things about his work that is never mentioned, for example, is his absolutely brilliant sense of humor. For those who doubt this, let me direct you to such books as *Dwellers in the Deep* and *Gather in the Hall of the Planets*, biting but hilarious satires of the fan and pro communities, respectively, or to such short stories as "A Delightful Comedic Premise" or "A Question of Slant." It's humor with a bite—and as it turned out, a lot of fans, pros, and critics objected to being bitten. Me, I figure that's *their* shortcoming, not Barry's.

Another thing that seemed to bother the Establishment was the sheer quantity of outstanding work that he was able to produce. After all, they claimed, no writer can turn out five or six excellent and ambitious novels in a year, right? Well, no writer *should* be able to, but Barry was always the exception to the rule—and out they flowed, in quantity and in quality: *Underlay, Overlay, Beyond Apollo, The Gamesman, The Last*

Transaction, The Destruction of the Temple, In the Enclosure, The Sodom and Gomorrah Business, Tactics of Conquest, Guernica Night, Galaxies, Herovit's World, and a host of others (along with 20 to 35 short stories a year)—each of them challenging, each written at the highest level of literary ambition, each filled with honest passion, each crafted with consummate skill, traits that were always his hallmark.

For example, back in the 1960s a lot of sf writers found that there was easy money to be made in the sex field, and started grinding out "adult novels" to supplement our incomes. There was Silverberg, and me, and far more of your current heroes than you might care to think about. But only one of us attacked these books with the same high level of skill and ambition reserved for our more serious work; only one of us signed his true name to them; only one of us produced books such as *Screen* and *The Spread* which, if marketed differently, would have been considered major works of mainstream fiction. Guess who?

Even though he stopped writing full-time more than a decade ago, Barry continues to turn out a flow of absolutely top-quality literature that, for any normal writer, would very nearly constitute full-time production. His Hugo-nominated collection of essays, *The Engines of the Night*, stands head and shoulders above all other works of science fiction criticism—and just to prove he hadn't lost the touch, he added a short story, "Corridors," to the 35 essays; it was immediately nominated for a Nebula.

He picks his shots a bit more carefully these days, but he has lost none of his skills. Perhaps the most heralded original anthology of the 1980s was *In the Fields of Fire*. Barry contributed a story entitled "The Queen of Lower Saigon," that was easily the best science fiction story of the year, probably the best ever written about the Vietnam experience, and was in fact so good that, for me at least, it ruined the rest of the rest of the book by making the other stories, all of them by writers of note and talent, seem simplistic and shallow by comparison.

This is a good and decent and honorable man, this Malzberg, possessed of an awesome talent that should be honored and cherished far more than it has been to date. I am delighted to see Readercon begin to make amends for past oversights, for writers—or men—of Barry Malzberg's ilk don't pass our way very often.

For ReaderCon 4 Program Book

10 REASONS WHY I HATE DAVID GERROLD

1. While still in his early twenties, David wrote "The Trouble with Tribbles," which was voted the most popular Star Trek script of all time. If it wasn't for David, there would probably be a million less Trekkies in the world. If there is a better reason to lynch him, I can't think of it.

2. It was David who, with Anne McCaffrey, cornered me at the 1969 worldcon in St. Louis and wouldn't let me go until I joined SFWA. There is no question in my mind that I would have won at least a Pulitzer by now, and probably a Nobel, if I hadn't spent so much time working on SFWA committees. (David himself dropped his membership in SFWA for almost a decade while turning out one bestseller after another, the swine.)

3. David wrote *When H.A.R.L.I.E. Was One* back in 1971. It really should have won the Hugo, but more to the point, it practically destroyed the field when one inept imitator after another tried to match David's sure hand dealing with cybernetic self-awareness.

4. David and I judged the 1978 worldcon masquerade in Phoenix, which that summer resembled the antiroom to hell. The only air-conditioned room in the city was the judges' deliberation room, and David therefore called for three separate run-throughs and eliminations, just so the judges could keep returning to air-conditioned comfort. Of course, I was the one who was blamed for it.

5. David wrote *The Man Who Folded Himself*, a work of sheer brilliance that made all future time paradox novels redundant. Just before I sat down to write mine, which would certainly have done the same thing even better.

6. David got the notion of charging a dollar apiece for his autographs at conventions, when the rest of us were doing it for free. Just about the time I was feeling morally superior to him, it was revealed that all the money he collected for those autographs went to charity. You can't imagine how

much I hate it when someone makes me feel like a moral midget. Especially someone like (ugh) David.

7. David began writing the *War Against the Chtorr* series, hitting the bestseller list with each of them. To add insult to injury, he came up with the plan of taking money to put fans into the books and having them die in horrible ways—and, of course, the money went to charity. This made it impossible for entrepreneurs like me to charge fans for killing them in gruesome ways while keeping the money for myself. One more black mark against him.

8. Because I am nothing if not generous and magnanimous, I decided to invite David to write for one of my anthologies. It was to be a one-time thing, just to prove to the world what I nice guy I am. And that blaggard screwed up the works again, by writing such a brilliant and well-received story that I had no choice but to commission 13 more for my next 13 anthologies. You've no idea of the psychic pain I endure each time a Gerrold story comes in that is too good to reject.

9. David is both thinner and hairier than I am. Can you think of a better reason to hate him?

10. I am a professional writer. It is the only thing people pay me to do. And yet, just because my anthologies have made David a household word (so is "cockroach," but let it pass), here I am writing about him for free. The only consolation I take is that he is so universally loathed—except by 20,000 fans and 3 million Trekkies, all of whom want to have his baby—that no other pro would write about him, even for money. So there.

(Mike Resnick is the Hugo-winning author of *Santiago, Ivory, Lucifer Jones*, the Kirinyaga stories, and about 200 other pieces of fiction that David Gerrold would give his eyeteeth to have written.)

For the Inconjunction XIV Program Book
Reprinted in the 1996 Tropicon Program Book

ABOUT MARK ARONSON, WHOM I ALMOST LIKE

I have a number of problems writing this brief biography of Mark Aronson, not the least of which is that I haven't really got anything nice to say about him.

For example: he is a fabulously successful advertising executive, a Vice President yet, and fully capable of buying me five times over with his pin money. And yet, though we've known each other for more than 20 years, the ingrate hasn't so much as made an offer.

Or take his hair. Please. I wake up every morning and start combing mine—3 back, 2 over, 3 back, 2 over, just trying to keep the sun off my ever-increasing bald spot—while Mark has so much hair that it not only covers his head but has slopped over to his chin as well. (And if there's one thing that I hate more than a hairy guy, it's a hairy guy who's over 40 years old.)

Fannishness? Well, without him and Lynne there wouldn't be a Windycon, and if there wasn't a Windycon, I wouldn't always miss my November deadlines. Mark's fault, no question about it, even though my hide-bound editors refuse to see it that way.

Ability? I thought I was doing pretty well when I got my short story word rate up over a dime a word. Mark—a man of few but very well-chosen words—gets over ten dollars a word. And I use really tough words like "cosmology" and "bifurcate" and "zap,"whereas Mark uses incredibly simple words like "Cadillac" and "Pepsi." It just isn't fair.

And speaking of unfair, who says he has to make me feel inferior by getting nominated for so many Emmy awards? I bought the first tuxedo I've ever owned when I was Toastmaster at this year's Worldcon; Mark has worn out five tuxedos just attending awards dinners where his work has been nominated.

He cheats, too. Most science fiction writers spend years honing their talents to the point where they can make you suspend your disbelief while they write about other worlds, whereas Mark can transport you to Nirvana just by picking up his violin and playing a few notes on it. And as if that weren't enough, while the rest of us were sweltering through the Midwest's worst summer of the century, Mark was actually being paid good money to sing with his chorale group in cool, comfortable Salzburg, Austria.

Perhaps worst of all is his sense of humor. He's not only a brilliant and witty public speaker, but every now and then—as with his now-classic detective story about Tucker's missing "Smooth"—he puts pen to paper just to embarrass the rest of us guys who write for a living.

Which is a roundabout way of saying that I'm not going to write anything nice about Mark Aronson after all, and Windycon can go find some other poor slob to blindly praise this half of their Fan Guest of Honor.

So there.

For 1988 Windycon Program Book

MICHAEL BANKS

So one day I'm sitting there, watching a ton of frozen dog food melt, and Mike Banks, who is visiting my kennel, says that fixing my refrigerator is child's play, and since I am desperate I tell him go ahead and I will pay him union rates (as long as they're not totally unreasonable, like more that $2.50 an hour). And while he's working on it, the air conditioner gives out, and he flashes me that confident grin and says air conditioners are even easier to fix than refrigerators and he'll take care of it for no extra charge, or at most a nominal one, and maybe he'll go into the appliance repair business because this stuff is so easy to do.

So he takes the refrigerator and the air conditioner apart, and lays all the pieces out semi-neatly on a table, and says he needs some parts and he'll be right back—and I do not see him again for the better part of two years.

Then he shows up at a meeting of the venerable Cincinnati Fantasy Group and says he's going to become a writer, and I figure that if he writes like he fixes air conditioners and refrigerators, his lovely wife Rosa is going to lose her girlish figure and get a job impersonating skeletons, because he is not destined to put an abundance of food on the table.

Which just goes to show why you should never trust science fiction writers to predict the future, because damned if Mike Banks doesn't go right out and do what he says he is going to do. First come about 200 articles on computers, and then some pieces on rocketry, and then a non-fiction book about writing science fiction (which in my greatheartedness I do not take as a personal criticism), and then some surprisingly good short stories, and then still more articles, and then he's collaborating with dead men for Baen Books, taking two-sentence outlines and turning them into 60,000-word pieces of literature, and then comes *The Odysseus Solution* with Dean R. Lambe, and suddenly I have to reappraise the situation, and I decide that if he could just repair refrigerators and air conditioners the way he can turn out saleable copy I could lease him out by the hour and become an instant millionaire, because along with everything else he has managed to solve the principle of perpetual motion, which is what he is perpetually in, and before you know it he's running the Science Fiction SIG on Delphi and giving out interviews all over the place and writing still more books on subjects ranging from computers to science fiction, and it occurs to me that the real difference between Mike Banks and all the other hopeful writers who were trying to break into print when he gave up molesting refrigerators for abusing keyboards is that they all *talk* about writing, but Mike *works* at it.

When the dust has cleared from his weekly endeavors he is likely to have written three or four articles and a short story and worked some on a novel and maybe done a little research on a non-fiction book, and he has very likely taught a college class on writing, and he has had time to turn Delphi into SFWA's home away from home, and he still has time to spend with Rosa and his kids, and somehow he also manages to be the Assistant Editor for *New Destinies*, and this is a definite boon to the field of science fiction, which needs a hell of a lot more guys like Mike Banks, and if he'd just come back to the kennel after all these years and finally fix the refrigerator and air conditioner I could probably be coerced into saying something complimentary about him.

For 1987 Rivercon Program Book

INTRODUCING LAN,
WHO NEEDS NONE

First of all, his name is Lan. George is just his fannish name, and Laskowski is the name he uses because he loves Polish jokes.

I wish I had enough space to tell you all about Lan's youthful exploits. The stories about the time he was a bouncer at the Blue Gibbon Whorehouse and Bagel Shop on the Macao waterfront would fill a book by themselves (and unquestionably will, as soon as I get the contract from Tom Doherty). And then there was the foggy morning he shot and killed seven Republicans, the heads of which are currently stuffed and mounted in his den, with only a slingshot and a copy of *The National Review* to use as bait. And his escape from the dungeons of Toledo, where he was incarcarated as a Michigan spy, is the stuff of legend.

But I digress.

On the other hand, when you get someone as multi-faceted as Lan, how can you avoid disgressions? I mean, you guys don't want to know that he is a devoted husband and schoolteacher. You want to know why he can simultaneously wear a tuxedo on his body and a dead baby raccoon on his head while accepting yet another Hugo Award, right? (The answer is simple: Maia makes him wear the tux, and the thing on his head, far from being a raccoon, is Cedric, the unborn twin brother he always wanted.)

OK, so much for Lan. Now let's talk about something *really* important: Me.

One of the things I like to do is read. And when it comes to fanzines, my favorite reading matter is *Lan's Lantern*, easily the best fanzine, bar none, to come out since the late lamented *Science Fiction Review*. Where else can you find 100-plus pages per issue of good reading, all available for $2 or a surly glare, whichever comes first?

Another thing I like to do is talk. And I must say that Lan is about the best listener I've ever found. Intelligent, thoughtful, sharp as a tack, amazingly well-read, interested in all things— and when he asks a question, he usually knows 90% of the answer before he opens his mouth. (Which is really very nice—it stays open for a shorter time that way.)

I also like to party. And when I'm at a con, the easiest way to find the best party is to follow Lan, who is not only a party in himself, but is invariably invited to the very best festivities . . . or maybe they are the very best festivities by virtue of his presence. Yeah, I know, I know: it's a radical theory—but they laughed at Einstein, too.

(Well, maybe they didn't exactly laugh at Einstein, but they hardly ever asked him to come out and play basketball with the guys, which just about broke his heart.)

Come to think of it, I like an awful lot of things, but I guess the thing I like best—at least, among those things not involving nubile young females—is writing. And when I write for fanzines, which I do from time to time to keep my Fannish Membership Card, Lan always gets my best for a simple reason: I like the company I keep in *Lan's Lantern*. So do a lot of other people: *Lan's Lantern* is a perennial Hugo nominee, and won the coveted award in 1986 and 1991, about four less times than it deserved, and about two more times than 99.8% of all fanzines will ever win it.

Back in 1986, I took a safari to Kenya. Lan asked to publish my trip diary. I thought he was crazy—I was naive enough to think his readers' interest was limited to science fiction and fandom, even if his wasn't—but I gave it to him. Since then, he's not only run diaries of my trips to Egypt, Tanzania, Botswana, Malawi, Zimbabwe, and Kenya again, but he's run trip diaries by damned near everyone else he knows who has ever left the country, to the point that *Lan's Lantern* not only runs the best articles and most thoughtful reviews of any fanzine around, but has also become the Rand McNally of the fannish community.

I suppose I should mention Maia, this person who has been hanging around with Lan ever since I've known him. Most of you aren't aware of this, but she was born with a plaster cast on her leg; it fell off a couple of years ago—the cast, not the leg— signaling her rite of passage to True Fannish Maturity. She is friendly and personable and pretty, but she's also got a mind like unto a steel trap, so be warned: if you're going to flim-flam a Laskowski, go after *him*. Only one Laskowski is a friendly, gullible dupe, and it ain't Maia.

Well, that's probably enough of an introduction about Lan, because if this isn't your first convention you probably know him better than you'd like to anyway. I regret that I can't be there to tell you about the time he was arrested for doing unspeakable things with three underaged femmefans, a dead chicken, an aqualung, and a jar of apricot preserves, but if you pass him in the hall, you might ask him about it.

Oh, and say hello to Cedric for me.

For Capricon 13 Program Book

SCOTT AND JANE DENNIS: SEMI-SECRET MASTERS OF FANDOM

Scott Dennis was born on the 7th anniversary of the first atomic bomb explosion, and spent his first eighteen years in Yellow Springs (where, amazingly, they have yet to erect a monument to him, even though all the regulars at the local pool hall still remember him coming around begging for bheer money.) He then spent 6 years at Johns Hopkins without getting a degree, which is almost as preposterous as walking by Larry Smith's huckster table without buying a Resnick book.

When everybody in America got thoroughly sick of him, he went to Italy for four years, where he worked as a translator, driver, gardener (not the Dozois kind), cook, and an olive and grape picker—all things that look great on a dust jacket and just terrible on a job application form. It is rumored that he never even killed anyone, which may well be why they sent him back to the USA in 1978.

We'll get back to Scott in a few moments, but two paragraphs of him is probably all that you can stand without a break, so let's turn to Jane Dennis, who, not to be outdone, was born on Columbus Day in 1951. (That's Harvey Columbus Day; Harvey played third base for the Missouri Geldings in the old Mid-Continental League, was a sucker for the slow inside curve ball, and had a .216 lifetime batting average. It's just a coincidence that his birthday happened to fall on the same day that Christopher stuck a flag in our soil on the mistaken assumption that he had reached Bombay and could finally get some shrimp curry.)

When she was growing up, Jane wanted to be a paleontologist. It was after someone told her that paleontologists hardly ever publish fanzines that she gave it up and became a Trufan instead. Her first convention was the 1969 worldcon in St. Louis—the very same one where Harlan Ellison gave the premiere performance of his I'm-Leaving-Fandom-Forever speech. Sam Moskowitz and Harry Warner, Jr. are still searching for a connection.

Deciding to remain in fandom, Jane promptly created the Kentucky APA and founded Rubicon (which I'll bet you didn't even know was losted). She also had more than a little to do with Louisville & Nashville fandom, and then created Lexfa and published *Lexfanzine*.

(She also created Alex Boster, born 9/22/73, but that's another story.)

Somewhere along the way she met Scott, who had metemorphised into a huckster upon returning to the States—it could have been worse; he could have turned into an accountant for St. Martin's Press—and soon found himself involved in the running of ConStellation, the 1983 worldcon. Scott did his job with such panache and elan that he has since worked on dozens of conventions, been on the committee of 6 Rubicons, and will co-chair the 1993 SMOFcon this December in Lexington.

Together Scott and Jane began publishing *Jane's Fighting SMOFs*, the first fanzine devoted to worldcon bidding, and while they are some 83 years late with the current issue, it remains one of the better publications within fannish memory.

They got married awhile back, cornered the world stationery and button markets (don't take *my* word for it: check out their table in the dealer's room), and have been Fan Guests of Honor at Concave and Armadillocon, this in spite of the fact that Jane had never been to a cave before and Scott bears only a surface resemblance to an armadillo.

Faced with a lifetime of living with Scott, Jane promptly threw herself into equestrianism. Her horse is called Queenie, which is not quite up there with calling your dog Woola or your cat Pyewacket, but what the hell, if Jane chose the name it must by definition be fannish. Scott has also gotten her interested in gardening, so much so that she has started a gardening APA.

(For the uninitiated, APA stands for Amateur Press Association. It also stands for Albanian Postal Authority, which probably doesn't apply here, as well as for Absolutely Perverse Anecdote, which *does* apply but which I have been forbidden to relate. Ask Dick Spelman about it at the parties.)

I would like to tell you about how they are two of the nicest, friendliest, brightest SMOFs around, but Bob Roehm, who is editing this thing, says if I do it would make them PMOFs (*Public* Masters of Fandom) and would ruin everything, and besides, he can't pronounce PMOF.

So you'll just have to hunt them up yourselves—follow the line of worldcon bidders, horseback riders, hucksters, fanzine publishers and gardeners seeking advice and you'll come to them—and introduce yourselves. They're pretty nice people, and they sell rare Resnick books at their table, which proves beyond any shadow of a doubt that they are true visionaries.

For Rivercon XVIII Program Book

SEVEN VIEWS OF KRISTINE KATHRYN RUSCH

#1: Kristine Kathryn Rusch is drop-dead gorgeous. This is perhaps not very important in a Guest of Honor, but it's damned important if you want *me* to write about said guest for free. And I happen to be madly in love with this particular Guest of Honor. I have no idea if she reciprocates my passion, but I figure it took me almost half a century of hard work just finding and falling for her, so it's hardly fair to make me responsible for what she feels too.

#2: Kris Rusch (us guys who are madly in love with her get to call her Kris) is as brilliant an editor as you're likely to find on this planet. The Hugo voters know that: they just gave her the first of what I expect will be many Hugos for editorial excellence. But the writers knew it quite a few years ago, even before she took over *The Magazine of Fantasy & Science Fiction* and gave new life to it. Even as early as the first couple of issues of *Pulphouse*, we knew we were dealing with a major talent. You think I'm exaggerating? Take a look at the names she corralled for those limited-edition hardcover issues, paying less money and promising less circulation than all the better-known prozines. When you find an editor like Kris, you're willing to work for free, just to be included in her publication. (Note to Program Book editor: please delete that last sentence before Kris sees it. I got carried away.)

#3: Cuddles (us writers who helped her win her Hugo get to call her anything we want) is also a superior short story writer. She has been nominated for Nebulas and Hugos and numerous lesser awards. She won the Campbell Award as the Best New Writer of the Year. But if you want the real proof of the pudding, pick up a Resnick anthology. Almost any of them. I have commissioned and bought 12 stories from her, and you don't sell me 12 stories (and a poem, come to think of it) unless you're just about the best there is. Especially when you live so far away that I can't even give you a friendly pinch from time to time as the mood strikes me.

#4: Ms. Rusch (a term of enormous respect) is one of the few writers who is equally at home—and equally brilliant—with both short fiction and novels. All doubters are advised (urged, ordered) to go right out to the bookstore, and after you've picked up the latest Resnick titles, make sure you stay in the R's long enough to buy her *Traitors* (from ROC) and *Sins of the Blood* (from Dell/Abyss). What you will find is that she can write riveting novels with the same remarkable facility that she can write riveting short stories, and when you get past her and me and a certain female person in Denver who I've lost 73 Hugos to, not an awful lot of us can do this.

#5: Greta Garbo vanted to be alone. Kris, on the other hand, can collaborate with anyone, even the golf-playing geek that she settled for marrying once she found out that I was off the market. She has co-authored some adaptations/novelizations with him (note that in a fit of jealousy I refuse to tell you his name, except to say that it is spelled Dean Wesley Smith) under the pen-name of Sandy Schofield, and they're as readable a batch of books as you could want. She co-edited *The Best From F&SF* (45th edition) with Ed Ferman and had enough charm, brains and clout to force him to let my story lead off the book (which is still available and which you should all rush out and buy, just as soon as you finish buying her novels). She is even collaborating with me on a short story. True, we've been working on it for almost a year and it's not quite 1,500 words long yet—but if *you* were working with her, would you be in a hurry to finish?

#6: Ol' Doc Rusch has come up with something that eluded even Einstein. (Well, actually there were two things that eluded Einstein. One was that he absolutely could not sink a jump shot from 3-point range. This is the other.) She has not only discovered the principle of perpetual motion, but has adapted it to her career. This is not a lady who edits an anthology a year, and writes a novel every 18 months, and writes a short story every half year. Not her. She edits 11 issues of *F&SF* every year. She edits anthologies. She writes at least 2 novels a year, usually more. She writes at least half a dozen stories a year, usually more. She conducts a writing workshop. She teaches. She attends conventions. My Ghod, she even cooks. (I've gotta end this paragraph; I'm getting exhausted just writing it.)

#7: There's also Kris Rusch the Femmefan. Really. She started just like the rest of us, except for her abundance of looks, talent and energy. She studied under Algis Budrys in his Writers of the Future seminars, and how much more fannish can you get? Less than a year ago, she contributed to a very fannish penny-a-word anthology I put together, and by law you can't get any more fannish than that. She is the most approachable writer/editor in the Western World (unless you are a gorgeous lady writer and you are approaching me). She is my friend, and I am sure that by the end of Tropicon she'll be your friend as well.

— Mike Resnick

(Mike Resnick is the author of "Seven Views of Olduvai Gorge" and several other stories that Kris Rusch was brilliant and perceptive enough to buy. And one or two that she was stoopid enough not to.)

For Tropicon XIII Program Book

ABOUT BARBARA DELAPLACE, WHO LIVES WITH THIS SKINNY HAIRY GUY

So Barbara Delaplace approaches me one day back in 1990 and says, "Teach me everything you know." Then she ruins it by adding, "About writing, not sex."

Well, let me tell you, teaching Barbara about writing is a lot like bringing coals to Newcastle, because if there has ever been a writer you could call a natural, it is her.

The first thing she writes is a brilliant story called "The Garden," which ends up in a *Twilight Zone* anthology. Then comes a story about Tom Dewey and the atomic bomb, the first of about 15 appearances for her in Resnick-edited anthologies, and I can tell, even from this story that is written to a rigid structure, that Barbara Delaplace is my kind of writer, because she is far more concerned about the human heart than the technology of the future, and while all of her stories have Ideas in them, the Ideas are secondary to the Characters, which is at it should be.

Over the next two years she produces and sells better than a story a month. Among them are such gems as "Black Ice," which I describe as Heinlein's *Magic, Inc.* brought up to date, and which promptly wins a HOMer Award; and "Farewell, My Buddy," which *should* have won an award; and "Painted Bridges," which is as good an explanation of Hitler's ability to gain followers as you're likely to find; and "The Hidden Dragon," which struck a responsive chord among editors and which she's sold about ten times; and a number of others, each meticulously crafted, each eminently readable, each unique unto itself. Of course she was nominated for the Campbell Award both years she was eligible for it.

And then she married this skinny hairy guy. I always knew I hated and distrusted skinny hairy guys, but until Barbara married hers, I didn't quite know why. Now I do. *She stopped writing for a whole year!* (Probably he spent all that time teaching her the stuff she didn't want to learn from me.)

I offered to marry her myself. This skinny hairy person she lives with suggested that it would be bigamy. I explained that of course it would be big o' me, paying for an extra woman, but that she was worth it.

Anyway, I miss my monthly Delaplace fix. So I want you all to meet her this weekend: partly because she's a wonderful and charming and witty lady, partly because its our duty to teach her to speak American rather than Canadian, but mostly because someone's got to pressure her to start producing that monthly Delaplace story again.

Why should *we* suffer just because *she's* on an extended honeymoon?

(Mike Resnick is the author of *Santiago, Ivory, Soothsayer,* and the Kirinyaga series. He has 3 Hugos, a Nebula, and 2,174 groupies. He bought the "big o' me" pun from Gardner Dozois, and wants a refund.)

[Note. Jack Haldeman died, tragically and far too young, of cancer, as this book was being prepared. I considered pulling this piece, and finally decided not to. Hell, he *was* a hairy skinny guy, and I miss him dearly—and I know he'd have been on my case in a New York minute if he thought I'd keep his beloved Barbara out of the book just because he left us 20 years too soon.]

For 1996 DeepSouthCon Program Book

10 LITTLE-KNOWN FACTS ABOUT JUDY TARR

1. She loves horses. Not the right kind of horses, to be sure, but for some reason she'd rather ride atop some incredibly stupid quadruped than stand cheering at the rail with a $2 ticket clutched in her hand.

2. She thinks she can't write science fiction. (She's wrong; I've wheedled a couple of sf stories out of her for my anthologies, and she does it better than about 98% of the journeyman sf writers.)

3. She laughs at my jokes. Sometimes.

4. She holds a Ph.D. from Yale.

5. She has never missed a deadline. Probably the threat to break both her kneecaps if she came in even a day late has a little something to do with it.

6. When she gets out of her riding duds and dresses up for Nebula banquets, she is drop-dead gorgeous.

7. She is one of the truly fine fantasy novelists extant, and she's never once cheated on an historical background.

8. She spends too much time riding with Editor Meacham and not enough time buttering up Editor Resnick.

9. There are very few subjects that anyone reading this will know better than she does.

10. I think she's neat.

For 1994 Tropicon Program Book

TEN REASONS WHY I HATE MARTHA BECK

1. She has more friends than I do. (Of course, she has more friends than *anyone* does, but that's another matter altogether.)

2. She's better-looking than I am. (This puts her 'way up there in the company of horned toads, moray eels, and the entire human race—except maybe for Jack Chalker and Gardner Dozois.)

3. She loves everything I write. (While this does wonderful things for my ego, it means that I had to find a less devoted pre-submission critic to avoid painful surprises.)

4. She will do anything for a friend in need. (This makes me feel intensely guilty and resentful, since what I mostly do for friends in need is send them to Martha.)

5. She is the Midwest's most loved fan. (Bob Tucker, on the other hand, is the Midwest's most *frequently* loved fan, but that's another story, and not suitable for a PG-rated biography.)

6. She has the nicest, friendliest husband in the world. (I don't even have an un-nice, unfriendly husband.)

7. She has a number of incredibly scarce items in her sf collection that I have coveted for almost 25 years. (This, of course, contradicts Item 4, but what's life—or Martha—without a few contradictons?)

8. She makes a fabulous Greek salad and she doesn't live in Cincinnati. (Pete Rose lives in Cincinnati. Johnny Bench lives in Cincinnati. *I* live in Cincinnati. Why won't she move here? What more reasons could she possibly want?)

9. She doesn't *go* to parties; she *is* a party. (While I wander the corridors at conventions, waiting fruitlessly to be accosted by oversexed groupies, Martha merely warms up the coffee, opens the door to her room, and instantly attracts all of fandom's Best People.)

10. She has never said a bad word about anyone. (Could it be that she doesn't *know* any bad words? What is she hiding?)

Of course, on those days that I don't hate her for the above reasons, I admire her—and I must admit that my admiration for Martha Beck is not totally unlike her appetite for hot fudge sundaes and hot young bellhops: bigger than all outdoors.

1988 Archon Program Book

BILL CAVIN:
JUST THE FACTS, MA'AM

The ConFusion Committee decided that Bill Cavin has accomplished so much and has been around so long that it would take not one but two biographers to do him justice. Leaving aside for the moment the question of whether it's really justice that he needs—as opposed to, say, mercy—they decreed that Bill Bowers and I should each tell you half of the Bill Cavin story. We flipped a coin, and I get to tell you about Cavin from the waist down.

My initial reaction upon finding out that I had to write about any portion of Cavin at all was "(expletive deleted)," which left only 499 words to go. Then I got to thinking about it, and I realized that Bowers, who is as untrustworthy as most slender guys with too much hair, would probably tell you nothing but lies about Cavin. It would therefore be left to a loyal and decent fellow like myself (you can tell by the Waistline of Nonaggression and the Bald Spot of Maturity) to set the record straight. This I shall now proceed to do.

What is Bill Bowers likely to tell you?

That Cavin cheats at poker. A vicious lie—and besides, even if he does, it hasn't helped him yet.

That Cavin is without convictions. Well, yes—but that's harder than you might think, especially considering his numerous arrests on morals charges.

That Cavin has abused his position as god-emperor of the Cincinnati fantasy group, and deposited its funds in his own secret Swiss bank account. Total hogwash. Cavin can't read Swiss. The last I heard, the money was in a Mexican bank. (He can't read Mexican either, but that's hardly my problem.)

That Cavin has the highest-priced table in the hucksters' room. I used to think so, too, but a careful study of the records shows that he pays $15 for it, just like all the other hucksters. (Having the highest-priced goods is another matter altogether.)

That Cavin frequently sleeps in his car at conventions so he can have more money for poker. Another vile canard. Anyone who has ever tried to sit in Cavin's Honda without swallowing his knees knows you can't sleep in the damned thing. What he does do in the middle of the night is sit there and twitch uncomfortably while waiting for some unsuspecting neofan with money to follow the trail of playing cards he has laid out from the con suite to the parking lot.

That Cavin has never gone on a diet. Wrong, wrong, wrong! In 1977, Cavin and I embarked on a series of diets together—we are currently on our 27th—and between us we have lost some 3,219 pounds, a figure which certainly constitutes a record for peacetime tonnage. Bowers is just jealous because we've never asked him to join us.

That Cavin is the best-loved fan in Ohio. Wrong again, Bowers. Cavin is the best-loved fan in America. Especially when he sits down at the poker table—but even (I grudgingly admit) when he doesn't.

(Okay, Cavin—I wrote that last paragraph word-for-word the way you dictated it. Now what about that date with C. J. Cherryh that you promised me in exchange for it?)

For 1983 ConFusion Program Book

LAURA RESNICK APPRECIATION

The dedication to my first major science fiction novel, *The Soul Eater*, which was published back in 1981, read: "To my daughter, Laura, with love and aggravation."

Fourteen years later not much has changed. I still love her, and she still aggravates me.

Well, maybe a little has changed. Since *The Soul Eater* appeared she has graduated Georgetown University on the East Coast and Weber-Douglas Drama School in England. She's lived in London and Palermo, been to 20 African countries, and just completed a return visit to South Africa.

In 1988 she won an award for Best New Series Writer in the romance field. In 1991 I enticed her into writing for a couple of my anthologies, and she was such a hit that soon Marty Greenberg and Dean Wesley Smith and a flock of other science fiction editors were begging her for stories. In August of 1993 she won an award for the Best Novel of the Year in the romance field, and less than a month later she won the Campbell Award for Best New Science Fiction Writer. (She was being charged by wild elephants at that very moment; I accepted for her, and I have to admit that it gave me a bigger kick than any of my own Hugo or Nebula awards.)

When she got back from Africa, one of her two publishers was no longer in business, and the other was no longer in the business of buying from Laura Resnick, more fools they. Being a typically insecure writer, she was sure she was going to have to find some other profession, at least on an interim basis. But then her hot new agent sold a romance to a new publisher for her biggest advance yet, and a few months later he just about doubled that advance for each of two fantasy novels for Tor. And just so she'll remember to care for me in my approaching dotage, I bought a 125,000-word memoir of her trans-African safari for Mike Resnick's Library of African Adventure. (It's *A Blonde in Africa*, and it'll be out next spring.) It's like pulling teeth to say it, but she's a better writer than I was at her age, and in all immodesty I was pretty goddamned good.

Now, I probably shouldn't be bragging about her, because

when she was 9 days old I proudly showed her off to her grandparents, then held her against my shoulder and gave her a friendly pat on the back. She promptly threw up all over my red-and-yellow Hawaiian shirt (in retrospect, it may well have been an editorial comment) and I never willingly touched or spoke to her again until she turned 30.

But long before she was 30, she was bright, vivacious, talented. And, oh yeah, aggravating.

The fact that she hardly ever listens to my advice (and, worse yet, proves time and again that she doesn't need it) notwithstanding, I love her as only a father can. Still, this is the real world, and her education *was* expensive. Puck Schimel has already offered me 40 cattle, 25 goats, and 5 camels for her hand in marriage. Do I hear a higher bid?

For 1995 ConText Program Book

CAROL RESNICK APPRECIATION:

I met Carol at the University of Chicago in 1960, and married her a year later in 1961. In the 34 years we've been together, I've learned a lot about her. To wit:

- She has a warm and friendly manner.

- Hidden beneath her warm and friendly manner is the most formidable intellect I have ever encountered.

- Her business sense is outstanding. In 1976, she bought a kennel that was losing money; she took it over and began making changes, and by 1980 it was showing a healthy profit; by 1990 it had made us financially secure for life.

- She is the most perceptive line editor I've ever had.

- She hates the limelight, or I would insist that she be listed as my collaborator on almost all my books and stories. I like to think that they'd still sell without her input, but I freely admit they wouldn't have half the quality.

- Her manners are as good as mine are bad.

- Her taste, in everything from opera to literature to clothing, is flawless.

- Her capacity for hard work makes me ashamed of my 14-hour work days.

- She never settles. If she does something, she does it with skill, class and style. She didn't just make costumes in the 1970s; she made costumes that won 4 of the 5 worldcons we entered. She didn't just breed collies; she made us America's leading breeders of champions three different years. She doesn't just correct my stories, draft by draft; she won't let the ambitious ones out of the house until they're award quality.

- In 34 years, she has never bored me. That's about 33

years, 11 months, and 29 days longer than anyone else.

I met Carol at the University of Chicago in 1960, and married her a year later in 1961. My only regret is that I wasted a whole year being engaged before I married her.

For 1995 ConText Program Book

ABOUT DICK SMITH AND THIS FEMALE PERSON HE LIVES WITH

OK, to begin with, I promise I won't do any bad jokes about *Uncle Dick's Little Thing*. Or about Uncle Dick's little thing, either.

The first time I actually met Dick Smith was at the 1984 ConFusion. I was the Guest of Honor, he was the Toastmaster, and he was very nervous about uttering a batch of terrible lies about a man he didn't know. (Not that it stopped him. Come to think of it, he's been doing it ever since.)

I, on the other hand, will tell you nothing but the truth about Dick, which should be twice as devastating.

Dick is the first fan ever to win the MAFF. (That's the Mid-Atlantic Fan Fund.) In fact, when he won it for the third year in a row, they retired the trophy.

Dick is such an ardent collector that he will only take one sip from a mint julep . . . because as everyone knows, once you take a sip, it's no longer mint. (I apologize. I bought that joke from Gardner Dozois. At a deep discount.)

Dick is the co-publisher of the Hugo-nominated *Stet*, which he cranks out on an old-fashioned Gestetner. (Rich Lynch to the contrary, there are no new-fashioned Gestetners. Thank Ghughu, Foofoo, Roscoe, and Ngai, just to cover all the bases.)

Dick is a software engineer specializing in real-time embedded systems. I have no idea what this means, but I suspect the end result is that one of Dick's systems can fuck up your business 87,315 times faster than you can do it yourself.

Dick, by the way, will not be the least bit annoyed with this introduction, because the truth of the matter is that he doesn't really care what anyone says about him as long as he is the topic of conversation.

Therefore, I'm going to talk about this female person that he lives with. Her name is Leah Zeldes Smith, and she was put on this Earth for one reason and one reason only: to torment me—a sweet, innocent, self-effacing, brilliant, devilishly handsome, multiple-Hugo-winning writer who never did her any harm.

Leah got into fandom by working in Phantasia Press publisher Sid Altus' dry goods store when she was a teenager. She is a woman of deep and strongly-held convictions, formost of which is Pros Should Pay For Everything. This, of course, goes against the Natural Order Of Things, and if pursued to its logical conclusion would produce Universal Chaos, or at least drastically cut down my convention schedule.

But I got even with her. I bought her first story. And her second. And her third. And I just assigned her fourth.

Suddenly you don't hear Leah saying that fans should be admitted to cons for free and pros should pick up all the expenses, do you?

Suddenly her standard greeting is no longer "Where's the N3F room?" but rather, "Where's the Tor suite and how many editors are here?"

Problem is, she's pretty damned good with a keyboard (especially if Dick didn't program the machine.) Before she started selling sf stories, she was a food editor and restaurant critic for a chain of newspapers. In fact, she still is. Her worldview carried over, too: fans shouldn't pay for cons, and restaurant critics shouldn't pay for meals. Nice work if you can get it, and she did.

As I sit here, I'm trying to remember a time when Leah wasn't producing a fanzine—and I find that I can't. She's been responsible for *Omekronicle, Imp, The SF Oral History Association Newsletter, Insufficient Funds, TANSTAAFL, Spirits in the Night,* and *Stet*—and she's worked on more conventions than most of you have been to.

Well, that's 350 words about Leah. Dick's eyes should be glazing over by now, so I'll mention him again. Seems he and Leah ran for DUFF back in 1993. Won, of course. Went to Australia. Became wildly popular with the Down Under crowd. Have been the American agents for Australia's 1999 Worldcon bid ever since. Between that and the two Hugo nominations and the pro sales, things are going so swimmingly that Leah has even forgiven Dick for that incident involving the four underaged femmefans, the dead chicken, the aqualung, the trapeze, and the bottle of apricot preserves.

Anyway, they were my friends when I sat down to write this . . . and who knows? They may be again someday. In the meantime, I urge you all to visit with them and get to know them this weekend, because fans (and people) of their quality are all too rare, and we really should cherish the ones we have.

For Armadillocon 17 Program Book

JACK WILLIAMSON

15 years ago, Jack Williamson was your Pro Guest of Honor at Rivercon, and I was one of your Fan Guests of Honor.

We've both come a long way since then. I have lost 86 Hugos to this female person from Denver, sold a few things here and there, and have finally achieved fame, if not fortune, as Laura Resnick's Father.

Jack has won a Hugo, and written a few more classics, and further enhanced his position as the unquestioned Dean of Science Fiction.

I would tell you how long I have been a Jack Williamson fan, but the answer would probably embarrass us both, and would surely discourage groupies from accosting us after 8:00 PM. Instead, I'll make a generic statement: it has been possible to be a Jack Williamson fan as long as there has been a science fiction field, because Jack was there at the start of it, a full decade ahead of Heinlein and Asimov and Sturgeon and van Vogt, and still strides across the science fiction galaxy like the literary colossus that he is.

It's probably common knowledge by now that Jack went out west in a wagon train, discovered *Amazing Stories* when he was a kid, decided he wanted to write that kind of Buck Rogers stuff for a living, sold his first story in 1928, and never looked back.

And it's true that he and Ed Hamilton seemed to take turns destroying and saving the galaxy—or at least the solar system—every other week. Jack's *Legion of Time* stories rivaled Doc Smith's Lensman books as the readers' favorite space opera series, and that was where he achieved his first measure of fame in our field.

But there was always more to Jack Williamson than met the eye.

When F. Orlin Tremaine announced that *Astounding* would feature what he called "Thought Varient" stories, Jack was first in line with the still-startling "Born of the Sun."

When John Campbell put out a call for brilliantly-written fantasies for *Unknown*, Jack turned in *Darker Than You Think*, which may well have been the best single novel that *Unknown*, the best fantasy magazine in history, ever published.

When it was time for hard science, Jack was there, using his Will Stewart pseudonym, with his *Seetee* novels of contra-terrene matter.

And when it came time to produce a masterwork for Campbell's *Astounding* Jack gave us "With Folded Hands," demonstrably one of the half dozen most important novellas ever written in this field.

And you know what the wild part is?

All that was more than half a century ago—and not only is Jack Williamson still with us, he's still at the top of his game. I think the highest compliment anyone could give him, and the highest he could aspire to, is this: his work has now appeared in eight different decades, and it has continued to improve with each decade. The Jack Williamson of 1935 was a pretty decent writer; the Jack Williamson of 1953 was a few levels of magnitude better; the Jack Williamson of 1979 was better still; and the Jack Williamson of 1996 is the best of all.

Do you know how rare it is for a writer to keep improving throughout his career? Do you realize the dedication it takes to keep honing your talent, day in and day out, for an entire lifetime? To the best of my knowledge, Jack is the *only* writer who can make that claim. (I might hedge a little on his oft-times collaborator, Fred Pohl. But no one else.)

Somehow you just know that anyone who tries so hard to please his readers is going to be a warm, friendly guy when you finally meet him, and if you haven't met Jack prior to this weekend, you've got a real treat coming—because along with being a living legend, he's an accessible, comfortable-to-be-with man who seems strangely unaware of the fact that he *is* a living legend. Sharp as a tack, of course, and witty, to be sure, but also a man who will go out of his way to put you at your ease.

He's also an incredibly honest, forthright man. If you doubt it, read his autobiography, *Wonder's Child*. (You know, a lot of our giants have written autobiographies: Asimov, Clarke, Pohl, and the list goes on and on. But only one has won a Best Non-Fiction Book Hugo for it, and that's Jack Williamson.)

In sum, he is such a decent and brilliant man that I almost wish I hadn't killed and eaten him in *The Williamson Effect*. On the other hand, I can truly say he's a man of excellent taste.

For 1996 Rivercon Program Book

TOASTMASTER:
JACK L. CHALKER

68 years ago, in a log cabin in Whittier, California, a baby boy was born to humble Quaker parents. Within six months, he had his first blue pinstriped suit and the beginnings of a natty-looking five o'clock shadow, and none who saw him could doubt that he had been touched by the hand of Destiny.

None of this has anything to do with Jack Chalker, but it makes a much more interesting story. In point of fact, Jack was born in a log cabin (well, plasterboard) in Maryland in December of 1944, and has only a nodding acquaintance with pinstriped suits.

He—Jack, not the other guy—discovered fandom at an early age, and fandom has never been quite the same. Ditto for prodom, which he decided to dominate a few years back, and which is still reeling from his onslaught.

Jack entered fandom in 1958—9 years before the creation of the Cincinnati Bengals, and 24 years before they wore those wonderful striped helmets to the Super Bowl, for those of you who need to put this in historical perspective—and began publishing a fanzine named *Mirage*, which made it to the final Hugo ballot in 1963. To show you the Svengali-like hold Jack has on the minds of fandom—especially pretty female fen—*Mirage* received 14 nominations for the 1964 Hugo, despite the fact that not a single issue was published in the previous year. In his spare time he founded Balticon (I'll bet you didn't even know it was losted), and ran it for the first four years.

Never content to have just one arrow in his quiver—(is that the proper analogy for a science fiction fan/writer/publisher? Maybe he's never content to have just one zap in his blaster. Oh, well, let it pass)—Jack is also an immensely successful specialty book publisher. His Mirage Press has produced everything from the original edition of *An Atlas of Fantasy* to Jack's own *An Informal Biography of Scrooge McDuck*. All were smashing successes, and today command unbelievably high prices from collectors. (You think not? Stop by Jack's huckster table sometime.)

The secret of his success as a pro is simple. Jack is a perfectionist. He decided, for example, to keep writing Well World books until he got it right: at last count he has five *Well of Souls* titles and about three zillion sales. His current bestsellers are *Lilith* and *Cerberus*, and I'm told on good authority that we can expect two more Lords of the Diamond books—and another few trillion sales—before he's convinced that he's done it properly. Among those works that pleased him the first time around are *A Jungle of Stars, And the Devil Will Drag You Under, Dancers in the Afterglow*, and *The Web of the Chozen*.

Civic-minded to a fault, Jack spent a number of years as treasurer for the Science Fiction Writers of America, collecting dues with unrelenting vigor and doling out money with the greatest reluctance, one of the reasons that SFWA is a little sounder today than when he joined it. Stranger, but sounder.

Throughout his fannish and professional careers, the essential Chalker has remained unchanged: he was, and continues to be, just your average, humble, hard-working, self-effacing egomaniac.

To say that Jack's favorite topic of conversation is his past, present and future fannish and professional projects is perhaps unfair. (For one thing, it implies that, at one time or another, he has seriously considered talking about something else.)

On the other hand, I must grudgingly admit that no one in recent years has had so profound an influence upon science fiction fandom and writing. (In fact, if he will ever deliver the latest chapter of our collaboration—he's eight months late with it, and counting—his place in the field's history would be secure, and I could get Guido Scarletti's Friendly Neighborhood Loan Service off my back, all in one fell swoop.)

Surely no biography of Jack Chalker, however brief, can be considered complete without some mention of his lovely wife, Eva, who has managed to take all the rough edges off his personality. (Friends of the aforementioned edges can still visit them, as they now reside around his middle.) Jack's latest fannish project (except on April 15 of each year, when it will take on all the aspects of professionalism) is the production, with considerable assistance from Eva, of a different sort of First Edition: David Whitley Chalker, who arrived between Thanksgiving and Christmas of 1981.

Anyway, I can't think of anyone I'd rather hear say nasty things about the Guest of Honor than Jack—and if he keeps writing at his current high level, I imagine it won't be too long before some Toastmaster is going to get up at a worldcon and say nasty things about *him*.

(P.S.—Jack is really a very friendly and accessible guy who loves signing autographs. So when you see a well-dressed, devilishly handsome, highly articulate man wandering around the convention, just walk up boldly and say that you want a Jack Chalker autograph—and I'll be glad to point him out to you.)

1983 Worldcon—Constellation Progress Report #1

BEAUTY AND THE GEEK

Kris Rusch is beautiful. It doesn't mean that much to her, but that's because she's on the inside looking out. It means a lot to me; I'm on the outside looking in. Or at, anyway.

Kris Rusch is talented. Immensely talented. That probably means something to her, but it means a lot more to the rest of us.

As a fantasy writer, she is the author of the fabulous books of The Fey, as well as *Traitors* and *The White Mists of Power*. In science fiction, her novels include *Alien Influences* and *Star Wars: The New Rebellon*. In horror, she's the author of *The Devil's Charm*, *Sins of the Blood*, and *Facade*. She's edited anthologies for Pulphouse and *The Magazine of Fantasy & Science Fiction*. Always expanding her horizons, she recently sold a pair of romance novels. She has a brilliant mystery-cum-mainstream novel out entitled *Hitler's Angel*.

Kris Rusch has unlimited horizons. She won a Campbell Award as Best New SF Writer. She won a Hugo Award as Best Editor. She has been nominated time and again for Hugos and Nebulas. She won the Ellery Queen Poll for Best Mystery Story.

Most meaningful of all, she bought almost every story I ever sent her when she was editing *Pulphouse* and *The Magazine of Fantasy & Science Fiction*. Now, *that's* talent.

In fact, it is my considered opinion that Kris Rusch has only one weakness. She's married to it.

Let me tell you about Dean Wesley Smith, who Kris chose to marry when she could have been an Official Mike Resnick Auxiliary Wife instead.

Dean is a wildly prolific and successful science fiction writer. He's one of the Old School, one of those writers who can turn out a book in a week . . . but whereas most of the Old School writers like me and Malzberg and Silverberg did our Old School writing under pseudonyms for editors-who-didn't-want-it-good-they- wanted-it-Thursday and published certain arcane subject matter ("the kind men like"), Dean writes his for a wildly enthusiastic audience which, unlike ours, doesn't wear raincoats and hang out near schoolyards but instead attends science fiction conventions.

Dean has been nominated for the Nebula, the Locus, and the World Fantasy Awards. He's the author of over 40 novels and more than 100 short stories, which would overwhelm just about any life partner except the one he happened to luck out and marry. He has collaborated with Kris on a number of books, most recently *Double Helix: Vectors* and *The Tenth Planet*, and in his spare time (???he has spare time???) he edits *Strange New Worlds*, a Star Trek new writers' anthology.

Dean is also the publisher of the late lamented Pulphouse and Axolotl Press, the most ambitious specialty press in the history of science fiction, which in its heyday published over 100 titles and magazines in a single year. He co-edited it with Kris in the beginning, then took over sole editorship when she moved to *F&SF*.

Dean was every bit as good an editor as Kris, which is to say he never once turned down a Resnick story.

So what is his deep dark secret? Why do I keep offering to run off with his wife to Bora Bora on the perfectly reasonable assumption that he'll never notice she's missing?

The truth is that Dean Wesley Smith has a secret life. You know how a lot of fans are computer geeks? And a few are Robert's Rules of Order geeks? Well, Dean Wesley Smith is a golf geek.

He's a former pro who isn't quite in a class with Tiger Woods and David Duvall, but now he's turning 50 and considering going on the Seniors Tour, where all he has to beat are duffers like Jack Nicklaus and Tom Watson. Dean chooses his conventions and his vacations based solely on the nearby golfing facilities. He actually prefers to leave his laptop back in Oregon than to go anywhere without his golf clubs.

I'm pleased to announce that in the course of my travels, I found the perfect golf course for him. It's the Cecil Rhodes Memorial Course in the Nyanga Mountains in Zimbabwe. If you hit it in the rough, you get eaten by leopards. If you hit it in the water, you get eaten by crocodiles. If you overshoot the green, you plunge 11,000 feet to your death. As soon as I make sure his life insurance is paid up, I plan to fly him out there and buy him a few rounds, then run off to Tahiti with his grieving widow.

I suppose I should tell you a little more about them. I edited some 20+ anthologies back in the early 1990s . . . and as any anthology editor will tell you, you soon find a handful of people you can count on to give you award-quality material on a week's notice, and once you find them you cherish them. To find two in the same house is really something rare, but neither Kris nor Dean was ever late on an assignment, and although they knew the stories were pre-sold, neither of them ever gave me anything but their best.

So much for talent and athletic aberrations. What Kris and Dean are best at is not writing, or publishing, or editing, or even buying Resnick stories. What they are best at is being themselves, than which no one is more fun to be with. Visit them in the con suite or wherever else Kris is signing contracts and Dean is hustling up a game of golf and you'll find yourself agreeing with me almost instantly.

For the 1999 Windycon Program Book

LEGENDARY LOU TABAKOW

He had a thick shock of hair as white as new-fallen snow, a jaw that Bob Kane would love to have drawn on the Batman (and frequently did), and a gravelly voice that sounded like a wire-haired terrior being combed against the grain.

He was my friend, the legendary Lou Tabakow, founder of First Fandom and God Emperor of CFG (Cincinnati Fantasy Group), and I'd like to tell you a little about him.

We knew him before we moved to Cincinnati back in 1976. You couldn't be in fandom and *not* know Lou, because he was just about the friendliest and most accessible fan in the world. He made sure that CFG always had a hospitality suite at Worldcons (a practice his successor, Bill Cavin, has continued), and sooner or later just about every member of the con would wander through the suite and run into Lou.

We moved because we had purchased a huge boarding and grooming kennel. It closed at one in the afternoon on Tuesdays, and Lou took it upon himself to make sure we became acquainted with our new town—so every Tuesday at noon, he'd pull up in his station wagon and wait for us to close up shop so he could give us that day's tour. (After awhile he got tired of sitting in the lobby, and most Tuesdays ended with Lou feeding dogs and cleaning runs so we could leave at one o'clock sharp.)

Now, a tour with Lou wasn't like a tour with anyone else. First of all, Lou loved to eat, but he hated meals—so we'd stop about every 60 to 90 minutes for coffee and maybe a piece of pie. Second, the word "upscale" was lost on Lou; his food of choice was whatever he could find at the nearest White Castle. Third, Lou had what at best be termed a quirky sense of direction.

How quirky? Well, I remember that once we were driving to Detroit for a convention, with Lou at the wheel. Detroit is four hours north of Cincinnati. Indianapolis is two hours west. Somehow, when we pulled into the Marriot *five* hours after we started, it was the Indianapolis Marriott.

Lou founded Octocon. Seems there was a funeral for a fan up north of Cincinnati, and everyone had such a good time at the funeral that Lou decided they should do it every year—the good time, not the funeral. So he found a hotel in Sandusky that had a swimming pool, a bowling alley, and exceptionally bad food—three of his absolute musts for anyone living the Tabakow version of the Good Life—and it became an annual event. Sandusky is a five-hour drive from Cincinnati. We didn't know that the first two years we went, because Lou drove us, and we mentioned to Margaret Keifer that we had no idea Sandusky was eleven hours away. (Well, eight hours, plus five stops for coffee-and.) Margaret remarked that she did it in five without breaking any speed limits, but that someone else found a new route that could shave an hour off that time. So the third year I drove, and sure enough she was right.

I think CFG members went to more conventions when Lou was around. He wouldn't permit them not to. He loved conventions, and he loved company, and he would do whatever it took to get people to go.

Once, when a girl remarked that she wanted to go but couldn't afford a room, Lou made a proposition to her: a single room cost $32, and a double was $36. He was going regardless, so if she'd put up the $4 difference he'd order a double and give her a ride. (And no, if you're thinking this was a sexual come-on, you didn't know Lou; he was too busy partying to have time for sex at a convention.)

Another time, Carol and I were still showing collies, and we told Lou we couldn't go to a Marcon in Columbus because we were going to be in a dog show in the same town that day. So he badgered the hotel until they agreed to let us keep the collies in the room with us *and* give us a convention rate. Then, when the show was over and we arrived at the hotel, he hunted up Sid Altus and a bunch of other fans and had them walk our dogs every couple of hours so that we'd have time to party.

Lou loved banquets. Lord knows why, because all he ate was dessert and coffee, but he'd travel just about anywhere to attend a con that had a banquet. That's probably why Midwestcon's only official function is the banquet. In our 50 years of existence we've never had a Guest of Honor or a program—but we *always* have a banquet.

He also loved gambling. I used to go crazy trying to get him to see the beauty that I saw in horse-racing. Never did. To me it was Seattle Slew versus Affirmed, locked in a classic head-and-head struggle, two superb athletes giving their all; to him it was the 2-horse and the 5-horse, and all he cared about was the odds.

He had a system for beating blackjack. He would deal out 10,000 hands, maybe 12,000, and when he knew he'd gotten all the bugs out of the system, he'd take a wad of cash to Las Vegas, prepared to break the bank.

I don't think he ever won. It was the damnedest system—it only worked in his living room in Ohio. In any state that allowed gambling, it was a dud. He could never figure out why.

He did a lot better playing pinnochle with his cronies at the local bowling alley, which was where you could find him any afternoon (unless he was at the track).

He lived for fandom. Every night he'd sit at his desk and get all his First Fandom business and CFG business up to date. Then, about one in the morning, he'd phone me—I was the only other CFG member he knew would be awake, since I write far into the night—and ask if I wanted to meet him for coffee. I'd finish the page I was writing, hop in the car, and meet him at one of the half-dozen all-night eateries that existed between our two houses. We'd talk for a couple of hours, load up on coffee (and Lou would have a piece of pie; I don't know why he never gained weight), and then go our separate ways.

One night he mentioned that he had a neat idea for a cute science fiction story. Ordinarily I wouldn't have taken much interest, but he was a friend, and more to the point, he'd sold some stories before.

(In fact, he won the 1955 Hugo for the "best unpublished story" of 1954. The story was "Sven," which made the cover of *Other Worlds* but was bumped when Isaac Asimov walked into Bea Mahaffey's office and offered to write a story while she waited. The magazine soon died, and "Sven" was never published. The "Hugo" was an Oldsmobile hood ornament.)

Anyway, the story had a cute gimmick, but I couldn't see any way to get more than a thousand words out of it without padding—and then it occurred to me that we could do a *lot* of stories like that if we got a continuing character, something like Ferdinand Feghoot but without puns. I suggested the name "Isaac Intrepid," Lou wrote a letter to Isaac Asimov requesting permission (Lou was one of the last people to still call him "Ike"), Isaac consented, and we sat down and ground out nine

600- worders in the next week or two, all based on science fiction premises. (Like, for instance, what happens if you travel into the past and shoot your father before you were born? Nothing—if your mother was unfaithful. That kind of thing.)

We started sending them to Stan Schmidt one at a time, and he bought four of them for *Analog* and Lou was back in print after a quarter of a century. (After his death, I sold all nine—four reprints plus the five Stan hadn't wanted—to another magazine, and surprised the hell out of Lou's granddaughter by sending her a check for half the money.)

Carol made a number of Worldcon masquerade costumes for us in the 1970s, and Lou, who was soon spending almost as much time at our house as his own, caught the costuming bug. So Joan Bledig, who was practically a member of our family, drove out from Chicago to visit, and decided to collaborate with Lou on a costume for the 1977 Worldcon. It was a very funny, very faanish costume (as befitted Lou) entitled "TAFF and DUFF, Two Visitors From the Planet FIAWOL," and it won awards for Best Presentation and Best Alien. Lou bragged about that for the next couple of years. He also realized he might lose the next time he wore a costume, so he decided to retire undefeated.

Besides, costumes were just a sidelight. Lou loved fans, and he spent his conventions in three locations: an easy chair in the hotel lobby, where he could spot every friend who entered; a chair in the CFG suite, where he could party all night; and a booth in whatever coffee shop was handy.

I still have so many memories of him. For example:

The Christmas Day he couldn't find any fans who were willing to leave their families to visit with him. He wound up treating Carol and me to dinner and taking us bowling in the middle of a blizzard.

We had a three-acre pond behind our house. A deep pond. When Carol didn't want to be bothered by the kennel staff (which at one point numbered 21 young women who could swear like sailors) she would take a rowboat and go into the middle of the pond where no one could bother her. One day I took Lou out in the rowboat. He remarked he hadn't been swimming for a couple of months, and he missed it. Next thing I knew he'd jumped overboard and, surrounded by ducks and geese and a turtle or two, field-tested the swim- worthiness of the pond for us.

The night that a nice, mindless summer entertainment called *Star Wars* opened, Lou somehow got free passes for every member of CFG, then did it again for *Alien*.

I remember that Lou practically owned the coffee shop at the Fontainbleu Hotel, home of the 1977 Worldcon. I kept count on one day, a Saturday: he had coffee and pie with 15 different groups of friends.

I can still recall every detail of a meal Carol and I had with Lou at the 1978 Worldcon. Lou had heard of this very nice roof-top restaurant. (We assumed he meant "penthouse"; nope, he meant "rooftop.") We got there, took an elevator to the roof, and stepped out into the rays of the late afternoon sun, which was more than hot enough to turn the tar on the roof into wet black goo. Lou and I immediately took off our jackets and ties. By the time the salads arrived, Lou had unbuttoned his shirt; it was gone before we hit the main course. Then, as the sun continued to beat down on us while we waited for dessert, stately, digni- fied, white- haired Legendary Lou looked around, saw that all the other diners except Carol were males, announced that Carol was officially a Tabakow and hence beyond embarrass- ment at what came next, and proceeded to remove his pants, finishing the meal in his shorts. He was unquestionably the most comfortable diner there.

And I remember the day he got his death sentence. He'd been slurring his speech a bit and had developed a slight limp. It looked like a tiny stroke, and he went in to find out what could be done about it. After a series of tests, they laid it on him—he had ALS, Lou Gehrig's Disease.

No one ever took it better. He knew he only had perhaps a year to function (and possibly a lot longer to live, which is the absolute horror of ALS, for the mind remains clear as a bell while the body loses all power), so he increased his fannish ac- tivities. He went to more cons, more parties, and I began get- ting an invitation to coffee at one o'clock just about every night. When he was no longer capable of driving, I'd pick him up and take him out to one of his favorite all-night restaurants.

His last con was the 1980 Worldcon, in Boston. He'd finally given in to the inevitable and started using a cane that Ray

Beam had brought for him. He was given the First Fandom Hall of Fame Award, and he partied later into each night than usual, as if he knew this was his last hurrah.

And then, with striking suddenness, he was gone. First to the general hospital for a tracheotomy to help him breathe, then another surgery that inserted a feeding tube when he could no longer eat, then off to a home where he spent his final days growing more and more feeble physically while remaining mentally alert as ever, and then, mercifully, it was over.

I still miss him. Not a day goes by that Carol and I don't think of him.

I tell people—and it's true—that if he had been alive these past 18 years, dragging me away from the keyboard for coffee four and five nights a week, I'd probably have produced a dozen less books.

You want to know something?

I'd rather have had Lou than the books.

For Challenger #10

I REMEMBER ISAAC

What kind of man was Isaac?

Let me tell you a story that took place in 1987.

I was in Westchester County, New York, to toastmaster a convention known as Lunacon. I got there a day early, and walked to the train station, where I planned to take a train to Manhattan, do a little shopping, meet my friend Barry Malzberg for a late lunch, and get a ride back with him.

Problem was, there were dozens of trains to choose from, and no one had given me a schedule. A little old lady—she must have been in her seventies—took pity on me, asked me where I was going, and since it turned out we were both waiting for the same train, she offered to ride with me and let me know where to get off.

We got to talking during the train ride, and I mentioned the reason I was in town, and she replied that she didn't know much about science fiction, but she had always wanted to meet the world-famous Isaac Asimov. And, without even knowing for a fact that he would be there, I told her that if she showed up on Saturday night, I'd be happy to introduce her.

I got off at my stop, went about my business, and thought no more of it—until 7:15 Saturday night, when the little old lady entered the hotel, walked up to me, and told me that she really only half-believed that this stranger she met on the train actually knew the celebrated Dr. Asimov, but since she only lived a mile away she thought she'd wander over and hope for the best.

As it happened, Isaac *had* come to Lunacon. In fact, he was sitting about 40 feet from me, flirting with some luscious and admiring young ladies, when I approached him to make the introduction. I figured he'd give her a quip and an autograph and then go back to pinching voluptuous bottoms, as was his wont . . . but instead, when he found out that this withered old lady had walked a mile through the snow to meet him, he made his excuses to the young ladies and spent the next hour charming my guest, even insisting she sit with him during the Jack Chalker Roast that I had been imported to emcee. You could tell by her face that he had more than made her evening; hell, the way he charmed her, he made her whole decade.

When she excused herself for a moment to call home and tell them she was staying for the roast, I walked up, thanked him, and told him that as a token of my gratitude I wouldn't insult him from the podium that night. He looked truly hurt, and insisted that not insulting him in front of all his friends would be the greatest insult of all.

And that's my fondest memory of the most approachable world- famous man it's been my pleasure to know.

For Foundation's Friends

DICK SPELMAN: FROM SMIF TO SMOF

Dick Spelman is what we in the trade—don't ask *which* trade; there's an excellent chance the Vice Squad might get their hands on a copy of the program book—call a man's man.

And for the better part of 20 years, the man whose man Dick was, was a probably a skinny, undersized wimp with thick glasses and a handful of cash, ready to buy a pile of science fiction books at Dick's huckster table. (To show you the depths of duplicity to which he could sink, he occasionally recommended a book which was *not* written by *me*. Thank goodness I never told him about my Asimov, Bradbury and Heinlein pseudonyms!)

These days, of course, he guzzles cheap white wine in the con suite, stays up most of the night, and passes the time pinching young femmefans when their backs are turned.

But there's more to him than Spelman the Huckster and Spelman the Dirty Old Man.

For example, back when the glaciers were still in California, there was Spelman the Dirty Young Man. In between his adventures in Maracaibo (I promised not to mention the pederasty trial, so I won't) and Samarkand (I can't remember if I promised not to mention the necrophilia arrest, so I'd probably better play it safe and not let you know about it), he served in the armed forces and spent most of his 8-year stint guarding a poker table on the third floor of the Luk Kwok Hotel in Hong Kong. It was there in Hong Kong that he first evidenced interest in his future profession, selling copies of Suzie Wong's diary to any client with a paltry $5,000 to spend.

On the way home, he obtained and sold copies of the Fleet's Pacific position to selected Russian and Chinese collectors, and within weeks of being mustered out and settling in California, he was selling Marilyn Monroe's unlisted phone number to various members of the Kennedy Clan.

One thing led to another, and before you knew it, there he was at every convention, selling Resnick books and various worthless imitations to a panting public, and proving that a hardworking bookseller could make a handsome living off science fiction. In point of fact, the acronym SMIF—Successful Mover of Infantile Fantasies (a term acknowledging his ability to sell an almost infinite number of four-book trilogies)—was created just for him.

Then, at the peak of his success, something happened. Something that was to change the face of fandom forever.

You all remember that little incident when Paul stopped for a beer at Tarsus, don't you? Well, one day when Dick was on the way to the dealer's room, a fannish angel appeared unto him and whispered a single word: "SMOF."

That was all it took. Suddenly it became impossible to hold a worldcon withiout Dick Spelman on the committee, or in charge of the huckster room, or both. A bidding party without Spelman was like a baseball diamond without home plate. A fanzine without favorable mention of Spelman was like . . . well, an anthology without a Resnick story. Unthinkable.

He moved to Chicago to be near the final resting place of Claude Degler, then realized that the heart of Trufandom lay further south, in Cincinnati, and moved again. Having become a multi-millionaire as a huckster and realizing that fandom had no money left to spend, he promptly sold his book business to an unsuspecting dupe, Larry Smith, and devoted himself full-time to forcing all his friends to eat at Cracker Barrel (he owns 800,000 shares of stock), breaking Wall Street (in case you wondered about all those homeless MBA's you saw lining the streets at ConFrancisco), and secretly correcting all the wrongs he found in fandom. (He missed the one about mailing all future Hugos to me and saving fandom the trouble and expense of balloting, but I presume he's working on it even as I write this.)

Anyway, he's mellowed in his dotage. He hardly ever drools when he's speaking, his eyes focus with far greater frequency, his hairpiece is usually on straight, his socks match (most of the time), and he doesn't walk into nearly as many walls as he used to.

He's really a very approachable guy, as long as you keep the above caveats in mind. He's probably the only fan I know who doesn't have a single enemy, he is unfailingly polite and attentive, he can amuse you on a wide variety of subjects, he's become a true party animal since selling the business, and he loves making new friends and meeting old ones.

Just don't mention the necrophilia bust.

(But he'll be happy to tell you about the four under-aged girls, the aqualung, the cattle prod, the trapeze, and the jar of apricot preserves. Really. Just ask him.)

(Mike Resnick is the Hugo-winning author of *Santiago*, *Ivory*, *Soothsayer*, *Purgatory*, and dozens of other books that Dick Spelman did his very best never to display face-up on his huckster table.)

For 1993 ConClave Program Book

PART III:
ARTICLES

I've been asked to write articles for dozens of different fanzines, and I've always tried to accomodate them. I think those where I've appeared most often in the last couple of decades would be Rich and Nicki Lynch's Mimosa, *the late George "Lan" Laskowski's* Lan's Lantern, Guy Lillian's *Challenger, and Timothy Lane's* Fosfax, *but I've written for everything from Edgar Rice Burroughs fanzines to the* SFWA Bulletin *to one-shots that no one has ever heard of. I find it almost impossible to believe that my first fannish articles appeared in 1963; after all, I'm only 32 years old, and sporting a full head of hair—or so I like to think.*

One of the nice things about being in some demand is that I pretty much get to write about anything that appeals to me, so along with all the Worldcon articles that appear elsewhere in this book, you have here a sampling that includes my favorite meals, museums and musicals, a memoir of my starving-writer days in the sex field, a serious survey of all the books devoted to fandom, and even a limerick history of science fiction.

MEMORABLE MEALS

Meals form one of the most important parts of my life. I sell books at meals. I sell short stories at meals. I buy short stories at meals. I hire agents at meals. I pitch stories to Hollywood at meals. I even proposed marriage to Carol at a meal.

Furthermore, Carol and I love to eat. We'll go 100 miles out of our way to try out a highly-recommended new restaurant. We've dined at 5-star establishments and dumps in both hemispheres. We've found unheralded restaurants that were strikingly good and world-famous restaurants that were shockingly bad.

And now, 60,000 meals or so from the beginning, I thought I'd share the most memorable with you.

SCIENCE FICTION MEALS

Most Expensive: This took place the Tuesday before the start of the 1998 Worldcon. We had just arrived in Baltimore, checked into the Marriott, went down to their coffee shop for lunch—and found that the stock market was in free fall. Someone had turned the television over the bar to MNBC, the all-day market channel, and between the moment we ordered sandwiches and drinks and the moment they arrived, we lost $8,200. Now, *that* was an expensive meal.

Most Profitable: This took place at the ABA Convention in New Orleans in 1986. I sat down at a long picnic table to have a very informal lunch with my Tor editor, Beth Meacham. During the first hot dog I described a couple of books I wanted to write next—*Ivory* and *Paradise*—and during the second hot dog she asked a bunch of questions and made a bunch of suggestions. She agreed to buy them as we were finishing our soda pop. Over the next 10 years, those two novels (including reprints, foreign editions, and movie options) were worth about a quarter of a million dollars to me.

Most Expensive Meal For Someone Else: In the fall of 1997, Miramax optioned *The Widowmaker* from me, and hired Carol and me to write the script. In February of 1998, they decided to introduce us to our director, Peter Hyams, and some of the execs who would be working on the film, so they flew us out to California for a business dinner. They bought us first-class airfare, of course, and since they did it on two days' notice, the tickets came to $3,800 for the pair. They put us up in a three- room penthouse suite at the 5-star Nikko Inn; I asked at the desk and found out that the rack rate was $1,300 a day. We were picked up by the longest limo anyone ever saw, and that limo and its driver were at our round-the-clock disposal; chalk up another $400. Finally, we met Hyams and the Miramax folk for dinner at the Four Seasons Hotel's 5-star restaurant. The tab came to $1,250 for ten of us, so we figure our share was $250. The entire meal and discussion lasted about 90 minutes. We flew home the next morning. Miramax's total outlay for a 90-minute dinner with the Resnicks: $5,570.

Most Break-Even: Lunch with Marty Greenberg at Noreascon III in 1989. He asked what I was working on. I told him I was writing "Bully!," an alternate history of Teddy Roosevelt (which would eventually be nominated for both a Hugo and a Nebula.) Somehow that gave him the notion of selling an anthology of *Alternate Presidents*, with me as the editor, and before he was finished, he had sold four more alternate anthologies to Tor, the titles being *Kennedys, Warriors, Outlaws* and *Tyrants*. Our gross income, including advances, royalties, book club sales, and foreign editions, came to about $81,000. But since I insisted on paying a word rate that would attract the best writers, and since Tor liked the notion of 140,000-word books, our net profit after paying the writers (and splitting royalties with them) was $7,700, which meant my share was $3,850 for editing 5 books. (OK, it's trivial, but why is it break-even? Because while people kept buying Resnick books, they were confronted with so many titles that they often bought the *wrong* Resnick books—anthologies, on which I got a quarter of the royalties, rather than novels, on which I kept 100% of the royalties—and we doped out that I lost about $3,800 in anticipated novel royalties while those anthologies were in the stores.

Most Potentially Expensive Meal: This was a breakfast at Little Governor's Camp in Kenya's Maasai Mara, and for doubters, I have the entire incident captured on videotape. Carol was just sitting down to eat when an enormous elephant smelled the citrus fruit on the table and mosied over to share it. Carol felt this was an unacceptable intrusion and refused to move. Jumbo kept approaching. Carol flexed her 130 pounds of muscle; Jumbo flexed his 13,762 pounds of muscle. Carol snarled and showed her fighting canines; Jumbo showed *his* fighting canines, which extended for about six feet from each side of his mouth. When Jumbo was literally eight feet from the table and tentatively extending his trunk, Carol finally retreated. Damned good thing, too; the cost of getting another Carol would have been prohibitive.

Most I'm-Glad-Our-Insurance-Was-Paid-Up Meal: I was in Philadelphia to deliver a speech, and of course Carol was with me. As always when we're in town, we stopped to visit Gardner Dozois and Susan Casper. Finally Gardner suggested we all go out to his favorite Philadelphia restaurant. We did. They seated us. We ordered. And—so help me—the restaurant burned down before the appetizers arrived. (I resisted the urge to walk to the nearest Greyhound station and scribble "For a hot time, call Gardner" on the wall.)

Biggest Tab For A Fannish Meal: This took place during Iguanacon, the 1978 Worldcon. We joined John Guidry for lunch at the Hyatt's atrium coffee shop. A few minutes later Tony and Suford Lewis sat down. So did Rick Katze. Lou Tabakow mosied over. By now the table was getting crowded, so we pulled another table over. It was immediately filled by Mark and Lynne Aronson and Bill Cavin and Jo Ann Wood and Pat and Roger Sims. Someone—I think it was Banks Mebane—broke out a deck of cards, and pretty soon there was a bridge game going on. Then someone opened up a portable chess set. We had to leave for a few hours. When we came back with Stu and Amy Brownstein, there were all-new faces at the table, but the card and chess games were still going on, and the tab was about three feet long. Each person tossed money into a coffee cup when he left, and when the last person reliquished the table about 30 hours later, the coffee shop's cashier raked in upwards of $500.

Most money wasted: This took place at the Nebula banquet that was held in San Francisco in 1990. Tor Books had five of the six nominees for best novel, and all five of us—me, Jane Yolen, Orson Scott Card, Poul Anderson and John Kessel—

were being treated to dinner by Tom Doherty. Just before the ceremony began, Tom surprised us by having Dom Perignon delivered to all three of the Tor tables to celebrate the publishing house's pending victory. And, of course, just about the time we popped the corks, it was announced that Elizabeth Scarborough, the one Bantam author, had beaten us all.

Longest Meal: the 1968 Worldcon banquet. I won't go into details here, since it's the subject of a forthcoming article elsewhere. But ask anyone who was there.

There is a Resnick Listserv (which is very much like a computer-driven apa for Resnick friends and fans) that is run by a fan called John Teehan, who also runs my web page. (You can visit the web page at www.MikeResnick.com and can join the Listserv from the web page.)

The discussions can be serious or trivial, and are definitely not limited to science fiction. At one point, we all listed the best and worst meals we'd had in restaurants, and since this article happens to be about meals, I thought I would repeat my own lists here.

BEST AMERICAN MEALS

1. **Doro's (Chicago):** My all-time favorite. It closed about ten years ago. In a country where almost all the 5-star restaurants are French, this was Italian. They served a wonderful soup with a poached egg in it, the best veal parmesan I've ever eaten (with some outstanding Fettucini Alfredo on the side), and a dessert tray to die for (but I always ordered the chocolate souffle).

2. **Le Francais (Wheeling, Illinois):** This is Carol's favorite restaurant, and most surveys rate it the best in America. French, but with a surprising assortment of game meats, exquisite sauces, a huge and very upscale wine list (I don't drink anything stronger than coffee, but I have been assured by many patrons that this is one of the best lists in the country), fabulous desserts. Not cheap, but we've blown maybe $3,000 there on 20 meals over the years, and we plan to go back for more.

3. Commander's Palace (New Orleans): In a city with such stellar restaurants as Antoine's, Arnaud's, Broussard's, Gallitoire's, and Brennan's, this one is clearly, easily the best. We've never had a bad appetizer, main course, or dessert (and Carol adds that she's never been touted onto a bad wine by the waiters).

4. La Caravelle (New York): I've never seen anyone rank this at the very top of New York's restaurants, but it's always in the top half-dozen, and it's my favorite. They have a fabulous pea soup that's heavy on the sour cream, they do unbelievable things with roast duck, and they make the best chocolate mousse in the country—and they're a safe and easy walk to the theaters, which is a major consideration in Manhattan.

5. Ritz-Carlton Dining Room (Chicago): All the Ritz-Carltons have fine dining rooms, but I think the one in Chicago is the best. Very French, except that they serve man-sized portions. They do fabulous things with sauces, both on their main courses and their desserts.

6. Nikoli's (Atlanta): This one affords eye-catching views from atop the Hilton, but if it were in a windowless basement it would still be the best restaurant in Atlanta. I actually enjoy their salads, and I *hate* green stuff. Very nice traditional appetizers and main courses (and the beef Stroganof was outstanding), and great one-and-two-person souffles for dessert.

7. Four Seasons Dining Room (Beverly Hills): Like the Ritz-Carlton chain, all the Four Seasons hotels have excellent dining rooms. This is the one we are usually put up at when we're flown to Hollywood, and the food is so good that even when a production company puts us in the Nikko Inn or the Beverly Hilton instead, they always take us here for dinner. (Breakfast is pretty good too. I always have coffee and eggs Benedict, Carol always has coffee and granola sprinkled with fresh fruit, and the bill—which we always charge to whatever movie company is putting us up here [usually Capella]—is always $45.00.)

8. La Maisonette (Cincinnati): This restaurant, about 17 miles from my house, has been a 5-star restaurant longer than any other in the country: 32 years. And it deserves it. More American than French despite the name, they have a venison dish in a rich brown sauce that is superb; a bottomless bowl of scallops in a thick wine sauce; great deserts; and surprisingly friendly service.

9. Lutece (New York): Haven't been here in a few years. When we went, it was the consensus #1 restaurant in New York. These days it doesn't make anyone's top ten. But the two meals we had there were truly memorable. Carol had fish dishes, I had meat once and duck once. I don't like mussels, but they had a mussel appetizer in cream sauce that I still remember, and unbelievable mousses and souffles for dessert.

10. Christini's (Orlando): I prefer Italian to French or American, and with the passing of Doro's (see #1), this is probably the best Italian restaurant left in America. (I haven't tried 'em all, but I've tried a hell of a lot of them.) Fabulous veal dishes, great pastas, everything you could want in a very upscale red sauce Sothern (much preferable to Northern) Italian restaurant.

11. Victor's (San Francisco): This one's atop the St. Francis Hotel. I don't even remember why we went there the first time; I know why we went back three more times. The main course was good, but not outstanding; the appetizers and the desserts were the best we've had on the West Coast except for the Four Seasons. They had so many wines that they have two stewards: a white wine steward and a red wine steward.

12. La Tour du Bois (Lake Geneva, Wisconsin): I believe this one's closed, too. It was at one of the resorts surrounding Lake Geneva. When we lived in Illinois, Carol and I spent a weekend there, then extended it another day so we could eat a third dinner at La Tour. Very French, high-cholesterol sauces over very French portions (i.e., not too big), but so damned many courses that it didn't matter.

BEST FOREIGN MEALS

1. **Chobe Game Lodge, Chobe National Park, Botswana:** The meal, eaten while watching a few hundred elephant drinking less than 75 yards away, consisted of an appetizer of eggs Florentine, a thick mushroom soup, ragout of impala (the best single dish I've ever had), and a dessert of trifle with an exquisite custard sauce.

2. **Ocean Sports, Watamu, Kenya:** They have a Giriama chef who was schooled in London, and could make a fortune if he'd ever leave his tribe and go to New York or Paris. The resort was run down; we couldn't figure out why our guide had recommended it—until we got to the dining room. Ex-pat Brits and Germans drive 100 miles each way just to eat here. Best Lobster thermidore I've ever had (that was dinner; I had a whole cold lobster with melted butter for lunch; then I had both meals again the next day, just to make sure I wasn't imagining how good they were the first time around) and a chocolate mousse that's even better than La Caravelle's in New York. Carol made serious inroads on the crab population before we were ready to move on.

3. **Mount Kenya Safari Club, Nanyuki, Kenya:** Their justifiably world-famous lunch buffet takes up about two dozen tables, with excellent hot and cold plates, cheeses, fruits, salads, desserts . . . but the *real* treat is to have a member (there are less than 100; our guide was one of them) take you to dinner in the Member's Dining Room, where you'll have the most memorable 10-course dinner on the continent.

4. **Livingston Room, Victoria Falls Hotel, Zimbabwe:** They specialize in my two favorite game meats—impala and Thompson's gazelle—but the best single meal I had there was kudu in an excellent sauce. Though landlocked, they have shrimp and lobster dishes, and far better desserts than one would expect from such a British-type restaurant. And no, you can't quite see the

Falls from the dining room—though if you eat outside you can. (Interesting footnote: the restaurant is right next to the I Presume bar. Honest.)

5. Last Days of the Raj, London: The single best Indian restaurant we've ever been to, it's on Drury Lane opposite the eternally-running turkey, *Cats*. There's a more popular Indian restaurant a couple of miles away, the Bombay Brasserie, which has better ambience but poorer (though far from poor) food.

6. The Carnivore, Nairobi, Kenya: An outdoor restaurant built along the lines of an open-pit Brazilian barbeque. The menu changes, but they always have six or seven different game animals roasting on a spit, and the waiters bring the meat to your table on a skewer, explain what it is, and slice off however much you want. Over our many trips there, we've had impala, hartebeest, eland, wart hog, Grant's gazelle, Thompson's gazelle, zebra, crocodile, topi, wildebeest, and half a dozen others. A great bar, for those who care about such things.

7. Petit St. Vincent's, Grenadines, Carribean: This is a small private island in the southern Caribbean, with eleven villas, none of which are within sight of the others. All you do here for a week or so is snorkel, sleep, and pig out at their 5-star restaurant. If you get up before noon, you can wander around (it's about a mile in circumference) and see dinner being caught. They also import beef and veal for those who don't like fish.

8. Bishopstrow House, England: Halfway between Bath and Stonehenge, this is an ancient manor that was split into two garden suites and maybe half a dozen rooms. We ate all but one meal in our suite, but the one we had in the restaurant was the single best non-Indian meal we ever had in England. Shrimp cocktail, excellent Yorkshire pudding and gravy, fabulous beef, and a seven-layer cake that was as moist as you could want. (I find most British pastries too dry.)

(This one also makes my Worst list, for totally different reasons.)

9. Royal Caribbean, Montego Bay, Jamaica: I think this is a Sandals now, but back when we were there it was still a unique hostelry, with the nicest beach of all the Montego Bay area resorts, including Round Hill (which is usually filled to overflowing with royalty and Hollywood celebs). We had about 30 meals here, and I can't recall a bad one. It's where Carol fell in love with Red Stripe beer, and I became a Jamaican coffee addict.

10. Ramses Hilton, Cairo, Egypt: The best meal in Cairo, with entertainment that includes belly dancers and an authentic whirling dervish. They serve a very interesting and exotic Egyptian coffee. It has much the same menu you might find in any Middle Eastern restaurant, but prepared with enormous flair and skill.

11. Ibis Grill, Nairobi, Kenya: Elegant food, elegantly prepared and served in elegant surroundings—the venerable Norfolk Hotel, temporary home to Teddy Roosevelt, Ernest Hemingway, King Edward, Robert Ruark, and (blush) the Resnicks on 4 different occasions. We always manage to have one dinner in the Ibis Grill. Fabulous cuts of meat, mouth-watering appetizers, adequate desserts. And if you have a cottage, as we always do, they'll walk the 50 or 100 feet and serve you your dinner on your porch while you relax and watch their aviaries.

12. Tamerind, Mombasa, Kenya: The Tamerind is known as the best seafood restaurant in Africa. It's in a former harem overlooking the harbor at Mombasa, but they also own a huge dhow, and you can make arrangements to eat on the dhow as it sails the Indian Ocean for the evening. And until you've had shrimp and crab and lobster in their unique sauces, partaken of their excellent wine and booze (so I'm told; I'm a teetotaler), and then danced to "Perfidia" and "The Blue Tango" while sailing out past Mombasa on a cloudless night, you don't know the meaning of the word Romance.

(One caveat: don't sit down to eat until the dhow makes it out of the harber, which smells *horrible* when the wind blows the wrong way.)

13. **Crane's Beach Hotel, Barbados:** Perched on a cliff overlooking the Caribbean, Crane's restaurant specializes in island fare—fish and poultry in spicy fruit sauces—but you can also get a 20-ounce steak or a huge slab of ribs if you ask for them. Probably the most interesting (and tasty) fruit plate I've ever seen; the dips tasted so good I still can't believe they were yogurt.

(Okay, so why didn't I list any Paris restaurants? Easy. We were there for the first time last spring, after a convention in Nancy—we'll have been there again before this article appears, and I might finally have some names to add to the list—and though we made reservations at Maxim's and a couple of other world-class restaurants, we were so exhausted from sightseeing that we kept canceling out and eating at local brasseries. Which is not to say that we didn't eat well, or pig out on wonderful souffles and quiches and mousses and crepes and the like; just that they weren't quite world-class. [But they would have cost three times as much in America, and you wouldn't have felt cheated.] Anyway, for anyone who stays on the Right Bank near the Seine, there is one brasserie in particular I'd like to recommend: Zimmer's, about two blocks from our hotel—Le Grand Hotel du Champagne, which is a mighty impressive name for a little 22-room hostelry in a 400-year-old building—which was open 24 hours a day, and which we kept visiting at 3 and 4 in the morning after we'd take a nap and get our second wind. It never disappointed.)

NEAR-GREAT MEALS
(which won't quite cost you a week's pay)

Stefano's, in Orlando, Florida. So far off the beaten track even the locals have a hard time finding it—but enough do to fill it up every night. Fabulous Italian food, and the whole family gets into the act: Dad cooks, Grandma supervises, and the next two generations serve as waiters, waitresses, hosts, hostesses, and buspeople. Superb veal dishes and pastas. Carol always asks for whatever the day's special is. Dad comes out from the kitchen every half hour to see how everyone's enjoying the food and talk about the joys of cooking. If you don't drink wine, you'll be out of there for about $11 a head for one of the half-dozen best Italian meals in the States.

Ocean Sports, Watamu, Kenya. I mentioned this as one of the two best foreign restaurants, but it qualifies here too, because it's surely one of the least expensive. How inexpensive? Try five dollars for a whole lobster, or twelve for lobster thermidore with a desert of chocolate mousse—and remember, I consider this not just a good meal, but a world-class one.

Idra, Greenwich Village, Manhattan, NY. I don't know if this one's still cheap, or even if it still exists. Great Greek restaurant on the second floor, above a Greek grocery store. We found it back in 1967. No one speaks English. You have to hold up three fingers and make a stabbing motion at your plate, all the while repeating the word "fork," if you need one. But the food makes up for it, and we never spent as much as ten dollars a plate, which is great anywhere but unbelievable in Manhattan. It's been about eight years since we were back.

Piccolo Mondo, Manhattan, NY. A great Italian restaurant on the East side, 1st or 2nd Avenue, somewhere around 62nd or 63rd Street (again, assuming it's still there; it's been six years since we were there. And I suppose I should point out that the reason we haven't gone back to our favorite cheap restaurants is that these days editors and publishers treat us to our favorite expensive ones.) Great linguini and fettucini, fabulous veal dishes, nifty pastries. Last time it was getting up around $20 a plate, but that's still dirt cheap for Manhattan.

The Greek Isles, Chicago, IL. We've been frequenting this one for close to 30 years. Outstanding saganaki, dolmades, pastitso, mousaka, Greek pastries. Alas, no belly dancers (but that just means they're serious about their food). It's maybe $15 a head, and worth double that.

Baboush, San Pedro, CA. Great Middle Eastern restaurant, where you sit on the floor and eat with your hands. Great belly dancers, too. A flat $20 a head no matter what you eat. Susan Shwartz and Lyn Nichols can vouch for this joint, because we took them there during the 1996 Nebulas. Marvelous decorations and ambience.

The Silo, Lake Bluff, IL. Home of the best (and most filling) pizza in the universe. You don't know the meaning of "deep dish" until they bring a 3-inch-deep pizza to your table here. Carol, Laura, Joan Bledig and I used to go there all the time when we lived in Illinois (and we still hit it occasionally); we would order a medium pizza for the table, and the four of us, none of whom can reasonably be termed a shy eater, never managed to finish one. Spread over a party of four, I'd say even a large pizza and a pitcher of beer probably doesn't come to $6 a head.

Montgomery Inn/Boathouse, Cincinnati, OH. Said to have the best ribs in the country. (Bob Hope has his private plane fly in for them twice a week.) But while the ribs are unrivaled anywhere I've ever been, the whole menu is excellent. These are sister restaurants with identical menus—one about 4 miles from my house in Montgomery, the other about 17 miles away, hanging out over the Ohio River. Their cheese onion soup, served only on Wednesdays, is one of the two best soups in the country (La Caravelle in NY has the other, and charges 8 times as much for it). You'll get out for under $20 a head.

Passage to India, Orlando, FL. The best Indian restaurant in the Orlando area—and because it's on International Drive in the tourist area, just about every hotel and tourist guidebook gives out half-price coupons to it . . . which means you can eat a huge and incredibly satisfying Indian meal in gorgeous surroundings for under ten dollars.

La Fondue, Manhattan, NY. One of the few midtown restaurants that don't cost an arm and a leg. Usually jammed at lunchtime, but if you go at 11:00 AM or 2:30 PM you'll probably get in. They make about 50 types of cheese fondue, and the best damned chocolate fondue you'll get anywhere, for a third of what you'll pay at any other restaurant within three blocks.

Zimmer's Brasserie, Paris, France. Paris is filled with hundreds of brasseries, and we stumbled onto this one as a matter of convenience, since it was only two blocks from our hotel on the Right Bank, maybe 3 blocks from Notre Dame in one direction, and 5 blocks from the Louvre in the other (for those who've been there, this'll help you get your bearings). Superb quiches, souffles, pastries, mousses, crepes and the like, open 24 hours, and I don't think we ever spent over $11 a person.

The Student Prince, Springfield, MA. When I was Guest of Honor at Boskone earlier this decade, the committee took me there four nights in a row. I was assured that it was not the only restaurant in town (we were beginning to wonder), but simply the best. A great selection of game meats. Not only venison, but even such exotic treats as bear and lion—and we never came to a dish we didn't like. Even today it's got to be under $20 a head.

The Chinese Dumpling House, Highland Park, IL. People drive here from Wisconsin, Indiana and Iowa, just for the superb Chinese food. The restaurant used to be a barbeque house, and though it's been there for 30 years, they haven't quite got around to taking down the cattle horns yet. The total lack of ambience doesn't keep anyone away. Their sizzling rice dishes are superb, and when you ask for your Setzuan dish to be hot, trust me, it'll take the enamel off your teeth. Even today, you can still have a fine meal there for under $15.

The Horseman, Karen, Kenya. A superb local restaurant in the Ngong Hills, unknown to tourists, frequented mostly by ex-pat Brits. Fine British dishes (far better than in Britain, in fact), with a mushroom soup and a brisket of beef that you can't beat anywhere on the continent. And you'll never pay as much as $12 for a complete dinner.

Julie's Waterfront, Orlando, FL. Carol insisted that I include this one, since we eat there quite often. But it's strictly for the ambience. They have a bar and you get bar food—hamburgers and the like—but you eat it under a swamp-cooler to keep the sun off your head while you watch otters, water skiers, and the occasional alligator frolic in the lake that comes to within fifteen feet of your outdoor table. The food truly isn't memorable, but we could (and do) sit there for hours, unwinding and watching the otters, who are the most playful and energetic beasts you can imagine. $8 a meal will do it, and that includes your beer.

The Athenian, Santa Monica, CA. Wonderful decor and ambience, and probably the best Greek meal you can get outside New York and Chicago. The pastitsio and mousaka were fabulous, and the Greek salad was outstanding. We've never spent $30 for the two of us.

MOST OVERRATED MEALS

Ernie's: San Francisco's most famous restaurant. The service was slow and surly, the meals poorly prepared, the menu uninspired. Even the chairs were uncomfortable.

Le Perroquet: Pricey Chicago restautant with an international reputation. You practically need to know the Secret Handshake to get the elevator to take you to the dining floor of this dilapidated Gold Coast building. Appetizers were excellent, a sadly undelivered promise of quality to come. The meal wasn't bad—but for the highest price in the most expensive area of an expensive city, "not bad" isn't good enough.

Bishopstrow House, England: A great meal, as I said elsewhere. So it wasn't the meal that was overrated. It wasn't even the service, since the meals were exquisitely served. It was the goddamned cultural conflict.

Let me explain. We're there with Pat and Roger Sims, and it's a chilly evening, and we sit down at the table, and when the waiter leaves the menus, I tell him I want a cup of coffee. He explains that coffee is served with desert. I explain that I'm cold and I want some coffee *now*. He explains that it simply isn't done. I explain that if he wants more than a halfpenny tip, it's gonna *get* done. This fight goes all the way up to the manager, who gives me all the same arguments about when civilized people drink their coffee and finally yields to my demand. And brings me a demitasse half-filled with coffee—maybe an ounce, if we're being generous. I drink it in one small swallow and tell him I want another. He looks around at his staff, and it is the same look King Henry II gives *his* staff when beset by Thomas Beckett, and it is a look that says "Will no one rid me of this meddlesome priest?" (for "meddlesome priest" substitute "barbaric American.") After arguing another ten minutes, I get a second half-filled demitasse, by which time my taste for coffee—and Bishopstrow House—has pretty much vanished.

Hotel Pierre, New York: The time is 1981. Carol and I have gone to Manhattan with Sid Altus, a good friend who would, for a time, become my hardcover publisher at Phantasia Press. During the day I visit editors and Sid goes sightseeing, and we meet for dinner and a play each evening. And on Sunday morning, because I've made a few book sales, I decided to celebrate by treating for brunch, and I not only invite Sid but Barry Malzberg and Lani Litt as well. Sid was staying at the Plaza, as we were, but we'd heard that the Hotel Pierre, an elegant establishment about a block away, had a truly memorable brunch, so we decided to go there. (I think it was the first time I met Barry, who has long since become my closest friend in science fiction, in person.)

So we eat, and the meal's as good as it's supposed to be. And the waiter comes by with a check, and I see that the bill has an area marked for me to include the tip, so, because it is a truly fine meal and a truly elegant restaurant, I scribble in a 20% tip, and the waiter takes my card and goes off to get it approved.

He comes back with the approved AmEx slip, and the price of the meal is filled in, and "Tip to Waiter" is filled in at 20%—but there is a line I've never seen before, which is "Tip to Captain." And no one has added up the total, because obviously I am expected to add a tip to the Captain, who nodded hello to us on the way in and has been invisible ever since.

And that pisses me off, because I feel they're trying to rip me off for extra tip money—had I known there was a separate area for the Captain, I'd have given 15% to the staff and 5% to him—so I leave the "Tip to Captain" column blank, add up the rest, write down the total, sign it, and hand it to the waiter. He lookos at it and frowns.

"Didn't you forget something?" he asks.

"Not a thing," I reply.

He comes by two minutes later to say, "The Captain wants to know how you enjoyed your brunch."

I tell him to tell the Captain that it's pretty good as brunches go.

Two minutes later he's back again. "The Captain wants to know if there is anything he can do for you?"

I reply that, for starters, he can stop sending me messages.

A few minutes later I get up to go to the men's room. The Captain follows me in and asks if he's done anything to offend me. I tell him that I am not in the least offended, but that I am not overmuch burdened by unwarranted guilt trips either: I pay 15% tips at normal restaurants and 20% tips at high class ones, and I don't care how he and the staff split it up, 20% is all he's getting.

Practically in tears, he points out that there is nothing in the box next to "Tip to Captain."

I tell him that we all have to learn to live with life's little disappointments, and that in the future it might be a good idea to let the diners know that he plans to extort a second tip from them after they've agreed to pay a generous first tip.

I left him mumbling about how he should never have left France. I returned to the table, did a little mumbling myself about how we should found a deli and grabbed some chopped liver and blintzes for a quarter of the price, and then the meal was over and we flew home.

Postscript: Carol just stopped by to tell me that if I don't stop biting my fingernails during Cincinnati Bearcats' basketball games, she's going to insist I add them to my list of "Favorite Meals" if I write a sequel. *Sigh*

For Challenger #11

MIKE RESNICK'S PREDICTIONS FOR THE 21ST CENTURY:

2001: "I'm back!" says Michael Jordan, accepting the $62 million the Chicago Bulls offer him for the 2001 season.

2003: Harry Warner writes his six millionth letter.

2004: The Zagreb Science Fiction Society, a wholly-owned subsidiary of NESFA, wins the bid for the 2007 Worldcon.

2005: *Star Wars—Part III*, opens on 3 screens nationwide, to mixed reviews ("Great effects, but shouldn't it have had a script or maybe some actors or something?") and mediocre business.

2006: Connie Willis' house collapses from the weight of her Hugos.

2007: The Mongolian Science Fiction Society, a wholly-owned subsidiary of NESFA, wins the bid for the 2010 Worldcon.

2009: Hillary Clinton, having lost her bids for the Senate (New York, 2000), Illinois (2002), Arkansas (2004), and New Jersey (2006), announces her intention to run for the Senate from Arizona in 2010. "I've always been a Cardinals fan, ever since I was a little girl," she tells the press.

2010: Hollywood producers assure Mike Resnick that they're planning to make *Santoago* "any day now."

2012: Best Editor Hugo trophy retired; Gardner Dozois sues, sells 24 Hugos on eBay to pay for his legal costs.

2013: Charlie Brown promises to give up control of *Locus* "just as soon as I can find a buyer and train him."

2015: Connie Willis' new house collapses from the weight of her Nebulas.

2016: Hillary Clinton announces her intention to run for President of NESFA. "The NESFA baseball team has always been my favorite," she tells the press.

2019: Men land on Mars. Two of them are former fans. Property values plummet.

2021: Department of Justice declares LASFS and WSFA are just fronts, sues NESFA for monopolistic practices. Rick Katze countersues Attorney General for bothering him during a Boston Celtics game.

2023: Roger Sims toys with producing 5th issue of his fanzine *Fantasyscope* when subscribers, who initially gave him money in 1947, threaten to riot.

2024: *Science Fiction Chronicle* comes out on time three issues in a row. Astronomers notice that the stars have stopped in their courses.

2026: "This may be our last issue of *Mimosa*," threaten Lynches. "We're definitely getting tired of it."

2029: "I'm back!" wheezes Michael Jordan, accepting a one-year $173 million contract to play for the Bulls during the 2029 season.

2033: Highmore, South Dakota wins the bid for the 2036 Worldcon under the astute leadership of Kevin Standlee.

2040: Star Trek fandom canonizes producer and actor. They are now Saint Big Bird and Saint Lenny.

2042: Star Trek fandom threatens to sue any scholar who suggests that science fiction existed before 1966. Star Wars fandom countersues, claiming that it began in 1977. Worldcon is canceled for lack of interest. World Mediacon draws 194,237, none of whom have ever read a book.

2050: "This is really my last season," swears Michael Jordon, accepting full ownership of the National Basketball Association in exchange for playing the final quarter of each game of the 2050 season.

2067: Men land on Saturn. Find the climate depressing. Go home.

2071: NESFA adds 174 more rooms to its clubhouse, making it larger than the World Trade Center.

2075: Men land on Neptune. Discover that Resnick was right: there *are* elephants there.

2081: Robert Jordan announces that the end of the *Wheels of Time* series is in sight. Stock market plunges.

2085: Pope converts to Ghughuism. NESFA appropriates Vatican's pornographic art treasury. Tony Lewis takes the filthiest books into the bathroom, announces his intention not to emerge until the 22nd Century.

2086: Harry Warner writes his 12 millionth letter.

2089: "Illegitimate Stepdaughter of Ol' Pointy Ears" becomes the 700th Star Trek spinoff to air on Fox TV network. "I don't see why that should be of any concern to anybody," says network prexy Throckmorton Roddenbury.

2092: Fosfax supports liberal candidate for dog catcher. Government shuts down for 72 hours.

2095: "The Ganymede Geldings have always been my favorite team," says Chelsea Clinton, buying a house on that distant moon and announcing her intention to run for its open Senate seat.

2098: Last lion dies. Last leopard dies. Last lynx dies. Last Latvian dies. Last Lithuanian dies. Last lesser kudu dies. It's a bad year for L's.

2099: NESFA publishes 8,000th book, dissolves government, declares war on Albania. When questioned by reporters, spokesman Mark Olson will only discuss NESFA's bid to host the 2102 Worldcon in Burkina Faso.

2100: Resnick shot in act by 6 jealous husbands. Smith and Zeldes immediately begin searching for some other poor schmuck to predict the 22nd Century.

For STET #9

THE LITERATURE OF FANDOM

The other night I was speaking to some eager young fans on one of the computer networks. They were curious about some aspects of fannish history, and I was regaling them with tales about past Worldcons and Claude Degler and Room 770, and one of them suddenly remarked that it was essential to get some of this stuff written down before the last of us oldpharts died and there was no one to codify fandom's history.

I explained gently that they had nothing to worry about, that we oldpharts had been codifying fannish history for the better part of 60 years, and that very few hobby fields were as well documented as science fiction fandom.

I even mentioned some of the book titles to prove my point. They'd never heard of any of them . . . which meant it was probably time for someone to write this article, so neofen will know where to look for the Holy Books of Fandom before the last of us oldpharts dies without telling them.

Now, this doesn't pretend to be a complete list of titles. It's just what I have managed to accumulate during my 35 years as a fan and a pro (which, I hasten to point out, are not mutually exclusive. I am, always have been, and always will be, a fan— the IRS's claims to the contrary notwithstanding.) Anyway, I think it's not unfair to say that if you read every word of every book I'm about to discuss, you'll stop being a neofan somewhere along the journey, and may actually be faunching for the secret handshake of Trufandom by the time you're done.

HISTORIES

The first book of major import has to be *The Immortal Storm*, by Sam Moskowitz (published by the Atlanta Science Fiction Organization Press in 1954, and later reprinted by Hyperion). It is nothing less than the history of American science fiction fandom, culminating with the first Worldcon in 1939, all described in incredibly minute detail.

Now, for those of you who may not know it, things did not go as smoothly at that first Worldcon as the participants might have wished. Moskowitz himself (a/k/a SaM, just as Forry Ackerman is a/k/a 4e) barred Don Wollheim, Cyril Kornbluth,

Fred Pohl, Doc Lowndes, and John Michel from entering, and the latter part of *The Immortal Storm*, told in the third person (though with Moskowitz as a major player), is an account of events leading up to, and including, what has come to be known as The Exclusion Act. Sometimes it's difficult to remember that these are *not* Kissinger and Disraeli SaM is writing about, but just a bunch of acne-faced kids with delusions of grandeur.

L. Sprague de Camp calls it "An extraordinary (if quite unintentional) study in small-group dynamics." Harry Warner, Jr. adds that "If read directly after a history of World War II, it does not seem like an anti-climax." An unnamed fan is quoted in *All Our Yesterdays* as calling it "Badly translated from the Slobbovian," a problem SaM would have again and again with his prose over the years.

Damon Knight devoted a short chapter of his book of criticism, *In Search of Wonder*, to *The Immortal Storm*. The title of the chapter was "Microscopic Moskowitz." How microscopic? Try this brief excerpt on for size:

"The membership never exceeded the original five, and since these five promptly split into two factions . . ."

I should add that there's a companion piece of sorts. It's Jack Speer's *Up To Now*, available in *A Sense of FAPA* (which will be discussed later), or as a stand-alone chapbook published by Arcturus Press in 1994.

It's Speer's version of fannish history in the 1930s, and actually pre-dates Moskowitz's book. Is it any gentler and kinder? Well, according to Joe Gilbert, it's "As if someone had gathered up all the hates, prejudices and petty jealousies that have clogged the pipes of the stream of life since the world was first begun."

So is it possible to write a history of fandom that *doesn't* gather up all the hates, prejudices, etc.?

It is if your name is Harry Warner, Jr.

Harry took up where SaM and Speer left off, and covered the next two decades of fandom in two volumes. The first, dealing with the 1940s, was *All Our Yesterdays*, far better written than its predecessors, and without any axes to grind, since Harry's primary interaction with fandom was through fanzines and letter-writing. It's a fabulous, informal history, covering all the high points, reporting on (for example) the initial meeting after the war between DAW (Wollheim) and SaM (the man who barred him from the first worldcon), filled with well over 100 photos, even indexed. It's a true treasure of fannish history and anecdotes.

Advent published *All Our Yesterdays* in 1969, and was set to publish *A Wealth of Fable* a few years later when Harry pulled the manuscript because, as he said in a letter to *Mimosa*, "Ed Wood submitted a list of things which he thought I should insert in my manuscript. Every one of these items had one thing in common: they concerned Ed Wood's activities in fandom or matters with which he had been closely associated."

Anyway, it was Joe Siclari and his Fanhistorica Press to the rescue. Joe mimeographed *A Wealth of Fable* and turned it into three "issues" of a fanzine in 1977, and that was the only form in which it was available until SCIFI Press and editor Rich Lynch finally brought out a fine-looking hardcover at the 1992 Worldcon. It's not even a sequel, but rather a continuation of *All Our Yesterdays*, heavily illustrated, obviously written by the same hand, chock full of the anecdotes that almost instantly become fannish legend.

A fascinating, though very localized history, was written by F. Towner Laney back in 1948. It was called *Ah! Sweet Idiocy!*, it was about his few years in LASFS (the Los Angeles Science Fiction Society), and it pre-dated Sen. Joseph McCarthy in accusing almost everyone the author knew of being either a homosexual, a communist, or both. The villain of the piece seems to be 4e Ackerman—yet it was Ackerman who footed the publishing bill. *Ah! Sweet Idiocy!* appeared serially in FAPA, and was later included, in its entirety, in Dick Eney's massive *A Sense of FAPA*.

Laney soon dropped out of fandom. He was married four times, and theoretically died on June 8, 1958. I say theoretically, because in the early 1980s I saw the name "F. Towner Laney" on the masthead of a computer magazine published in New York, and how many F. Towner Laneys can there be in the world?

Well, I've referred to *A Sense of FAPA* twice now, so I might as well tell you about it. Back in 1962, Dick Eney collected some of the most interesting items that had ever run in FAPA— fandom's very first apa, which is still going strong in 1997—and published them before they could be lost forever. Its 370+ pages encompassed tons of artwork and articles, including Speer's history and Laney's idiocy. In a way, it's a rival history of fandom, by people who had no idea they were contributing to fannish history until Eney put all their old articles and cartoons together in one fat fannish volume. You'll also find "Mutation or Death," John Michel's propaganda tract that drew the battle lines between the Futurians and New Fandom, and some wonderful excerpts from Redd Boggs' immortal *Skyhook*, Bob Silverberg's *Spaceship*, and other now-classic fanzines.

DICTIONARIES AND ENCYCLOPEDIAS

The first fannish encyclopedia—a dictionary of fannish terms and their origins, actually—was Jack Speer's *Fancyclopedia*, published in 1944 by Forrest J Ackerman. It ran over 100 mimeographed pages.

It was succeeded in 1959 by *Fancyclopedia II*, edited by Dick Eney (and with co-editorial credit to Speer). *Fancy II*, one of my two or three favorite fannish books, runs 184 single-spaced pages, with 19 pages of Additions and Corrections and 24 pages of The Rejected Canon. A fabulous book, which is equally adept at discussing the X Document, telling you how to mix an Atomic cocktail, or displaying the floor plans to the Tucker Hotel. Jack Chalker's Mirage Press printed a facsimile edition in 1979.

Eney also published the *Fancyclopedigest*, which was to be a bridge to *Fancyclopedia III*. When he ceased publishing, the project was taken over by some Los Angeles fans, who announced a pending publication in 1984. As I write this, it's only 13 years overdue, barely half as late as *The Last Dangerous Visions* (also a Los Angeles project, now that I come to think of it), and I still have some slight hope of seeing it during my lifetime.

A much more recent and somewhat less ambitious publication is Elliot Weinstein's *The Fillostrated Fan Dictionary*, published in two parts by "O" Press in 1975. It comes in two volumes, totaling 171 pages, and may even have more definitions than *Fancy* (the fannish term for *Fancyclopedia II*). But the reason I prefer *Fancy* is that it gives anecdotes and histories of the terms, while *Fillostrated* simply gives definitions.

Halfway between a (small) dictionary and an (equally

small) encyclopedia is *The Neo-Fan's Guide*, written by Bob Tucker back in 1955. It has been reprinted a number of times, to the best of my knowledge without ever being updated. The most recent copy I've seen was published by Mike Glyer in 1984, though Dave Truesdale tells me that Ken Keller published the authorized 7th edition in 1996. I think its popularity is a combination of two things: Tucker's continuing status as fandom's most beloved member, and the fact that, unlike, say, the *Fancyclopedia*, is it quite small and hence inexpensive to print. It really *is* for neofen; if you could find the fanzine in which this article appears, you're past needing it.

Finally, there's Roberta Rogow's *Futurespeak: A Fan's Guide to the Language of Science Fiction*, published by Paragon House in 1991, and much too limited and media-oriented for my taste.

PROCEEDINGS

For a while there, I had high hopes that I could revisit every Worldcon since 1962 just by reading the transcript, but alas, it was not to be. Still, three of them did see print.

The first was *The Proceedings: Chicon III*, the complete, heavily-illustrated transcript of all the panels and speeches from the 1962 Worldcon, edited by Earl Kemp and published by Advent in 1963. To me, the highlights of this book are Bob Bloch's lecture on Hollywood, and Ted Sturgeon's Guest of Honor speech.

Then came *The Proceedings: Discon*, the 1963 Worldcon transcript, also with close to one hundred photos, edited by Dick Eney and published by Advent in 1965. The best thing in this one is a panel with Asimov, de Camp, Lieber, Ley and Brackett that addressed the question, "What Should a BEM Look Like?" There's also a fine Guest of Honor speech by Murray Leinster, who seems to have been forgotten a little faster than most of our giants, and if you never experienced Isaac Asimov as a toastmaster, this will show you what you missed.

Finally, Leslie Turek edited the profusely-illustrated coffee-table-sized edition *The Noreascon Proceedings*, the main-track transcsripts of the 1971 Worldcon, which was published in a coffee-table-book format by NESFA Press in 1976. Highlights include a panel with Asimov and Cliff Simak, and another with Asimov, Marvin Minsky, and Larry Niven.

By then, Worldcons had gotten so large that it was impossible to glean even a hint of their flavor from a single track of the proceedings, and to print the entire proceedings—which has occasionally run to 15 and more tracks of programming, from 8 to 14 hours a day, during a 5-day weekend—was simply not feasible.

PHOTO BOOKS

The continuing growth of Worldcon eventually spelled fini to a series produced by Jay Kay Klein, science fiction's unofficial photographic historian. Surely no one who has ever been to a Worldcon has been able to avoid Jay Kay and his flash camera—but not all that many people know that in 1960 he published his *Convention Annual #1, Pittcon Edition*, a memory book filled with hundreds of photos and captions from the convention, covering panels, speeches, masquerades, the Hugo ceremonies, lobby lizards, and dozens of parties.

This was followed in rapid succession by *Convention Annual #2, Chicon III Edition*, in 1962; *Convention Annual #3, Discon Edition*, in 1963; and *Convention Annual #4, Tricon Edition*, in 1966. Jay Kay was all set to publish a fifth book, from 1974's Discon II, but the Worldcon had grown so huge by that time that even with help, he could barely identify half the fans in the photos, and so he retired the series.

Looking back on them, I think the Klein photo books gave even more of a sense of what the conventions were really like than the various Proceedings did, since Jay Kay not only photographed every panel, but also thoroughly covered the art shows, the huckster rooms, the masquerades, and just about every party that was thrown on Worldcon weekend. Until we invent a time machine, these photo books are probably the closest you'll ever come to experiencing — or re-experiencing — those early 1960s Worldcons.

There were two more memory books, published only months apart—and both, while slickly produced, were far less thorough than the Klein books. In 1984, Steve Francis edited *Memories of NorthAmericon*, a photo book of the 1979 NasFic that was held in Louisville, Kentucky—and just a few weeks later, Massachusetts Convention Fandom brought out the *Noreascon Two Memory Book*, the photo book of the 1980 Worldcon, edited by Suford Lewis. (They have since published the *Noreascon III Memory Book*.)

It's been quite a while since the last photo memory book was produced, yet I know fans cherish them; hopefully some future committee(s) will reestablish the practice.

PRO/FAN MEMOIRS

As science fiction has reached larger audiences, and its practitioners have become more famous, it was inevitable that some of the leading professionals would be asked to write memoirs and autobiographies—and since so many pros came up through fandom, especially in the early days, many of their recollections also concern fandom.

The most important, and delightful, of these is Damon Knight's *The Futurians*, published by John Day in 1977 (and later brought out in mass market paperback). Damon chronicles the group of teenagers who banded together in New York in the late 1930s, determined to have an effect on the field of science fiction—and considering that their numbers included Don Wollheim, Fred Pohl, Isaac Asimov, Damon Knight, Robert Lowndes, Cyril Kornbluth, Virginia Kidd, Judith Merrill, and James Blish, among others, I think it's safe to say they did just that. Knight chronicles their interior and exterior feuds (and one can be forgiven for feeling that, for their first couple of years of existence, they lived only to feud), follows them as Wollheim, Pohl and Lowndes nail down editorial jobs and begin buying from each other (and by 1943 they controlled more than half the prozines in the field), and then traces them to the present day, with Isaac becoming an international superstar, Wollheim metamorphizing from communist to capitalist and starting his own very successful publishing company, Kornbluth dying far too young, John Michel dying in almost total obscurity. It's a difficult book to put down.

There's a collection of six novelette-length autobiographies, edited by Harry Harrison and Brian Aldiss, entitled *Hell's Cartographers* (an editorial tip of the hat to Kingsley Amis's ground-breaking collection of essays about science fiction, *New Maps of Hell*). It was published by Harper & Row in 1975, and three of the six autobiographies—by Fred Pohl, Damon Knight, and (peripherally) Robert Silverberg—deal with fandom.

Fred Pohl also wrote a full-length autobiography, *The Way The Future Was*, published by del Rey in 1978, which covers much of his life in fandom before he turned pro. Isaac Asimov's *In Memory Yet Green*, published by Doubleday in 1979, does much the same, though Isaac was never as heavily involved in fandom as many of his contemporaries. Surprisingly, Robert Bloch's *Once Around the Bloch*, published by Tor in 1993, contains almost nothing about fandom, though Bloch himself was the best professional friend fandom ever had. (He wrote me that he had included a number of fannish anecdotes, especially about himself and Bob Tucker, but that they were later excised.)

Some passing references are made to fandom in some other memoirs, most notably Lloyd Arthur Esbach's *Over My Shoulder* and Jack Williamson's Hugo-winning *Wonder's Child*, but in truth these are so pro-and-publishing-oriented that they don't really qualify for mention here, despite their outstanding quality.

Finally, David G. Hartwell's *Age of Wonders*, published by Walker in 1984 and since reprinted by Tor, has perhaps the best analysis of the symbiosis between prodom and fandom that has ever been written. It took a pro editor, rather than a fan, to write a general book for the sf-reading public that explained in simple, straightforward terms the historic connection between fandom and sf, the pervasive influence of fans on the literature through fanzines, conventions, awards, and the graduation from their ranks to professional status of dozens of writers. Anyone even mildly acquainted with the field knows this is true, but it wasn't until Hartwell's book that it was stated so clearly that people who *weren't* acquainted with fandom would know it too.

COLLECTIONS

My other favorite fannish book, along with *Fancyclopedia II*, is Bob Bloch's *The Eighth Stage of Fandom*, a collection of 49 articles and poems, plus some hilarious filler ads. Bloch made his reputation as a writer of psychological horror, but he was also one of the field's master humorists, and that sense of humor was never on better display than here. The book was published in hardcover and trade paperback by Advent in 1962, and 30 years later Wildside Press reprinted it in hardcover. It was editor Earl Kemp's idea, and a damned good one; I love this book.

Bloch's second fannish collection was *Out Of My Head*, published by NESFA Press in 1986. It contains 22 stories and articles, including the first new Lefty Feep story in four decades.

Another fine fannish writer turned pro was the late Terry Carr. His most interesting collection was *Fandom Harvest*, a hardcover containing some 20 articles—including such classics as "The Hieronymus Fan" and "The Infinite Beanie"—and published in Sweden (but with English text) by Laissez Faire Produktion AB in 1986.

Terry also authored another collection of fanzine articles, *Between Two Worlds*, the flip half of a hardcover double with Bob Shaw's delightful collection, *Messages Found in an Oxygen Bottle*. This two-in-one book was published by NESFA Press in 1986, when Terry was the Worldcon's Fan Guest of Honor and Bob was its Toastmaster. Terry's half of the book has 5 pieces, including the classic "Night of the Living Oldpharts"; Bob's has 9 pieces, including the text of perhaps his most famous speech, "The Bermondsey Triangle Mystery."

Another Terry Carr product was *The Cacher of the Rye*, a parody by "Carl Brandon." Brandon was more than just a pseudonym; he was a fictional creation—a black California fan—that Terry foisted on fandom, and at one time most of fandom believed Carl was an actual person. The book begins with a long article by Carr explaining how and why he created Brandon, then presents the story, and ends with a thorough index of every article and story ever credited to Brandon and who actually wrote them (Carr did the bulk of the writing, but he was helped from time to time by Boob [sic] Stewart, Ron Ellik, and a handful of others who were in on the secret.) The story itself is a semi-loving criticism of fandom, which also manages to take a shot or two at Dianetics.

Another half of a convention double book was *In and Out of Quandry*, by Lee Hoffman. (The flip side is A. Bertram Chandler's *Up to the Sky in Ships*.) *Quandry* was the best and most important fanzine of the early 1950s, Lee was its editor, and this hardcover contains 9 articles from it, including "The Bluffer's Guide to Publishing a Fanzine" and "A Surprise for Harlan Ellison." It was published by NESFA Press in 1982, when Lee was the Fan Guest of Honor at the Chicago Worldcon. (Chandler was the Pro Guest of Honor.)

The 1996 Worldcon Guest of Honor book, *The White Papers*, published by NESFA Press, not only contained some brilliant stories by James White, but also most of his fannish writing as well.

Paranoid/Inca Press brought out a couple of Bob Shaw chapbooks back in 1979, each a sheer delight. The first is *The Best of the Bushel*, a collection of 13 articles, and second is *The Eastercon Speeches*, containing five of his always-hilarious "Serious Scientific Talks" from 1974 through 1978. A later book, *A Load of Old BoSh* (published by BECCON in 1995) collected ten of Bob's Eastercon speeches. (A word about these speeches: Bob Shaw ranks with Bob Bloch and Isaac Asimov as one of the funniest natural talents ever to hit science fiction's Toastmaster circuit, and his collected speeches are almost a textbook demonstration on how to delight an audience, without letdown, for a full hour.)

Perhaps the most famous single collection of fannish writing ever put together is the massive *Warhoon 28*, published in hardcover by Richard Bergeron in 1978. This contains more than 600 pages, single-spaced, by Northern Ireland's legendary Walt Willis, arguably the greatest fan writer of all. This enormous tome contains, among other things, installments 1 through 44 of his classic column, "The Harp That Once Or Twice"; the 36 chapters of "The Harp Stateside,"his memoir of his first American visit; the 20 chapters of "Twice Upon A Time,"the story of his return visit to America; and 21 segments of the mostly-autobiographical "The Subcutaneous Fan." There are also a number of convention reports, some fan fiction, and various other examples of Willis' literary art. A very worthwhile volume.

More recently, NESFA Press published a pair of fannish collections, both of which were nominated for Hugos. First came Teresa Nielsen Hayden's *Making Book*, in 1994, which included 15 articles from fanzines; and then, in 1996, multiple

Hugo winner Dave Langford's *The Silence of the Langford*, which includes more than 50 articles and reviews and incorporates the earlier Langford collection, *Let's Hear It For the Deaf Man*.

And, he said immodestly, I have edited a number of anthologies about fandom: *Alternate Worldcons* (Pulphouse, 1994), *Again, Alternate Worldcons* (Old Earth Books, 1996), and, with Patrick Neilsen-Hayden, *Alternate Skiffy* (Wildside Press, 1997). These were all semi-pro publications. I also edited a mass market anthology of recursive science fiction, *Inside the Funhouse* (Avon, 1992), which includes some stories about fandom.

Finally, there is a totally different type of collection, and a must-have for any serious student of fandom. This is *Science Fiction Fandom*, edited by Joe Sanders and published by Greenwood Press in 1994. The book contains 26 articles which cover fandom in various countries, its history, collecting, conventions, apa's, Fanspeak, and just about everything else you need to know about science fiction fandom. It's not cheap—I believe my copy cost $50.00—but it's worth every penny of it.

I should add that some books consisting of fanzine articles, such as *The Conan Reader, The Conan Swordbook* and *The Conan Grimoire*, all from the two-time Hugo-winning fanzine *Amra*, have nothing to do with fandom; whereas the numerous *Fanthologies*, which collect the best fan articles of the year, would be of interest to anyone who enjoys fine fannish writing. (The *Fanthologies*, by the way, are sponsored by the annual Corflu convention, with a new volume appearing every year. As I write these words, they're up to 1993.)

NOVELS

There have actually been seven professional novels about science fiction fandom. Six are set at conventions. Perhaps even more surprisingly, five of them are murder mysteries. Or maybe it isn't so surprising at all.

The two best—both of them quite brilliant—are by Barry Malzberg, writing early in his career under the pseudonym of K. M. O'Donnell (his tribute to Henry Kuttner and C. L. Moore, who often wrote under the pen name of Lawrence O'Donnell; hence K(uttner) M(oore) O'Donnell.) The first is *Dwellers of the*

Deep, half of a 1970 Ace Double, in which fandom must save the universe from alien invaders. The second, *Gather in the Hall of the Planets*, a 1971 Ace Double, takes place at a Worldcon, and for months after it came out fandom's (and prodom's) favorite game was trying to figure out who was who, because every pro and fan in this mordantly funny book has a real-life analog. (Both are included in an omnibus volume from NESFA Press, *The Passage of the Light*, which was edited by Tony Lewis and myself.)

Gene DeWeese and Buck Coulson wrote a pair of murder mysteries set at Worldcons. *Now You See It / Him / Them . . .* (Doubleday, 1975) takes place at the 1974 Discon II, and *Charles Fort Never Mentioned Wombats* (Doubleday, 1977) is set at the 1975 Aussiecon.

Perhaps the most famous novel about fandom—or at least the best-selling one—is Sharon McCrumb's *Bimbos of the Death Sun* (Windwalker Books, 1987). The fandom is not one I much care for—the convention it's set at is mostly media and gaming—but it's a fine mystery, and in fact won an Edgar Award. She later produced a sequel, *Zombies of the Gene Pool*.

Finally, there's William Marshall's *Sci Fi* (Holt, Reinhart and Winston, 1981), in which a murder takes place in Hong Kong at the All-Asia Science Fiction and Horror Movie Festival. Again, fandom—but not necessarily as we know it.

Peripherally, there's another novel—Niven, Pournelle, and Flynn's *Fallen Angels* (Baen, 1991)—in which thinly-disguised fans appear and *Mimosa* itself is mentioned, but this, unlike those already mentioned, is not a novel *about* fandom and/or conventions, but merely a science fiction novel in which some of the characters are fans. I suppose if you stretch the definition far enough, you could even include Frederic Brown's delightful *What Mad Universe?*, since the entire story takes place in a universe imagined by a goshwowboyoboy teenaged fan (or, more accurately and confusingly, presumed by an editor to be a universe that this particular fan would create — and even that's not exactly right, but it's close enough.)

There are two more books that must be mentioned. Neither is a professional novel, but each was co-authored by a pro, and their place in the history of fannish literature is secure. I'm referring, of course, to the classic work of fan fiction, *The En-*

chanted Duplicator, by Walt Willis and Bob Shaw (a Hugo-nominated writer as well as a fan). This completely charming allegory follows the adventures of Jophan as he sets out to find the Enchanted Duplicator and publish the Perfect Fanzine. It was originally published in Belfast, Northern Ireland, in 1954, and has been reprinted so many times I've lost track of all the editions.

Then, 37 years later, Willis teamed up with another fan-turned-Hugo-nominated-pro, James White, to produce *Beyond the Enchanted Duplicator . . . To the Enchanted Convention*. It was published by Gerry Sullivan's PROmote Communications in 1991, and to be honest, it's not up to the level of its predecessor, though it's still an enjoyable read.

FANZINES AND PROZINES

Remember a book called *Seduction of the Innocent*, by Frederic Wertham, M.D.? It's the study that suggested Batman and Robin did more together than fight crime, that the Phantom Lady was the logical successor to Gypsy Rose Lee, and that William Gaines of E. C. Comics was in league with the devil. In the end, it was the prime reason the Comics Code was created.

Well, that same Frederic Wertham began seeing his name reviled in one fanzine after another—the editors thoughtfully sent copies to him, since he couldn't purchase them on the newsstands—and lo and behold, a few years later he wrote a flattering, if shallow, study of them, called it *The World of Fanzines*, and sold it to Southern University Press, which published it in 1973.

The only other book about fanzines would be the *Fanzine Index* by Bob Pavlat and Bill Evans, which purports to list every fanzine "From the beginning through 1952." Assuming that it was published in 1952, I've never seen an original; but it was reprinted (I assume) and published (I know) in 1965 by Harold Palmer Piser.

A lovely, nostalgic book, one that demonstrates exactly what fannish enthusiasm is all about, is *A Requiem for Astounding*, by Alva Rogers, an issue-by-issue study of the golden days of John Campbell's *Astounding*, in which Rogers' less-than-scintillating prose is more than compensated for by his boundless enthusiasm. He imparts that sense of almost unbearable anticipation he—and so many other fans—felt while waiting for each new issue, the agony of not knowing the end of a Heinlein or van Vogt serial for weeks on end. It was published in 1964 by Advent, which tried to recapture the magic in 1986 with *Galaxy: The Dark and Light Years*, by David L. Rosheim, but while *Galaxy* was a fine magazine, in ways even better than Campbell's, the book is a failure. Far from being the adulatory fan that Rogers was, Rosheim didn't even read *Galaxy* during Horace Gold's editorship; and since he can't capture the sense of enthusiasm Rogers imparts, what remains is a simple recounting of the stories—which has been done better by many other writers and critics.

MISCELLANEOUS

A chapbook of absolute brilliance is *The Best of Elmer T. Hack*, by Jim Barker and Chris Evans, a BFA/Hack Press Publication, printed in England in 1979. Elmer T. Hack is a cartoon character, a science fiction writer who represents the hack of your choice. The comic strips are hilarious, and there are some mock biographical tidbits and an interview of sorts. Delightful.

Fandom is For the Young, or One Convention Too Many, by Karen "K-Nut" Flanery and Nana Grasmick, a vanity hardcover published by Vantage Press in 1981, is not very well-written, and far too media-oriented for my taste. Then there's a wonderful little chapbook called *Love's Prurient Interest*, by Cathy Ball, published by the Norman Oklahoma Science Fiction Association in 1983. I still don't know if it's a parody of fandom set in a romance book, or a parody of romance books set at a science fiction convention, but I do know I liked it enough to purchase it for my 1988 anthology, *Shaggy B.E.M. Stories*, where it appeared alongside parodies by Asimov and Clarke and didn't have to take a back seat to either.

Closing out the miscellaneous section are a pair of one-shots by Earl Kemp. Both are in symposium form (i.e., numerous answers to the singular question posed by the title). The first, *Who Killed Science Fiction?*, published in 1960, won the Hugo Award; the second, *Why is a Fan?*, is as valid today as when it was published back in 1961.

SO WHAT'S NEXT?

That takes care of my library, and should provide a sufficient answer to those neofen who were afraid we doddering old folk would take all this fannish history to the grave with us.

So what's next? Well, as fandom both grew and splintered, it became obvious than neither Harry Warner nor any other single author could do justice to an entire decade of fannish history. But we have three decades to catch up with—the 1960s, 1970s and 1980s—and in three more years we'll have a fourth.

Well, cheer up. Trufandom, never willing to let an opportunity to publish slip by, is currently, under the leadership of Rich Lynch, preparing the definitive history of fandom in the 1960s. And after he collapses and dies of overwork, I'm sure The Widow Nicki will be more than happy to take over and organize the authors who will codify the 1970s and 1980s.

As for me, I look forward to planting flowers on their graves (right next to Algernon's), and reading those soon-to-be-assembled histories.

For Mimosa #21 *(slightly revised for this book)*

UH . . . GUYS—
MY NAME ISN'T KORIBA

Let me begin with an immodest statement: the Kirinyaga stories are pretty good pieces of fiction.

The fans think so. The first one won a Hugo, and the second was nominated for a Hugo.

The pros think so. The first two were Nebula nominees, the third is currently leading the list of recommendations for the 1991 Nebula, and the fourth, though it's only been out for a month (I'm writing this in late August), has already secured a place on the 1991 Nebula Preliminary Ballot.

The publishers think so. They have appeared in the two most prestigious prozines in the field—*F&SF* and *Asimov's*; Tor bought the only novella in the cycle as a lead title for a Tor Double; and a number of publishers have asked for the chance to bid for them when the stories are finally collected in book form.

The critics . . .

Well, um, yeah—the critics.

The fact of the matter is that these little fables have driven the critics to distraction. I have been accused of everything from racism to sexism to jingoism to (name the "ism" of your choice here). In fact, about the only thing I *haven't* been accused of is poor writing—so, since we all agree that the Kirinyaga stories are well-constructed and well-written, I think it might be interesting to see just what it is about them that so annoys the critics.

The narrator of all the Kirinyaga stories is a fanatic named Koriba. He is a fictional construct. He is based on many Kikuyu I have met, but none of them are named Resnick. He—and the real-life sources from which he was drawn—deeply believe in the traditional Kikuyu lifestyle. He feels that the intrusion of Western culture has destroyed that lifestyle, and his notion of Utopia is a return to the way things were before the Europeans showed up to bring them the dubious benefits of civilization.

Resnick, on the other hand, believes in air-conditioning, running water, electricity, and microwave ovens. It is important that you keep this in mind as the article progresses. Just keep saying to yourself: Resnick is a writer, and Koriba is his fictional construct. (There. That wasn't so hard, was it?)

(Well, maybe it was, as witness:)

Rebecca Ore, writing to *The New York Review of Science Fiction* (which I am convinced exists solely to keep me from becoming over-confident in my gifts, such as they are), says, "Is Resnick's space-bottled African culture ever sexist!"

Uh . . . that's not *Resnick's* African culture, gang—and therein lies the crux of it. This isn't Resnick's Africa; it is the Kikuyu's Africa as it existed in 1885, and as it exists today. Women are second-class citizens, no question about it. In fact, there is no word for "woman" in Swahili; the closest one can come is *"manamouki,"* which means "female property,"and applies equally to women, cows, sows, bitches, mares, and ewes. Pay attention now: this isn't the way Resnick *created* it; it's the way he *found* it.

I'm not even sorry that it offends Rebecca. It was supposed to; hell, it offends *me*. But is it valid to criticize the author for representing a society as it exists, rather than as we wish it would exist?

"I'm all for cultural relativism that's not imposed by an elite whose life is going to be much the same whether peasants or electric fixtures hold the lights while they party," concludes Ms. Ore.

Roughly translated, this means: I am all for cultural relativism as long as it is imposed by an elite with whom I find myself in agreement. So are we all—which is one of the reasons that colonialism came into being in the first place.

Now, the driving force behind Koriba's motivation in the first few Kirinyaga stories is to free his people from all Western influence, even if that means they must give up all those things that Resnick holds dear: Monday night football, automatic transmissions, computers, paved roads, blood pressure medication, and so forth. Not a story goes by that Koriba doesn't give numerous examples of exactly how (in his opinion) the Kikuyu culture became corrupted by exposure to Western influence.

Gordon van Gelder, writing in *The New York Review of Science Fiction*, concludes his excoriation of "Kirinyaga" with the following paragraph:

"Given my penchant for venturing to Africa every ten years, I expect I'll return to Kenya three or four years from now.

With luck, I'll be able to spend as much time in the country as I'd like, be able to make new friends and share experiences, and perhaps impress upon some people the ideals in which I believe. Ideals I hadn't realized I still felt strongly about until I read 'Kirinyaga'."

Words to warm a writer's heart: I actually made the man think, and reexamine his beliefs.

On the other hand, I don't seem to have made him think very deeply or very rationally: he knows at a gut level that his cherished beliefs are right and the Kikuyu's are wrong, and he's already planning on going to Kenya to give them still further exposure to White American Middle Class Values. Obviously, this is just what they need. (Contributions for Mr. van Gelder's headstone may be sent to this address. Remember to include postage, as we shall almost certainly have to mail it to Kenya.)

Robert Killheffer, writing in (surprise!) *The New York Review of Science Fiction*, has absolutely no knowledge of things African, so he proceeds to tell his readers why "Kirinyaga" doesn't apply to American Indians. And why shouldn't he? I mean, after all, they're non-white and non-high-tech, so they must be a) identical, and b) in serious need of Western culture, right?

Now, it was after Killheffer's article appeared that I wrote to *The New York Review of Science Fiction* and suggested that since everyone who had thus far attacked the "Kirinyaga" stories seemed woefully ignorant of Third World cultures in general and the Kikuyu culture in particular, I would be happy to supply all future critics with a recommended reading list if they would just take the trouble to request one.

The aforementioned Mr. van Gelder affixed a postscript to my letter, recommending Marjorie Shostak's *Nisa: The Life and Worlds of a !Kung Woman*. Nothing wrong with that, I suppose—except that the !Kung are hunter-gatherers and the Kikuyu are agricultural; the !Kung live almost 3,000 miles away from the Kikuyu and possess a stone-age culture, while the Kikuyu had worked with iron and had an incredibly complex social structure long before the Europeans arrived; and the !Kung have been hunted to the brink of extinction by their neighboring tribes, whereas the Kikuyu are the dominant tribe of East Africa. But what the hell—they're all non-white, non-Western, and non-high-tech, so what's the difference, right?

Now, lest you think this is a grudge match against *The New York Review of Science Fiction*, let me assure you that it isn't. They actually haven't mentioned the Kirinyaga stories for the past six months, and have contented themselves with criticizing the dedication pages to my most recent novels. But that, alas, doesn't mean the ignorance of our own world among science fiction critics has ceased. Heinlein pointed out in "Solution Unsatisfactory" that you can't embargo knowledge; perhaps he should have pointed out that the same holds true for ignorance.

Gardner Dozois, who told me that nothing receives hate mail at *Asimov's* like the accurate depiction of Third World cultures (hi, Lucius!), has been forwarding it to me quite regularly. Perhaps the most outraged came from a Dr. Anne Rubin, who pointed out that female circumcision *hurts*, and that I was a crude, evil, barbaric man (as well as a sexist pig) for suggesting that it should exist in Kikuyu culture.

Well, the truth of the matter is that I didn't suggest that it *should* exist anywhere in the world. I am guilty only of pointing out that it *does* exist in Kikuyu society, whether Dr. Rubin likes it or not. More to the point, almost 80% of all black African women from *all* African cultures undergo circumcision ceremonies (female circumcision is a euphemism for clitoridectomy, for those of you who haven't figured it out yet.) I think what drives Westerners craziest about the situation is that whenever well-meaning missionaries and/or colonial governments have tried to put an end to the practice, it has been the *women*, not the men, who have protested most vehemently and refused to give up their cherished rite of passage to adulthood.

(It might be well to point out here that some 34 years ago, Robert Ruark wrote a best-selling novel about Kenya. It concerned the Mau Mau Emergency, and was entitled *Something of Value*. The title was not picked at random: when you take away a people's culture, you must replace it with something of value, or you've got a big problem on your hands—a fact that seems not only to have eluded the British and the French and the Italians and the Belgians and the Portugese, but at least some of the people who find fault with the Kirinyaga stories for not toeing the party line, said line being that If We Believe In It, It Must Be Right—And Don't Bother Me With What All Those Illiterate Savages Think.)

Anyway, let's try a different magazine. *Locus* points out in reviewing "For I Have Touched the Sky" and "Bwana": "Koriba's advice now borders perilously close on self-deprecating racism."

Now you know—Koriba's a racist.

Well, not really. What Koriba has pointed out in every story is that the Europeans' culture is not evil in itself—after all, it works just fine for the Europeans—but it is wrong for the Kikuyu. If the Europeans were a) black, or b) polka-dot, would this still be a racist statement, I wonder?

Anyway, the *Locus* commentary goes on to ask: "Is this the best we can do, to return to the primitive? A dismaying thought . . ."

Yes, it *is* a dismaying thought. It's a dismaying practice, and in the stories more than one character suffers considerably because of it. But it is Koriba's dismaying practice, not Resnick's. Honest. Resnick just sits at his computer and transmutes what he has seen in Africa into science fiction stories.

But this does point out another blind spot among the reviewers and critics. So much science fiction is actually a presentation of the author's impassioned arguments in favor of some point of view, a fictionalized polemic as it were, that no one (always excepting the readers and the writers) seems willing to acknowledge that having a narrator take a position that is totally in opposition to what the writer believes (and what he hopes the reader believes) is a legitimate literary device.

So perhaps it's time for a lip-reading exercise. Ready? Here goes. Read my lips:

Koriba is wrong. His Utopia won't work. There will be 10 stories in the cycle, and Kirinyaga is already crumbling around the edges in the fourth story. The author doesn't believe in the viability of Koriba's Utopia—but Koriba does, and for the character (who, let us never forget, is a fanatic) to ring true, he must never doubt that it is both possible and viable.

I shudder to think what the critics would make of a story that fairly and truthfully represented Ayatollah Khomeni or Saddam Hussein. (Actually, I know what they'd think. As Gardner Dozois and Barry Malzberg and others have said, make 'em aliens and you can do anything you want with 'em. Just don't tell anyone that they might actually exist as human beings; it makes people uncomfortable. This seems to have held true for my novel, *Paradise*, which is nothing but a thinly disguised allegory of Kenya's history—but because my Kikuyu became fur-covered aliens called Bluegills, not a single voice was raised in protest to any of their beliefs or attitudes. Curious, isn't it?)

In reviewing "The Manamouki," *Locus* pointed out that "Today's lesson from Kirinyaga is that people with different ways must be rejected or disharmony will result." This is a difficult concept for Americans to swallow, since we live in a melting-pot—but the history of the world (and not just the Third World) would tend to show that people with different ways must be rejected or disharmony will result.

How different must the ways be? Not very. Idi Amin slaughtered 300,000 of his fellow Ugandans; his successor, Dr. Milton Obote, slaughtered 400,000 more; and *his* successor, General Okello, wiped out another 400,000. How the hell different can one Ugandan be from another? (The answer, for those critics who have stopped burying their heads in the sand long enough to take a breath, is: different enough.)

In fact, as I sit here writing this (late August, 1990, three days before taking another trip to Africa in search of story material to make the critics twitch), the death total in Soweto has topped 600 for the month. These were not blacks who were killed by whites. These are blacks—Xhosa and Zulu—whose ways were different enough from each other that they temporarily forgot exactly who has been oppressing them lately . . . so, leaving aside whether he understood what the story was really about, maybe the lesson the *Locus* reviewer received from "The Manamouki" was not totally invalid when applied to the world which he inhabits.

Charles Platt's credentials as a critic are well-known in the field. He and I have entered a long correspondence about the Kirinyaga stories, which will be published in Charles' own fanzine in the next few months, but I'm sure he won't mind my quoting two paragraphs of it here, since they constitute what I believe to be the core of his arguments:

"Personally, I think it is an outrage that science fiction, which has the potential to do great good by stimulating the imagination and encouraging a problem-solving attitude toward the future, is used in such a way that it may encourage the reverse: hobbling the imagination and turning away from problems that seem too difficult to face. This is the mood of the times, among many people scared of technology, and *your stories are encouraging it* [italics his]. You show primitive people on a space colony freely choosing to go back to traditions such as clitoral circumcision, voodoo, and child sacrifice, because the alternative was even worse. To leave it at that, and never even imply a third path might exist, is a disgraceful piece of oversimplification.

"It is also a paternalistic, racist insult to African tribes who have happily transcended the superstitions and barbarisms of their past. Would they agree with you, that European ways are not their ways, and cannot ever work for them? More likely, they'd be furious with you for writing a story in which they are shown as savages who can never hope to become anything more than savages without fucking up their world."

That second paragraph is so culturally myopic, so offensive to people who live in a complex society that resents the intrusion of our Western values, so typical of the reaction that the Kirinyaga stories have received from a handful of critics, one scarcely knows where to begin.

But probably I should begin by addressing the initial paragraph and pointing out (this is a recorded message) that my name isn't Koriba. *I* don't hold his truths to be self-evident; *he* does. The fact that a third path might exist has of course occurred to Resnick—but Koriba is a fanatic, and precious few fanatics see a plethora of alternatives to what they believe. (I also find it difficult to believe that someone finding my story stuck in the middle of a science fiction magazine will forthwith eschew all technology, but let it pass.)

(I suppose I should add, parenthetically, that Koriba has *never* referred to the Kikuyu as "savages" or as "barbarians," nor do he or Resnick believe them to be. That choice of definitions we leave to Caucasian critics.)

As for African tribes who have happily transcended the superstitions and barbarisms of their past, I'm very tempted to say "Name three" (but only because I'm polite: "Name one" is just as tough a question.) Certainly we all know that Uganda had just a little bit of trouble adjusting to life as an independent nation . . . but because these nations are non-white and non-high- tech, we—and our press—tend to overlook the fact that none of the other sub-Saharan nations are doing a hell of a lot better.

In the Central African Republic, the self-proclaimed Emperor Bokassa slaughtered literally 70% of his country's population; Equitorial Guinea's dictator matched that number *and* burned the treasury, just so no one else could spend it; President Joseph Mobutu has banked all five billion dollars of aid we've sent to Zaire, while at the same time his people have actually deserted the cities and gone back to living in the bush; Hastings Banda, the American-educated President of Malawi, has the best-trained death squads on the continent; the majority Shona tribe of Zimbabwe has been waging an off-and-on war of genocide against the minority Ndebele tribe for more than a decade; Tanganyika and Zanzibar did not become Tanzania until more than a million Arabs had been slaughtered; the death toll in the Mozambique revolution recently passed the three million mark; the first thing the free slaves who settled Liberia did was sell the people they found there into slavery; even the placid, gentle Bushmen of the Kahahari have been hunted to near-extinction by their neighbors in Botswana, Namibia, Zimbabwe, and South Africa.

In 1973, no less than four African presidents had indulged in cannibalism; when Julius Nyerere retired as President of Tanzania in 1985, he was only the second president in African history to retire voluntarily (as opposed to dying in office, being killed in office, or being thrown out of office); and 35 sub-Saharan nations are currently listed as human rights violators by Amnesty International, including the two most modern, capitalistic, high- tech, Westernized countries—South Africa and Kenya.

Now, that's an unpleasant catalog, and I have a feeling that a lot of critics such as Charles and those others I've quoted would prefer that we just sweep these facts under the rug, since they conflict with their worldview—but if it is the job of the fiction writer to examine the human condition, he hamstrings himself artistically by starting with false premises, however unpleasant the truth may be.

When I set out to write the Kirinyaga stories, I thought that if properly done, they could be powerful and they could move people—but I never anticipated that they could place so many critics so uncomfortably face-to-face with their own beliefs. These were going to be (and I think *are*) simply little fables, morality plays if you will, told from a point of view that, while existing in the real world, is as alien to us as any character ever created on Mesklin or Barsoom or Arrakis.

I think, in retrospect, that if I'd have made Koriba a native of Mesklin or Barsoom or Arrakis, the series might have come out, pleased some readers, failed to make a single critic uncomfortable, and vanished without a trace.

All things considered, I'm glad I didn't.

Postscript: the mail just arrived—and I find that a friend, who is probably laughing his head off, has sent me the text of a speech that was given at a recent convention in Chicago. The gist of it is that Resnick may think he's created a Utopia, but it sure as hell isn't a Utopia for women.
Sigh

For Science Fiction Review #5

ORLANDO SAFARI DIARY

Lyn Nichols and Louise Rowder, influenced in their formative years by my safari diaries, asked me to post an Orlando Trip Diary, and in a moment of total weakness, I agreed. So here it is.

I should begin by saying it's all Ray Herz's fault.

Well, his and Christini's.

We had never been to Orlando before Ray invited me to be Guest of Honor at Oasis II back in 1989. We decided to take a few extra days to see the various attractions. MGM/Disney was newly opened, not very big, and hideously over-crowded, so we left before noon and decided to have lunch. Someone had told us that there was a fabulous restaurant named Christini's on Dr. Phillips Boulevard, just a couple of miles from our hotel. We went there, only to find that it didn't serve lunch and was open only for dinner. So we figured we'd drive around a little and see what else was open—and drove, quite by accident, to a gorgeous, upscale residential area a mile away, an area known—depending on where in it you happen to be—as South Bay or Bay Hill. We were charmed by it. And, after a couple of minutes of driving through it, we looked at each other and said, you know, we could *live* here.

We've been going back at least once a year, scouting upscale areas, checking prices, etc. This was our sixth trip, and we essentially wanted to check out builders and architects in case what we wanted wasn't on the market when we sell our home (which we plan to put up for sale next February or March).

Tuesday, Sept. 27, 1994:

We landed at Orlando's spacious and truly beautiful airport, rented a Lincoln Town Car (I don't change horses, or cars, in mid-stream), grabbed a couple of gyros sandwiches at the Mercado kiosks, and checked into our hotel, a Fairfield Inn just off International Drive that Dick Spelman had discovered: $34 a night, including free breakfasts, free newspapers, free coffee, free faxes, and free local phone calls. We then set out to check all the upscale developments in the southwest quadrant of the city and suburbs. There's some lovely stuff there.

We dined at Chatham's Place, arguably Orlando's best restaurant; it's not for every night—it was $100 for the two of us, and I don't drink; steep but worth it—but wonderful for special occasions. Later that night we went out for coffee to the Peabody's all-night coffee shop, the B-Line Diner, where none of the waitresses had any memory of Magicon. I guess holding the masquerade elsewhere makes a difference.

Wednesday, Sept. 28:

We drove to the northeast quadrant and checked out Riverwalk and Riversbend. Lovely homes and forested setting at Riverwalk, but we ruled it out; it's at least an hour from all the things we want to move to Orlando for. (And no, Disney isn't one of them; after 6 trips, we've yet to set foot inside the Magic Kingdom, and plan to keep our record intact.) We stopped to shop at the Belz Outlet Mall—175 national chains in 6 buildings—and while I do not know to this moment what Carol bought, I know I got a pair of Johnson & Murphy shoes that retail at $122 for $46. Carol's foot started hurting then—she's going in for foot surgery on October 20—so I dumped her off at the hotel. Then I decided to drive through the Bay Hill/South Bay area that had attracted us to Orlando in the first place. It's perhaps 2 square miles, and as I drove through it, captivated again by its ambience, I stopped and wrote down the address of every "For Sale" house that looked to be about the size we wanted. Then I stopped by a real estate office, found a hungry employee, and laid these 35 addresses on her, promising that she could be our agent next spring if she would order her computer to give me readouts of the addresses. It took less than an hour—16 were too large or too small or too expensive or too inexpensive (yes, a house can be too inexpensive: we *have* to spend X dollars or pay taxes on the difference) . . . but when the dust cleared, there were 19 houses with the proper square footage (3800 to 4300), the proper amenities (enough wall space, swimming pool and hot tub, etc.), and the right addresses—and if our house sells for anywhere near its appraised value, we can afford all but two of them. So I took all the readouts back to the hotel, showed them to Carol, and we decided that since this is the slow season, they'll probably have 30 houses in our range and with our requirements comes springtime, and since we both prefer this area above all others in Orlando, it's almost a dead certainty that we'll be buying an existing house here when we finally decide to make the move.

Dick Spelman and Pat and Roger Sims had arrived during the day, and we met them for dinner at the excellent steak and seafood restaurant, Charlie's Lobster House, in Mercado Center. Also joining us was Linda Dunn, whose company had sent her down to Orlando for a week's seminar on something esoteric concerning computers, and who was floating on air over having just made a sale to Analog. (Prior to that, she had sold a couple of stories to Marion Zimmer Bradley, one to me, and a couple elsewhere.) It being a clear and lovely night, we played miniature golf at the Pirate's Cove course right next door. Then I dropped Pat and Carol off, Linda went to her hotel, and I treated The Guys to desserts at the B-Line, which I think is destined to become my late-night hangout when I move here, just as the Perkins 4 miles away is now.

Thursday, Sept. 29:

We were up bright and early (ugh) and went to Sea World, which I hadn't seen in 5 years. The dolphin and whale shows are enjoyable, but the truly fascinating things are the walk-through displays of a coral reef and "Terrors of the Deep," where you take a tunnel through the middle of a 300,000- gallon aquarium filled with sharks, baracudas, eels, and what- have-you, all swimming beside, above and below you. It was hot and humid, and Carol and I left before the others. We drove through South Bay/Bay Hill again, and jotted down about 10 more addresses with *very* discreet "For Sale" signs I had missed the first time through. Then I popped over to the airport to pick up my father, who was arriving in late afternoon in Terminal B (Dick was picking up his sister, Betty, in Terminal A at just about the same time), and we all met for dinner at The Butcher Shop in the Mercado Center—a fine restaurant where you can get a 28-ounce steak or a 33-ounce prime rib—and we were joined by Linda Dunn again. (With 8 of us at the table, it started feeling like a Midwestcon.) After dinner, we dropped Carol and Betty off at the hotel, and took another shot at miniature golf, where I came in 3 strokes below par. Probably even as I write this they're erecting a bronze statue of me somewhere near the course entrance.

Friday, Sept. 30:

We all made our annual pilgrimage to Busch Gardens, the one theme park we never skip, since it's really a zoo with all kinds of African glitz added. Their "Serengeti" area, seen via an overhead monorail, is 300 acres of African plains game, all unfenced and free to mingle (except for the lions), and includes kudu, sable, giraffe, buffalo, rhino, hippo, nyala, impala, wildebeest, and Thompson's gazelle. And what fun it is to watch them hosing down and scrubbing the baby elephants, who just live for their baths and can't stop wriggling and squealing with pleasure!

Busch is maybe 90 minutes each way from Orlando, but as you drive down Interstate 4, you are hardly bored, since there's about a 30-mile stretch where literally 70% of the telephone poles have osprey or bald eagle nests atop them. Dick and Betty drove to Clearwater to eat dinner, but we were too tired to join him, so we returned to Orlando and ate at one of our favorite restaurants, The Phoenician, which specializes in exquisite Lebanese food. Everyone else collapsed. I took a long dip in the pool to cool off, then mosied over to the B-Line with Joseph Heller's *Closing Time*, and read and drank iced coffee for a couple of hours; a sequel to *Catch-22*, which I consider the finest American novel of this century, it's very good when Yossarian is onstage and very boring when he's not.

Saturday, Oct. 1:

While my father went off with Dick and Betty to look at retirement homes—Dick doesn't need one, and probably won't for more than a decade, but he lives by the Boy Scout motto of Be Prepared—we took Pat and Roger out to look at Bay Hill, and to see the condos they and Dick had been scouting out. We'd never eaten Brazilian food, so we stopped for lunch at Cafe Brazil just off International Drive, and liked it enough that we decided to go back to it once more before leaving town.

We drove over to Merritt Island on the Atlantic Coast in the afternoon; half of it is Cape Canaveral, the other half—the half we always visit—is a national wildlife refuge. There's a beautiful trail for cars that covers 17 miles and has 11 viewing stops/platforms, and of course you can stop whenever you want if you see something interesting. Of the 7 or 8 trips we've made there, this was the most gratifying: we saw alligators, wild boar, deer, and a vast array of birds. No one felt like a fancy dinner when we got back, so we went to a fern bar and then played miniature golf, where I busted par *again* and seriously considered turning pro.

Sunday, Oct. 2:

We had brunch at a Friday's on Colonial Drive with about 20 Orlando fans, where Steve and Sue Cole and Dave Ratti and Lloyd McDaniel gave Carol far more information about insects, mildew, and dry rot than any of the guide books told her, and mighty useful it was. Then we cut out to look at open houses. This was the 3rd time we've checked open houses in Orlando, and we've come to the conclusion that they only put white elephants on the market. We've never seen a truly good one yet on a Sunday. Still, we hit every one there was in South Bay/Bay Hill, eight in all, and then went to the somewhat overrated Ming Court for a Chinese dinner, where Jack Haldeman, who had been at the brunch, joined us again. Beautiful building, food nothing special.

After dinner Jack, Roger and I hunted up a bar with a big screen and sat down to watch Shula the Dolphin go up against his son, Shula the Bengal. Our beloved 0-and-5 Bengals were actually leading with a minute to go in the first half. The Dolphins had a 10-point lead 3 minutes into the 3rd quarter, and Roger and I agreed that if we didn't score on our next possession, we'd leave. So the Bengals fumbled, and we left . . . and found out the next morning that if we'd stayed 8 more minutes, we could have watched them set a record by turning the ball over on 5 consecutive possessions. We drowned our sorrows with chocolate sodas at the B- Line and emerged feeling a lot better than Shula the Younger.

Monday, Oct. 3:

We spent the morning letting Dick show us the condos he was interested in—they were all in one development, yclept Sandlake Pointe, about a mile from South Bay—and then went out to do some shopping. One thing we like about South Bay/Bay Hill is the convenience. It's barely walking distance to the Dr. Phillips Center, which has a very upscale supermarket, a larger and less upscale one, 5 restaurants, and about 75 other shoppes (right: shoppes, not shops). It's maybe 3 miles from the

175 discount stores at Belz. It's no more than 2 1/2 miles from all the International Drive restaurants—and while most of International Drive is cheap tourist stuff, the restaurants at Mercado (and maybe a dozen others as well) are excellent quality, and I'm already a late-night B-Line addict. It's perhaps 12 miles from the airport. And it's about 6 or 7 miles from the Florida Mall, the biggest shopping mall in Florida, containing 206 stores (including 6 "anchor" department stores) under one roof, and another 200 stores accessible without leaving the parking lot. The complex is 4 blocks by 4 blocks. For those who are into amusement parks—and we're not; for most of them except Busch, once every two or three years is plenty for us—its about 5 miles from Sea World, 3 miles from Universal, and perhaps 10 miles from Disney. (However, there are great restaurants and fireworks displays at EPCOT, and with a yearly pass I can see us popping over there every couple of weeks just for dinner and a light show.)

In the afternoon, we went to MGM/Disney with Pat and Roger. I don't know what foreigners think of this particular theme park, but I am convinced it taps a racial memory among Americans. Very small compared to, say, EPCOT, easy to do the whole thing in 4 or 5 hours, and when you come out the first thing you want to do is go to your local Blockbuster Video and rent out the entire "Classics" section. We all met up at Caruso's Palace, a gorgeous building on International Drive, with, for a change, food even more fabulous than the decor. Swam in the hotel's pool and even convinced Carol to come with me to B-Line for coffee.

Tuesday, Oct. 4:

We hit the last few developments, just to be thorough: MetroWest, Sunset Lakes, a few others . . . saw Waterford Pointe again and reconfirmed our decision to build there if we can't find a standing house in South Bay/Bay Hill . . . dropped my father at 3 apartment complexes where he found out they offer the same facilities and much the same floor plan he has in San Diego and charge less money . . . and ate in a charming "ladies' lunch"-type spot, the Parramore House, in Windermere. We spent a couple of hours checking out a list I had obtained of all the lakefront properties for sale in Windermere, found they were much too, shall we say, optimistically priced, stopped at

Belz and the Florida Mall again, and met Dick and Pat and Roger for a final dinner at the Bubble Room, which is fast becoming my favorite Orlando restaurant. The food is excellent and the helpings enormous, but it's the decor that gets me: old photos of Hollywood stars, old pieces of sheet music, and quite possibly every toy sold between 1938 and 1948. You walk through the place—and it takes literally hours—and relive your childhood (at least, if you were born in 1942, as I was). We tried a new miniature golf course, Congo River, where I came in 19 strokes over par and decided to stick to sf writing after all.

Wednesday, Oct. 5:

Pat, Roger and Dick all left for Cincinnati in the morning. We stopped by a new set of discount outlets right next to Belz, where I bought a $425 sports jacket for $99; and a just-opened Saks Fifth Avenue outlet called Off Fifth, where I got an autumn safari jacket, retail $179, for $51. I collect cloth patches (badges? labels?) from all the African camps and parks we stay at; Carol says when we get home she'll so them all onto the safari jacket.

We had lunch at the Florida Mall, which has some 35 or 40 kiosks in their food section, including Darbar's, which used to be my favorite Indian restaurant in the whole damned country. (It closed its doors on Dr. Phillips Boulevard and is looking for a new location, and is keeping its hand in by serving fabulous Indian meals for a pittance on paper plates and styrofoam cups at the Mall.)

After lunch we drove down to Kissimmee, where we spent an hour or two in the World of Orchids, a wonderful exhibit with at least 6,000 orchids in bloom. (Carol used to raise them in our greenhouse, until they began dying by the hundreds during our African trips; now she raises hardier stuff, but she still loves orchids). Also stopped by a swimming pool place to look at models and ask some stupid questions in case we have to build rather than buy. I did some writing in the hotel (Actually, I wrote almost every night, but seem to have forgotten mentioning it til now), cooled off in the pool for an hour, and then we all went to the B- Line for a late-nite dinner of Eggs Benedict and other temptingly- presented cholesterol.

Thursday, October 6:

Slept late for a change. In the early afternoon, after another lunch at Cafe Brazil, we went to Universal, with free passes thoughtfully supplied by local fan Julia Kitzmillo. We'd never been there before; they were constructing it on our first trip, and we never had time on any subsequent Orlando excursion. I give it an A for set decoration; their remakes of Hollywood and New York streets of 50 and 60 years ago felt exactly right. On the other hand, I give it an F for crowd control; they could learn a helluva lot from Disney. We waited in line 35 minutes for the E.T. ride (which, I have to admit, was worth it . . . *once*), and 83 minutes for the 5-minute King Kong ride, which was definitely *not* worth it. Everywhere you looked there were endless lines. There is also a Central African Pavilion somewhere; I asked the 3 or 4 employees who worked closest to the sign announcing it, but none of them seem ever to have heard of it before. Beautiful park, stupidly and ineptly and infuriatingly run.

For dinner we went over to Mercado and tried Josie O'Day's, their Mexican restaurant, which was acceptable but not memorable. Walking thru the Mercado shops, I discovered something called the Conch Republic, where I picked up a half dozen of the Guayabera shirts I'm always wearing in warm weather. And, of course, one last trip to the B-Line, where I'd gotten 4 of the waiters and waitresses reading my books.

Friday, Oct. 7:

We checked out, drove north to Apopka to check out another pool builder; he had 5 pools on display and answered all our questions (which were based on the literature we'd been given at the first pool place we visited). Then we drove to the Wekiva Springs State Park, an absolutely beautiful 6400- acre tract that's still inhabited by black bear, deer, wildcats, and a zillion birds. We drove through it for an hour, then walked around some lovely lagoons for another couple of hours. (When we go back, we've decided to rent a canoe and let Carol do her bird- watching from the water.) After leaving the park, we had lunch at the first of a chain of delis to hit Orlando—Toojay's by name; they're too good *not* to be opening branches down on the south side any moment. Great chopped liver, fabulous blintzes, a *real* deli. Then we went to the airpoint and came home, and found out that Spelman had already put in a bid on the condo he liked in Sandlake Pointe and will probably beat all the rest of us to Orlando.

Oh well—at least we'll have a place to stay next time we go looking.

(Postscript, 2001: Dick Spelman moved to Orlando in late 1994, and Pat and Roger Sims moved down there in 2001. We still live in Cincinnati.

(Carol contracted breast cancer a few years ago. The doctors caught it early, cut it out, radiated her, and cured her completely. But she remains under a Cancer Watch, and since she has complete faith in her local doctors—and Cincinnati is one of the top cancer centers in the country—we've elected to stay here for at least a few more years, until there is no question that the remission is permanent.)

For the GEnie Network

WHAT WORKS FOR ME

I've been going about my writing in pretty much the same way for close to two decades. It's idiosyncratic, and it won't work for you unless you're married to Carol, but I was asked what works for *me*.

Carol is my wife, my uncredited collaborator, and the best line editor I've ever known. You're going to have to take that as a given.

When I get a notion for a book or a story (and so help me, I don't know where they come from, but after you train your mind to think in certain patterns, you'll find that you get dozens every week), I bring it to her and we discuss it. And then we discuss it some more. And then still more. Carol has also trained herself, over the years, to spot ideas and characters that play to *my* strengths, rather than to urge me to write those stories she would choose to write were she at the keyboard. Anyway, once a story has been decided upon, we work out every detail, every setting, every major character. Only when we've got it blocked out do I go out and do my research, on those occasions that research is necessary.

Finally, after a few weeks or a few years (yes, we're always working on 5 or 6 projects at once), when there's nothing left to discuss, I sit down and start to write. I'm not one of those people who can sit there and look at a blank computer screen or a blank piece of paper and wait for inspiration (or let a story "grow organically," which has become a more popular definition of the practice.) When I go to work, I know what every character is going to do or say, if not precisely how they're going to do or say it. I've heard authors state that their characters frequently take on lives of their own and run away with the story. Not mine. *I* pull the strings, *they* go through the motions; if it ever starts working the other way around, then I haven't thought the piece out well enough and I go back to the mental drawing board.

If I'm writing a novel, I'll try to avoid the heavier cerebration for at least 10,000 words or so—after all, half of our potential audience is under 21, and I don't want to scare them off. By the same token, I've long since given up using a thesaurus, on the assumption that if *I* have to look it up, so will my reader, and I think the most important quality a writer can bring to a piece of work is *accessibility*. There is no concept so deep or so difficult that it can't be stated in terms the average reader can comprehend—*if* a writer is willing to spend a little extra effort searching for those terms.

I'll usually work four or five nights a week, from perhaps 10:00 PM to 4:00 AM, when the rest of the world is sleeping the sleep of the innocent and there is no one around to bother me. I try to do a draft of a chapter in a single sitting, or two sittings at the very most, just so it will read as if it's all of a piece. (By the same token, I don't read fiction when I'm writing fiction. I don't swipe ideas or characters, but I inadvertently borrow authors' voices. If I *do* read some fiction, Carol can usually tell who the author was by reading the first couple of pages I write that evening, before I get my own voice back.)

Carol gets up before me—hell, the whole world gets up before me—and I always leave the previous night's work on the breakfast table for her to go over it. On first (and sometimes second and occasionally third) drafts, her line-by-line notes will be more voluminous than the manuscript she was reading. When I get up we'll discuss what I did right and wrong, and that evening I'll sit down and do it again . . . and keep doing it again until I get it right. I rarely move on to the next chapter until the previous one is set in stone. When the changes and corrections are properly minor, I'll fix it in the afternoon and finally move on to the next chapter that evening.

Once a chapter seems to be done, I'll read it aloud. Not for an audience; in fact, usually I'll do it alone in my office. This is because of my passion for accessability—and what seems grammatically correct on a page will occasionally sound or feel wrong, and I never want to make the reader stop and re-read a sentence or a paragraph because he didn't comprehend it the first time, or because it seems sluggish or obscure.

When the book is halfway done—and, a few million words into my career, I can usually tell you exactly how many pages the book will go by the time I hit page 50—I take a couple of days off and Carol and I each read the finished section to make sure that it flows properly—for just as two correct sentences don't always belong next to each other, sometimes two chapters are just fine when read separately but are jarring when placed back-to- back.

The process continues for the remainder of the book, and indeed picks up steam. I don't know about other writers, but I'm immortal when I begin a book—but when I have less than, say, 100 pages to go, I am aware of the fact that any moment I may wrap my car around a tree, and they'll farm out the final pages to the worst writer I know. So the last 70 or 80 or 100 pages are done at high speed, usually with nothing but coffee, sandwiches, and occasional naps. Then the book is complete, no one has been hired to destroy my artistic vision (such as it is), and I'm immortal again.

All of my novels are important to me—you'd have to be crazy to make such an investment of time and psychic energy into a project of that length that you considered trivial—but the same is not true of my short pieces. Some of them are works of serious ambition—the Kirinyaga stories, the Teddy Roosevelt stories, some of the others—and I attack these the same way I attack my novels. But a number of them are pieces of fluff—I love writing humor, and science fiction and fantasy short stories are just about the only places you can get away with it on a regular basis—and these I show to Carol only when they're completed, if at all. I don't know why; maybe I'm just more secure in my gifts as a writer of funny short stories.

Do I always listen to her? No.

Does it make a difference? Well, everything I write sells sooner or later . . . but I've never had Carol approve a book or story that didn't sell the first time out of the box. I'm slick enough and industrious enough so that I could still make a decent living without her collaboration . . . but I think the quality of my work would suffer considerably.

So that's how I do it. You can a) steal my secret weapon, or b) devise your own methodology.

For the SFWA Bulletin

HUNTING LAKE

In my life, I have written a grand total of three fan letters to writers. One of the recipients, Barry Malzberg, became my closest friend and occasional collaborator. Another, humorist Ross Spencer, also became a good friend. The third was African writer Alexander Lake, who died on Christmas Day, 1961, a month before I wrote to him. I've always regretted not meetiing Lake, who has been virtually forgotten by the American reading public, despite a number of bestsellers.

I recently moved *Resnick's Library of African Adventure* from St. Martin's Press over to Alexander Books. The primary reason was to bring Lake back into print.

Sounds simple, right? I mean, hell, all editors do is sit on their judgment all day and see what comes in the mail.

Well, sometimes it's not *quite* that easy. Take Lake, for example.

Hell, take the whole damned chronology:

1954: I buy the paperback edition of *Killers in Africa* at age 12, take it to summer camp with me, read it in its entirety once a week for two months. From that day to this, I am fascinated by all things African, I take 5 safaris, I write 13 books and 18 short stories set in Africa, and I never forget that it is Alexander Lake who awakened this passion in me.

1988: St. Martin's Press buys Tor Books. St. Martin's also publishes Peter Capstick's *Library of African Adventure*, a series of classic reprints.

1989: *Ivory* becomes a Nebula and Clarke nominee for Tor right after *Santiago* hits #3 on the bestseller list, and the nice people at Tor look about for ways to keep me happily in their stable. I tell them that if Capstick ever dies or gives up editing the Library, I want to take it over.

1991: St. Martin's informs me that Capstick has moved to a different publisher, and I can edit the Library. I tell them that the first two authors I want to bring back—they've each written two books—are Alexander Lake and John Boyes, a scalawag who was one of the Kenya pioneers and at one time was the white king of the Kikuyu. They reply that they'll reprint the Boyes books, which were written in 1910 and 1928 and are in the public domain, but with so many classics available for free they won't spend a penny to purchase the Lakes, which we all assume are still under copyright. I reluctantly agree—after all, no one else is beating down my door to edit books about killing animals in this Politically Correct year of 1991—and I select three books, by Boyes, F. C. Selous, and Arthur Neumann, for publication, writing new introductions for each.

1992: Alexander Books, which specializes in small editions of trade paperbacks, is feeling expansive and approaches me about writing a mystery novel and editing a line of mass market science fiction. I agree, and suggest that I'd also like to bring the reprint series over from St. Martin's Press, which isn't making any money on them anyway and would probably be happy to let them go, so that we can at least make an attempt to get Lake's books back into print. The publisher, Ralph Roberts, has never heard of Alexander Lake. I loan him copies of *Killers in Africa* and *Hunter's Choice*; he calls back two nights later—he loves them, and he'll start up the African reprint line as soon as I'm ready.

January, 1993: In an attempt to find out who owns the rights to Lake's books, I write to Doubleday's accounting department and ask who they are sending his royalty checks to. Their records only go back to the 1970s, and no royalties have been paid out since then. It takes them a mere 3 months to tell me that.

April, 1993: Ray Feist suggests that I write to the Doubleday legal department to find out what literary agent represented Lake during the contract negotiations. (If he did it himself, I'm out of luck, and the search—and project—ends here.) Doubleday takes four months to respond that Lake was represented by the McIntosh and Otis Agency.

August, 1993: I write McIntosh and Otis and ask who owns the rights to Lake's books. They write back to tell me that they've never heard of Lake. I write back and suggest they check their files back to the 1940s. They write back to say that they did, and they've still never heard of him. This correspondence takes nine weeks.

October, 1993: Once more I write to the Doubleday legal department and tell them that McIntosh and Otis has no record of representing Alexander Lake, and could they please check the contracts again? They do, and finally direct me to Elizabeth McKee of McIntosh, McKee and Dodds. I write to her and ask who owns the rights to Lake's books. No answer. I write again. No answer. I phone. She's out of town on an extended vacation.

January, 1994: Ms. McKee writes to tell me that yes, she did indeed represent Alexander Lake in the early 1950s, but she has had no word from him or his literary estate in more than a third of a century. She no longer has any records telling her who his literary heirs are. She has no idea where to look.

February, 1994: I call my own literary agent, Eleanor Wood, explain the problem, and ask for suggestions. She gives me the number of the Copyright Department of the Library of Congress. Maybe, she suggests, the books are public domain. If *Killers in Africa*'s copyright wasn't renewed in 1981, it's mine for the taking; if it *was* renewed, at least I'll be able to find out who renewed it.

March, 1994: I call the Copyright Department. They ask what years the two books were originally published, then tell me to send them $40.00 for each title to track down the copyright status. I send them a check for $80.00 on my birthday, March 5.

June, 1994: It is now two years since Alexander Books has agreed to publish *The Resnick Library of African Adventure*, and Ralph understandably wants to know where it is. I tell him that I moved it from St. Martin's for the express purpose of publishing Alexander Lake, and I'm not giving him any other titles until I know beyond all doubt the Lake is unobtainable. He runs his own copyright check—evidently publishers have access to the Copyright Department's data—and can't find a renewal. I agree that if they're public domain we'll publish them, but I won't be satisfied until I get it in black-and-white from the Copyright Department. Ralph mutters and grumbles, but agrees to postpone the *Library* until 1995.

July and August, 1994: I call the Copyright Department weekly, trying to find out what happened to my request. I never get the same person twice, and no one there seems to know what's going on.

September, 1994: I give up trying to get a response out of the Copyright Department. I promise WorldComm that if I still haven't determined Lake's copyright status by the end of the year, I'll give them a different title to kick off the new line.

October, 1994: *Finally!* The Copyright Department tells me that Lake's children, Storm Alexis Lake-Bartel and Richard K. Nelson, renewed the copyrights, and gives me their addresses as of 1987: Storm is at a post office box in La Honda, Richard is in San Mateo. I call Ralph Roberts to tell him the news. Now comes the tricky part: if either of them say No, that's the end of it, and my dream of bringing Alexander Lake back into print is dead . . . so I have to decide which of them is more likely to say Yes. All I have to go on is their names. There's a son, Richard, who *should* be called Lake and isn't (I don't know at the time that he's a stepson; for all I know, he's a blood son who hated Lake and took on a stepfather's last name to spite him); and there's a daughter, obviously married, who could reasonably be expected to have dumped Lake's name but chose to keep it: Lake-Bartel. Easy choice. I write to the daughter. And two weeks later the letter comes back, Address Unknown.

November, 1994: My very last chance is to make contact with the son. I write to the San Mateo address. It comes back, Address Unknown. I am so close and so far away, I hate to think of what it's doing to my blood pressure. I try to get Storm's phone number from the La Honda operator; no record of a Lake-Bartel. (It turns out that she got divorced sometime after 1987 and is once again going under the name of Lake.) Then I try to get Richard's phone number from the San Mateo operator. I don't have much hope; it's a common name—there are probably ten Richard Nelsons in any fair- sized city. But just for once, Fate is on my side. Thank goodness he uses that middle initial, because while the operator doesn't have a Richard K. Nelson at the address the Copyright Department gave me, she *does* have one in the area code. I take the number, call, leave a message on Richard's answering machine, he calls back, and five years after I start jockeying to bring *Killers in Africa* and *Hunter's Choice* back into print, I finally make contact with the two people who can make it possible, and a week later we're in business.

Easy job being an editor, right? If I make a dime an hour for the time I put in, I think I'll be ahead of the game.

Anyway, as I write these words, *Killers in Africa* is in print, and *Hunter's Choice* is a month from publication and will be in print long before any of you read this. Two-thirds of my Good Samaritan work is done: I got Lake back into print, and I got all of Barry Malzberg's recursive science fiction back into print in one big volume (*Passage of the Light*, written by Barry, edited by me and Tony Lewis, published by NESFA, and you should all run right out and buy it.) If I can just get Ross Spencer's hilarious Chance Purdue novels back into print—and I'm working on it; it should be a fait accompli by the time you read this—I'll feel like I've paid my dues in full.

Since some of you may be wondering what all the fuss is about, here's the introduction I wrote for *Hunter's Choice* which will hopefully whet your appetites:

When we reprinted Alexander Lake's first book, *Killers in Africa*, last spring, we promised you that if it sold at all well, we'd be following it up with his *Hunter's Choice*. The sales figures are in, the readers have spoken, and here it is—another book by that most readable of all authors of Africana.

Encountering an Alexander Lake book is very much like sitting around an African campfire and letting an old pro spin tales of his youth—but while *Killers in Africa* was strictly about hunting, and was divided into chapters about various animals, *Hunter's Choice* is a true potpourri of tales guaranteed to tweak anyone's sense of wonder and adventure.

It even has a chapter unique to African books. Every hunter will happily tell you about the chase and the kill, and then regale you with how wonderful that kudu or impala tasted—but only Alexander Lake tells you, delightfully, *how* to cook that beast once you've killed it.

Ever wonder how to trap sixty monkeys armed with nothing but twenty gallons of bad booze? Trust Lake to supply the hilarious answer.

Could anyone—even Lake's brilliant tracker, Ubusuku—possibly kill the Big Five armed only with a hand axe? Lake describes the hunt that was initiated by a two thousand pound bet (the pre-World War I equivalent of a $100,000 wager) between an American hunter and Lake's employer, Nicobar Jones.

Lake even recounts a jungle murder, and the recovery of three of King John's emeralds.

And, of course, he tells these tales within the framework of his life: an American, with American attitudes and an American way of looking at things, who made his way across the African continent as a professional hunter. He recalls his clients, both good and bad, humorous and tragic, with a contagious fondness.

It is amazing to me that this book could have remained out of print for close to forty years, for it is a pure delight from the first page to the last. Still, while Lake was obviously a happy and contented man, true fame eluded him until the last decade of his life.

He was born Alexander James Lake in Chicago, Illinois, on July 29, 1893. His father was a Methodist minister, and the family moved to South Africa in 1908. Lake went to Jeppestown High School in Johannesburg, and then attended the Marist Brothers College, where he captained the rifle team that represented the Transvaal at the All-British Empire Shumaker Cup. His team came in second, but he himself set a record of 10 bull's-eyes in 33 seconds, which brought him to the attention of the famed trader Nicobar Jones, who hired him as a meat hunter, a job that took him to Portugese East Africa, Tanganyika, Kenya, Uganda, Northern Rhodesia, and German Southwest Africa. Within a couple of years he was a fully-fledged and licensed white hunter.

He took time off from his hunting career to fight for the American forces as a pilot in Europe during World War I, then went back to his beloved Africa for another twelve years, after which he returned to the United States, working as a reporter and editor for a number of newspapers in the Pacific Northwest. Then Africa called to him once again, and he returned there in 1937 for three more years. When he came back to the States in 1940, this time to stay, he met and married his wife, Mildred, and began writing anything that would sell: African reminiscences, business articles, even some pulp fiction.

Says his daughter, Storm Alexis Lake: "He loved being the center of attention, and he was fascinating and fun to be around. He loved life and lived it to its fullest, with a very wild first 40 years. When he met and fell in love with my mother, he became tamed and settled down for the first time in his life. It's amazing what a good woman can do for a man! Once a heavy drinker, after meeting my mother he never touched alcohol again."

After World War II ended, he and Mildred bought a home on the Pacific Coast near the California/Oregon border, and he finally started cracking the major markets—*Look, Collier's, Time, Reader's Digest*—with his accounts of Africa and hunting. His main markets, however, were *Field and Stream* and *Argosy*, where he delighted in debunking the myths of African hunting and setting the record straight.

Killers in Africa became a bestseller in 1953, and *Hunter's Choice* also made the bestseller lists a year later. These led Lake to a job as a consultant and writer for Sol Lesser, producer of the Tarzan films. (In fact, Lake may well be the reason that Gordon Scott was allowed to speak in sentences, rather than monosyllables. At least I'd like to think so.)

Finally, in his last few years, Lake began researching his father's missionary work in Africa. This in turn led him to investigate reported answers to prayer, and that led to two more bestsellers, *Your Prayers Are Always Answered* and *You Need Never Walk Alone*. He died on Christmas Day, 1961, while working on a biography of his father.

I discovered Alexander Lake when I was eleven years old. I picked up a copy of *Killers in Africa*, and had read half of it in the bookstore before my mother realized she was either going to have to buy the book or leave me in the store overnight. A few months later I bought *Hunter's Choice* with money I had earned mowing lawns, and from that day forward I knew two things: that someday I would visit the wonderful continent that Lake had made come alive on the printed page (I have, 5 times now, with more trips planned), and that I would find some way to make my living from Africa (that took a little longer, and considering that I became a science fiction writer, it was a lot more difficult—but I managed. I would confidently suggest that no other science fiction writer, dead or alive, has set 13 books and 22 works of short fiction in Africa or African analogs, or received as many major and minor awards for them. And of course, a lot of Lake's reminiscences have been appropriated, thinly-disguised, in my fiction.)

Before we go any further, I want to tell you a little something about the cover to this edition of *Hunter's Choice*. At first glance it appears to be a scene from Chapter 6 ("Don't Spoil the Heads") of this book, but if you'll look at it closely, you'll see it's really from *Killers in Africa's* chapter on elephants. The giveaway is the figure of Lake himself, on the ground beneath the elephant. The African with the axe is, of course, Ubusuku.

So why didn't we run it on *Killers in Africa*? Simple. I didn't know Storm Alexis Lake then. Over the past few months she has graciously gone through her father's old notes and magazine articles as we try to find enough uncollected material to create a brand-new Alexander Lake book. During one of our phone conversations, she mentioned that she and her brother owned this remarkable painting of her father's miraculous escape from a wounded elephant, rendered by an artist named Kahn. Before she was through describing it, I knew we had the cover for *Hunter's Choice*.

By the way, as the editor of this series, I do try to be thorough, and when it came time to publish *Hunter's Choice*, I thought I would see if I could find a negative opinion, since mine is one of unmitigated praise. Well, I checked every review ever written, and I finally found one, in the September, 1954 issue of *African Wild Life*, published by the South African Wild Life Society, of which less than 2,000 copies were printed. (How's *that* for thorough?)

The reviewer, who uses only his initials—D.E.N.—takes Lake rather severely to task for two misstatements: that lions charge in "forty-foot leaps" and that the lion "is the fastest animal on Earth."

Well, they once measured the stride of the great race horse, Swaps, and it turned out to be 33 feet 8 inches, so I have to assume that Lake—who probably did not have a measuring tape handy when charged by lions—was wrong.

As for his statement that the lion is the fastest animal on earth, I'm sure he was as aware of the cheetah's 65-mile-per-hour speed as everyone else. What you have to remember is that we aren't the only creatures who know lions have very little stamina; lions know it too. Hence, unlike the cheetah, who spots his meal a quarter mile away and then runs it down across open territory, the lion rarely charges more than sixty yards. If he hasn't caught his prey by then, he usually gives up. Now, there is no question that the cheetah is the fastest animal on earth, but it takes him a little time to work up to his top speed, whereas the lion is going full speed with his first stride. I've seen them both in action, and I'd be willing to bet Lake was right—*if* you limit it to the length of ground a lion charges (and since Lake was more aware of a lion's limitations than most men, why would he describe a longer race?) So much for D.E.N., whoever he or she was.

Okay. I've gone on long enough, and you've got a wonderful book to read. I think if I were to choose a single word to describe *Hunter's Choice*, it would be *evocative*. Lake's description of his office, or Ubusuku's hunt, or the mystic power of a Zulu witch doctor, or the Sunday baseball games in Johannesburg, or a lonely Christmas Eve in the bush . . . well, if they don't make you wish you'd been there, then somebody shorted your soul in the areas of Romance and Adventure.

Written for Lan's Lantern, *appeared in* Fosfax

A LIMERICK HISTORY OF SCIENCE FICTION

by Mike Wadsworth Resnick

1926

At the start, Hugo brought out *Amazing*,
In spite of some serious hazing
From lawyers and writers.
(It seems that the blighters
Sought cash for their written star-gazing).

1939

John Campbell then surveyed the field,
And said, "Now this drivel must yield.
I shall draw a fine line
With writers like Heinlein,
And think of the power I'll wield!"

1949

Tony Boucher at once saw the light,
And he said (sounding quite erudite):
"I don't give a fig
If the concept is big —
My authors must know how to write!"

1950

Then Horace Gold quickly appeared,
And he wasn't the failure we'd feared,
Galaxy was afire
With wit and satire —
And the poorer stuff all disappeared.

1964

Then along came Mike Moorcock, who said:
"SF is most certainly dead.
Who wants to re-hash
Even more of this trash?
I'll give them the New Wave instead."

1978

Judy-Lynn del Rey said, "Lester,
Our readers will never dig Bester,
But with cute fuzzy robots
There's no ifs and no buts,
You'll be a most happy investor."

1984

A mirrorshade crowd made the scene,
And said, looking hungry and lean,
"With punks made of cyber,
And no moral fiber,
We'll sweep the bestseller list clean."

1996

When Lucas from college departed,
His vision to film was imparted;
The books have been pleasant,
But quite adolescent —
And now we're right back where we started.

For Lan's Lantern

INTRODUCTION TO FANTASTIC CHICAGO

by Mike Resnick, Chicagoan emeritus

Chicago has always been a hotbed of politics, graft, baseball teams that never quite live up to their potential, more graft, excellent ethnic restaurants, still more graft, and—believe it or not—science fiction.

In the beginning there was E. E. "Doc" Smith, who was the dominant science fiction writer of the 1930s. To quote John Campbell's statement a couple of decades later, "Doc Smith gave us the stars; we're still waiting for the next break-through." Doc, of course, was the first science fiction writer ever to be Guest of Honor at a Worldcon.

And speaking of Worldcons, 1991 will mark Chicago's fifth. (Compare that to New York, home of the editors and publishers, with 3, and the Los Angeles area, home of most of the writers, with 4.)

Which makes sense. Chicago has always had an active fan group, and it's always housed its fair share of writers, too. Back in the 1940s, *Amazing Stories* (the best-selling science fictiom magazine of all time when Ray Palmer was editing it) was published in Chicago, and was mostly written (and ghost-written) by local writers. *Other Worlds* and *Imagination* were also born (and died, probably none too soon) in Chicago. The first, and probably best, of the non-fiction specialty publishers, Advent Books, has been a Chicago institution for more than three decades now, and other Chicago specialty presses have followed in its wake.

The 1952 Worldcon, which finally got around to honoring Hugo Gernsback a year before we started giving out little rocket ships bearing his name, was chaired by Julian May, who has since become a best-selling writer in the field. At various times Fritz Leiber, Frank Robinson, Harlan Ellison, and a host of other major writers have worked out of the Chicago area.

Back when I lived here, we had a little club called the Windy City Writers Conference, and at the last meeting I attended prior to moving to Cincinnati in 1976, it included George R. R. Martin, Algis Budrys, Gene Wolfe, Phyllis Eisenstein, Tom Easton, and Tom Reamy. At the same time, such fans as Martha Beck, John and Joni Stopa, Mark and Lynne Aronson, and Bob and Anne Passavoy were establishing credentials that would make their names synonymous with Fandom.

Today you've got a new generation of pros and fans emerging from the Chicago area, and there's no doubt in my mind that they'll be the professional superstars and fannish legends of 2010 or thereabouts.

And with such a history as that, it's only natural that a number of science fiction stories have been set in future or alternate Chicagos. After all, the East and West coasts may spend all the money, but the City of the Big Shoulders has always paid the bills.

Therefore, it is absolutely fitting that this, the fifth Chicago Worldcon, should publish an anthology of Chicago stories edited by Guest of Honor Martin H. Greenberg, who is indisputably the most influential anthology editor in the history of the field.

Marty lives in Green Bay, which makes him almost a Chicagoan. His complete bibliography would fill a book longer than this one, and the most amazing thing about that bibliography is that he created it without making a single enemy along the way. If there is anyone in the field who is easier to work with — and I say this both as a frequent contributor to his anthologies and an occasional co-editor of them — I haven't found him; if there is anyone with a more commercial sense, nobody has found him; and if there is anyone walking the Earth who is simply as out-and-out *nice*, then Marty must have been cloned when no one was looking.

So here you have it: a fine tribute to almost six decades of the Chicago science fiction community, presented by the one man best able to unearth and assemble these stories.

Enjoy.

THE BEST AFRICAN MOVIES

Steve Silver has requested (read: cajoled, begged, and threatened to hold his breath until he turned blue) that I select and discuss the best films ever made about Africa.

I usually don't write about films, because people usually ask me to write about science fiction films, and I believe the good ones can be counted on the fingers of one mangled hand. But Africa is another matter: there are quite a few good ones, well over a dozen, which is a lot for any one category.

So let's get going.

1. *Zulu* (1964).

This is not only the best African movie ever made for theatrical release, but quite possibly the best war movie as well. It stars Stanley Baker, and features Michael Caine's screen debut.

It's based on a true story. In 1879, four thousand Zulus swept out of the hills and massacred a British column of 1,500 men at Isandhwana. (That story is covered in the much inferior prequel, *Zulu Dawn*, starring Peter O'Toole and Burt Lancaster.) The next morning they attacked a little outpost at Roarke's Drift, some 12 miles away.

Roarke's Drift had 128 men, many of whom were sick or injured. Yet those 128 men held the Zulus off and fought them to a standstill. More Victoria Crosses were presented to the defenders of Roarke's Drift than in any other British military action in history. The movie is a pretty fair representation of what happened, and is absolutely riveting from start to finish.

2. *King Solomon's Mines* (1950).

This one is much the best of four versions of H. Rider Haggard's classic novel of African adventure. Stewart Granger is perfect as Alan Quatermain, the quintessential white hunter who is weary of it all but is talked into one last impossible undertaking. Deborah Kerr is outstanding as the woman who hires him (in the book it was her husband, but Hollywood needs love interests, and this one was better than most.)

The scenery, from desert to savannah to highlands, is ex-

THE BEST AFRICAN MOVIES

quisitely photographed, the wildlife stampede has never been equaled, and Granger seems right at home in the part—as well he should be. He played an almost identical part in *The Last Safari*, a nice but not-quite-outstanding film, and often went on safari himself between films.)

3. The Gods Must Be Crazy (1980).

This is about as charming as movies get to be. Produced, written and directed by the remarkable Jamie Uys, it tells the story—with huge amounts of humor—of the Noble Savage encountering Civilization and overcoming it.

N!xau and the Bushmen are wonderful, and somewhere along the way, Uys found one of the finest physical comedians, Marius Weyers, ever to work in film. From the first scene to the last, the is an ansolutely captivating fable, a charmer on the level of *Harvey* or *They Might Be Giants*.

4. Trader Horn (1931).

This may have been Hollywood's most ambitious undertaking ever. It was the first feature film to be shot on location, it took a couple of years to complete, and a star (Edwina Booth) and a number of crew members died from diseases they picked up there.

This is based on the two-time bestseller (first when it was presented as non-fiction, again after it was unmasked as fiction), about Aloysius Horn, an old African hand who trades up and down the Dark Continent's rivers back in "the earlies," and winds up finding every explorer's dream—a white goddess.

The dialog is absolutely charming, most of it lifted from the book, and Harry Carey delivers it well. A very young Duncan Renaldo, later to become TV's Cisco Kid, co-stars. But the real star is Africa itself, brought to American screens for the first time in a feature film. (Martin and Osa Johnson had brought back the first of their silent documentaries, *Simba*, two years earlier.)

You can see Africa as it was 70 years ago, when it seemed like the animals would go on forever, and the natives didn't climb into their blue jeans and t-shirts when the cameras stopped grinding. A Romantic film, with a capital R.

261

5. *The African Queen* (1951).

Bogart's Oscar winner, well-deserved, with an equally powerful performance from Katherine Hepburn, and a small but memorable cameo by Robert Morley. A classic tale of love and adventure, beautifully told by the master director John Huston.

There's been even more written about the making of the movie than about the movie itself. The novel (later a Clint Eastwood film) *White Hunter, Black Heart* was an expose of Huston's obsession with killing an elephant to the point where he ignored the safety of all involved in the film. Hepburn, too, wrote a book about it.

But when all is said and done, it is the film that is the masterpiece, and the rest, however fascinating, is just associated material.

6. *White Mischief* (1987).

Originally I was a bit disappointed in this film, which stars Charles Dance, Greta Scacchi, and Joss Ackland. It's taken from a book about the murder of a member of Kenya's "Happy Valley" crowd, and most of the book deals with the facts of the murder and the court case.

Then I watched it again, and realized that director Michael Radford had told a totally different story, using the murder merely as a plot device to hold the film together. Kenya was largely populated by remittance men, second sons, dillitantes and no-goods who were no longer welcome in British society. (There was an old saying: "Are you married, or are you from Kenya?" It was said than an entire generation of colonists was conceived on the pool table of the plush Muthaiga Club.)

The movie is actually about the now-vanished days of sex, drugs, drink, parties, and total irresponsibility, and how—because of the murder—they finally came to an end. I was guilty, the first time I saw it, of the cardinal sin of reviewing (in my head, anyway) the movie I wanted to see rather than the one Radford wanted to make. I've seen it four times since then, and have appreciated it more each time.

7. *Mountains of the Moon* (1990).

An old-fashioned, big- budget historical adventure film, the type almost no one makes any more. This is the story of the search for the source of the Nile, and of the friendship between Sir Richard Burton (whose life I science-fictionalized in *A Miracle of Rare Design*) and John Hening Speke, which eventually turned into a bitter rivalry and hatred.

Excellent acting jobs by Patrick Bergin and Iain Glen, and thoughtfully directed by Bob Rafelson. It's not anywhere as romantic as Hollywood would have made it in 1935 or 1960, but it *feels* right.

8. Dingaka (1965).

The very first film by the multi- talented Jamie Uys, who wrote and directed it. This is the flip side of *The Gods Must Be Crazy*, a serious story of the Noble Savage running head-first into Civilization.

It ostensibly stars Stanley Baker, but the true star and the major character is the African played by Ken Gampu, who finds that whether he obeys the law of the tribe or the white man, he breaks the law of the other.

It's just a little out of balance, because to get funding for the film Uys had to spend too much time on a totally meaningless marital crisis between Baker and Juliet Prowse, but the film's virtues—the power of the story, the power of Gampu's acting, and the best musical score ever in an African film—more than make up for it.

9. The Kitchen Toto (1988).

Almost unknown in America, though it's in a few rental stores, this is a powerful and relentless Kenyan film about a small boy, a "kitchen toto," who finds himself trapped in the violence of Mau Mau in 1953.

It's grim, it's accurate, it's well-acted, and director Harry Hook is in total control of his material. I don't think there's ever been a time when this one could have been made in America.

10. Out of Africa (1985).

The only African movie ever to get the Oscar for Best Picture, it's taken from the classic book by Karen Blixen, who just missed beating Hemingway out for the Nobel Prize. The photography is beautiful, Meryl Streep gives the performance of her life, and Klaus Maria Brandauer is excellent as Bror Blixon, about whom numerous books have been written and a good movie should someday be made. No expense was spared, and every penny can be seen on the screen.

So why do I rank so many African films above it?

Two reasons. The first is Robert Redford, who is hideously, fatally wrong for the role. (Denys Finch-Hatten was a balding, well-spoken Etonian, not a California beach boy).

The other is that the film, like the book, doesn't lie in any particular about Karen Blixen's life, but the whole thing is nonetheless a lie. She went home almost every year, spent less than seven years total in Africa though she owned the farm for well over twice that long, took other lovers before Finch-Hatten, was advised by every colonist she knew not to try to grow coffee at her farm's altitude, found new ways to scam living money out of her family every year. None of that was in the book, and it wasn't in the movie, but given the number of Blixen biographies that have been published over the years, it's common knowledge—and since it is common knowledge, I consider it a cop-out that the film tried to present her as a tragic, put-upon heroine. She was one of the most brilliant writers of this or any century; that ought to be enough.

11. *Born Free* (1966).

A truly heart-warming movie about Joy Adamson's extraordinary experiment: to successfully reinsert a human-raised lion into the wild. You couldn't ask for two better people to play the Adamsons that Bill Travers and Virginia McKenna, and James Hill directed the film to perfection.

(Side note: Travers and McKenna—and Hill—made two non- fiction films set in Africa, and both are available in video rental stores: *An Elephant Called Slowly* and *Christian the Lion*. Since they're scripted, I don't list them with the documentaries, but they're both good enough so they should be mentioned *somewhere*.)

The logistics of making *Born Free* must have been enough to drive everyone wild. These weren't trained circus lions, but real African lions, raised by George Adamson. As such, no single lion could do everything the film required. There were four separate Elsas—a car-riding Elsa, an animal-herding Elsa, etc., and the same for most of the others. It is a film that time hasn't diminished, done with love and care.

12. The Gods Must Be Crazy II (1990).

Okay, so Jamie Uys isn't perfect. This one's not quite as good as the original, simply because he has too damned many story lines to keep track of, and while he eventually ties them up, the constant back-and- forth dilutes the power of the fable.

Still, he came up with another top-notch physical comic, this time in the voluptuous person of Lena Farugia. N!xau is back, but has almost nothing to do but ran endlessly after a truck. There are two wonderful children, two hilarious soldiers, and a captivating gangster. It's not up to the first one, but it's still a lot of fun.

Honorable mentions:

White Hunter, Black Heart
The Last Safari
The Naked Prey
Mister Johnson
Sands of the Kalahari
The Air Up There
The Ghost and the Darkness

MADE FOR TELEVISION DIVISION:

1. The Flame Trees of Thika (1981, 7 hours).

It's not fair to compare this film to theatrical releases, because it occurs in 7 one-hour episodes. Of all the countries in Africa that I have been to, Kenya is the one I love and keep returning to. This movie demonstrates much of what I love about it.

It's based on Elspeth Huxley's two autobiographies, *The Flame Trees of Thika* and the first part of *The Mottled Lizard*, and is the story of her childhood in Kenya from about 1910 until the start of World War I. Hayley Mills puts in the best performance of her life at Elspeth's mother, Holly Aird plays Elspeth (but with a different name in the film), and David Robb is her father.

It is the simple story of a British family that buys a plot of farmland, emigrates to Kenya, and tries to make a go of it. Except that, given the location and the era, it's not simple at all.

Farmers in Nebraska and Iowa don't have to face man-eating lions, rampaging elephants, and spear-carrying tribes that don't know what you're doing on their land but know that you didn't buy it from *them*.

It's told with charm and grace, the literate script does Huxley proud, the score is hauntingly beautiful, and director Roy Ward Baker has never been better. As I said, this cannot properly be compared with a theatrical release, but I think it is probably my favorite of all African films.

2. *Shaka Zulu* (1986, 5 hours).

This is the second of the two African masterpieces made for television. The historical Shaka started out with a kingdom no larger than a couple of football fields. By the time of his death 12 years later, he ruled a kingdom three times the size of France. This is his story.

Shaka is brilliantly portrayed by Henry Cele, while the British company that finally makes contact with him features Edward Fox and Robert Powell. They learn his story as we do— through a fascinating, historically accurate two-hour flash-back, in which we see him come to young manhood and totally reinvent the art of warfare. The efficacy of his methods speaks for itself.

So historically accurate was Shaka's village that a tour company bought it when the film was done, and it has become a pricey place to stay while visiting Zululand. Another histori-cally accurate feature was the clothing, or lack of it—an awful lot of the female leads are bare-breasted, which has caused the movie to be cut by as much as two hours when playing on com-mercial TV, so make sure you see it on cable or rent it from a store. Either way, it's worth your time. If I could rank this with the theatrical releases, it would surely make the top five.

NORTH AFRICAN DIVISION:

There have been a lot of films made in Egypt and other parts of North Africa. I assume these were not what Steve meant when he asked me to rate the African films, but there are a few that bear mentioning.

1. The Wind and the Lion (1975).

A wonderful, romantic adventure film, *very* loosely based on an historical incident. Sean Connery is fine as the Raisuli, the last of the Barbary Pirates, and Candace Bergan probably puts in the most believable performance of her life as an American woman he kidnaps. John Huston has a wonderful cameo, the music is superb, and the photography is outstanding. John Milius, one of my favorites, wrote the script and made his debut as a director.

But it was Brian Keith as Teddy Roosevelt that captivated me. Some of you may be aware of my fascination with Roosevelt, and that I've written half a dozen alternate history stories about him. Well, this is the film and the performance that first aroused my interest. Prior to this, I'd always thought of Roosevelt as nothing more than a jingoist, or a buffoon who runs who the stairs yelling "Charge!" (courtesy of *Arsenic and Old Lace*). But after watching the fascinating and intelligent presentation of Roosevelt in *The Wind and the Lion*, I went out and bought every book by and about him that I could find, so this film holds a special place in my heart.

Just on merit alone, it would surely make the top 3 or 4 theatrical releases if I had not seperated North Africa out from the rest.

2. Khartoum (1966).

A fine adventure film that will show you (assuming you ever wondered about it) why a government went to war over a man it despised ("Chinese" Gordon), and why it fell when it could not save his life.

Charlton Heston plays General Gordon, and plays him well. Richard Johnson is good in a secondary part. Ralph Richardson is fine in a cameo. But it is Lawrence Olivier who steals the film as the Mahdi, the Expected One, the bloodthirsty fanatic who at one time controlled most of North Africa.

This is a film about the siege of Khartoum, and as such it's excellent, but it also goes a long way toward explaining two mysteries: Gordon's character, and why Khartoum has such historical importance.

SPECIAL NOTE:

Lawrence of Arabia (1962).

I'll be brief. This is, by far, the greatest movie ever made. When ranking films on an all-time list, there is *Lawrence of Arabia* and there is everything else. It's as simple as that. And since parts of Lawrence take place in Egypt and the Sudan, it qualifies as at least a part-African movie.

FEATURE-LENGTH DOCUMENTARIES:

Thanks to PBS, feature-length documentaries are now an extinct species. But there were some good ones while the species lasted.

1. *The African Elephant* (1972).

A beautiful film, and incidentally the last theatrical documentary ever made about Africa, this was photographed by Simon Trevor and narrated by David Wayne. It follows an African elephant from almost the moment of his birth to his 5-ton adolescence, and closes with some exceptionally rare footage of Ahmed of Marsabit, the huge tusker who was the only elephant ever protected by Presidential Decree.

2. *Animals Are Beautiful People* (1974).

Yes, it's Jamie Uys again, with his one "documentary." I put the word in quotes because it doesn't qualify as a documentary by the strictest definition of the word; there are too many staged shots. But it's done with that wonderful Uys wit, and that makes it a keeper. You'll see elephants get dead drunk on fermented fruit, the world's clumsiest lioness, and some of the most fascinating beetles you can imagine. A delight, as per usual with anything by Jamie Uys. (He died last year, and boy, are we African film buffs going to miss him.)

3. *Simba* (1928).

A silent film, this was the first documentary about African wildlife ever to hit the American theaters, and is the film that made Martin and Osa Johnson superstars. (It's available on videotape, as are half a dozen of their other documentaries, from the Martin and Osa Johnson Safari Museum in Chanute,

Kansas.) It's fascinating to watch, if only to see the incredible hardships a 1920s safari had to undergo. Loading a reluctant camel could take half a day and cost a couple of broken limbs; driving across a rocky country with no roads could kill a car in a day; just crossing a croc-infested river without four-wheel drive was a study in logistics. And along with everything else, you'll get to see something that hasn't taken place in over half a century: a group of Maasai elmoran (young warriors) go lion-hunting armed only with their spears.

Honorable mention: *In the Blood*. Roosevelt descendants go on a nostalgic safari, retracing Teddy's footsteps, led by white hunter and author Robin Hurt and accompanied by *Village Voice* publisher and African novelist Bartle Bull.

Everyone is welcome to disagree with me. (You'll be wrong, but don't let that stop you.) But in the meantime, I hope I've pointed you to some films that have escaped your notice. It's a hell of a continent.

THE GREAT ERB REVIVAL

It's hard to imagine it today, but 40 years ago Edgar Rice Burroughs was considered a children's writer. Only a handful of his books were in print, eight or nine Tarzan titles, and they were published as a matched, cheap ($1.00 apiece) set of hardcovers by Grosset & Dunlap. The only place you could find them was in the Juvenile or Young Adult section of your local bookstore.

Mars? Venus? Pellucidar? If you were born after 1940, there was an excellent chance you didn't know they existed. Yes, ERB Inc. reprinted the Mars and Venus books, but their distribution was dreadful. For example, in Chicago, where I grew up—the second-biggest city in America—only one establishment, Carson Pirie Scott (a department store, not a bookstore) carried the ERB reprints.

All that was soon to change.

I still remember the first of the Ace reprints—it was half of *The Moon Maid* (Ace specialized in splitting any ERB book that was, well, splittable) with a cover by Roy Krenkel.

Science fiction by Mr. Tarzan? Science fiction that wasn't set on Barsoom or Amtor?

I bought it. So did thousands of others.

And pretty soon we began to realize the full extent of ERB's vast imagination—Africa, Mars, Venus, Pellucidar, the Moon, Poloda, Caspak, the Niocine, the Apache books, the cowboy books. And we discovered two brilliant artists who came to be associated with him in the 1960s as J. Allen St. John had been in the 1920s and 1930s—Frank Frazetta and Roy G. Krenkel.

And just about the time Burroughs fans thought things couldn't get any better, especially after that long drought when so much of his work was out of print, presumably forever . . . why, Dick Lupoff took over the editorship of Canaveral Press. Not only did they print hardcovers of known titles, but they began bringing out brand-new titles as well, titles that had been unpublished during his lifetime.

Then ERB, Inc. got into the act itself, bringing out *I Am a Barbarian*.

With this plethora of Burroughs titles, of course fandom began getting organized. The Burroughs Bibliophiles were

formed at the 1962 Worldcon in Chicago, and Vern Coriell res-
urrected the *Burroughs Bulletin*. Pete Ogden was publishing
ERBania, and then Camille Cazedessus brought out *ERB-dom*
and Paul Allen followed with *The Barsoomian*.

New artists started getting noticed. Jeff Jones was probably the best of them, but there was Larry Ivie, and Neal Mac-
Donald, and Bob Barrett, and a host of others.

In 1965, the Burroughs fans, declining to follow the
Worldcon across the ocean to England, held their first independent Dum-Dum in Chicago. It was a smashing success.

By 1966, the Burroughs Wave was riding high. *ERB-dom*
became the first (and only) Burroughs fanzine to win the Best
Fanzine Hugo. The Barsoom novels were nominated for Best
All-Time Series (along with Tolkein's *Lord of the Rings*,
Heinlein's Future History, Doc Smith's Lensman series, and
the eventual winner, Asimov's *Foundation Trilogy*.) Frank
Frazetta picked up the Hugo as Best Pro Artist (an award Roy
Krenkel had won three years earlier).

New titles were appearing all the time. *Tarzan and the
Madman*. "The Wizard of Venus." *Tarzan and the Castaways*.
"Savage Pellucidar." *I Am a Barbarian*. A two-in-one hardcover
of the *Tarzan Twins* books, which had been prohibitively expensive for a third of a century. Word came that they'd uncov-
ered *Marcia of the Doorstep*. Irwin Porges was working on his
massive ERB biography. The Burroughs family hired Bob
Hodes to run the corporation, and soon Hodes had Tarzan and
John Carter back in the comic books, and plans were afoot for
the movie that eventually became *Greystoke*.

And then, not overnight, not so fast that anyone noticed it,
the wave was gone. Oh, the Burroughs books remained in print
for the most part, and before too long George McWhorter began
a new and beautiful incarnation of the *Burroughs Bulletin*, and
the Dum-Dums continued, and Disney made a mint on its animated Tarzan movie—but that first flush of excitement was
gone.

The Dum-Dums haven't been held in conjunction with the
Worldcon for twenty years now, and that's probably fitting,
since neither seems to have any great interest in the other. Burroughs, who once couldn't get onto the shelves of some public li-
braries, is now so respected that two years ago I was asked to

write an introduction to the University of Nebraska's reprint of *The Land That Time Forgot*.

ERB and his work are on dozens of web pages. Colleges now concede his importance to the field of science fiction. Major movie studios have renewed interest in Tarzan. Disney will be coming out with a John Carter film before too long. ERB is here to stay this time.

But there will never again be the excitement and the sense of discovery his work generated in the 1960s. He's better known, better respected, more widely read now, his fandom's better organized, his reputation has been rebuilt—but I wish you could have been around *then*, when the world was just finding him again.

It was really something.

For the ERBmania web page

HOW FANDOM HAS CHANGED

Leah Zeldes has asked me to discuss how fandom has changed since Carol and I first discovered it back in 1962.

First, let me tell you how it hasn't changed:

1. It's still a white middle-class phenomenon. There are no more blacks than there ever were—which is to say, almost none—and there's not really any more money, given the boom economies of the Reagan and Clinton years.
2. As I've said elsewhere, its greatest virtue remains the fact that it is so all-encompassingly tolerant, and its greatest shortcoming is that it has so much to be tolerant of.
3. Editors still ask old-time fans and fans-turned-pros to write articles on how fandom has changed.

So . . . how *has* it changed?

Well, the biggest change began in 1967, when the Trekkies discovered us at Nycon III. I still have a photo from the masquerade of seven Mister Spocks, each of whom thought his costume would be unique. From that day to this, fandom has become more and more media-oriented. Large groups of fans now insist that "real" science fiction began with this pointy-eared guy in 1966, while other, almost equally-large groups, say that no, it began with the flight of the *Millennium Falcon* in 1977. And the wild part is that they *mean* it.

Boiled down, it comes to this: I can remember when the vast majority of fans at a Worldcon either read or wrote science fiction. Today, they are outnumbered by those who merely *watch* it.

There was a time when almost every fan wanted to be a writer, except for those who wanted to be artists. These days most fans are content simply to watch endless TV reruns and bad new movies with expensive special effects—and far more disturbing to me, a majority of those who want to become writers want to write only Trekbooks or Wookiebooks. Here we are in the field that allows the greatest play of imagination, that has the least restrictions on the kind of story one tells, and all these fans want to tell twice-told tales in a third-hand universe. I find it both appalling and incomprehensible.

Other changes?

Well, the demographics of fandom for one. When we got into fandom, you could attend maybe four or five cons a year: Worldcon, Philcon, Midwestcon, Westercon, maybe one or two others. Today there have to be more than 400 cons a year, and special interest cons—from Trekcons to filkcons to costumecons to whatever—have spread across the land in some quantity.

Still more changes?

Huckster rooms used to sell just books and magazines. Look at them today.

Since more pros came from fandom in the olden days, more pros continued to write for fanzines.

The advent of the computer and the modem means that an increasingly large number of fans indulge in most of their fanac online. This makes for less con and club attendance and less opportunity to meet your fellow fans in the flesh, but to compensate, it makes for enormous amounts of accessible fanwriting. You can now read every word of every issue of multiple Hugo-winning fanzine *Mimosa* for free, just by logging onto their web page . . . or you can see hundreds of photos and read dozens of long-lost fanzines over on Joe Siclari's fanac.org web page.

Back in the 1960s there was so much less science fiction being published that a dedicated fan could keep up with almost all of it. Today, according to *Locus*, there are better than 1,700 sf and related books published every year, plus ghod knows how many prozines and semi-prozines.

Since fandom was smaller, it was a unified whole. The Burroughs Bibliophiles, the Hyborean Legion, the Count Dracula Society, all held their annual meeting at Worldcon. The Burroughs people broke away in 1980 and have never come back, and a lot of other interest groups—even literary ones—have split off to have their own conventions.

There was more interaction between pros and fans. Oh, you still get a few pros who spend most of their time at cons with fans (and invariably these are pros who came up through fandom, a common occurance in the 1960s, a relatively rare one these days). When there was no money in the field—and there wasn't any to speak of for the longest time—pros could relax and mix with fans. Today, with tens and hundreds of thousands of dollars per book at stake, very few pros can ignore the opportunity to meet face-to-face with editors and publishers and to swap insider news with other pros, and this of course takes away from the time they can spend with fans at conventions.

There was a time when if you read Advent's annual book, you read just about all the non-fiction amd criticism that was published in and about the field. Today you'd have to read a book a week to keep up with it.

Sound grumpy? Well, fandom—and what it's become—can be disappointing at times . . . but it's still a way of life, and a very enjoyable one, where interesting people of like minds can get together in a bond of friendship, and where the word "party" doesn't bring forth images of drunken people, nose candy, and date rapes.

They say you can choose your friends but not your family.

They're wrong.

We chose our family back in 1962. These days we meet with the local branch of it (the Cincinnati Fantasy Group) every two weeks, and look forward to its annual reunion, yclept Worldcon, like a kid looks forward to Christmas.

So I guess maybe it hasn't changed all that much after all. At least, not in too many meaningful ways.

MY FAVORITE MUSEUMS

I've been to France five times in the past three years. And although I've always been there as a guest of some convention committee or other that was hundreds of miles out of Paris, I've managed to spend a few days sampling the joys of Paris on each trip.

The most fabulous building I've ever seen in my life is the Louvre. I think it must be about a mile from one end to the other, and it has four—and, in places, five—levels. And it does have the Mona Lisa, and the Venus de Milo, and the Winged Victory, and more famous art than any other museum in the world. But what it mostly has are 4,000 or 5,000 paintings of the crucifixion, and I am first, partially color-blind, and second, an atheist.

Which is a roundabout way of saying that I love the building, but I'm not especially enamoured with what's inside it.

A few weeks ago (I'm writing this in November of 2001) I went to the Orsay, a nearby Parisian museum, with Gardner Dozois, Susan Casper and Kristine Kathryn Rusch. It boasts the greatest collection of French impressionists ever assembled.

After an hour I stopped pretending I cared about French impressionists, left my companions, and took a long walk through the Tuilleries, the exquisite gardens behind the Louvre. It was time to admit to myself that, for whatever reason, these world-famous museums simply don't appeal to me.

And that, of course, suggested an article about the museums that *do* appeal to me.

So here are my favorites, in order. I don't expect anyone who doesn't share my tastes, A to Z, to agree with me.

1. The National Museum of Racing.

This is horse racing's Hall of Fame, and I have been a horse racing fanatic for half a century (and at one point a weekly columnist for well over a decade.) There are brilliant paintings by Richard Stone Reeves and others, all kinds of memorabilia, and names that are evocative of equine greatness—Kelso, Man o' War, Ruffian, Citation,

Seattle Slew, Native Dancer, Secretariat. There are films and videotapes of the great races, silks of the great farms like Calumet and Claiborne, no end of things to look at.

And the Hall of Fame isn't just for horses. Every year a trainer and a jockey are also inducted. The last time I was there they were building an addition so visitors could see exactly how a race horse is cared for.

2. The Nairobi Museum.

Not a huge museum, but then, Kenya's not a huge country. The museum has the stuffed remains of Ahmed of Marsabit, the magnificent elephant who's shown up in a few of my stories. It's got a rifle that was used by John Boyes—and Boyes appears in three of my stories, and I've also brought his two classic books back into print in the *Resnick Library of African Adventure.*

There are stuffed (taxidermied?) animals of every species that occurs in Kenya. There is a huge display of the Emergency (yclept the Mau Mau) and the opening days of Independence. There are displays of tools, weapons, and tribal insignia of almost all the Kenyan tribes. There's even a large snake and reptile park right across the street. Fascinating place for anyone interested in Kenya's history (especially from 1890 to about 1970) and fauna.

3. The Royal Tyrell Museum.

The finest prehistory museum in the world. The museum is run by Dr. Phil Currie, a former science fiction fan and now one of the world's two or three preeminent paleontologists. They've got more than 20,000 dinosaurs that they're still cataloging prior to assembling.

The Tyrell is located in the middle of Canada's Alberta Province, a treasure trove of dinosaur fossils, but they're not limited to Alberta. Phil was part of the group that found the feathered dinosaur in China, which essentially ended all the bickering and finally proved that dinosaurs did indeed evolve into birds. He was also in the expedition that discovered the largest carnivorous dinosaur of them all, one that dwarfs T. Rex, down in South America. Phil's specialty is carnosaurs, so the museum has an exceptional collection of them.

Also, most of the great museums are just huge rectangular buildings that were erected and then filled with whatever they decided to specialize in. Not the Tyrell—they *knew* what their exhibits would be, and the museum, which is only about 20 years old, was designed and created expressly for the exhibits it holds.

4. The Field Museum of Natural History.

I'll be honest. I don't know if this is any better than the American Museum of Natural History in New York, but it's the one that I grew up with and probably visited over 300 times before we finally moved from Chicago to Cincinnati. (My only job prior to freelancing full-time was a 5-minute walk from it; I spent almost every lunch hour there.)

It's always had a fine African exhibit. Carl Akeley Hall, named after the great hunter, naturalist and taxidermist, is unsurpassed. There are a pair of battling bull elephants in the main entry foyer that never fail to inspire awe—and these days Sue the Tyrannosaur, the most complete T. Rex ever found, stands about 60 feet away from them.

The dinosaur exhibits have always been outstanding, ditto the Indian and Ocean exhibits, and they've reproduced the waterfront avenue of a shabby South Pacific town, circa 1930, that's wildly evocative. And as a man who spent hundreds of hours in their library (on the not-open-to-the-public third floor), I'll vouch that I've never seen a more thorough one.

5. The Gene Autry Museum of Western Americana.

When we first heard of this place, during a Guest of Honor stint at Loscon, we thought it would be a little storefront with a few posters from Autry movies and maybe a 45 rpm record of Gene singing "South of the Border" in his distinctly nasal voice.

Boy, were we wrong! The Autry Museum is an $80 million dollar building that seems like Valhalla to a couple of grown-up kids (Carol and me) who were raised on cowboy movies. The permanent exhibits include stagecoaches, saddles and outfits that look almost too fancy for Roy Rogers and Trigger (the fashion plates of all B-movie cowboys and horses). There's a display of every variety of Colt ever man-ufactured, including a Buntline Special. There are some life-sized Disney animatrons that re-enact the Gunfight at the O.K. Corral every few minutes. There is a lot of space devoted to Western movies, from William S. Hart through Clint Eastwood. It takes most of a day to go through the place.

Each month there's a new featured display—one month it was the fabulous furniture created by cowboy ac-tor George Montgomery; another time it was illustrated lit-erature—magazines, comic books, paintings—devoted to the civil war; one month there was a huge collection of John Wayne memorabilia.

And they have a *great* gift shop with books and CDs I've never seen anywhere else.

6. The American Museum of Natural History.

Almost a sister to Chicago's Field Museum, with one major difference—they have a section devoted to Theodore Roosevelt, who, as Resnick readers know, happens to be my hero. Roosevelt and his family were generous with his memorabilia, and it's a very impressive display.

Their taxidermy sections are fine, though I think the Field's are better. Their tribal exhibits from around the world are probably better than the Field's. They've refur-bished their dinosaur exhibit, and it's very impressive (but the Field has Sue).

Excellent evening programs, and a very thorough gift shop.

7. The Cairo Museum of Antiquities.

A one-of-a-kind museum. Other museums around the world present Egyptian exhibits, but they fade into insig-nificance next to this one. It's got the first painting in his-tory. It's got most of the King Tut collection. It's got pillars and carvings, sphinxes and stone pharoahs, it's got every-thing.

You'll need an interpretor when you go through it—most of the cards and labels are not in English—and last year you needed a bodyguard just to approach it, though hopefully that situation has improved. There are so many large and small Egyptian artifacts on exhibit that even a non-museum type could easily spend a week there. And there's a lovely fountain and pond just outside the entrance.

8. The Kentucky Derby Museum.

A museum devoted to a single race—one that the man of the street thinks is the most important on the calendar, whereas horsemen will tell you that winning the Breeders Cup Classic or the Belmont Stakes will do far more to enhance a horse's value. Still, to the public at large, the Derby is the Big One.

There are videos of the past 75 or 80 Derbies. Silks of the winning jockeys. A few of the golden trophies that have been returned to the museum (which is on the grounds of Churchill Downs, just a 5-minute drive from the annual Rivercon site, and 10 minutes from Rivercon's successor, ConGlomeration). There are winners' bridles, saddles, saddle blankets, horseshoes, everything you can think of relating to the Derby. You can do the place thoroughly in 90 minutes (double that if you watch the videos, which I always do), and when you leave you'll know more than you'll ever need to know about the Run for the Roses.

9. The Martin & Osa Johnson Safari Museum.

Martin and Osa Johnson were the first documentary filmmaker superstars. Martin began by going to the South Seas with Jack London, but soon married the teen-aged Osa and set up shop in Africa, bringing back the first legitimate footage anyone had ever seen of African animals in the wild, or African tribes at home.

Their first film, *Simba*, followed them on a safari to Lake Paradise, the Mount Marsabit location that would be their home for four years, It contained a lot of footage of elephants and antelope, and ended with the Maasai's rite of passage to adulthood: a lion hunt in which the young warriors were armed only with spears.

The museum displays most of the artifacts Martin and Osa brought back from Africa. It contains not only *their* bestsellers (both were authors, writing of their adventures), but also possesses a library of over 10,000 volumes—and it sells videotapes of almost all their movies. Its unlikely location is in Osa's home town of Chanute, Kansas.

10. The Smithsonian (especially its Natural History Museum).

This is the big one—the history and future of the United States in a number of impressive buildings. The aeronautical exhibits are fascinating—hell, *all* the exhibits are fascinating—but the one that most interests me is the Natural History museum. Not up to the Field or the American, but nonetheless an excellent display.

11. The British Museum.

A fascinating museum. If an object of worth existed anywhere in the Empire and wasn't nailed down, the Brits found a way to bring it back and put it on display in the British Museum. There's an Egyptian galley, a Roman temple, you name it and they've got it. I think the only reason the pyramids are still in Egypt is because they couldn't figure out how to ship them to London.

It goes on forever, and is endlessly fascinating, but there's actually very little *British* on display.

12. The Louvre.

OK, I'm not moved by crucifixions, and I suspect Venus looks better with arms, and I think Mona Lisa is a plain-looking and totally uninteresting woman—but this is still the most fascinating building in the world, with enough stuff so even color-blind atheistic art-haters like me can find something to admire (I liked the room with all the Reubens paintings, and of course I liked the Egyptian exhibit). If you're in Paris, then even if you are no more impressed with classic art than I am, you owe it to yourself to visit the Louvre for one day at least.

13. The Salvador Dali Museum.

So who are my favorite artists? Well, at the top there are Simon Combes and David Shepard, two of the premiere wildlife artists in Africa. I persist in thinking that Walt Kelly's *Pogo* was not only the best-written comic strip in history but the best-drawn as well, and I love Kelly's artwork, *Pogo* and non-*Pogo* alike.

And I like Dali. I discovered him in high school back in the 1950s, and while Picasso was (and remains) incomprehensible to me, Dali struck a responsive chord. The museum, down in St. Petersburg, Florida, has maybe 50 of his paintings on display, a nice gift shop, and a fascinating tour that tells you enough about his totally strange life and marriage that you want to run right home and write a novel about it.

14. The La Brea Tar Pits.

It's not up to the Tyrell, but then, nothing is. This Los Angeles museum is situated over the tar pits, and that means it tends to specialize in what gets pulled out of the pits—mammoths, sabre-tooths, and other mammals that lived from 10,000 to 25,000 years ago.

The displays aren't numerous, but they *are* interesting, it's easy to reach if you're in the L.A. area, you can go through the thing in an hour or so, and as all the Bantam writers who attended the 1996 Worldcon will attest, they put on one hell of a banquet.

There are a few museums we haven't been to yet that I have a feeling would surely make my list. Right off the bat, there's Dr. Jack Horner's Museum of the Rockies, which is said to be the greatest paleontological museum in the United States (the Tyrell's in Canada). I've never been to The Pro Basketball Hall of Fame, and since it's the only sport besides horse racing that I'm truly passionate about, I plan to get up to Springfield, Massachusetts and see it one of these days. There's the Exotic World Burlesque Museum and Hall of Fame out in Helendale, California that I'd love to see now that I'm a Dirty Old Man. Finally, I'm on the track of a Doc Holliday Museum, another character who keeps showing up in my books and stories; this particular museum is supposed to be run by his family members in the Deep South, rather than out West where he laid his claim to immortality.

There's one that *should* make the list, but probably never will, and that's The British Museum of Natural History. They have everything it takes to make the Top Ten—except intelligence.

I went there in 1984 to examine the tusks of the

Kilimanjaro Elephant, prior to writing *Ivory*. They were not on public display, and I had to write ahead to make arrangements to see them. When I got there I spent two hours looking around the museum, and I found that its African fauna collection, which I'd looked forward to seeing, was much less interesting that I'd anticipated. Then I met the official who was to escort me to the tusks. We went down to the basement, and suddenly I was surrounded by literally hundreds of the most impressive African trophies I'd ever seen. I asked why they weren't on display. Same reason as the ivory. They weren't shot on license; therefore they were poached, and the Politically Correct museum refused to display anything that was poached.

Makes sense—*except* that this entire collection was shot and donated by F. C. Selous, generally considered to be the greatest African hunter of all time (my own choice would be W.D.M. "Karamojo" Bell, but that has nothing to do with this story), and Selous, who died fighting the Germans in Tanganyika in 1917, brought back the vast majority of his trophies before there *were* hunting licenses.

Go figure.

For Challenger #15

TIME CAPSULE

My fandom is dying.

It's been dying for years. It'll be decades more before the last remnants are gone, and I have every hope and expectation that it will outlive me.

But it *is* dying.

I can remember when every fan at a worldcon (well, 95% of them, anyway) was an avid science fiction reader, and most of them aspired to write it professionally someday. Today, those Worldcon attendees who read and write science fiction are far outnumbered by those who are content merely to watch it.

I can remember when Midwestcon, the most faanish of conventions, drew close to 400 people. These days it's a rarity for it to pull more than 140.

I can remember not only when every fan read fanzines, but when there were a lot of fanzines worth reading. Today there are maybe six or seven, surely no more than ten.

So, since I'm feeling my mortality today, I'd like to consider what I'd put in a time capsule, for fans—or what passes for fans in 2100 A.D.—to open and learn about us.

I am only going to select things that I myself possess. (We ran into this problem once before, when I wrote "The Literature of Fandom" for *Mimosa 21*. So let me state it again: these are *my* preferences, based solely on what I have within the four walls of my house. If yours differ, I have no problem with that . . . until you start writing in and telling my why *your* choices should have been *my* choices.)

They probably won't still have VCRs then, so I'll have to pack one in the capsule. And then I would include the following videotapes, some professional, some semi-pro, some totally amateur:

- *The 1989 Worldcon 50th Anniversary Banquet.* Asimov toastmastered, and perhaps 20 pros and fans gave brief speeches about their first Worldcons or their love of Worldcons.

- *FAANS*, the lovingly-made half-hour movie starring Roger Sims, Larry Tucker, Bob Tucker, and a goodly portion of midwestern fandom.

- *Uncle Albert's Videozine #1*. This gave complete coverage to a typical regional con, the 1984 ConFusion. If there was ever a second issue, I'm not aware of it.
- *Galaxy Quest*. The Hugo-winning box-office smash, which brought fandom to the general public in a much less frightening manner than *Trekkies*, which came out the same year.
- The 1988 and 1998 Hugo ceremonies. I'm sure there are others in existence (I have a couple of truncated ones), but these are the only two complete ceremonies I have on videotape.
- The 1972 and 1974 worldcon masquerades (I have these as film transfers to tape), and the 1982, 1986 and 1991 masquerades complete as video originals.

Then would come the books and the one-shots:

- *Fancyclopedia II*, compiled and edited by Dick Eney
- *A Sense of FAPA*, the huge compendium edited by Dick Eney
- *The Enchanted Duplicator*, by Walt Willis and Bob Shaw
- *The Chicon III Proceedings*, edited by Earl Kemp
- *The Discon Proceedings*, edited by Dick Eney
- *The Noreascon I Proceedings*, edited by Leslie Turek
- *Warhoon #28*, the enormous hardcover collection of Walt Willis' fanwritings
- *Science Fiction Fandom*, edited by Joe Sanders
- *Dwellers of the Deep*, by Barry Malzberg (writing as K. M. O'Donnell), the best novel ever written about fandom.
- *The Futurians*, by Damon Knight
- *The Game of Fandom*, by Bruce Pelz
- *The Eighth Stage of Fandom*, by Robert Bloch
- *Out of My Head*, by Robert Bloch
- *Fandom Harvest*, by Terry Carr
- *The Immortal Storm*, by Sam Moskowitz

- *All Our Yesterdays*, by Harry Warner
- *A Wealth of Fable*, by Harry Warner
- *Why is a Fan?*, edited by Earl Kemp
- Jay Kay Klein's memory albums from Chicon III, Discon I, and Tricon
- The Noreascon I, II and III memory albums
- The 1979 Nasfic memory album

And finally there would be two or three sample issues of each of these fanzines:

- *Mimosa*
- *Science Fiction Review*
- *STET* (especially #9)
- *Amra*
- *Duende*
- *Quandry*
- *Granfalloon*
- *Beabohema*
- *Lan's Lantern*
- *Hyphen*
- *Slant*
- *Challenger*
- *Double Bill*
- *Outworlds*
- *Dimensions*
- *Luna*
- *Oopsla*
- *File 770*
- *Rhodomagnetic Digest*

There would be a few other books, one-shots and fanzines, too; I'm creating this off the top of my head, and when I go through all my boxes of stored treasures and memories I'm sure

I'll find more that I wish I'd included. Oh, and there'd have to be a propeller beanie, even though I've never worn one.

But this list would be sufficient to show them what my fandom was like before it died twenty or thirty years from now.

And I think, along with all the tapes and books and zines, I'd also include a little note:

Dear Citizen of 2100:

I hope you are living in the Utopia we envisioned when we were kids first discovering science fiction. I am sure you have experienced technological and medical breakthroughs that are all but inconceivable to me.

But I have experienced something that is probably inconceivable to you, at least until you spend a little time studying the contents of this capsule.

I wish I could see the wonders you daily experience. But you know something? As badly as I want to see the future, to see what we've accomplished in the next century, I wouldn't trade places with you if it meant never having experienced the fandom that this capsule will introduce you to.

Enjoy.

I certainly did.

For Mimosa #27

HOW I SINGLE-HANDEDLY DESTROYED THE SEX BOOK FIELD FOR FIVE YEARS
(And Never Even Got A Thank-You Note from The Legion of Decency)

There has always been a field where a writer who was fast, facile, and willing to work under a pseudonym could make a quick buck or two. In the 1930s, it was the hero pulp field, where various diverse hands became Maxwell Grant to write *The Shadow* and Kenneth Robeson to write *Doc Savage* and *The Avenger*.

By the 1960s the money was to be found in the adult book field, where Bob Silverberg, Barry Malzberg, Marion Zimmer Bradley, myself, and a number of other future science fiction writers learned our trade while paying our bills.

I wrote a *lot* of sex books under more than 150 pseudonyms. But early on it occurred to me that I could make even more money by building a little creative factory of writers who were just as fast as I was, and even hungrier.

It worked like this: I'd find a new sex book publisher, and write two or three books for him. (It was always a him . . . .and given a choice between good and Thursday, he always wanted it Thursday.)

He'd pay about $1,000 for the book—royalties were never mentioned, and certainly never received—and after I'd sold him a few to prove I could give him what he wanted and make my deadlines, we'd usually come to an understanding: he would guarantee to buy a book every four (or six, or eight) weeks from me if I would guarantee to deliver the proper number of pages on time.

Then I would find (and, usually, train) writers who were hungrier than me to write these 200-page masterpieces for $500. After I edited the first couple, I'd pay a trusted assistant $50 to edit all future books, and then I'd pay a typist $50 (a quarter a page, the going rate for a book back then) to type the edited manuscript—and I'd make $400 for setting it up.

I'd pocket that $400 two or three times a week, in addition to what I was making with my own writing and editing, which wouldn't be too bad today and was incredibly lucrative for a kid in his mid-20s back in the late 1960s.

It was a nice set-up. I had maybe three guys writing full-time, another one editing part-time, and we kept two work-at-home typists busy. There was only one fly in the ointment: Greenleaf Classics.

Greenleaf was the biggest publisher of dirty books around. (And when I say "dirty," I mean soft-core. All this stuff pre-dates Linda Lovelace, Larry Flynt, *Screw*, and that whole crowd.) They published close to 500 new titles a year. Their publisher, Bill Hamling, was the former editor of *Amazing* and publisher of *Imagination*. Their editor, Earl Kemp, had won a Best Fanzine Hugo for *Who Killed Science Fiction?*, and also chaired the 1962 Worldcon in Chicago. I knew Earl, having joined Chicago fandom just before he left to edit sex books in California.

So what was the problem?

Greenleaf only paid $600 a book. Once I farmed a book out for $500, paid $50 for the editor, and $50 for the typist, I had broken even—and after I paid for postage, I was in the hole.

It drove me crazy. There *had* to be a way to get Earl to come up with $1,000 a book or more. I had the manpower to supply him with 50, even 100 titles a year, but at his prices I simply couldn't afford to do so.

Now, while I was doing all this free-lancing, I was also editing a weekly tabloid called *The National Insider*, which was second only to *The National Inquirer* in circulation. And one of the things I did as editor was to buy photos of "nudie" movies (not the *Deep Throat* kind, which hadn't captured the public yet and was confined to stag smokers, but rather the Russ Meyer kind, with lots of nudity but no legally actionable obscenity).

The guy I bought them from was a fellow named Marv Lincoln, who took publicity photos for about half the nudie movies that were made in California. After I'd been dealing with him for awhile, I thought I saw a way to give Earl something so special that he couldn't get it anywhere else and would *have* to fork over four beautiful digits for it. I asked Marv to find out how much it would cost me to buy 100 black-and-white photos from a nudie movie, plus the rights to novelize the script. (Well, actually, I never saw a script; I was happy to novelize it from the publicity brochure, which probably had more words than the script anyway.)

He came back to me a couple of weeks later with a price: $400.

Okay. I would pay Marv $400. But now, with 100 8x10 photos, I only needed a 100-page book rather than 200 pages, so I could pay my hungry writers $250 instead of $500. And my editor and typist would each get $25 instead of $50. So my total expenses would be $700.

I called Earl and hit him with the idea. He offered $1,200 a book and we were in business.

I delivered about 20 books to him in two months. It felt like stealing.

Then the first couple came out. I had a couple of science fiction paperbacks on the stands back then; they sold for 50 cents apiece. Sex books were going for $1.95. Earl charged $3.95 for the sex books with the 100 photos in them—and they sold like hotcakes.

I always wondered who took the publicity photos for the *other* half of the nudie industry, the half Marv Lincoln didn't take.

I soon found out. It was none other than Bill Rotsler, longtime fan and perhaps the greatest cartoonist in the history of fanzines.

And pretty soon Bill was selling Earl just about as many of these illustrated novelizations as I was. (I have no idea if he wrote them himself or farmed them out—but farming out was a pretty common practice back then.)

[Note: After this article appeared, Earl told me that he assigned *all those books to Rotsler.]*

Title after title sold out. And of course there had to come a day when Earl and Bill Hamling asked themselves The Question: if we can charge $3.95 for a book with *some* text and 100 photos and sell out, what can we charge for a book with 200 photos and *no* bothersome text at all?

They printed up a handful of such books and sold out at $7.95 apiece. Their next step was to explain to me that they no longer needed any novelizations, and then they contacted all the photographers directly.

Publisher after publisher followed suit. After all, why sell 50% of your print run at $1.95 when you can sell all of it at $7.95 and not have to pay any writers for the privilege?

And that was that.

Oh, eventually they began publishing hardcore photos and one by one they were busted and shut down, and a few years later adult novels ("the kind Frenchmen like") made their reappearance, but by then I had stockpiled enough money to quit the field—thank Ghod!—and was preparing for a full-time career as a science fiction writer.

And that's the story. Except that, almost 30 years shutting down the field, I'm still waiting for my commendation from Jerry Falwell and my medal from the Legion of Decency.

For Mimosa #26

MY FAVORITE MUSICALS

To the best of my knowledge, there is only one other art form that requires the suspension of disbelief to the same extent that science fiction does, and that is the musical theater. Indeed, it took his collaborators a few years to convince Larry Gelbart to write the libretto to the brilliant Tony winner, *City of Angels*, because he wasn't convinced that an audience would buy the notion of a hard-boiled private eye breaking into song.

So it's probably natural that I've loved musicals for as long as I've loved science fiction (which is all my life, minus the first half-dozen years or so.) Carol and I have probably seen close to 200 different musicals, and my musical theater library—scripts, records, audio tapes, studio demo tapes, performance tapes, CDs, videos, bootleg videos, and DVDs—is somewhere between extensive and vast.

So since I find myself a lot closer to the end than the beginning, I think perhaps it's time to share my list of favorites with you (as well as the megahits I *don't* like.) Who knows? You might find a show or two you weren't aware of. At the very least, it'll give you something to argue about the next time you see me.

1. Sweeney Todd.

Quite simply, this is the American musical come of age, with Stephen Sondheim's finest score. This is probably as close as a musical can get to opera while remaining identifiably a musical. We saw it with both Len Cariou and George Hearn in the title role, and Angela Lansbury opposite each of them. They were the best roles any of them will ever have. [Original cast CD is available. The video is currently out of print; there is some talk about releasing it on DVD in a year.]

2. Falsettos.

It's become a cult hit, but it's much more than that. In fact, it's the first work of theatrical brilliance to be influenced by Sondheim (Broadway's current reigning genius) rather than Rodgers & Hammerstein (Broadway's antiquated innovators of 60 years ago), and William Finn, who, like Sondheim, writes both music and lyrics, produced a sung-through show (i.e., no dialogue/libretto) that is hilarious and heartbreaking at the same time. [Available on CD; no official video, but there are bootleg versions of at least 4 different casts, ranging from Broadway to regional.]

3. Pacific Overtures.

A case could be made that this Sondheim score is every bit as good as *Sweeney Todd*'s—but the libretto, about the opening of Japan, tries to cover a bit too much ground. This one has Sondheim's favorite song ("Someone in a Tree") and Carol's favorite Sondheim song (the absolutely tragic "A Bowler Hat"). [Original cast CD is available; there are two bootleg versions on video, including the original cast in a performance that was broadcast only in Japan back in 1976.]

4. City of Angels.

A brilliant conceit, with libretto by Larry Gelbert and featuring Cy Coleman's finest score. This is the story of a mystery writer who is selling out to Hollywood, and it is also the story he's busily emasculating, told on one half of the stage in black and white, while his own story is told, in color, on the other half. It also qualifies as fantasy, because at one point the private eye steps out of his own story to confront the author and castigate him for selling out. [Both the American and the London casts are available on CD; there is no official video, but bootlegs exist of the Broadway, national, and London companies as well as a college performance.]

5. Grover's Corners.

Tom Jones & Harvey Schmidt, authors of THE FANTASTICKS and the only team that approaches Sondheim in talent, wrote this adaptation of OUR TOWN in 1985. Mary Martin was to star, and when she died of cancer, their funding fell through and they lost their option on the property before they could refinance it. It was performed for only three weeks in Lincolnwood, Illinois and never again—but I have a tape of the performance, and an unbelievably moving demo tape of the score and (condensed) libretto, and I'd have to say that this is their finest work. It contains my favorite Jones/Schmidt song, "Time Goes By." [There is no official record or CD, but bootleg audios exist of the demo and the performance. There are no known videos.]

6. Ain't Supposed To Die A Natural Death.

This all-black musical piece by Melvin van Peebles, set in the ghetto, ran for a year on Broadway back in 1971, and was so powerful—and so frightening and disconcerting to white audiences—that to the best of my knowledge it has never been revived. Van Peebles wasn't much of a musician—the melodies, such as they are, are all rather pedestrian jazz riffs—but his lyrics proved him to be the most powerful poet of our age. [The record is out of print. There is no CD, and there are no known videos.]

7. 1776.

The Pulitzer-winning musical about the signing of the Declaration of Independence—and the wild part is that even though you know how the play is going to end, halfway through you are almost willing to bet that we'll never get there. Unlike most musicals, this one didn't feel a need to give you a song every five or ten minutes; there is one 22-minute segment containing nothing but (fascinating) debates about independence. [Available on CD. The movie used the original Broadway cast, and it is available on video—but don't buy it. The DVD will be out next year, with 40 minutes they cut out of the film restored to it. There's also a bootleg video of the recent revival, and another of a regional cast.]

8. The Fantasticks.

The longest-running show in American history, it's fast approaching its 40th (and final, or so they say) birthday. A beautiful, charming piece of whimsey, with a perfect score by Jones & Schmidt and a libretto (most people don't realize this) that Jones wrote in blank verse. I was fortunate enough to see Jerry Orbach create the role of El Gallo; his performance has never been surpassed by the 60 or 70 succeeding El Gallos. There was a mediocre television adaptation in 1964, and an absolutely horrible movie released last year. You wouldn't think you could un-polish a 24-carat diamond of a show that badly. [Available on CD, both the original cast and a later version. There is no official video of the play, and the movie isn't worth watching; there are at least three bootleg videos of regional performances of the play.]

9. Follies.

Another work of art from Stephen Sondheim, with what is actually a pair of scores—a rich romantic contemporary one, and a second score filled to overflowing with pastiches. James Goldman's book gets more criticism than it deserves; it's too grim for most Broadway audiences, but it's actually quite good. [Original cast, London cast, concert, and 2001 revival cast are all available on CD, and a video and DVD of the concert are available. There is no official video of the play, but at least five regional and revival casts have been captured on bootleg videos.]

10. Man of La Mancha.

Don Quixote set brilliantly to music with Mitch Leigh's greatest score. I've seen it with both Richard Kiley and Raul Julia in the lead, and it was easily a Top Ten play. I've also seen it with both Jose Ferrar and Keith Andes in the lead, and it was mediocre at best. Here's a play that *really* requires a top-notch performance from its leading man. Pay no attention to the movie—it stunk. [Original cast is available on CD; so, I think, is a later British cast. There is no official video of the play, but there are at least two bootlegs, one featuring Raul Julia, the other a regional cast.]

11. Baker Street.

One of three Sherlock Holmes musicals. (The other two are the mediocre *Sherlock Holmes—The Musical*, and the truly dreadful *Holmes!*) This one had definitive performances by Fritz Weaver as Holmes and my all-time favorite musical actress, Inga Swenson, as Irene Adler. Great songs by Ray Jessell, vigorous dances, and more humor than you would expect. Hasn't been performed in 35 years; it's past time for a revival. [Original cast record is out of print; no CD has been made yet, and no video is known to exist.]

12. Sunday in the Park with George.

Sondheim's Pulitzer winner about the life of George Seurat—or, more to the point, about the creation of art. It contains my favorite of his songs, "Finishing the Hat"—which I suspect is the favorite song of the vast majority of writers and artists who see the show. [Original cast CD is available; so are the video and DVD.]

13. Celebration.

Another Jones & Schmidt play. An allegory about the Winter Equinox, and about youth and age, it should have been performed on a small off-Broadway stage like *The Fantasticks,* rather than in a huge Broadway theater where it lost all its intimacy and charm. The play flopped—I blame the theater, not the cast or material—but all small-theater revivals have been successful. [Original cast CD is available. There is no official video, but at least one amateur cast bootleg exists.]

14. A Little Night Music.

Sondheim's third Tony winner in a three-year period (following *Company* in 1971 and *Follies* in 1972), the show is an adaptation of Ingemar Bergman's *Smiles Of A Summer Night*, and every song is a waltz of some sort. "Now" may contain the wittiest lyrics of the decade. Beautiful, moody, evocative. [The original cast and the London cast are both available on CD. A terrible movie version is available on video; avoid it at all costs. There is no official video of the play, but the New York City Opera revived it and aired it on PBS, and thousands of copies of that telecast exist.]

15. West Side Story.

The libretto doesn't wear well and the slang is almost ludicrous today—but Bernstein's music, Bernstein's (uncredited) and Sondheim's lyrics, and (especially) Jerome Robbins' choreography remain among the best. This was the first major conceptual breakthrough since *Oklahoma!* some 14 years earlier. Warning: almost all revivals, lacking Robbins' choreography, are almost painful to watch. The movie wasn't as good as the play, but it was better than most Hollywood adaptations. [Original cast CD is available, as are a number of revivals, here and abroad. No official video exists; there are at least two bootlegs of rather poor semi-pro productions. You'd probably be better served by the video or DVD of the movie, despite the embarrasingly poor performance by Richard Beymer.]

16. 110 in the Shade.

Jones & Schmidt's adaptation of J. Richard Nash's *The*

Rainmaker. This is easily their most melodic score, and it makes you realize that if Harvey Schmidt had gone off on his own, by now he'd be acknowledged as the logical successor to Aaron Copeland. The score, alas, is a lot better than Nash's adaptation of his play. I should add that Inga Swenson's performance was the best I've ever seen by a woman in a musical. (The best by a man would be George Hearn in *Sweeney Todd*, Richard Kiley in *Man of La Mancha*, or Robert Morse in *How To Succeed In Busine*ss.) [Original cast and the complete New York City Opera revival are available on CD. There is no official video, but there is a bootleg of the NYCO revival.]

17. Carnival!

After writing one score for Gwen Verdon and another for Jackie Gleason, Bob Merrill was finally given a chance to write for two real singers, Anna Maria Alberghetti and Jerry Orbach, and he responded with his greatest score in this Tony-winning adaptation of the movie *Lili*. [Original cast CD is available; two regional videos are known to exist.]

18. Sophisticated Ladies.

This wasn't really a play, but a big-budget revue consisting of 30 Duke Ellington songs performed by one of the most talented set of dancers ever assembled, and an orchestra directed by Mercer Ellington, the Duke's son. A delight to both eye and ear. [Original cast CD is available. The official video exists, but is currently out of print. There is no DVD.]

19. Take Me Along.

Bob Merrill's excellent score highlights this adaptation of *Ah! Wilderness!* The score is especially outstanding when you realize it was written for non-singers Jackie Gleason, Walter Pidgeon, and Una Merkel. The O'Neill play loses none of its charm here, and this is the show that made Robert Morse (who *could* sing) a major Broadway star. [Original cast CD is available. There was no official video; one bootleg of a regional cast is known to exist.]

20. It's a Bird, It's a Plane, It's a Superman!

Pay no attention to the horrible, emasculated version of this that played on late-night TV a couple of decades ago. The Broadway show was a delight, with a wonderful Strousse and

Adams score, a pair of hilarious star turns by Jack Cassidy and Michael O'Sullivan, a proper Superman in Bob Holliday, and sets that looked like they were comic book panels. [The original cast CD is available; except for bootlegs of the TV abortion, no video is known to exist.]

21. Fiorello!

The musical biography of Fiorello H. LaGuardia, New York's most beloved mayor (until September 11, 2001, anyway). It won every award in sight, was sold out for close to three years, made Tom Bosley a star in his first role—and never toured on the assumption no one outside of Manhattan would care about it. It was never revived, which is a crying shame, because this was clearly the best play of its year, one of the five or six best of its decade. [Original cast CD is available; no video is known to exist.]

22. The Threepenny Opera.

You must be careful here, because there are a number of translations. The best is the Marc Blitzstein one, which brought Lotte Lenya to America and gave Jerry Orbach his first professional role. The Kurt Weill score has always been brilliant, and Blitzstein has done much the best translation of Bertold Brecht's lyrics. There are two German movie versions, neither very good, and a more recent American version titled *Mack The Knife*, starring Raul Julia and the rest of the revival cast; it's not great, but it's better than you might expect. [Original cast CD is available. So are a number of non-Blitzstein versions. No video of the play is known to exist, though there is a commercial video of the Julia movie.]

23. Philemon.

Jones & Schmidt's deepest, heaviest musical. Fine score, fine libretto—but performed on a tiny stage with a minimalist cast, orchestra (2 pieces) and props, as is their wont, it almost collapses under its own weight. Just as *Celebration* needed this kind of treatment, this needs the Broadway treatment that *Celebration* received. Still, it beats the hell out of most of its competition. [An original cast record is out of print; no CD has been made. There was never an official video, but the original cast performed the play on PBS in 1977, and bootleg copies of that performance exist.]

24. The Bone Room.

Jones & Schmidt's artiest play, this is about a menage a trois at the Natural History Museum between a young girl, an old man, and Death. It was shown to invited audiences only, for 6 performances back in 1977. I think it's brilliant, but it will never be performed again, because they cannibalized a number of its songs for their future plays, especially *Colette Collage* and *Mirette*. [No CD exists, but there is a bootleg audio of the play in performance. No video is known to exist.]

25. Assassins.

Sondheim's most daring conceit, a musical—not quite a play, but far more than a revue—about history's presidential assassins. Each song evokes the era in which the assassination (or attempted assassination) took place, and the lyrics are outstanding, as usual. This play was sabotaged by history twice. It was set to move from off-Broadway to Broadway when the Gulf War broke out, and the producers decided Americans wouldn't want to watch a musical with this subject matter, so they cancelled it. It was scheduled for a February, 2002 Broadway revival when September 11, 2001 rolled around, and it got cancelled again. [Original cast CD is available. There is no official video, but at least five different bootlegs of New York and regional casts are known to exist.]

26. Cabaret.

Kander & Ebb's most powerful play (but not their best score). Bob Fosse ruined it by turning it into a movie with incidental nightclub music, rather than the full-fledged musical play it originally was—and the recent revival, though they made better use of Allan Cummings' emcee than they did with Joel Grey's original, managed to cut "Meeskite" and some of the other songs, to the play's severe disadvantage. It seems to be the kind of play everyone wants to tinker with, which is a shame, because they did it right the first time. [Original cast and revival cast CDs are available. There is no official video, but at least three regional cast bootlegs are known to exist, as well as a bootleg of a top pro cast, including Cummings, that was televised in England.]

27. Big River.

People have tried making musicals of Mark Twain's books before, but no one ever got it right until they hired Roger Miller to do his one and only Broadway score. Suddenly everything fell into place, and even Twain would be pleased with what *Huckleberry Finn* became. [Original cast CD is available. There is no official video, but at least two regional cast bootlegs are known to exist.]

28. How to Succeed in Business Without Really Trying.

Fine score by Frank Loesser, one of the all-time great performances by Robert Morse. It won the Pulitzer and all the other awards, but the humor is a little old today, it's a bit too sexist, and Matthew Broderick's recent lackluster starring stint just shows how necessary Morse was to the play. The original cast starred in the movie, which wasn't as good and lost half a dozen songs, but wasn't bad as movie versions go. [Original cast CD is available. There has never been an official video of the play, but a bootleg of the recent revival is known to exist. And the movie is available on video and DVD.]

29. Jacques Brel Is Alive and Well and Living in Paris.

A musical revue of Brel's songs, as translated by Mort Schmumann. The original cast, with Schumann and Elly Stone, was much the best, but any competant cast is a delight. They also made a pretty good movie out of it, again with Schumann and Stone. [Original cast CD is available. The movie video is long out of print; no DVD exists. There is no known video of the play.]

30. Into the Woods.

Sondheim turns a bunch of fairy tales into a dark, grim, adult entertainment. Far from his best score, but so far above average as to put you in awe of what he can do when he's not at his sharpest. [Original cast CD is available. Video and DVD of the original cast are available.]

31. La Cage Aux Folles.

Far better than the original movie of the same title, or the Nichols/May remake titled *The Bird Cage*, primarily because this concentrates on the two middle-aged lovers rather than "their" son and his fiance. I think it's Jerry Hermann's best score, and George Hearn and (especially) Gene Barry were out-standing. [Original cast CD is available. There was no official video, but two Broadway bootlegs—the original opening night cast and the closing night cast—are known to exist.]

32. Zorba.

Kander & Ebb's greatest score. There were two versions of this play. The original starred Herschell Bernardi, opened in 1969, and was the better version. The 1982 revival was watered down, made less grim and more palatable to Broadway theatergoers (who are usually out-of-towners and aren't paying $75 a seat for thoughtful entertainment)—but it had Anthony Quinn, and though the former is the better play, Quinn made the revival *seem* better through the sheer force of his perfor-mance in the role he seemed born to play. [Original and revival CDs are available. There was no official video, but a bootleg of the Quinn revival is known to exist.]

33. New Girl In Town.

The earliest of Bob Merrill's three superior scores, this is the adaptation of Eugene O'Neill's *Anna Christie*. (*Take Me Along*, his next score, was from O'Neill's *Ah! Wilderness*! Obvi-ously he had an affinity for that particular playwrite.) Gwen Verdon and Thelma Ritter co-starred, and tied for the Best Ac-tress Tony. It's a nice score, and a nice play, but not up to Merrill's next two, which have already been mentioned. [Origi-nal cast CD is available; no video is known to exist.]

34. Candide.

Leonard Bernstein's richest, most luscious, most melodic score, and the lyrics—both the original's by Comden and Green, and the revival's with some new lyrics by Sondheim—are fine . . . but the play never quite knows if it wants to be an opera, an operetta, or a musical. [The original cast and at least two re-vival casts are available on CD. There was no official video, but the New York City Opera revived it and performed it on PBS, and thousands of copies exist.]

35. Passion.

Sondheim's most recent play, until *Wise Guys* reaches Broadway, and hence his most recent Tony winner. This story of a man who rejects a wealthy, loving sexpot for a sick, ugly,

MIKE RESNICK

death-obsessed woman is lovely to listen to, but very hard to believe. [Original cast CD is available. A video of the original cast
is available; it has not yet been made into a DVD.]

36. Company.

Sondheim's first Tony winner, a witty but totally (and purposely) plotless play about marriage. I love the songs, but sue
me, I like plots, and I also find the basic philosophy off-putting.
[Original cast and recent revival are available on CD, and a
video and DVD of the making of the original cast album are
available. No official video of the play was made, but there was
a performance on British TV, and hundreds of copies have
made their way to the States. There are also at least two bootleg
videos of regional casts.]

37. Colette Collage.

Years ago, Jones & Schmidt mounted a major play for Di-
ana Rigg, called *Colette*, based on the life of the writer. It folded
in Seattle before it ever got to New York. The songs were brilliant, of course, but the book needed work, and the costs were
such that it was cheaper and easier to fold it. But years later,
they brought out *Colette Collage*, a rewrite of the original show,
keeping most of the songs, adding a batch more, and tailoring it
for the small stage for which they have such an affinity. It was
much better received, and has been revived again and again.
[No CD exists of *Colette*, though there are audio bootlegs of both
the score and the entire show in performance. The original cast
CD of *Colette Collage* is available. No video of any version is
known to exist.]

38. Destry Rides Again.

The musical version of the classic James Stewart/Marlene
Deitrich movie starred Andy Griffith and Delores Gray, and
was brilliantly choreographed and directed by Michael Kidd.
[Original cast CD is available. No official video was made, but a
bootleg of a regional cast is known to exist.]

39. Greenwillow.

The lovely fantasy novel by B. J. Chute was Frank
Loesser's only flop, but it was the book that was weak, not the
score. Tony Perkins starred as Gideon Briggs, the young man
cursed with wanderlust, and while his voice isn't much, he was

well-trained and managed to hit all the right notes in a score that was written for a much better singer. [Original cast CD is available. No video is known to exist.]

40. On the Town.

Leonard Bernstein's first Broadway score, and still one of the two or three best of the 1940s, with witty lyrics by Betty Comden and Adolf Green. Great choreography by Jerome Robbins. The plot was silly then and embarrassingly silly now. There's a Gene Kelly/Frank Sinatra movie version that dumped all but three Bernstein songs and replaced them with songs by a studio hack. Some exec is burning in hell for that at this very moment. [Original cast CD is available. No video of the show is known to exist, but PBS ran a concert of the score, and it was later released as a video.]

41. Irma La Douce.

Don't let the horrible Jack Lemmon/Shirley MacLaine non-musical movie fool you, *Irma La Douce* was originally a musical, and a very fine one. Imported from France and starring Elizabeth Seal and Clyde Rivell, it took Broadway by storm and won its share of awards. I don't think it's ever been revived, and I've no idea why not. [Original cast CD is available. No videos are known to exist.]

42. Guys and Dolls.

Frank Loesser's first megahit, revived umpteen times. I like the score and I love Damon Runyon, and probably I should rank this a bit higher, but Runyon was funnier and Loesser's done better scores. The play's pleasant, but *How To Succeed* was funnier and in this day of Sondheim and Finn and Jones & Schmidt, it's just a little too simple and Rodgers-and-Hammerstein-ish for me. [Original cast CD and various revivals are available. A bootleg of the recent revival with Nathan Lane is known to exist. Skip the movie until they get around to dubbing a real singer for Marlon Brando.]

43. A New Brain.

William Finn's latest, a semi-autobiographical and hilarious sung-through play about his brain tumor. The cast recording would put this in the top 20 . . . but the cast recording left out seven or eight mediocre songs. Still, the man's style is unique and fascinating; no one, not Sondheim, not anyone, sets today's language to music quite as well. [Original cast CD is available. There is no official video, but a bootleg of the original Off-Bradway cast exists.]

44. Gypsy.

Brilliant Julie Styne/Stephen Sondheim score, and a role—Mama Rose—that middle-aged actresses kill for. Three of them have won Tonies for it, Ethel Merman for the original, and Angela Lansbury and Tyne Daly for revivals. Roz Russell out-acted all of them in the film, but the film was pretty weak. Bette Midler was the most-awaited Mama Rose of all in the TV version, but she turned out to be just about the weakest of them. (I'd say of all the Roses I've seen, Betty Buckley was the best.) Sondheim says it's the last outstanding musical of the old Rodgers-and- Hammerstein type, and he might be right . . . and that also might be why I don't rank it any higher, though I keep paying my money to see each new Mama Rose. [Original cast CD is available, as are a few others; no official video was made, but at least two bootlegs, one with Buckley, are known to exist. Videos of the movie and the TV version are available, but they're not very good versions of the play.]

45. Minnie's Boys.

If GYPSY is the dark side of being a stage mother, and it is, then MINNIE'S BOYS is the light side. This is the musical biography of Minnie Marx and her sons, who just happened to grow up to be Groucho, Harpo, Chico, Gummo and Zeppo. Some hilarious stuff here, and some fine songs, but it takes too long to get going. I saw a truncated version at the Cincinnati Conservatory of Music two years ago, and it was far better than the original for just that reason. [Original cast CD is available; no video is known to exist.]

46. South Pacific.

OK, I had to stick one Rodgers and Hammerstein play in the top 50, and this is much their best. Their finest score, their most powerful story, no stupid dream ballets, no endless Cabins of Uncle Thomas. Too many kids—a typical R&H fault—and too many chorus numbers (another), but it's from a wonderful James Michener collection, and it's an acknowledged classic. [Original cast CD is available, as are some revivals. No official video was made, but a film-to-video bootleg transfer of Mary Martin in the 1951 London presentation is known to exist.]

47. The Music Man.

Robert Preston and Barbara Cook were outstanding. Paul Ford was pretty good. Some of the songs were very nice. But it's just too sweet and too old-fashioned for my taste (and yes, I saw the original cast. I'm ancient, remember?) The movie was a fair representation, though Shirley Jones is no Barbara Cook, Buddy Hackett was an embarrassment, and the production numbers were 76 times bigger and noisier than necessary. [Original cast and recent revival CDs are available. No official video was made, but a bootleg of the recent revival is known to exist. The movie is available on video and DVD.]

48. A Funny Thing Happened on the Way to the Forum.

Sondheim's first hit, and a very funny, very traditional play. The humor's a little broad, and the actors in every version I've seen (4 or 5 at last count) all seem to feel compelled to chew the scenery. The movie wasn't much. [Original cast CD is available. No official video was made, but at least two regional bootlegs are known to exist. The movie's available on video and DVD.]

49. Chicago.

Another example (PIPPIN was the first) of Bob Fosse uncanny ability to make something out of nothing as a director—except that this time he got to direct Gwen Verdon, Jerry Orbach, and Chita Rivera, which certainly made his job easier. A couple of nice songs, a couple of nice dances, nothing really memorable. [Original cast and revival cast CDs are available. There was no official video, but at least two bootleg videos, one of the revival, one of a regional cast, are known to exist.]

50. The Lion King.

Silly story, good but not outstanding music—but this one belongs in the Top 50 for two reasons: the greatest and most imaginative costumes ever seen on Broadway, and some wildly creative choreography. [Original cast CD is available. No official video was made, but at least four Broadway and national company bootlegs are known to exist.]

51. I Do! I Do!

Jones & Schmidt's biggest Broadway hit, this was based on *The Fourposter*, and filled an entire Broadway stage with a cast of only two. (The fact that they were Robert Preston and Mary Martin didn't hurt.) Fine score, though I prefer all their others. So did they; after this, they never wrote for the Broadway theater again, prefering the small stage and their notion of ritual theater. [Original cast CD is available. There is no video of the original, but there is a video of the revival starring Hal Linden and Lee Remick; it has not yet been released on DVD.]

52. The Producers.

Yes, it's hilarious—but it's not very creative: every funny line, with one obscene exception, is from the movie. The music and lyrics are amateurish, and while Nathan Lane was outstanding, Mathhew Broderick added absolutely nothing in the Gene Wilder role. Maybe it was because it was such a poor year for theater, but this play got ten times the hype—and awards—that it deserved. [The original cast CD is available, as is a video of the making of the CD. There is no official video of the play, but at least three different bootlegs, all featuring the original cast, are known to exist.]

53. Donnybrook.

A musical based on *The Quiet Man*, starring Art Lund and Eddie Foy, Jr. Better than its 3-month run would imply, but not up there in classic territory. Joan Fagan, in the Maureen O'Hara role, was much the best thing about it. [The original cast record is out of print. There is no CD, and no video is known to exist.]

54. Riverwind.

A lovely off-Broadway play, set at a small country resort on the banks of a Midwestern river. One of the best off-Broadway scores I've heard, with charming dialogue, but the play is totally forgotten today. [Original cast record is out of print. There is no CD. No video is known to exist.]

55. Sunset Boulevard.

Okay, I suppose we have to have an Andrew Lloyd-Webber show somewere in the top 60, middlebrow and derivative as he is. This score is his most melodic, though *Evita* is better. But this has a single line that elevates it above his others. It comes from Norma Desmond, the silent movie queen (and, in true Lloyd-Webber style, is repeated umpteen times before you can make your way to an exit): "We taught the world new ways to dream." [Original London cast, original New York cast, and at least two other cast recordings are available in CD. There is no official video, but bootlegs with Patti LuPone, Glenn Close, Betty Buckley, and Elaine Paige are known to exist.]

56. Man with a Load of Mischief.

Another forgotten off- Broadway play with a brilliant score. This one starred Reid Shelton and Virginia Vestoff very early in their careers. [The original cast record is out of print. There is no CD. No video is known to exist.]

57. In Trousers.

William Finn's prequel to *Falsettos*. The songs, individually, are excellent . . . but this is a sung-through musical, and they don't hold together as a unit anywhere near as well as *Falsettos*. [Original cast CD is available. There is a bootleg audio of the revival with Chip Zien. There was no official video, but at least one regional bootleg is known to exist]

58. Merrily We Roll Along.

Terrible play, but with a brilliant Sondheim score. You're better off listening to it than watching it, trust me. [Original cast and revival cast CDs are available. There was no official video, but at least three bootlegs, including the original cast, are known to exist.]

59. Evita.

Lloyd-Webber's best score, derivative and repititious as it is. Problem with it as a play (as opposed to the movie, which was an improvement except for Madonna replacing Patti LuPone) is that every important thing happens offstage. [Original cast and various other cast CDs are available. There was no official video, but at least three bootlegs, including the original cast, are known to exist. The film, which is visually stunning but, as I say, lacks LuPone's stellar performance, is available on video and DVD.]

60. Promises! Promises!

Burt Bacharach's only Broadway score, for the Jerry Orbach hit based on *The Apartment*. Very enjoyable light entertainment. The play is mildly funny, the music is mildly pleasurable, and were it not for the immensely-talented Orbach, the play would have been totally forgettable. [Original cast CD is available. There is no official video, but a regional bootleg featuring George Hearn in a supporting role is known to exist.]

61. Cry For Us All.

Based on the prize-winning Off-Broadway drama *Hogan's Goat*, this was Mitch Leigh's first score after *Man of la Mancha*. The play folded early on, despite the presence of Robert Weede and Joan Deiner, and it probably deserved to—but the score was excellent, and requires those near-operatic voices to do it justice. [The original cast record is out of print. There is no CD. No video is known to exist.]

62. Shinbone Alley.

Originally just a record (not unlike Lloyd-Webber's early endeavors) featuring Carol Channing and Eddie Bracken, they finally turned it until a full-fledged musical play. It's based on Don Marquis' "archy and mehitibel" story-poems, and just about every character in it is a cat or a cockroach. Charming, and not at all juvenile, no matter how the description sounds. [Original record, titled *Archy and Mehitibel*, is out of print. There is no cast recording, and no CD of the original record. No video is known to exist, but there is an out-of-print full-length animated cartoon of the play, with Channing's and Bracken's voices, also titled *Shinbone Alley*. Finally, there was a PBS version almost 40 years ago with Tammy Grimes and Eddie Bracken, in black and white, and video bootlegs are known to exist.]

63. The Most Happy Fella.

Frank Loesser's most ambitious score, but I found the play slow-moving and very hard to believe in. [Original cast CD is available. There is no official video of the original cast, but there *is* a video available of an opera company's revival of it.]

64. Bye Bye Birdie.

Forget the (ugh) movie, and the (double ugh with yogurt on

it) TV production. The Broadway play, with Dick van Dyke, Chita Rivera, Susan Watson, and Michael J. Pollard was a pure delight. [The original cast CD is available. No video of any legitimate theatrical version is known to exist.]

65. Lost in the Stars.

Kurt Weill's wonderful score highlights a serious show with a rather antiquated and awkward book, based on Alan Paton's classic *Cry, the Beloved Country*. [The original cast CD is available. A true-to-the-play movie was made starring Brock Peters, but the video is long out of print. No performance video is known to exist, and there is no DVD of any version.]

66. Wonderful Town.

The weakest of Leonard Bernstein's four produced Broadway scores (he had a dreadful unproduced one, 1600 PENNSYLVANIA AVENUE, with lyrics by Alan Jay Lerner), but mediocre Bernstein is like mediocre Sondheim—head and shoulders above 97% of his competition. This was a musical version of MY SISTER EILEEN, starring Roz Russell, which was later (1952) produced on television back when television still had artistic ambitions. (It lost them long before 1960.) [Original cast CD is available; there is no CD of the TV version, but there is an out-of-print record of it. There is no official video of any version, but a bootleg of the TV version is known to exist.]

67. Mack and Mabel.

Robert Preston and Bernadette Peters in a musical version of the lives of Mack Sennett and Mabel Normand. The score is charming, especially the opening number; the play doesn't live up to it. [The original cast CD is available. No video is known to exist.]

68. Mirette.

A children's musical about a high-wire walker in Paris, written by Jones & Schmidt. It does exactly what it set out to do, but it *is* for children. [There is no CD, but there are bootleg audios of the demo tape and a performance tape, which are very different from each other. No video is known to exist.]

69. Damn Yankees.

Pleasant show, pleasant score. History has come full cycle. This play only works when you can hate the New York Yankees, so no one performed it in the late 1960s, the early 1970s, or the early 1990s. Now it's popular again. [Original cast CD is available. No video of the original cast is known to exist, but there is a bootleg of the revival starring Jerry Lewis, and videos of the movie, with original Broadway players Ray Walston and Gwen Verdon, are commercially available.]

70. Anyone Can Whistle.

Sondheim's early show about madness and sanity. His music became more sophisticated (his lyrics were already there), but the score is acceptable; it's Arthur Laurents' libretto that fails here. Ambitious, but eventually unsuccessful. [Original cast and concert recordings are available on CD. There is no official video, but one regional bootleg is known to exist.]

71. Evening Primrose.

Not a Broadway play at all, but a written-for-TV musical that was performed only once, back in 1967. By Stephen Sondheim and James Goldman (Goldman collaborated with Sondheim on *Follies*, won a Tony and an Oscar for *The Lion in Winter*, and wrote original screenplays for *They Might Be Giants* and *Robin and Marian*—a far more talented writer than his more famous brother William), it's based on John Collier's horror fantasy about people passing themselves off as mannikins in a department store, then moving about at night. Fine songs, but totally unnecessary to the story. [Two studio recordings are available on CD, one as *Evening Primrose*, one on a Mandy Patinkin CD. There is also a bootleg audio of the original cast. There is no official video, but bootlegs of the TV show are known to exist.]

72. Nine.

The Tony winner, starring Raul Julia, based on Fellini's 8 1/2. Here's one where I find the staging and performances fascinating and the score mediocre. [Original cast CD is available. There is no official video, but bootlegs of the original cast and national company are known to exist.]

73. KISS OF THE SPDIER WOMAN.

Based on the straight play (and movie) of the same name, starring Chita Rivera, this is another one where I liked the score least of all the parts. Excellent staging and lighting. [Original cast CD is available. There is no official video, but a bootleg of the original cast is known to exist.]

74. THE PHANTOM OF THE OPERA.

Typical of Lloyd-Webber. So much spectacle, so much money thrown into the production, that it takes quite a while to realize that it's only got one acceptable song, or that most songs are re-used endlessly. [Original cast and various other cast CDs are available. There is no official video, but at least seven different bootlegs, including the original cast, are known to exist.]

75. ONCE UPON A MATTRESS.

It's only half the show without Carol Burnett, who became a star more than half a century ago thanks to this play, but it's got pleasant melodies and some of the humor still holds up. [Original cast and revival cast CDs are available. Burnett performed it twice, with totally different casts, in two completely different (and truncated) versions on television, and bootlegs of both exist. There is no known video of the actual play in performance.]

76. CAROUSEL.

Pleasant tunes, with only "Soliloquy" possessing any depth. Typical Rodgers and Hammerstein play, which is to say, they stop the play to deliver a pop/hit song and maybe do a little dance, and then get back to the play. Again. And again. The words "integrated whole" seems to have been absent from their lexicon, as well as that of most of their immediate imitators. [Original cast and various revival casts are available on CD. The movie wasn't much, but it's available on video and probably DVD. There is no official video of the play, but at least two videos of regional casts are known to exist.]

77. YOU'RE A GOOD MAN, CHARLIE BROWN.

A little too sweet and a little too preachy, but it does possess a certain charm. [Original cast record is out of print; revival cast is available on CD. There is no official video, but one regional bootleg is known to exist.]

78. Bring On The Noise, Bring On The Funk.

Wildly innovative show that tells the history of America as a number of black dances. I don't like the music much, but I love the audacity of the concept and the skill of the performers. [Original cast CD is available. No video is known to exist.]

79. Marry Me A Little.

Interesting show, cobbled together out of songs Sondheim cut from other plays. (They've done this in a number of Sondheim revues I haven't covered here—*Side By Side By Songheim, Putting It Together*, and *You're Gonna Love Tomorrow*—but they *were* revues; this attempts to be an integrated play.) Needless to say, the music is better than the storyline, which had to be stretched totally out of shape to accomodate all these diverse songs. [Original cast CD is available. There is no official video, but one regional bootleg is known to exist.]

80. Kiss Me, Kate.

Okay, it's a dinosaur, and it's been done to death—but how can I keep Cole Porter's best score off the list? And while it's overly familiar, some parts are still funny. [Original cast and some revivals are available on CD. There was an inferior movie with a top-notch cast that's available on video. No video of the play in performance is known to exist.]

And now, the moment you've all been waiting for: Megahits that didn't make the list, and why:

A Chorus Line.

A play should have more than dancing. I couldn't find a story anywhere in this, and I actually found the music annoying.

Camelot.

Every scene was nice—but there were so *many* of them. I felt like I'd read all 250,000 words of the book when the play finally let out. (Halfway through the second act I was tempted to turn to the usher and say, "Let my people go!")

Cats.

Same fault as *A Chorus Line*. Brilliant dancing, totally without any meaning. (What do I mean? Every dance in *West*

Side Story furthers the plot. Every dance in CATS serves no purpose except to show you that the performers can dance.) Pedestrian score, mediocre lyrics, story line a four-year-old would find infantile.

Fiddler on the Roof.

It's a nice story, but they didn't have to tell it three times. Act I: Tevye's oldest daughter marries against his will; he learns to live with it. Act II: Tevye's middle daughter marries against his will; he learns to live with it. Act III: Tevye's youngest daughter marries against his will; he learns to live with it. Yawn.

Hello, Dolly!

Totally out of balance. Created as a star vehicle for Carol Channing (and as a movie it was a star vehicle for Barbra Streisand.) But it's not *about* Dolly, who is actually a supporting character. It's about two clerks off on a wild weekend in New York. Dolly gets all the production numbers, but the clerks carry the plot and are the ones you care about.

The Sound of Music.

This one is so disgustingly sweet that it could send entire sections of the audience off to the hospital in diabetic comas.

Chess.

Brilliant opening number, goes straight downhill musically from that moment on.

My Fair Lady.

Tricky, leaving it off my list, because it's a pleasant play. But every witty line in every song is George Bernard Shaw's. All Alan Jay Lerner did was find mundane lines to rhyme with them. I suspect I'm punishing it for a lack of creativity rather than a lack of quality. (*The Producers* was equally uncreative, but at least Mel Brooks stole from himself.) Had *My Fair Lady* been an original, it would have come in somewhere between 30th and 50th.

Les Miserables.

It was a pretty dull story when I read it, and it was a pretty dull play when we saw it. Great sets don't disguise mundane music and uninspired lyrics. We came awfully close to walking out of this one, and we almost never do that.

Oklahoma!

Just too primitive. Leave aside the fact that Laurie was *interesting* in *Green Grown the Lilacs* and that Hammerstein wrote her as dull and uninteresting in *Oklahoma!*, any play that has a dream ballet with guest dancers is too much of a dinosaur for me. (If you haven't seen it—is there *anyone* who hasn't seen it?—Curly and Laurie don't do their own dancing in the totally unnecessary dream ballet.)

The King And I.

Not quite as many disgustingly cute kids as *The Sound of Music*, but close. And "The Cabin of Uncle Thomas" may have been wildly innovative in 1949, but it's an embarrassment these days.

Redhead.

The ultimate star vehicle, it won a batch of Tony awards with an incredibly silly plot, songs only Gwen Verdon could sell, and choreography only Gwen Verdon could dance to. Another make-something-out-of-nothing Bob Fosse show. It closed the day Verdon left the cast, has not been revived in 40+ years, and will never be performed again—nor should it be until they find a way to clone her.

Oliver.

A simple prayer (though usually aimed at Rodgers and Hammerstein plays): Lord, save me from cutesy-poo kids and syrupy sentimentality in Broadway musicals.

Mame.

A star vehicle with terrible songs for the star to sing. What could be more unnecessary?

Hair.

What can I tell you? I hate rock music.

Rent.

Over-hyped megahit with inferior plot, music and lyrics.

As long as I'm unloading a lifetime's worth of musicals, let me just mention some, each of which had something to recommend it, but none of which were capable of making my Top 80:

Brigadoon
The Saint of Bleeker Street
Allegro
Street Scene
Pipe Dream
Paint Your Wagon
Saturday Night
La Plume de Ma Tante
Miss Saigon
Milk and Honey
Godspell
Flower Drum Song
Ernest in Love
Call Me Madam
Sideshow
The Life
Starlight Express
Jesus Christ, Superstar
Oh, Captain!
Jamaica
Finian's Rainbow
Pal Joey
Can-Can
Saratoga
Do I Hear a Waltz?
The Baker's Wife
Woman of the Year
Top Banana
No Strings
Her First Roman
Half a Sixpence
Funny Girl
What Makes Sammy Run?
Golden Boy
Pickwick
Sweet Charity
The Apple Tree

On a Clear Day You Can See Forever
Illya Darling
Dear World
Prettybelle
Applause
Coco
Purlie
Two Gentlemen of Verona
Raisin
Seesaw
Skyscraper
Tenderloin
Little Shop of Horrors
Kismet
Shenandoah
The Cradle Will Rock
Aspects of Love
Pippin
Teddy and Alice
The Full Monty
Li'l Abner
Ben Franklin In Paris
On the Twentieth Century
Grand Hotel
The Rink
Tom Jones
Snoopy
Showboat
Stages
Merlin
The Steel Pier
Working
Berlin to Broadway with Kurt Weill
Ballroom
Peter Pan
The Human Comedy
Carmen Jones
The Golden Apple
King of the Whole Damn World
Grind

Stop The World—I Want To Get Off
Smile
Dreamgirls
The Mystery Of Edwin Drood
Once On This Island
Nick and Nora
My Favorite Year
Beauty and the Beast
We Take the Town

There are more, of course—but this should be enough to hold you for awhile.

And that's it—50+ years of watching musical plays and a couple of evenings of evaluating them. I've still got to see Jones & Schmidt's new one, *Roadside*, which opened off-Broadway three days before I wrote this, and like everyone else I'm waiting for Sondheim's long-overdue *Wise Guys*, and I missed *Ragtime* a couple of years ago and am still trying to catch up with it, but while they may someday be added to the list, they won't knock anything off.

As pasttimes go, this was (and remains) one of the more enjoyable ones.

For Burstzine #1

PART IV: SPEECHES

I give a lot of speeches. I've toastmastered a Worldcon and maybe a dozen regional conventions, I've probably given 25 or 30 Guest of Honor speeches, and while I never charge conventions, I do deliver a number of speeches elsewhere each year for money.

So, in this technological age, it's only natural that some of my speeches would be recorded, and a few would actually get transcribed. I'm including a couple of toastmaster gigs and a brief banquet speech here, plus one that was written expressly to be read aloud by Tony Lewis for a convention I was unable to attend.

SKYLARK PRESENTATION:
A Message from Mike Resnick

It is a long-standing tradition that the most recent winner of the Skylark Award hands it out to the new winner at the Boskone banquet. Obviously that is not going to happen this year. One look at this year's speaker—the receding forehead, the unkempt appearance, the beady little eyes that reflect no spark of intelligence—will convince even the most unobservant among you that the person reading this is not the devilishly handsome and incredibly talented Mike Resnick.

However, while I cannot be with you this weekend, at least I can speak to you through this semi-literate drone and let you know why I am not here to share in the festivities. While you are all enjoying the usual winter sports connected with Boskone—hockey, ice sculpting, and listening to Rick Katze deny that he's secretly plotting to chair Noreascon IV—Carol and I are out here in Hollywood, sweltering in the 72-degree heat and slowing starving to death on a meager daily menu of cavier, pate de fois gras, and pheasant under glass, while being forced to drink gallons of 1953 Dom Perignon. (At least it's from the North slope.)

It seems that, after almost 6 years of futzing around, they are finally, really and truly, making a movie out of *Santiago*—(Tony: pause 30 seconds for riotous applause to subside)—and since Carol and I have written the screenplay (in fact, we have written it 10 times at last count), they have flown us out for one of a number of what are called story conferences.

Let it be known that this is to be a Major Production that spares no expense. In fact, you can reach us by writing to us in care of the Beverly Hilton.

Well, in care of *a* Beverly Hilton, anyway. Our producers thoughtfully arranged for us to stay with Beverly, the key grip's maiden aunt, who lives out in the Mojave Desert and offered us an unfinished room over her garage.

On the other hand, we have as much clout and input as any screenwriting team in history. Which means slightly less than the producer's nephew's wife's hairdresser, about the same as the men's room attendant, and just a shade more than Dimitri

Tiomkin, who hasn't scored a movie in 20 years and has been dead even longer than that.

The story conferences themselves are at least as science fictional as anything ever written by Lois McMaster Bujold. My favorite comment from yesterday's session was, "Why *can't* one of the twins be black?"

They haven't cast the film yet. They keep saying they want the biggest, most expensive star around, but we keep holding out for Mel Gibson instead of Michael Jordan.

Anyway, so much for Hollywood. I want you to know that I remain my sweet, humble, lovable self, and no matter how many millions I make and how many Oscars I win, I will always cherish the memory of you totally insignificant people who have been bit players and extras in the rich tapestry of my life.

(Tony: Pause 2 minutes until standing ovation has subsided.)

But I digress. We've got a Skylark to present. And the first order of business is to ask why we call it a Skylark, since it is fitted with a Lens and would better be called the Kimball or the Lensman. But after 3 days of the kind of answers one gets at story conferences—"Sure we can do the Audrey Hepburn Story, but let's get an Audrey with hooters"—I'm sure as hell not going to be the one to question it.

The Skylark Award goes to that person who best personifies the qualities that made the late E. E. "Doc" Smith beloved of fandom. But since no one has written any Skylark or Lensman books lately, or messed around with doughnut formulae (ask the drone here to explain that reference later), we tend to give it to a pro or a fan who's a kinda sorta nice guy and doesn't vote against NESFA at worldcon business meetings. I figure I won mine because I've overslept every business meeting since 1963, and after all these years I still can't spell NESFA, WSFS, or BNF.

Nonetheless, I am enormously proud of my own Skylark, and carry it with me everywhere I go. Usually I put it in a window where everyone can see and admire it. Unfortunately, I seem to be running in bad luck these past twelve months, as I have had 3 hotels, a Polish laundry, and a pornographic bakery shop go up in flames around me.

I mentioned this to Jane Yolen, who suggested, as usual,

that I put the Skylark where the sun never shines. But since I don't know where the New York publishers hide their accounting ledgers, I have not yet been able to do this.

Ah, well, I'm due to judge the Miss Nude Beverly Hills Pageant in a couple of moments, and you must be getting tired of hearing Tony Lewis screw up my priceless prose, so let's get on with it: in this Politically Correct year of 1996, one of the Skylark winners is Gay.

The other is her husband, Joe.

Gay Haldeman is a world traveler, and wherever she goes she brings a little sunlight with her. She has worked, credited and otherwise, on conventions for a third of a century. She has helped more writers than just Joe, and more fans than you can shake a stick at. (Well, more than *I* can shake a stick at, anyway—and Teddy Roosevelt and I both carry pretty big sticks.)

As for Joe, the record speaks for itself: multiple Hugo winner, multiple Nebula winner, past president of SFWA, screenwriter, filksinger, and one of the more dangerous poker players around.

I congratulate Gay and Joe Haldeman, the very worthy winners of the 1996 Skylark Award for lifetime achievement in science fiction.

For the 1996 Boskone banquet
Read Aloud by Tony Lewis

MIKE RESNICK'S TOASTMASTER SPEECH AT NOLACON II, THE 1988 WORLDCON HELD IN NEW ORLEANS.

Good evening, and welcome to the Awards Ceremony of the 46th World Science Fiction Convention.

Well, actually, that's not exactly true. If you'll check the third revision of the second printing of your program book . . .

There, that wasn't so bad. You know, I met Bob Shaw one night this week. He toastmastered this in Atlanta, and he assured me that no matter how used I was to public speaking, when I actually got around to Toastmastering the Hugo ceremonies I was going to be nervous. I explained to him that very few things make me nervous, except for muddy racetracks and overly aggressive redheads named Thelma.

But here we are, and I think maybe he was right. For the past few weeks I've been having this recurring dream, and in this dream I'm sitting right over there, and John Guidry introduces me, and I get up, resplendent in my tuxedo, walk to the microphone, open my mouth—and I haven't anything to say.

So yesterday I scribbled some notes, and last night I dreamed that John Guidry introduces me, and I walk to the microphone, and I know exactly what I'm going to say—but I'm not wearing any pants.

I'm afraid to look down.

Anyway, when the Nolacon committee invited me to be Toastmaster, I asked what the job entailed, and they explained that my primary function was to introduce the pro and fan Guests of Honor. I've been flown here at great expense to do just that—so you can imagine my dismay when I found out that they already knew each other.

So instead, as long as I'm here, I might as well hand out these little rocket ships.

At least I get to do it in New Orleans, which is a fascinating town just now recovering from a veritable plague of Republicans.

When you consider that mankind took his first tentative footsteps across East Africa four million years ago, and two hundred thousand generations later we are confronted by a Presidential contest between George Bush against Michael Dukakis, you can only draw one logical conclusion: Darwin was wrong.

So much for politics. On the plus side, New Orleans is also the home of Risen Star, the remarkable racehorse who won this year's Preakness and Belmont Stakes by huge margins. I freely admit that I'm a devout horse-racing fan, and I think you'd be surprised at how many science fiction writers are. Pat Cadigan, who's up for a Hugo tonight, is well known as a great horse follower. Her only problem is that the horses she follows are even greater horse followers.

Speaking of bettors, the former governor of Louisiana, the very colorful Eddie Edwards, was quite a gambler himself. It was at this very podium in this very hotel, while awaiting trial for borrowing money from the Louisiana State Treasury to go gamble in Las Vegas, that he called a press conference and offered 8-to-5 odds that he'd beat the rap.

Not bright, but colorful.

Anyway, the story of Risen Star, who is currently recovering from a bowed tendon—for you fans in the audience, that's the equine equivalent of Twonk's Disease—is really quite uplifting. Ten percent of his earnings are given to the New Orleans branch of the Little Sisters of the Poor.

It was a inspiring thing to do, and I went out looking for them in the French Quarter last night. I couldn't find them.

I did find several Big Sisters of the Poor. They're on almost every street corner, along with their business agents.

Speaking of the Quarter, I hope most of you have had a chance to get there. In places, it's almost wilder than the Orlando party.

My favorite store is no longer there, but it was until about two years ago, and it was known as the Endangered Species Shop. From the name, you'd think they specialized in selling science fiction novels to which there were no sequels, but in point of fact it sold ivory and animals skins and the like, and why it wasn't picketed by 20,000 students is beyond me, but it did go the way of all endangered species.

Bourban Street is the Quarter's huckster room, and it's probably as hard to walk from one end to the other without being accosted by some fast-talking salesman as it is to walk through our huckster room without Dick Spelman trying to sell you a complete set of Dumarest of Terra for only $1,600.

$2,300 if you include New Orleans tax.

These days Bourban Street seems to be divided into three equal parts, not unlike Gaul, but Bourban Street's parts seem to be t-shirt shops, brass shops, and strip joints featuring performers of indeterminate gender.

For you celebrity watchers in the audience, I should point out that the Hugo nominees are all sitting in these cordoned-off areas up front. The committee has asked that you neither pet nor feed them until the awards are finished.

Actually, some of them will probably spend all night here, since a number of the hotels won't be honoring Worldcon reservations until next Wednesday—which, coincidentally, is the very same day the next-to-final Progress Report is going out.

Fifth class.

That means the mailman tosses it on the road and hopes you trip over it.

Now, before we go any further, it's my unhappy duty to point out to you that the practitioners of science fiction, who write about longevity and immortality with such optimism, are themselves not exempt from the limitations that the Star Maker has placed upon all other mortals. Science fiction has been harder hit than usual this year, and among the departed are four former Worldcon Guests of Honor: C. L. Moore, Alfred Bester, Clifford D. Simak, and perhaps the tallest giant of them all, Robert A. Heinlein. The complete list of our departed friends is on the necrology page of your Program Book, and we ask for a moment of silence for them at this time.

<pause>

Before we give out the Hugos, I've got a few bits of business to do. Just before I came out here Algis Budrys slipped me five dollars and asked me to plug one of his books, so I want you all to know that Algis is responsible for the sale of half a million copies of *Rogue Moon*.

I know I sold mine.

For those of you who are following the pennant races, we

have some late scores for you: 3 to 1, 6 to 5, and tied at 2-to-2 in the top of the eleventh inning.

On a more serious note, the Sheraton Corporation has asked me to announce that Dave Kyle is now banned from the use of the swimming pool.

He leaves a ring.

At this point, I suppose I should draw your attention to the fact that for the first time in many years there is no screen on the Hugo stage. We offer no apologies for this; it was done purposely. We feel that the Hugo Award ceremony is the one of the last bastions of the written word and of serious illustrative art, and if you absolutely must have pictures with your awards, we suggest a re-run of *Lost In Space*.

Before we get around to presenting the awards, and we've got an awful lot to present this year, I think it's time we showed our appreciation to the diligent workers who have been working on the Worldcon. I'm only going to introduce two by name— President Justin Winston and Chairman John Guidry—but would everyone involved please stand up and take a bow?

Now I tried this at Opening Ceremonies and it didn't work, so I'm going to try it again. We have a couple of dignitaries from across the various drinks, and we're going to try to introduce them once more. The TAFF winners—Lilian Edwards and Christina Lake. And the DUFF winner, Terry Dowling.

Before we get to the Hugo Awards, we have some awards that are traditionally given out at the Hugo Ceremony, and the first of these is the Big Heart Award, given out by Forest J Ackerman.

<Ackerman gives out Big Heart Award to Andre Norton>

I'd be remiss if I didn't once again point out our Professional Guest of Honor, Donald A. Wollheim. Take another bow, Don.

And our Fan Guest of Honor, who hasn't spoken to me since the Roast, Roger Sims.

For our next special awards, we have two gentlemen from Japan who are going to be presenting the Japanese Hugos.

<Japanese Hugos are given out.>

Our final special award is the First Fandom Hall of Fame Award. And this year we will have multiple awards, given by multiple presenters, all directed by the singular Mark Schulsinger.

<First Fandom Hall of Fame awards are given out.>

The Hugo Ceremony wasn't always the prestigious ceremony that it has become. The award wasn't created until 1953, when the very first one went not to a novel or a short story, but to Forry Ackerman as the Number One Fan Personality.

They made such an impression on fandom and Worldcon committees that they were dropped in 1954 (and Bob Silverberg has been trying, during his various Worldcon Toastmaster gigs, to give out the 1954 awards ever since.)

They were back in 1955, and to show you how seriously they were taken, the legendary Lou Tabakow won a Hugo for the Best Unpublished Story of the Year. And Sam Moskowitz, arguably one of the two or three most identifiable fans in the universe, won a Hugo as Science Fiction's Mystery Guest.

However, they were back again in 1956, and since anything that happens two years in a row becomes a fannish tradition, we began taking them seriously and there's never been any suggestion since then that they should be discontinued.

Now, categories have changed over the years. On occasion there were only two categories for fiction, and there was a time when if all the fans in the world were laid end to end—as I'm convinced happened outside the Cincinnati suite last night—they could still only win one Hugo between them.

Categories continue to evolve, even this year. I was personally hoping to open the envelope for the Least Anti-Social Behavior by a Best-Selling Author Not Under the Influence of Alcohol, if only to announce that there were no nominees. But instead this year's new category is entitled Other Forms, which in these days of explicit inter-species sex truly boggles the mind.

Now, the Hugos are just one small part of Worldcon, and as I hand them out I'm going to be recalling to you incidents from other Worldcons, because most of us don't win Hugos.

For our first award, Stan Schmidt, the editor of Analog, will be giving out the John Campbell Award for Best New Writer. And if Stan wonders where the envelope is, it's right here.

<Stan Schmidt presents Campbell Award to Judith Moffett>

More work goes into a Worldcon than meets the eye. Some of that work involves the creation of the Hugo Award itself. In 1973 the rocket ships didn't arrive on time, and the committee was forced to give out wooden bases to the winners.

I should point out that professional artist Ned Dameron, who did the cover to the Program Book, has designed the bases for this year's Hugos, which are the first ever to be shown in actual flight.

<Best Fan Writer award is presented to Mike Glyer. This and all subsequent awards are presented by Mike Resnick>

The 1971 Worldcon was held at Boston's Sheraton Hotel, and it had an open-air swimming pool which could be seen from all rooms above the fifth floor, where it resided. One night I walked into your Fan Guest of Honor Roger Sims' suite on the 23rd Floor, and everyone was playing cards or reading or talking. There were no empty couches or chair, no place for me to sit down, and I was exhausted from lugging a bunch of books with me all day.

So I walked to the window, looked down, had a wonderful idea, walked to the center of the room, and announced that there were 500 naked people in the pool. You never saw a room empty out so fast, as they all made a mad rush to the elevators and stairs.

Well, I sat down in the empty room, and started reading some of the things I'd bought in the huckster's room. But the room stayed empty. And stayed empty. And finally, a couple of hours later, Roger, red of face and short of breath, entered the room, and said, "We thought you were kidding."

I said, "Do you mean I wasn't?"

And that is the origin of skinny-dipping at Worldcon.

There's a postscript to that story. The next evening it was about 45 degrees and raining, and some 2,000 hopeful voyeurs gathered by the pool, waiting for the previous night's skinny-dippers, all of whom had the intelligence to stay inside where it was warm and dry.

<Best Fan Artist is presented to Brad Foster>

1972 was the year that Worldcons outlawed peanut butter. They really did. It seems that there was a fan who came to the masquerade in a costume of his own creation, as an underground cartoon character called The Turd. And his entire costume was about ten quarts of peanut butter spread across his pudgy little body.

But he hadn't realized that at Worldcon masquerades there are numerous bright lights, and before the evening was over the peanut butter had turned rancid. He ruined every costume that he brushed against and did considerable damage to the walls and curtains.

<Best Fanzine is presented to the Texas SF Inquirer>

The 1968 Worldcon was held in Berkeley, California at the Claremont Hotel, later to be known in fannish legend as the Transylvania Hilton.

Worldcons were just beginning to get big at that point, and the Claremont had hardly any rooms, so most of us stayed at sleazy downtown Berkeley hotels. (There are no unsleazy downtown Berkeley hotels.)

Now, Worldcon was held at the same time as the Democratic Convention in the city of Chicago, and the local Hell's Angels decided to protest Chicago police brutality by killing a Berkeley cop. Suddenly all the hotels were cordoned off, and reaching the Claremont became a feat equivalent to climbing the Berlin Wall and getting to the other side.

I remember one night I went out to get something cold to drink, and I had three Berkeley policeman accompanying me. I bribed each of them with a chocolate malt so we could out quickly the next morning. It took two and one-half hours to get to the Claremont anyway, which was when I realized, perhaps for the first time, that to outsiders such as policemen in the real world, we look even stranger than Hell's Angels.

<Best Semi-Prozine is presented to Locus>

Prior to 1968, Worldcons weren't large enough to fill a single hotel, let alone the three and four we regularly fill these days, and we frequently found ourselves sharing a hotel with another convention.

Yes, I'm coming to that one, but first I want to tell you about 1966, because it was at Tricon in Cleveland that we shared the hotel with a convention of Scotsmen who donned their kilts, pulled out their bagpipes, and marched up and down the corridors all night long serenading us with bagpipe music.

I think it was first, and I believe the only, case in history where the members of a Worldcon complained to a hotel that the mundanes were making too much noise.

<Best Professional Artist is presented to Michael Whelan>

In 1967 we shared New York's Statler Hilton Hotel with a convention of Scientologists. To this day I still don't know who converted more of which to what.

But 1967 was also the year that an impassioned group of fans called Trekkies made their initial appearance at a Worldcon. At first we thought we might have a little fun running them off the premises, but then cooler and wiser heads prevailed, and explained that the show was on its last legs and we'd obviously never hear from it or them again.

So much for science fiction's ability to predict the future.

<Best Editor is presented to Gardner Dozois>

Every Worldcon is allowed to present one special award. In 1963 it was given to Isaac Asimov, right in the middle of his schtick about how he deserved awards more than anyone but had never won one. It was the only time I've ever seen Isaac speechless.

This year's special award will be presented by John Guidry and Justin Winston.

<The SF Oral History Society is presented with a special award>

I want to say just a little more about the Science Fiction Oral History Association, because too many people don't know about it. They have more than 20,000 hours of recorded tapes and interviews, many with people who are no longer around. They have major speeches and addresses which will never be given again. They are underfinanced and underappreciated, and I hope all of you will take it upon yourselves to start supporting them. I'm sure they have a room or a booth here where you can find out what they are doing and how you can help. They're all we have; without them, we have no history.

Except for me. I'm going to give you a little more.

Now we come to the category of Best Dramatic Presentation, and along about this time you must be wondering why we even bother listing the ever-present No Award, since it never seems to win.

Well, it did win in 1958 for Best New Author, but more to the point, it has triumphed in this particular category, Dramatic Presentation, more often than Gene Roddenbury, Stephen Speilberg, or Stanley Kubrick, which makes it a formidable contender.

<Best *Dranatic Presentation is presented to* The Princess Bride>

The 1977 Worldcon was held in the Fontainbleu Hotel in Miami Beach. There were signs posted everywhere you could see that the residents should leave no crumbs on the floors. At first we thought this was merely because the maids were lazy—which indeed they were—but one night while going from one tower of the Fontainbleu to the other, we stumbled across a small army of palmetto roaches.

I had never seen a palmetto roach before. I hope to God I never see a palmetto roach again. They'd make dandy trophies if you could just figure out a way to kill them without endangering your own life.

We immediately turned around, went back to our room, and scrubbed down the floor.

<Best *Other Form is presented to* The Watchman>

Worldcon voting wasn't always carried out quite the way it is nowadays. Prior to 1970 we voted only one year in advance, and there were no such things as mail order ballots. Those of you who survived the parties to the extent that you could crawl out of bed at nine in the morning and attend the business meetings heard somebody say something about the restaurants in each city and then you voted.

One year a Midwestern fan decided to enter a gag bid—for Tijuana. It didn't take a whole lot of votes to win in those days—40 to 50 were usually quite sufficient—and when the perpetrator saw how well-received his proposal was, he did a very quick head count, and at the last moment he and his wife both voted for one of his main competitors. It's probably a good thing that he did: Tijuana, complete with its rent-by-the-hour hotel, missed being in the final runoff by a single vote.

<Best *Non-Fiction is presented to* Michael Whelan's Works of Wonder>

The 1976 Worldcon in Kansas City was billed as "the ultimate Worldcon," and the proprietors, in the months leading up to it, became positively paranoid that people were going to try to get out of paying. So they announced that along with the normal convention badges that everyone wears, they were going to come up with a unique identification system that could not be replicated in a single weekend—and in the days and weeks leading up to the convention, that became the primary topic of fannish conversation.

Not to keep you in suspense, what it turned out to be was a hospital bracelet with your name imprinted on it . . . and now that a dozen years have passed and Ken Keller is no longer so sensitive about such things, I think I might as well reveal that a number of fans went to a local hospital, found a septigenarian lady who was due to be released that Friday, convinced her not to take her bracelet off, and managed to get her into every function including the masquerade and the Hugo ceremony.

<Best Short Story is presented to "Why I Left Harry's All-Night Hamburgers" by Lawrence Watt-Evans>

Phoenix can be a pretty hot town. It certainly was during the 1978 Worldcon, with the temperature rising to 120 by day and rarely dropping under 100 at night.

One evening I went out for dinner with the legendary Lou Tabakow. Lou had heard about a fabulous rooftop restaurant not far from the hotel, and nothing would do but that we should go to that one and avoid the crowds. What he didn't know was that this was not a penthouse, but literally a rooftop restaurant, with no screening and no shade—and of course no air conditioning, since it was outside.

We sat down, ordered drinks, and removed our ties before they arrived. Our jackets were gone by the time we got our salads. I had my shoes and socks off long before the main course arrived. Then dignified, white-haired, legendary Lou, who in his time was both a professional writer and a worldcon chairman, looked around before dessert came, saw that we had all male waiters and that no one else was crazy enough to be dining on the roof, and finished this 4-star meal in his underwear, which is my one lasting memory of Iguanacon.

<Best Novelette is presented to "Buffalo Gals" by Ursula K. Le Guin>

I remember everyone at the 1983 Baltimore Worldcon telling us they were going to make a profit. I remember everyone at the 1984 Los Angeles Worldcon assuring us there was no way they could possibly make a profit.

I don't know about you, but I feel much more secure knowing where our future fantasists are coming from.

<Best Novella is presented to "Eye For Eye" by Orson Scott Card>

I don't have any stories from Brighton last year. Everyone who went with me is still there looking for the Corn Exchange.

So we'd better get on with our major award, the Hugo for Best Novel of the year.

<Best Novel is presented to The Uplift War by David Brin.>

There are going to be some very unhappy people tonight, if there aren't already. I think the audience should acknowledge that even making a Hugo ballot, no matter how much they aspire, is something that most people will never do, and give all the nominees one final ovation.

<long standing ovation>

I have been asked to announce that the New Orleans Lagnappe Dance will be held in the Marriott Mardi Gras Ballroom at eleven o'clock, so you don't have to run, you have plenty of time to get there.

I've also been asked to announce that all Hugo winners are due onstage for photographs as soon as the Hugo ceremony is over.

And finally, I've been asked to announce that the Hugo winners are due onstage now.

Thank you and good night.

For Challenger #14
(Transcription, from videotape)

1989 WORLDCON BANQUET SPEECH

Note: I was blinded by the spotlight and couldn't read my speech, so I gave what I could remember of it. This is the whole thing.

Our first convention was the 1963 Worldcon in Washington, D.C.—Discon I—and I can remember it as if it were yesterday. I was 21, Carol was 20, and a year earlier we hadn't even known that fandom existed.

The total attendance was about 400. Rooms were $7 a night. The banquet was $3 (and everyone was furious about it.)

A Frazetta cover painting went for $70, the highest price of the auction, and people doubted it would ever be equaled. (I think the same painting sold 20 years later for something like $18,000.)

Everyone agreed that things were looking up for the field. Some of the better writers could even foresee the day, not far off, when they could make about $7,500 a year from their science fiction—provided that Bob Silverberg would stop selling 30 stories a month.

There were no regional parties, because there were only three regional cons in the whole world, and they didn't have to compete for customers.

There were no mail ballots for site selection. You dragged yourself out of bed on Sunday morning, listened as various pros told you which city had the better restaurants and various fans told you which city had better bookstores, and then you voted.

The nightly entertainment was provided by future Worldcon bidders, each of whom reserved one evening to sponsor a bheer blast for the entire convention. The costume ball *was* a costume ball, complete with a dance band.

There was a special interest group that constituted at least 20% of the membership—and no, it wasn't the Trekkies. They came a few years later. It was the Burroughs Bibliophiles, all of whom wore suits and ties (as did almost everyone else.)

The Hyborean Legion spent most of its meeting debating whether there would ever be enough interest in Robert E.

Howard to get at least a couple of the Conan books reprinted in paperback.

Femmefans were outnumbered almost ten-to-one, female authors by an even wider margin.

The huckster room sold books and magazines. Period.

Fans who actually read science fiction outnumbered those who didn't.

The convention wound up with a play, written and performed by the pros, just the way summer camp used to end with a play put on by the counselors.

There was no social schism between fans and pros. Hell, most of the pros had *been* fans . . . and an awful lot of the fans were on the road to becoming pros. There was an almost tangible sense of community among the members of the convention.

I was the greenest of neofans, and fully expected to be ignored by everyone, but before I had been there for two hours Doc Smith—*Doc Smith himself!*—bought me a cup of coffee and spent half an hour talking to me.

Sam Moskowitz gave me the first of many condensed courses on the history of science fiction.

Jack Chalker, who was only 19, and I, who at 21 should have known better, both remarked at a party that we planned someday to earn our livings writing sf—and I was amazed that not a single person scoffed at the notion, and indeed everyone seemed to encourage it . . . the very first words of encouragement I had ever heard except from Carol.

Stan Vinson, an old-time Ohio fan who I had known only through correspondence, bought me a book that he knew I wanted and couldn't afford, and for the next 15 years refused to let me reimburse him.

Bob Tucker taught me my first 50 fannish words.

Lester del Rey and Sprague de Camp invited us into the darkened recesses of a pro party.

John Campbell sat me down in a corner and explained what his latest editorial *really* meant.

Ed Wood sat me down in another corner and explained why good science was far more important than good writing.

Then Fritz Leiber came over and gently explained why I shouldn't necessarily believe anything John Campbell or Ed Wood told me.

The legendary Lou Tabakow hijacked us to the Cincinnati Suite and insisted that we think of it as home at every Worldcon we attended.

The N3F (National Fantasy Fan Federation) made sure I went home loaded with half a hundred fanzines.

We even met the Chicago fan group which, unbeknownst to us, had been meeting regularly across the street from our apartment for years.

If there was an unfriendly fan or pro there we never met him.

That was the main impression we carried away from Discon I: the feeling that we had found ourselves among friends we had had all our lives but simply hadn't met until then.

Things have changed over the years. Nowadays when I come to the Worldcon it's at least as much for business as for pleasure—but that wonderful feeling of community remains unchanged.

There is an old adage that you can choose your friends but you can't choose your family, to which I reply: Bunk!

We chose our family 26 years ago and have been coming back to its annual reunion ever since.

Appeared in File 770:83

2000 RIVERCON SPEECH

Since this is the very last Rivercon—at least until I speak to Sue and Steve Francis in a day or two and set them straight about things—I think it's an appropriate time to look back. After all, science fiction has been my life, and Rivercon has been a very important part of it—especially on Sundays, when we go to the Galt House for brunch and I get my annual fix of Rebecca sauce.

Then I feel guilty and usually go on a diet as soon as I get home. So does Bill Cavin. He and I have gone on 38 diets together and have lost 1,614 pounds, a record for peacetime tonnage. To put it in layman's terms, between us we have lost 14 entire Nicki Lynches.

But I digress.

I was about to point out that a lot has changed over the years.

We were so poor that when we got into science fiction we couldn't afford a dog or a cat. My only pet was Silver Charmer—a paper clip.

God, I loved that paper clip! It never once argued about the Nebula rules or the Worldcon site selection rotation plan. (Well, only when it got drunk or came into contact with a NESFA mailing.)

Back then, an endangered species was an animal that was on the road to becoming extinct. Today it's a science fiction novel to which there are no sequels.

We had no such thing as Virtual Realty. If a one-eyed steel-toothed guy with a broadsword, a loincloth and a bad attitude came after you, you'd damned well better be faster than he was or you were in deep shit.

Back then we said that no science fiction television show would ever have the wit, style or elan of *Maverick*. They have since proceeded to prove it 73 times. And counting.

Back then George R.R. Martin was a harmless chess tournement director. Today he's our most dangerous writer. You think not? I picked up his latest hardcover at Larry Smith's table and got a triple hernia.

Back then Kelly Freas had won so many Best Artist Hugos that Worldcon committees were seriously considering retiring the award. I am convinced that if he had Bob Eggleton's hair, he'd still be winning them.

Back then Jack Chalker had only written 43 Well of Souls books. Then he *really* got busy.

Back then we all expected Bruce Pelz to win a few Hugos for Best Short Fiction, given the skill he displayed writing the LACon I Financial Report.

Of course, some things have stayed the same.

Big Julie Shwartz still comes to these things with a gorgeous woman on each arm—which would be okay except that he's not into sharing.

Dick Spelman still goes through the dealers' room and makes sure that no Resnick books are ever displayed face-up, a hangover from his huckster days.

Dave Kyle still invites innocent young girls up to his room to examine his Hugo—in spite of my warning them that Dave hasn't had a Hugo in years.

And of course, the longest-standing trufan of then all, Forry Ackerman, hasn't changed at all. Not even his socks. And I've been meaning to talk to him about it.

Now, there are certain guests that I have been asked not to insult.

Therefore, I won't tell any short jokes about Roger Sims. I have a feeling they'd go right over his head anyway.

I will not tell you what Rusty Hevelin said when the judge asked him what he was doing with the four girl scouts, the aqualung, the trapeze, and the dead chicken.

I will not ask Esther Friesner what it was like to play left tackle for the Green Bay Packers before her operation.

And I will not explain that our 1998 Toastmaster writes science fiction as Hal Clement only because he has appeared in more than 100 porno films as Harry Stubbs.

I've just been told that if I introduce every former guest and toastmaster now, and let each of them stand up and take a bow, by the time we're finished the ice cream should be completely melted, and then you'll never realize that Sue Francis only bought half the usual supply and pocketed the rest of the money (or wasn't I supposed to say that?)

Anyway, here is the list of those fans and pros who have honored Rivercon with their presence, and whom Rivercon has honored in return.

[[[Reads the names of the 47 former guests in attendance.]]]

Now grab a quick 5,000 calories apiece, and then To Your Scattered Parties Go.

[[[Mike, who is the only person to be Pro Guest of Honor, Fan Guest of Honor, and Toastmaster at Rivercon is given a plaque declaring him to be a Triple Crown winner.]]]

Thank you very much for this. I'm deeply honored. I also want to point out that the only two other living Triple Crown winners, Seattle Slew and Affirmed, both command stud fees in excess of $100,000 despite the fact that neither of them has ever sired a Campbell winner, from which you may draw the logical conclusion.

Appeared in Fosfax

PART V: INTROS TO FANNISH BOOKS

Much to the dismay of my creditors, all of whom have expensive tastes, I seem to find myself doing more and more fannish projects these days. Including the editing of books that appeal almost entirely to fannish interests.

Here are the introductions to four of them.

INTRODUCTION TO
ALTERNATE WORLDCONS

First, let me set the scene for you.

The time is Labor Day weekend, 1993. The place is, of course, San Francisco. The venue is ConFrancisco, the worldcon that will never live down the nickname of ConFiasco. The location is the Cincinnati hospitality suite at the Marriott Hotel.

The committee is not very happy with those of us who chose to room in the Marriott. We've taken about 60 rooms, plus this suite, and they're not getting any credit for the room/nights.

The people in the suite aren't all that thrilled with the committee, either. When the committee blew this hotel and wound up with the party hotel being six blocks away from the convention center—six *uphill* blocks—we made up a name for ourselves that didn't sound like "worldcon," blocked 60 rooms, and quickly filled them with pros and old-time fans.

We were in the nicest hotel in the area. We were in the closest hotel to the convention center. Our elevators worked. We should all have been wildly happy.

But we weren't.

There was the three-hour line for registration. There was the endless line for the masquerade, at which hundreds of people were turned away. There was the high-handedness and out-and-out rudeness with which many of the panelists were treated. There was an endless backstage wait at the Hugo ceremonies. There was this, there was that, there was the next thing. Read some con reports in the fanzines; they'll fill you in.

Anyway, it's Sunday night and there we are, maybe twelve or fifteen of us, seated around the huge mahogany table in the designated smoking room of the suite, bitching about ConFiasco.

And, as always, someone says, "Could be worse."

"How?" asks somebody else.

"Could have been in Zagreb."

Yeah, that's right. Zagreb, Yugoslavia, was one of the losing bidders for the 1993 worldcon, just before the whole damned country went up in flames.

But because these are nothing if not imaginative people sitting here, someone else decides to argue that a Zagreb worldcon would have been better than this one, even *with* bombs flying through the air.

Pretty soon someone else is arguing that the Boat (a 1988 bid for a worldcon on a cruise ship) would have been better than Nolacon II. And a couple of old-timers start guessing what Syracon in 1967 might have been like if New York City hadn't aced them out of it and put on one of the poorer worldcons in history.

And I'm sitting there at one end of the table, listening to all this, and Dean Wesley Smith is sitting at the other end, probably wondering what the hell he'd wandered into. And my brain is still in a rut from selling *Alternate Tyrants* to Tor Books a few hours ago, and the reason it is in a rut is because I went through 23 *other* "alternate" pitches before Patrick Nielsen Hayden finally agreed to the Tyrant book, and all I can think of is alternate dinners and alternate autograph sessions and maybe going to an alternate party—and suddenly I realize that I am listening to the genesis of an anthology called *Alternate Worldco*ns, and I yell across the table to Dean that I want to edit it and will he publish it, and he gets this incredibly dopey smile on his face (yeah, even dopier than usual) and says, yes, he'd love to publish it.

Well, everyone else thinks we're crazy and they keep busy imagining what would have happened if Barsoom had beat Chicago in 1940 and really important things like that, and I lead Dean off to the next room to talk business, and damned if we don't have a deal within the next ten minutes.

So we come back to the room that gave it birth, and announce that *Alternate Worldco*ns is now in business and I'll be commissioning stories and Dean will have the book out in time for the 1994 worldcon, and suddenly authorial eyes blink open and authorial ears perk up, and I am surrounded by potential contributors, and I realize it is time to separate the wheat from the chaff, so I say that I view this as a Trufannish project and will therefore pay Trufannish wages of a penny a word.

You wouldn't believe how fast a crowded room can empty out.

But then they start thinking of stories they want to tell, and one by one, shyly, apologetically, begrudgingly, furiously, they begin returning, and I begin making assignments, and word gets out and the next day I assign the rest of the stories.

They've been drifting in over the past half year—at these prices you don't lean too heavily on the writers until it's 11:59 at the Well of Souls—and here they are, a labor of love that will make no one rich (except maybe Dean and me), but will charm your socks off and will perhaps get you thinking about your favorite alternate worldcon so you'll be ready to write the story when this edition sells out and Dean gives me three million dollars for the sequel and I raise the rates to a munificent two cents a word.

INTRODUCTION TO
AGAIN, ALTERNATE WORLDCONS

*Alternate Worldcon*s made its debut at the 1994 World Science Fiction Convention, which was held in Winnipeg.

I've never seen anything sell like that before. Not even hotcakes. Serious, award-quality Resnick novels should sell half that well.

Let me tell you how it was: Dean Wesley Smith, the publisher, shipped a few hundred copies to Winnipeg. By Saturday they were all gone. By Sunday fans were offering $40.00 and $50.00 for this $9.95 book despite the fact that they knew there were hundreds of copies available from the publisher and that they'd find them at all the upcoming conventions.

How could I not produce a sequel? Your humble editor, true to his word, promised a raise in word rates if the first volume was a bestseller. No more of this fannish penny-a-word stuff.

So here we have *Again, Alternate Worldcons*, with a brand-new publisher (Michael Walsh), a brand-new word rate (a fabulous penny and a quarter a word), all new authors (except for Dick Spelman, who hasn't been new in close to two-thirds of a century, and Leah Zeldes, who promised to run those photos of me and the four girl scouts and the dead chicken and the trapeze and the apricot preserves on the Internet if I didn't ask her for a story) and the same old editor (me).

So enjoy . . . and if enough of you buy it, I promise that the book that makes it a trilogy will pay a whopping penny and a half a word. Before taxes.

Editor's Note (skip this unless you've got a thing for boredom):

When the original *Alternate Worldco*ns came out, I was contacted by numerous irate SMOFs who informed me that the word "Worldcon" was the singular possession of the World Science Fiction Society, and that I was doubly damned to hell: first, for not asking their permission to use it, and second, for having the audacity not to capitalize it when I did use it.

I replied that while I didn't acknowledge that anyone owns a word and could prevent me from using it—especially when I became a shareholder in the corporation that claims to own it simply by paying my worldcon (excuse me: Worldcon) dues, I would be happy to insert any statement or disclaimer they wanted, both in this book and in all reprints of the old book.

All that took place close to two years ago. Since none of them have seen fit to contact me again, despite the fact that the publication of this book was common knowledge (and indeed the book was delayed a year while not one but two publishers went belly-up, one permanently, one temporarily), I have swiped the wording of one of Kevin Standlee's footnotes and instructed the typesetter to insert it on the copyright page of both books. I am also, you will note, using the Politically Correct capitalized version of Worldcon in this introduction, though I will not force any writer to do so in his/her story.

I am doing this because I am a Nice Guy (note caps). But no one will ever convince me that I need permission to use the word Worldcon.

Or even worldcon.

INTRODUCTION TO
ALTERNATE SKIFFY

Introduction #1[1]

It's all Patrick's fault.

You see, he was the purchasing editor of the Alternate series for Tor. You know the books—*Alternate Presidents, Alternate Kennedys, Alternate Warriors, Alternate Outlaws*, and so on.

Problem is, Patrick likes to be begged. Or at least proposed to. And there are a limited number of viable Alternate books. And I hate thinking up viable Alternate book proposals.

So one night we were having dinner at a Worldcon, or perhaps it was a Nebula banquet, and the conversation went exactly as follows:

Mike: All right, then, how about *Alternate Diseases of the Big Toe*?

Patrick: Right or left?

Mike: Yes.

Patrick (after a thoughtful pause): I don't think so. Whether we chose the right or left toe, we'd alienate half our readership.

Mike: Okay, how about *Alternate Secretariat Tales*? In one he's a gelding, in another he's a milk horse, in a third he's magically transformed into the Lone Ranger's Silver . . .

Patrick: No, I hear Bantam is doing *Alternate Man o' War Stories*. This would be too close.

Mike: Okay, no way you can say no to this next one—what do you think of *Alternate Michael Jordans*? In one story, he

---

1   Patrick Nielsen Hayden wrote the other introduction.

could walk away from basketball in his prime and pursue a career as a minor league outfielder . . .

Patrick: Silliest thing I ever heard of. Forget it.

Mike: I give up. I can't think of any more Alternate skiffy stuff.

Patrick: That's it!!!

Mike (looking around quickly): What is, and how many legs has it got?

Patrick: That's the next Alternate book— *Alternate Skiffy*!

Mike: Oh, no! You're not sticking me with a book called *Alternate Skiffy*, and how much are you paying for it?

Patrick: I like it so much, I'll edit it with you, and we'll split the money.

So that's the story. Patrick is co-editing this volume because he is dead certain it'll enhance his reputation for editing Works of Quality. Me, I'm doing it for my half of the $108,350 advance that remains after shelling out a penny a word to all the writers. (It was too large a sum to fit on the contract, but Patrick and Publisher John Betancourt promised that they'd remember it.)

Now Patrick's going to give you his version of an Introduction. Since I'm writing mine first, I have absolutely no idea what he's going to say, but if it differs in any detail, however slight, from my own, I'd advise you all to stand clear of him, because you never know which way he'll fall after God strikes him dead.

INTRODUCTION TO
GIRLS FOR THE SLIME GOD

ME AND THE SLIME GOD

November, 1960 was a pretty interesting time to be around.

Kelso was just wrapping up the first of his five Horse of the Year titles.

A womanizer who makes Bill Clinton look like a monk with vows of celibacy won the presidency from a Richard who makes Shakespeare's villain of the same name look like a choir boy.

Ngo Dinh Diem crushed an army revolt in a little country called Vietnam that most Americans couldn't find on a map. (Oh, hell, let's be honest—most Americans *still* can't find it.)

America's first submarine armed with nuclear missles put out to sea.

And the November *Playboy* hit the stands.

Now, you might think that last item is pretty minor, and perhaps it is, but the first four have nothing to do with this book, whereas the November, 1960 *Playboy* is responsible for it.

I think it was one of the half-dozen or so issues of *Playboy* I ever bought. It's not a magazine that does much for me, once I get through staring at the photos. In fact, that issue is the only one I've ever kept. I still have it, and I still open it up every year or so.

But not to the photos.

I bought it because, as I was thumbing through it at the newsstand at the ripe old age of 18, I came to a series of science fiction pulp covers in glorious color. Then, as I looked more closely, I realized that they were parodies of pulp covers, drawn by Will Elder of *Mad* and *Little Annie Fanny* fame.

They illustrated an article called "Girls for the Slime God," by William Knoles, a wonderful tongue-in-cheek piece of nostalgia about all those old science fiction pulps that featured BEMs (Bug-Eyed Monsters, for the uninitiated) ripping the clothes off the heroine, and usually sporting titles like the one the article itself bore.

As you'll learn, though most of the magazine covers promised such goodies, only one magazine—*Marvel Science Stories*—
delivered on that promise, and then only in its first two issues.

Knoles began quoting from the magazine, especially from a
story called "The Avengers of Space," which is all about space
heroine Lorna's futile attempts to keep her clothes on for more
than a page at a time, and a funny thing happened—I fell ever-
lastingly in love with poor Lorna and her ill-fated obsession to
keep getting dressed.

Now, I wasn't the only person who read that article. Isaac
Asimov did, too, and he immediately produced an amusing fictional answer entitled "Playboy and the Slime God," which ran
in the March, 1961 *Amazing Stories*.

Fast forward to 1963. I finally found the first two issues of
Marvel Science Stories, which contained "The Avengers of
Space," "The Time Trap," and "Dictator of the Americas," the
three stories that were quoted extensively in Knoles' article.
(They cost 50 cents apiece; I doubt that you could buy the pair of
them for much less that $150.00 today.) Carol and I were as
dead broke as most young couples, and got our entertainment
as cheaply as possible—and I can still recall the night that we
sat down and read "The Avengers of Space" aloud to each other,
the rule being that one of us read until he or she cracked up
with laughter and then the other took over.

I also noted an interesting thing. Not all the stories, even in
these two issues, were the sort Knoles remembered so fondly. In
fact, there were just the three I mentioned above. And two of
the three were written by the prolific Henry Kuttner, who later
went on to write—in collaboration with his wife, Catherine L.
Moore—the Gallagher stories, the Baldy stories, "A Gnome
There Was," *Fury*, "What You Need," and a host of other semi-
classics.

Only the short story, "Dictator of the Americas," was written by someone else—in fact, by a name I'd never encountered
before, James Hall. When I went through my various indexes
trying to track him down, I discovered that "James Hall" was a
pseudonym of Henry Kuttner's.

(Kuttner used a *lot* of pseudonyms. One legend, perhaps
apocryphal though it makes sense given the tenor of the times,
is that he had to invent "Lewis Padgett" and "Lawrence

O'Donnell" because, after the shocking tales of Lorna and her fellow heroines, no editor would buy from him. In a poll taken in the late 1940s, both Padgett and O'Donnell ranked higher than Kuttner in the readers' affections.)

So *Playboy* published the article, and Isaac responded to it, and I bought and read the stories, and that was that. Except, as I mentioned, I fell in love with Lorna—and so, in a very platonic way, did Carol.

Now, Carol had been creating costumes for us to wear in the World Science Fiction Convention masquerades all during the 1970s. We had won in 1973 and 1974, lost in 1976, and won again in 1977. All of them had been beautiful and elaborate, and soon most of the costumers were imitating her approach, so she decided to do one last costume to show everyone that beautiful and eleborate wasn't the only way to go, and then retire from competition. What she came up with was an old-fashioned burlesque skit featuring Lorna, Captain Shawn, the BEM ("a teratological baroque spawned by no sane world"), and a Mime who would hold up speech balloons as the actors froze in pulp poses. Her only criterion was that the entire costume for all four of us had to cost less than $100.00.

"The Avengers of Space" won Best in Show at the 1979 NorthAmeriCon held in Louisville, Kentucky, and suddenly there was renewed interest in Lorna and the Knoles article and Isaac's story and the whole damned Slime God milieu. I was just starting to sell regularly and make a name for myself in the science fiction field, and it occurred to me that I could put together a book called *Girls for the Slime God* that would begin with the Knoles article, then run the three Kuttner stories (two of which were novellas and would bulk it out), follow them with the Asimov story, and finally maybe even run the script for our costume.

The one thing I knew was that this wasn't a mass market book. Not that sex doesn't sell, but rather that if you don't love the field, if you can't read these with a sense of delight and nostalgia and realize how far we've come, then they're just more fodder for critics who constantly judge science fiction by its worst examples. (Let's be honest here: Kuttner wrote these for a bottom-of-the-barrel market just about 60 years ago.)

One small press after another enthusiastically agreed to publish *Girls for the Slime God*, only to run into problems. Phantasia Press went dormant. Pulphouse closed its doors. Others had other problems. But now Gordie Meyer has elected to make it his company's very first publication, and all's well that ends well.

So she's back, blushing and chilly, eluding BEMs and heroes with equal desperation.

Lorna lives!!!

PART VI:
THE RESNICK LISTS

Over the years the members of my Listserv have ranked (and argued) just about everything from books to movies to meals.

If you don't feel you know me after reading all the articles in this book, there's probably very little likelihood that you ever will, but just on the off chance . . .

THE 15 BEST SCIENCE FICTION AND FANTASY NOVELS

1. *Star Maker* (Stapledon)

2. *Herovit's World* (Malzberg)

3. *Last and First Men* (Stapledon)

4. *Dimension of Miracles* (Sheckley)

5. *Galaxies* (Malzberg)

6. *The Demolished Man* (Bester) [magazine version]

7. *The Stars My Destination* (Bester)

8. *Dandelion Wine* (Bradbury)

9. *The Martian Chronicles* (Bradbury)

10. *The Voyage of the Space Beagle* (van Vogt)

11. *City* (Simak)

12. *Way Station* (Simak)

13. *The Once and Future King* (White)

14. *Cosmicomics* (Calvino)

15. *The Dying Earth* (Vance)

THE 10 BEST SCIENCE FICTION FILMS

1. *Forbidden Planet*
2. *The Road Warrior*
3. *Blade Runner*
4. *Dr. Strangelove*
5. *2001: A Space Odyssey*
6. *The Terminator*
7. *A Clockwork Orange*
8. *Charly*
9. *The Matrix*
10. *Them*

THE 10 BEST FANTASY FILMS

1. *Field of Dreams*
2. *Harvey*
3. *The Wonderful Ice Cream Suit*
4. *The Mummy* (Brendon Fraser version)
5. *Something Wicked This Way Comes*
6. *Sinbad the Sailor* (Douglas Fairbanks Jr. version)
7. *All That Jazz*
8. *Conan the Barbarian*
9. *Fantasia*
10. *Portrait of Jennie*

(After 30 years I still do not know if *They Might Be Giants* and *Black Orpheus* are fantasies. If they are, place them first and fourth on the list.)

THE 12 BEST FILMS
OF ALL TIME

1. *Lawrence of Arabia*

2. *They Might Be Giants*

3. *The Maltese Falcon*

4. *Mask of Dimitrios*

5. *The Flame Trees of Thika*

6. *The Quiet Man*

7. *The Wind and the Lion*

8. *Casablanca*

9. *Zulu*

10. *Field of Dreams*

11. *The Magnificent Seven*

12. *L. A. Confidential*

MY 25 FAVORITE FANZINES
(and their editors)

1. *Science Fiction Review* [a/k/a *The Alien Critic, Psychotic,* and *Richard E. Geis*] (Richard E. Geis)

2. *Amra* (George Scithers)

3. *Quandry* (Lee Hoffman)

4. *Mimosa* (Rich and Nicki Lynch)

5. *Challenger* (Guy H. Lillian III)

6. *Duende* (Will Murray)

7. *Dimensions* (Harlan Ellison)

8. *Hyphen* (Walt Willis)

9. *Lan's Lantern* (George Laskowski)

10. *Slant* (Walt Willis)

11. *Algol* (Andy Porter)

12. *ERB-dom* (Camille Cazedessus, Jr.)

13. *Pulp Era* (Lyn Hickman)

14. *Extrapolation* (Tom Clareson)

15. *Double: Bill* (Bill Mallardi and Bill Bowers)

16. *Riverside Quarterly* (Leland Sapiro)

17. *Rhodomagnetic Digest* (most issues by Don Fabun)

18. *Tangent* (Dave Truesdale)

19. *OtherRealms* (Chuq von Rospach)

20. *Science Fiction Commentary* (Bruce Gillespie)

21. *Luna* (Frank Dietz)

22. *File 770* (Mike Glyer)

23. *Delap's F&SF Review* (Richard Delap)

24. *Thrust* (Doug Fratz)

25. *Energuman* (Mike Glicksohn)

THE 5 MOST INFLUENTIAL SF EDITORS

1. John Campbell
2. Horace Gold
3. Mike Moorcock
4. Judy-Lynn del Rey
5. Gardner Dozois

THE 5 BEST RESNICK NOVELS

1. *Paradise*
2. *Kirinyaga*
3. *Ivory*
4. *Santiago*
5. *The Return of Santiago*

MY 5 FAVORITE RESNICK NOVELS

1. *The Outpost*
2. *Adventures*
3. *The Soul Eater*
4. *Santiago*
5. *Stalking the Unicorn*

MY 15 BEST SHORT FICTION STORIES

1. "For I Have Touched the Sky"
2. "Seven Views of Olduvai Gorge"
3. "Winter Solstice"
4. "Barnaby in Exile"
5. "The Elephants on Neptune"
6. "Mwalimu in the Squared Circle"
7. "The 43 Antarean Dynasties"
8. "A Little Knowledge"
9. "Bully!"
10 "The Light That Blinds, The Claws That Catch"
11. "Hunting the Snark"
12. "Hothouse Flowers"
13. "Kirinyaga"
14. "The Pale Thin God"
15. "Here's Looking at You, Kid"

THE 5 WORST WORLDCONS I'VE ATTENDED

1. Baycon (1968)
2. Nycon III (1967)
3. ConFrancisco (1993)
4. St. Louiscon (1969)
5. ConStellation (1983)

THE 12 BEST FILM SCORES

1. *The Magnificent Seven* (Elmer Bernstein)

2. *Lawrence of Arabia* (Maurice Jarre)

3. *The Professionals* (Maurice Jarre)

4. *Picnic* (George Duning)

5. *The Wind and the Lion* (Jerry Goldsmith)

6. *The Quiet Man* (Victor Young)

7. *Dingaka* (traditional tribal)

8. *The Great Escape* (Elmer Bernstein)

9. *The Flame Trees of Thika* (Ken Howard and Alan Blaikley)

10. *Field of Dreams* (James Horner)

11. *Raiders of the Lost Ark* (John Williams)

12. *For a Few Dollars More* (Morricone)

THE 25 BEST WESTERN FILMS

1. *The Magnificent Seven*
2. *The Good, The Bad, and the Ugly*
3. *The Professsionals*
4. *The Searchers*
5. *True Grit*
6. *Red River*
7. *The Rounders*
8. *The Shootist*
9. *McCabe and Mrs. Miller*
10. *Support Your Local Sheriff*
11. *She Wore A Yellow Ribbon*
12. *Tombstone*
13. *For A Few Dollars More*
14. *Once Upon a Time in the West*
15. *Unforgiven*
16. *The Outlaw Josie Wales*
17. *Cat Ballou*
18. *A Fistful of Dollars*
19. *From Noon to Three*
20. *Butch Cassidy and the Sundance Kid*
21. *The Gunfighter*
22. *High Noon*
23. *Pale Rider*
24. *Red Garters*
25. *Stagecoach*

THE 25 BEST COMEDY FILMS

1. *The Ritz*
2. *Duck Soup*
3. *The In-Laws*
4. *Ruthless People*
5. *Serial*
6. *Monkey Business* (Marx Bros. version)
7. *The Cheap Detective*
8. *The Pink Panther*
9. *A Christmas Story*
10. *Mr. Blandings Builds His Dream House*
11. *School for Scoundrels*
12. *Horse Feathers*
13. *I Was a Male War Bride*
14. *Doctor in the House*
15. *Animal Crackers*
16. *The Wrong Box*
17. *Young Frankenstein*
18. *A Fish Called Wanda*
19. *The Gods Must Be Crazy*
20. *The Producers*
21. *Radio Days*
22. *Galaxy Quest*
23. *Best in Show*
24. *Brain Donors*
25. *Monty Python's Life of Brian*

I just saw *My Big Fat Greek Wedding* while proofing these galleys, and would rank it in the Top Ten, possibly even the Top Five.

THE 12 BEST AMERICAN MEALS

1. Doro's (Chicago)
2. Le Francais (Wheeling, Illinois)
3. Commander's Palace (New Orleans)
4. La Caravelle (New York)
5. Ritz-Carlton Dining Room (Chicago)
6. Nikoli's (Atlanta)
7. Four Seasons Dining Room (Beverly Hills)
8. La Maisonette (Cincinnati)
9. Lutece (New York)
10. Christini's (Orlando)
11. Victor's (San Francisco)
12. La Tour du Bois (Lake Geneva, Wisconsin)

THE 12 BEST FOREIGN MEALS

1. Chobe Game Lodge, Chobe National Park, Botswana
2. Ocean Sports, Watamu, Kenya
3. Mount Kenya Safari Club, Nanyuki, Kenya
4. Livingston Room, Victoria Falls Hotel, Zimbabwe
5. Last Days of the Raj, London
6. The Carnivore, Nairobi, Kenya
7. Petit St. Vincent's, Grenadines, Carribean
8. Bishopstrow House, England
9. Royal Caribbean, Montego Bay, Jamaica
10. Ramses Hilton, Cairo, Egypt
11. Ibis Grill, Nairobi, Kenya
12. Tamerind, Mombasa, Kenya

THE 12 BEST AFRICAN FILMS

1. *Zulu*
2. *King Solomon's Mines* (Stewart Granger version)
3. *The Gods Must Be Crazy*
4. *Trader Horn*
5. *The African Queen*
6. *White Mischief*
7. *Mountains of the Moon*
8. *Dingaka*
9. *The Kitchen Toto*
10. *Out of Africa*
11. *Born Free*
12. *The Gods Must Be Crazy II*

Made for TV Division:

1. *The Flame Trees of Thika*
2. *Shaka Zulu*

North African Division:

1. *Lawrence of Arabia*
2. *The Wind and the Lion*
3. *Khartoum*

Documentaries:

1. *The African Elephant*
2. *Animals are Beautiful People*
3. *Simba*

THE 25 BEST MUSICALS

1. *Sweeney Todd*

2. *Falsettos*

3. *Pacific Overtures*

4. *City of Angels*

5. *Grover's Corners*

6. *Ain't Supposed to Die a Natural Death*

7. *1776*

8. *The Fantasticks*

9. *Follies*

10. *Man of La Mancha*

11. *Baker Street*

12. *Sunday in the Park With George*

13. *Celebration*

14. *A Little Night Music*

15. *West Side Story*

16. *110 in the Shade*

17. *Carnival!*

18. *Sophisticated Ladies*

19. *Take Me Along*

20. *It's a Bird, It's a Plane, It's Superman!*

21. *Fiorello!*

22. *The Threepenny Opera*

23. *Philemon*

24. *The Bone Room*

25. *Assassins*

THE 12 BEST PERFORMANCES BY AN ACTOR IN A MUSICAL

1. Richard Kiley (*Man of La Mancha*)
2. Robert Morse (*How to Succeed in Business*)
3. George Hearn (*Sweeney Todd*)
4. William Daniels (*1776*)
5. Tom Bosley (*Fiorello!*)
6. Raul Julia (*Man of La Mancha*)
7. Len Cariou (*Sweeney Todd*)
8. Gene Barry (*La Cage Aux Folles*)
9. Mako (*Pacific Oversures*)
10. Robert Preston (*The Music Man*)
11. Jerry Orbach (*Carnival*)
12. James Naughton (*City of Angels*)

THE 12 BEST PERFORMANCES BY AN ACTRESS IN A MUSICAL

1. Inga Swenson (*110 in the Shade*)
2. Gwen Verdon (*Redhead*)
3. Barbara Cook (*Candide*)
4. Angela Lansbury (*Sweeney Todd*)
5. Patti LuPone (*Evita*)
6. Ethel Merman (*Gypsy*)
7. Inga Swenson (*Baker Street*)
8. Joan Diener (*Man of La Mancha*)
9. Elizabeth Seal (*Irma La Douce*)
10. Glynis Johns (*A Little Night Music*)
11. Lotte Lenya (*The Threepenny Opera*)
12. Alexis Smith (*Follies*)

MY 10 FAVORITE TV SHOWS

1. *The Prisoner*

2. *Maverick*

3. *Columbo*

4. *The Avengers*

5. *Sherlock Holmes* (PBS)

6. *Mission: Impossible*

7. *Tales of the Gold Monkey*

8. *A Touch of Frost* (PBS/A&E)

9. *The Night Stalker*

10. *Star Trek* (original)

(Note: I stopped watching all network shows in the early 1980s.)

THE 25 GREATEST RACE HORSES OF THE 20TH CENTURY

1. Seattle Slew
2. Citation
3. Man o' War
4. Dr. Fager
5. Kelso (g)
6. Swaps
7. Native Dancer
8. Colin
9. Count Fleet
10. Ruffian (f)
11. Forego (g)
12. Secretariat
13. Buckpasser
14. Affirmed
15. Damascus
16. Cigar
17. War Admiral
18. Sysonby
19. Alydar
20. Tom Fool
21. Landeluce (f)
22. Graustark
23. Bold Ruler
24. Spectacular Bid
25. Round Table

(g) = gelding; (f) = filly

MY 12 FAVORITE MUSEUMS

1. The National Museum of Racing

2. The Nairobi Museum

3. The Royal Tyrell Museum

4. The Field Museum of Natural History

5. The Gene Autry Museum of Western Americana

6. The American Museum of Natural History

7. The Cairo Museum of Antiquities

8. The Kentucky Derby Museum

9. The Martin and Osa Johnson SAafari Museum

10. The Smithsonian

11. The British Museum

12. The Louvre

MY 10 FAVORITE ZOOS

1. San Diego Zoo

2. Cincinnati Zoo

3. Brookfield Zoo (Chicago)

4. New Orleans Zoo

5. Bronx Zoo

6. Lincoln Park Zoo (Chicago)

7. San Diego Zoo Park

8. St. Louis Zoo

9. Miami Zoo

10. Calgary Zoo

MY 15 FAVORITE AFRICAN GAME PARKS

1. Ngorongoro Crater (Tanzania)

2. Hwange (Zimbabwe)

3. Chobe (Botswana)

4. Samburu/Buffalo Springs (Kenya)

5. Aberdares (Kenya)

6. Maasai Mara (Kenya)

7. Serengeti (Tanzania)

8. Etosha (Namibia)

9. Mana Pools (Zimbabwe; see above note)

10. Queen Elizabeth II (Uganda)

11. South Luangwa Valley (Zambia)

12. Moremi Reserve (Botswana)

13. Amboseli (Kenya)

14. Tsavo (Kenya)

15. Meru (Kenya)

MY 3 FAVORITE HISTORICAL CHARACTERS

1. Theodore Roosevelt

2. John Boyes

3. Doc Holliday

THE 5 BEST BASKETBALL PLAYERS

1. Michael Jordan
2. Wilt Chamberlain
3. Oscar Robertson
4. Julius Erving
5. Bill Russell

THE 5 BEST BIG BANDS

1. Xavier Cugat
2. Jimmy Dorsey
3. Glen Miller
4. Tommy Dorsey
5. Desi Arnaz

THE 5 BEST MYSTERY WRITERS

1. Raymond Chandler
2. James Ellroy
3. Dashiell Hammett
4. James Cain
5. Ross MacDonald

THE 5 GREATEST NOVELS I'VE READ

1. *The Last Temptation of Christ,* by Nikos Kazantzakis
2. *Moby-Dick*, by Herman Mellville
3. *Catch-22*, by Joseph Heller
4. *Huckleberry Finn,* by Mark Twain
5. *Star Maker*, by Olaf Stapledon

THE 5 BEST FILM DIRECTORS

1. David Lean
2. Sergio Leone
3. John Huston
4. Jamie Uys
5. John Milius